THE
BONE WARS

A NOVEL

ERIN EVAN

Published by Inkshares, Inc., San Francisco, California
www.inkshares.com

Edited by Adam Gomolin
Cover design by M.S. Corley
Interior design by Kevin G. Summers

ISBN: 9781942645665
e-ISBN: 9781942645672
LCCN: 2017955470

First edition

Printed in the United States of America

Magic is just science we don't understand yet.
—Arthur C. Clarke

A myth is a way of making sense in a senseless world.
Myths are narrative patterns that give significance to
our existence.
—Rollo May

For my mother.
As usual, you were right.

And for my father.
See, Mom was right.

ROCKS, PEBBLES, SAND

Molly

FOR AS LONG as I could remember, all I ever wanted to do was dig in the dirt. To look for treasure.

Sure, I did other normal kid stuff. I'd play hopscotch or swing on the monkey bars. Ride my bike with my friends. Binge Netflix. But as soon as I could get away and be alone, I'd find myself at a park, poking and kicking at the soils to get to the layers of stone underneath. Once exposed, I'd carefully break apart the layers, looking. Always looking.

Eventually I'd find something. I always found something. Rocks, no matter how broken, tell a story. If it was small, I'd bag it and take it home for my collection. If it wasn't small, I'd end up digging until dark, dreaming about the day I'd find real treasure.

My dad realized I had a passion and wanted to nurture it. At dinner parties, he'd parade me about, proudly noting that his four-year-old was still into her "dirty habit." It was an inside joke that horrified adults who had no sense of humor.

My mother was less understanding. I knew she only wanted the best for me. "Look up, Molly!" she'd say. "You're missing the world."

Yet my eyes never left the ground.

The day I left for Montana was no different. I leaned my head against the plane's window and squinted down at the ground. I couldn't see any small rocks, but I could see Glasgow, Montana. It was a gray-and-black sprawl dotting a brown-and-yellow landscape of small hills and grasslands. The town felt slow, even from a thousand feet in the air. I bet people waved when you passed, hosted potlucks on the weekends after the big high school football game, and went to church in their Sunday best.

I closed my eyes and leaned back in my seat, my fingers toying with the gold ring on my leather necklace. Five hundred years ago, Glasgow didn't exist. It was a vast, grassy prairie punctuated by Indigenous settlements and vast swaths of buffalo and pronghorn antelope.

Ten thousand years before that, this land was on the outer edge of the enormous Laurentide Ice Sheet. It was a cold, harsh world for the humans who survived on fifteen-foot-tall mammoths that they hunted with nothing but stone-tipped spears and guts of steel.

Sixty-six million years before that, this land was near the coast of the enormous Western Interior Seaway, a vast body of ocean water that cut right through North America. Dinosaurs such as *Tyrannosaurus rex* hunted in its forests and open areas for dinner while small mammals—including our ancestors—hid in terror at the possibility of being on the menu. Eventually these animals died, either by bad luck or old age, and some were buried under mud, silt, and sand. Their fleshy parts decomposed, leaving their bones behind.

Over time, those bones were slowly replaced with minerals. Petrified into immortality. Transformed into the *real* treasure. A treasure that was often hiding in plain sight, and could be overlooked if you didn't know what you were looking for. It was the kind of treasure that people kill for.

Fossils.

Those of the dinosaur ilk, more precisely.

Okay, I don't know for *sure* if anyone has actually murdered for dinosaur fossils. But I do know that plenty of people have gotten hurt looking for them. While the hunt was thrilling, for me, it was really about something else. Something deeper. For me, it was the endgame of finding that new, revolutionary fossil. An ancient truth hidden right under our feet.

I was going to Montana to hunt that treasure.

It was easy to see why so many people were obsessed with dinosaurs. Dinosaurs were one of the most successful animals to ever live on earth. The first dinosaurs appeared roughly 230 million years ago and the last ones died sixty-six million years ago. They basically ruled the planet for over 164 million years. Think about it. 164 million years. The first *Homo sapiens*— modern humans—only appeared three hundred thousand years ago. The age of the dinosaurs was called the Mesozoic era, and it was broken into three distinct periods: the Triassic, the Jurassic, and then the Cretaceous. The whole Mesozoic was so long that some of the best-known dinosaurs never even saw one another. For example, the famous bony-plated *Stegosaurus* thrived in the Jurassic period about 150 million years ago. However, *Tyrannosaurus rex* lived at the end of the Cretaceous period, about sixty-six million years ago. There were fifty million to one hundred million years between these two incredibly famous dinosaurs. Not once did they ever see each other, let alone fight, contrary to the whims of every single child who owned a dinosaur toy set.

Scientists have found about seven hundred dinosaur species in the fossil record so far, but considering their lifetime on the planet and the fact that their distant cousin, the modern bird, currently stood at about eighteen thousand species, I thought it safe to say we were still missing a lot.

I smiled as I stretched my body, moving my cramped legs as best as I could, sore from all my traveling over the past few hours. That would change soon. I'd be digging for dinosaurs.

"How are you doing, young lady? We're running a bit late," an overly caffeinated voice chirped near me. I turned to look at the air steward, the only other passenger on my flight. She was tall and blond. So blond. "But we'll be landing soon." She pointed a perfectly manicured nail toward my window. "Probably a cow delay."

Okay, I'd bite.

"Cow delay?"

She nodded emphatically. "Oh, yes. Old Mike Spencer's ranch shares a fence line with the airport. He's terrible at keeping it up. His cows get on the tarmac now and then."

Definitely not like home.

I gave her a shrug and reached down to grab my headphones from my backpack. I plugged them into my phone and brought up Dr. Sean Oliphant's TED Talk. Soon, Oliphant's familiar clipped speech filled my ears.

"Imagine a world millions of years ago that looks almost exactly like this one. Can you do it? Just try." Oliphant laughed gently, his tone cheerful as he walked across a brightly lit stage. He was wearing a crisp white button-down with a navy suit jacket and beige slacks. The uniform of the Television Scientist. After giving the audience another encouraging smile, he waved his arms out toward them. On cue, the camera turned to the front row. All eyes were on this man. I didn't blame them.

"I bet you can. Geologists call this idea the Law of Uniformitarianism. It's the idea that what's happening today, at least in terms of geologic processes, is what occurred in the past. Not much in that respect has changed. There was the sun. There was rain that fell from the sky, eroding the land. There was snow and ice. Floods, droughts. Landslides, earthquakes. The world operated the exact same way. And there was life.

Many animals were familiar looking. Four-legged creatures that ambled about the world, like amphibians and lizards. Fish and clams in the oceans. And insects like the amazing cockroach." I heard a few chuckles mixed with disgusted titters in the background. "No, I'm serious." Oliphant grinned. "The amazing cockroach. Arguably the most successful animal in earth's history. Laugh all you want. It evolved about three hundred million years ago and lived through multiple extinction events. It's still going strong, especially in my kitchen." Oliphant gave the audience a knowing smile, and there was another round of laughter.

"But, while all this feels and looks familiar, the world was fantastically different in a significant way. It was filled with our ancestors. Precursors to our modern animals. For example, this guy." Oliphant clicked a small remote. Behind him, the screen lit up with a picture of a long, four-legged creature. It had a bulky head filled with sharp teeth and a long tail. But its most distinctive feature was the spiny sail protruding from its back. "For millions of years, *Dimetrodon* wandered forests, eating smaller prey. This prehistoric reptile was a giant of the land; it was the length of a small car."

Click.

Another picture, and the familiar shape of a flying *Pteranodon* filled the screen, its body and beaked skull tiny in comparison to its massive wings. "Fast forward millions of years, and reptiles were not only on the land, but also in the skies and oceans. They evolved into flying *Pteranodons*."

Click.

"Or swimming plesiosaurs. An oddity in the ocean, the giant plesiosaurs had a bulky body, flippers, and a long neck, perfect for streaking through the sea to catch fish."

Oliphant took a deep breath and walked along the stage. Behind him, a picture of a *Tyrannosaurus rex* filled the screen.

"But the strangest, in my opinion, was this diverse class of animals. I'm talking, of course, of the dinosaur." He pointed at the screen behind him. "That crazy reptile relative! How dare it not conform to the standards of the day? How dare it not be a slow, lumbering reptile, like a good Mesozoic crocodile or lizard! No. It was like that city cousin we all seem to have who has tons of piercings and tattoos and works in a coffee shop spouting poetry and man-buns while slinging espresso."

He paused and looked around the room, a slight smile on his face as the audience chuckled.

He continued, "The crazy dinosaur decided to be different. What did it do? Well, it decided to evolve their legs under their body. What fantastic posture. So very different from the lumbering sprawling leg and hip arrangement their country bumpkin cousins had, and still have today. Take a look at a modern lizard. They have only side-to-side motion when they walk or run. It was the same back then. But not dinosaurs. No, no. They evolved into something new. Then, those crazy dinosaurs, well, they just had to diversify to take advantage of their faster hip setup. Fill in some niches and exploit new food opportunities. And boy did they do that. Some ate meat. Some ate plants. Some did both. Because of this, they evolved into a diverse group of animals. Some had scales, some feathers. Some were as tiny as a dog. Some were as giant as a redwood. Some walked on two legs, others four. Some were real rebels and went back and forth between the two. And they have captured our imagination for the entirety of the insignificant time that *Homo sapiens* has been around, digging them up, putting them back together, categorizing them, bringing them to life in books and films.

"As many of you are well aware, I'm a vertebrate paleontologist with a focus on dinosaurs. I dig in the ground because I truly believe it's critical to learn about our past. We learn from our past to strengthen our future, to be better people. Even if dinosaurs are as far from humans as can be, they still had a lot of relatable similarities. Some lived alone, others in groups, for example. Through my research at Nest Valley in Montana, I was able to prove the complex social structures of dinosaurs, dinosaurs people assumed were lumbering, solitary idiots. In actuality, they laid their eggs, raised their young, and juveniles lived nearby, relying on the old adage of strength in numbers to survive predators. We know a lot. This is especially impressive considering academic paleontology is really only one hundred and fifty years old—"

Just then, I heard a rumbling noise over my headphones, and felt the plane shift. I stopped the video and removed my headphones in time to hear the pilot's crackling voice echoing through the cabin, giving us some sort of direction. But it was hard to make out over the whine of the engines.

"I guess the cows moved," I said to the air steward.

I felt a rush of cool air hit my face as I walked through the entry door to the airport terminal. The terminal turned out to be a small, empty room with dingy carpet and several unoccupied desks.

An email from Nakasogi Industries said I'd won their prize to fund my internship, and a second email from my crew boss, Sarah Connell, told me to be at Glasgow Airport on that date and at that time. So there I was. By myself, apparently.

While I waited for Sarah to arrive, I opened my small backpack to double-check I had everything I might need for the day, just in case we went right to the dig from the airport. I paused at the worn children's book near the top. I touched its cover and spine with my fingers, tracing the title's familiar angles and ridges.

Dragons of the World.

The front door swung open, and I jerked my head up. A tall man in a dusty T-shirt, canvas pants, and heavy boots strode into the room. His face was square and his sunburned cheeks were covered with gray stubble.

The classic field look. This was probably my ride.

"Hi," I said with a small wave.

Gold-rimmed aviator sunglasses hid his eyes, but I could tell that he was boring holes right into me. He stopped and stared down at me for a few seconds. Man, he was really tall.

"You're the kid who's working on our dig this summer?" he finally asked.

"Yeah, but I'm no kid."

"Sure you're not," he said. "What are you, eleven?"

"I'm sixteen!"

He groaned. "I thought Nakasogi Industries was sending us someone with experience."

"I've got two years of field experience and four years of museum—"

"That's two years not enough," he said.

Who the hell did this guy think he was?

Before I could say anything, the man snorted. "Okay, kid, don't get your hackles up." He reached down and swung my larger backpack over his shoulder. He glared at me over the rim of his sunglasses. "This it?"

"Um, yeah." I shrugged the smaller backpack onto my back.

He turned and headed for the exit.

"Wait! Where's Sarah Connell?"

"At the site. Let's get moving before the jackalopes eat her alive."

What a charmer.

PLASTER OF PACHY

Farnsworth

HEAT AND DUST hit my face as I banged open the terminal door. Welcome to Glasgow, Montana. A large dust devil whirled around just beyond the boundary of the airport, lifting debris from the rocky terrain.

Kids don't belong on digs. Especially an inexperienced West Coaster. She'll probably force me to stop at an organic farmers market to look for vegan soy burgers for lunch.

The rubber of her boots squeaked as she ran to catch up to me. Probably fresh out of the box.

After a few steps, I glanced behind me. She was a small, slight thing, barely filling out her jeans and T-shirt. She had a heart-shaped face and wide, green eyes. Her dark brown hair was tied behind her head in a ponytail that swung back and forth as she ran to keep up.

"At least you're dressed like a paleontologist," I said.

She stopped and looked down. "What else would I be wearing?"

"You'd be surprised." I tossed the girl's larger black backpack into the truck bed. It hit with a loud thud.

The girl's head jerked up. "Hey, watch it! That's my stuff." She frowned, a teenager's edge to her tone.

What was her name again? Sarah told me, but I wasn't listening. I'd polished off too many beers at Murphy's last night, and Sarah knew how and when to strike.

I looked hard at the girl before opening the driver's side door. "It's fine," I said.

She stood on her toes and peered into the truck bed for the pack.

"Those are fossils," she said. She pointed to several round white blobs in the truck bed. Her voice was high, and her face was glowing red. "You just leave fossils in your truck while you go pick up people at the airport? Aren't you afraid of somebody damaging them, or stealing them?"

"Kid, people out here are a lot more honest than in San Francisco. I told you already, they're fine. Now are you coming or not?"

Instead of opening her door, she climbed up onto the truck's wheel and leaned forward to inspect the fossils. They were jacketed in plaster-of-Paris, with the smaller ones in cardboard boxes.

"What is that label, pachy? As in part of a Pachycephalosaurid?"

I wanted to yell at her to get into the truck, but I leaned over to look. Sure enough, I saw Sarah's handwriting on one of the smaller white blobs nestled within a bed of newspapers in a large cardboard box.

> *Pachy sp.*
> *(D or S?)*
> *skull, disartic.*
> *UWY-FP-112*

"This is part of a Pachycephalosaurid skull?" she said.
"Pretty good guess, for a beginner."

"Not a guess. It's labeled pachy sp., as in a *Pachycephalosaurus* species. And it's a piece of the skull since it's labeled as disarticulated." She leaned forward again. "Whoever labeled this probably thought it was either a *Dracorex* or a *Stygimoloch*."

Interesting. Didn't expect her to know that.

Pachys were a dinosaur species that lived during the Cretaceous, about sixty-six million years ago. They had skulls that were dome-shaped and thick. Some paleontologists believe they banged their heads to fight or to display their prowess for a mate—like goats or elk do today. It was a relatively obscure dinosaur, compared to movie stars like *Tyrannosaurus rex* and *Triceratops*.

The heat from the sun caused my stomach to roil. My head still felt like I had bashed it into a keg of beer. I should be lying down, or drinking some hair of the dog. Not hanging out with a tween. But something the kid said made me pause. "Why either of those two?"

"Based on the location of the dig. We're going to be working the Hell Creek Formation, right?" She looked at me for confirmation.

I slow-waved for her to continue. She narrowed her eyes again.

"Because they are both known to have lived during that time in this area." She scrambled into the truck.

I climbed into the driver's seat and my truck roared to life. She was old and had a lot of miles, but she was reliable. Not unlike yours truly. I accelerated as we left the airport.

"Okay," I said. I'd give her a bonus round. "What is the full species name of *Dracorex*, and what does it mean?"

"*Dracorex hogwartsia*." She didn't hesitate, not a millisecond. "It means 'Dragon King of Hogwarts.' Named for the Harry Potter book series. Give me something hard."

"So you have a library card. What do you know about fieldwork?"

"I already told you. I've worked in the field for the last two summers. And a library card? Dude, we use computers. It's all on the internet."

Since there wasn't anyone else on the road, I turned to really look her over. She was facing me, her arms crossed against her body. Her eyes were a ferocious emerald. She'd mastered the art of the glare, at least.

"Okay, two years. But doing what, exactly?" I said. "Playing tourist, with an outfit that caters to your whims? 'Hand me a rock hammer please, I'd like to prospect for a fossil before we have our root beer?'"

"I was at Nest Valley," she said. She turned back to look out the front window.

"Well, there you go," I snorted. "Oliphant's dig."

She nodded. "I went to his field camp the first summer I ever dug dinos. I didn't meet Dr. Oliphant, though," she said. Her anger forgotten, she was an enthusiastic, rambling kid. "But I did end up working for one of the grad students last summer," she continued. "Nick Stone was from Yale. He was almost finished with his PhD." She looked out the window. Her voice shifted lower, and I heard a trace of sadness. "That's why I'm here. Because I can't work for Nick again. He's done with his fieldwork. At least for now."

"Well, this isn't Nest Valley, kid. We expect you to work hard here."

"I can do that. Nick's site was a small quarry. A few isolated skeletons and lots of plants."

"Maybe, but I don't know this Nick, and I don't know what you were doing," I said. "All I know is how I work, and how Sarah likes to run her dig. This is paleontology at its best: snakes, 110-degree heat, spiders, scorpions, backbreaking work. We're not going to babysit you. In turn, you may learn a thing or two."

I half expected another outburst of anger from the girl. Instead, she nodded thoughtfully and looked out the window.

"It was really cool getting to work on Dr. Oliphant's dig," she said.

"Sure it was."

"What?" the girl asked.

"Nothin'," I replied. I extended a hand to her. "Derek Farnsworth."

She paused for a moment, then clasped her hand with mine. "Molly Wilder."

We drove south along Route 24 near the Fort Peck Reservoir. All around us were the prairie grasses, bushes, and small hills common in eastern Montana. But as we approached Fort Peck Reservoir, the terrain changed. Millions of years of savage storms, expanding ice, and an unforgiving sun had carved this part of Montana into a strange array of colorful hillsides, ravines, and coulees. Perfect hunting grounds, if you were a pirate.

In the distance was a large mesa and steeply graded badlands, their white-yellow tops a stark contrast to the cloudless, cerulean sky. "That's where we're going," I said, pointing at the mesa.

I grew up on these lands, prospecting for fossils with my granddad. I knew how lucky I was. All around Glasgow and Fort Peck were rocks filled with plant and animal remains. Millions of years ago, this area was a mixture of rivers, deltas, and bogs that flowed east, down away from the relatively newly formed Rocky Mountains into the low-lying western shore of the giant Western Interior Seaway that split the continent into Appalachia and Laramidia. Cycads, katsura, magnolias, and palm trees shadowed the land with a cool, protective canopy. Moss and ferns gave the smaller animals, such as snakes, lizards, frogs, and ancient rodents, cover. When animals died, sands and muds covered their bodies, entombing them. Eventually, time turned clays, silts, and sands into sedimentary rock, and the bones and imprints into fossils. Millions of years recorded in a few inches of sandstone and mudstone.

The particular formation we were working in was the Hell Creek, and it represented a time in earth's history called the Late Cretaceous, so about sixty-six million years ago. In my humble opinion, if you were looking for dinosaur fossils, the Hell Creek is where you wanted to go. You could find a pachy like the one in my trunk. You could find a *Triceratops*. There were a lot of them out here. I've also found a lot of hadrosaurids or duck-billed dinosaurs. All of those fossils get a good price, so I'm not complaining.

But the Hell Creek is so much more. Yes, dinosaurs were the dominant land animal during the Mesozoic, and they ruled the continents for about 165 million years. But I often meet people who assume that dinosaurs swam and flew, which is just plain wrong. Actually, the seas and sky belonged to other, equally huge and terrifying reptiles.

While fossils of ancient crocodiles, turtles, and fish were dotted throughout the Hell Creek Formation, we'd also found the remains of swimming reptiles like the giant mosasaurs. The mosasaurs were a short-necked group of reptiles that looked like fifty-foot swimming Komodo dragons. We'd also found evidence of plesiosaurs, a long-necked group of reptiles that dominated the seas for over 130 million years. In the skies, flying reptiles such as the giant pterosaur *Quetzalcoatlus* glided over the tree canopy, searching for fish, small reptiles, and even small dinosaurs to eat. The pterosaurs were the family of flying reptiles that are the first known vertebrates to have evolved to fly. Take that, Wright brothers.

Like dinosaurs, the pterosaur family had a lot of variety. Some pterosaurs had crests on their heads for ornamentation, some did not. Some had tails, others had only little stubs on their rears. They were a beautiful bunch of animals.

"And here we go," I said as I slowed the car and pulled off onto a service road. The truck bounced and groaned with effort as we drove along, dust billowing out from the tires. I slowed down a bit. Molly grabbed her armrests as we jostled and bounced along the road.

"So, who are you? What's your job?" she asked.

"I'm assisting Sarah Connell on the site."

"Aren't you a little old to be an intern?"

"I'm not an intern. I'm not even with the University. I'm a fossil hunter."

"What?"

I heard the surprise in her voice.

"I'm a commercial fossil hunter. I dig for fossils, and then I sell them."

Holding on to the steering wheel with my left hand, I fished a dirty business card out of my right pocket. "Take it." Molly grudgingly reached for it like it was something on fire. Her fingers pinched its corner, and she pulled it toward her face.

After a long moment without a response, I glanced at her. She was staring at the card, her face wrinkled in disgust.

Here it comes. Every damn time.

"You sell fossils," she finally said with a slight edge to her voice. "You sell them before anyone can even study them. You destroy the sites before we get the data."

"Life is shades of gray, kid. The paleontologists that succeed in this business are the ones who work hard and literally *find their bones*. Doesn't matter if it's for a university or a museum or a client. It's all the same. Try to keep an open mind."

She didn't respond. I slowed the truck down. We were nearly at the mesa's edge. The dirt road to the bone quarry bended southwest around the mesa, so I followed its perimeter. After a few moments, we'd driven into a wide gully that separated the mesa from a large, towering butte farther to the south. Both landforms were whitish yellow, with bands of brown, gray, and pink.

I carefully followed the other tire tracks along the stream bed that separated the mesa from the butte. Dried-up streams were the best places to look for fossils. Water eroded rocks and rubble from the nearby hills and deposited the fossils in stream beds, where we discovered them during the drier months. Finding that large tooth in this stream was what led Sarah and me to concentrate our search for fossils in this area in the first place.

A few minutes later, we parked next to Sarah's newer but equally dirty F-150. Nearby, Sarah and the other students had already unloaded supplies into a pile near the bottom of the mesa.

"Right on time." I turned off the truck's ignition. Molly was looking at me. She seemed a bit unsure, maybe even nervous. Her fingers toyed with a gold ring attached to a leather necklace around her neck.

I pointed at Sarah. "Well, there's your new boss."

She hesitated.

I pulled my glasses down. She wasn't the only one who could glare.

"Scram. Your science awaits."

That did the trick. She threw the door open and jumped out. I got out too, gravel and sand crunching under my boots.

She slammed her door closed and raised a hand to shade her eyes from the bright sunlight.

"Hey," I called.

She turned to look at me. I reached into the bed of my truck and quickly felt around. My fingers brushed against soft fabric, and I pulled up one of my caps.

"You need a hat out here." I walked around and stood in front of her, pushing the cap onto her head. "Welcome to Montana, Molly."

Letter from Rev. William Buckland to Gideon Mantell, 1824

My dear Mr. Mantell,

I was excited to read your last letter, and thank you for your detailed drawings. They suggest your newest fossils from the Tilgate formation here in England are from my *Megalosaurus*, although the color does not match. However, that is to be expected based on the distance that they were found from my own site. Fossils can show color variation based on location, as you know. Based on the size of your fossil, I estimate the *Megalosaurus* grew to be the size of about eighteen yards in length. Quite impressive! The Bible speaks of "when there were giants on the Earth," and these fossils demonstrate the accuracy of that statement. I plan on discussing my *Megalosaurus* fossil and your finds at the February's Geological Society meeting in London. I hope you can attend.

I will visit when I can, and you can show me where the quarryman found your fossils. My students can be overwhelming this time of year. You will laugh when I tell you that I still plan on taking my students to the mud flats just outside

Oxford after a storm. They will get a first-rate introduction to the slippery properties of mudstone when it is wet! I plan on not telling them to bring a change of clothing. I myself will teach from a horse.

Yours etc.
William Buckland

PS Since writing you above, I did wonder whether you could provide a more detailed drawing of the teeth, to confirm the serrations. I wonder whether the number is correct.

DINO DAMAGE

Molly

I YANKED THE baseball cap off my head and gave it a look over. It was one of those trucker caps that had a cloth patch in the front and mesh in the back. It had a *T-rex* skull with two rock hammers crossed behind it, like a pirate flag. Written underneath in raised lettering was "Glasgow Geological Institute."

It was much cooler than the old A's cap I brought from home, but I didn't want to owe this fossil hunter anything. No matter what he said, he was still the guy who tooled dinosaurs away from the rest of us. I handed it back to him.

"No, thank you."

"Take it," he growled. "You're a kid. It'll give you some cred with the experts." He slammed the hat back onto my head and pointed toward the group near the trucks. "Go. You're not getting any smarter standing here." Then, in a crunch of dirt and gravel, he walked away.

I snapped my mouth shut and whirled around. It was Sarah Connell I had to impress, not this Farnsworth guy. I was her intern, and she'd be the boss of my life for the next two months.

I took a deep breath and looked around to take stock of my surroundings. In front of me was a large, flattop mesa, its sides broken by steep sawtooth-shaped divides that exposed brightly colored layers of sedimentary rock. It had classic badland structuring, which was different from anything I'd seen in California. Badlands were steeply sloped sedimentary rock formations that formed by wind and water erosion. They had very little vegetation, and hardly any topsoil. Often, they'd come in bright colors: reds, whites, pinks, yellows, and occasionally browns. This one favored a yellow-white coloring, with some red.

A few feet away were two women and a man, standing in a circle near a stack of pickaxes, bags, buckets, and a large red cooler. The trademark tools of paleontology.

"Welcome, Molly!" the taller of the two women called out. I guessed she was Sarah. She looked to be in her late twenties. She had curly dark hair, streaked with purple and white, the white probably plaster-of-Paris. Tattoos covered one of her arms, a chaotic tangle of dinosaurs, fossil skeletons, and flowers. "No trouble with your flight?"

"Just a little cow delay." I smiled sheepishly.

Sarah nodded like that was totally normal. "Glad the old man didn't leave you hanging at the terminal," she said loudly. I turned around and saw Farnsworth as he determinedly dug around his truck bed, not looking in her direction but moving his hand high enough to give her an offensive gesture.

"Let's get started." She chuckled. "This is Karolin and Dean, undergrads from Wyoming." Karolin was a tall blond woman with blue eyes. Dean was shorter and stocky, with dark hair and a bearded face mostly covered by aviator sunglasses.

Sarah pivoted and pointed up toward the middle of the mesa. "Our bone quarry is up there. We've spent the better part of the spring digging a shelf that contains the layer of bones we're excavating."

I nodded and pulled at the straps of my backpack to make sure it was secure. Right below the edge of the quarry was the beginning of a huge talus pile. I learned about talus piles my first summer. They formed when erosion breaks rocks from their original home on a cliff or mesa or something, then drops them onto the ground. I hate them. It was hard to walk on them. Rocks slipped and slid underneath your boots, and they could be really sharp. I had to climb a few last summer and I still had scars from when I slipped and fell.

"Grab a bucket, and let's go," Sarah said. She grabbed one side of the large red cooler and Karolin grabbed the other. Together, they headed to the base of the talus slope.

I reached down and grabbed a large orange plastic bucket filled with burlap strips, and the nearest large tool, a pickaxe. I looked up again toward the mesa. It was enormous, about as tall as a four-story building. While the sides were cut with sharp divides, there were also a few ledges and smaller lips formed by harder rock layers that wouldn't give in to Mother Erosion. As a result, the striated mesa looked a bit like a giant, highly decorated turtle shell.

"Crazy, huh?" Dean grinned at me, pushing his sunglasses onto his forehead. "There's even a small cave on the northern side of this mesa, that way."

"I didn't see any cave as we drove in," I said.

"Yeah, it's not that visible from the service road, but it's there," Dean said, moving past me up the slope.

I took a deep breath and followed him. Scrambling up the slope, it took only a minute to get to the edge of the terrace. It was surprisingly large, about thirty feet across, and mostly flat. At the end of each side of the terrace was a sloping wall of sandstone, like bookends. At one side was a large white tent, the kind you'd expect to see in an adventure movie with Indiana Jones. Dotting the floor of the terrace were random fossils of dinosaur bones. Dean moved across the terrace, removing tarps laid out the night before to protect the fossils from the weather. Some of the fossils were entirely exposed, and familiar shapes started to knit together in my mind. Only a few feet away I saw what looked like a large femur bone; its brown coloring sharply contrasted with the yellow-white rock matrix that surrounded it.

"Where would you like me to start?" I asked Sarah.

"Come with me. I'll give you the grand tour of the quarry in a minute, but I want to show you something first."

The tent was large, about the size of one of those massive family tents I'd seen camping, and its interior was dark and cool. I blinked quickly to allow my eyes to adjust from the bright sun. In the middle of the tent, a blue tarp covered a fossil as big as a dining room table. Peeking out from under the tarp was an exposed cross section of plaster and layers of burlap covered in white plaster-of-Paris.

I looked up at Sarah. She was smirking and the area around her eyes was crinkled.

"Lift the tarp, Molly."

I lifted the tarp and moved it aside. In front of me sat a large chunk of Hell Creek Formation, and in the middle were several large, brown vertebrae.

"Do you know what you're looking at?"

Well, kind of. I could tell that they were large vertebrae, five of them in a row. And while finding verts was not uncommon in bone beds, finding five this huge, and together like that, was interesting. What large dinosaurs lived in this area during the Cretaceous? More importantly, what dinosaur would get Sarah this excited?

"*Tyrannosaurus rex*?" I half expected her to laugh. Instead, she nodded enthusiastically.

"Yup. Right in one."

I let out a squeal. Outside, I heard Dean and Karolin laughing.

I was embarrassed. I was used to being the youngest at digs, but I did try to act like an adult.

"That was my reaction, too!" Dean yelled.

I'd seen their skeletons in museums, but those were just replicas, casts made of plaster. Throughout the whole world, scientists had only discovered about forty complete or semi-complete T-rex skeletons. So while they're not the rarest dinosaur ever, it was pretty awesome to see one in real life.

Tyrannosaurus rex.

The King of the Dinosaurs.

They were the apex land-dwelling predators in the late Cretaceous and lived about sixty-eighty to sixty-six million years ago. A *T-rex* grew as tall as twenty feet and was about forty feet from its snout to the tip of its tail; its skull alone was about five feet long. So its head was almost the same size as me.

"This is all we have so far. We're still looking for the skull, arms, legs, and tail, but no luck so far," Sarah said.

"Why did you move it in here? Why not leave it out and finish the cast? Or move it to a lab?" I asked.

"Well," Sarah said, standing up. "Fossil thieves. Since this is a *T-rex*, we didn't want to leave it out, exposed. *T-rex* fossils can go for a lot on the black market."

"Does that happen a lot around here?" I asked.

"I've had it happen at other digs around the world."

I whipped my head around toward the voice. Farnsworth stood at the tent entrance, leaning against the frame.

"Now show her the special part," said Farnsworth.

Even backlit by the sun, I could make out his grin.

Sarah cleared her throat and then crouched down toward the fossil, motioning for me to do the same.

I raised my eyebrows. "Like, this *isn't* the special part?"

Sarah looked at me. For a moment, I saw something wash across her features. Sadness. But in the next moment, it was wiped away. The happy Sarah was back.

"Look closer at the fossils. See that four of the vertebrae seem to have cracks in them, unlike that fifth one? And see how they look shorter than that fifth one, like they were smashed by something?"

I nodded. As I thought about this, I played with my leather necklace. On it was my mother's ring. It was small and gold, with flowers adorning the sides.

"Maybe before they fossilized, the verts got squished by an outside force," I said. "Like a tree fell on the *T-rex* as it died, and smashed it up. Or, as they fossilized, the sands squished them as they were pressured into sedimentary rock."

"Squished? Find that in a textbook?" Farnsworth jabbed.

I glared at him and he smirked.

"Good reasons, Molly," Sarah interjected in my defense. "But touch that vert, right there." She pointed to the top of the middle vertebra, at the base of its broken arch. I gently touched the cool rock, and as I probed, I felt a very deep hole in the vertebra, not really visible from where I was crouched.

"Do you see those cracks?" I squinted to where she was pointing. Small lines appeared to be radiating out from the hole my finger was touching. I looked back at her and nodded.

"Here's my theory. If you were looking at this *T-rex*'s back from above, when it was alive, you'd see that something had bit down into the *T-rex*. I think compaction caused these cracks and breaks."

"You think these were caused by another dinosaur?" I looked up at her face. "As in . . . this is dino damage?"

But *T-rex* didn't have enemies, except for other *T-rexes*.

"Show her." Farnsworth's voice boomed through the tent.

She looked at me again, like she was taking me in. I wondered if she was remembering herself at my age. Or maybe just wondering whether I would be able to put together whatever puzzle they had.

Then, as before, Sarah just smiled and walked over to one of the coolers. She leaned over and grabbed a yellow backpack. She unzipped it and reached inside, pulling out something wrapped in toilet paper.

"Last spring, when I was looking for fossils near this mesa, I found this." She carefully unwrapped the toilet paper and held up a white, conical-shaped object. "This is a plaster cast of a tooth. The real tooth is back at Derek's lab. But this tooth is what led us to look around here. After a few days of digging, we found this bone quarry."

"Can I see it?"

"How do I know that I can trust you, Molly Wilder?"

"You can."

"I can? Do you pledge yourself to the scientific method and all it holds dear?"

"Yes."

"Will you search for the truth, at all costs?"

"Yes."

Her brown eyes bored into mine. They had little gold flecks that warmed as a smile spread across her face.

"Well, all right then."

Sarah slapped it to my palm. It was cool against my skin, maybe ten inches in length, and thick. And while it was slightly curved, like a *T-rex* tooth, I could immediately see a huge difference. *T-rex* teeth had two serrations, one along the front, and one along the back. These serrations helped the tooth cut up its meal, like the serrations on a steak knife.

But this tooth had four rows of small raised lines along its backside, as well as one along its front. This was not a *T-rex* tooth. I looked back up at Sarah.

"We think another, bigger dinosaur did this to the *T-rex*. I think that gouge you felt in the *T-rex* vert is damage from another, unknown dinosaur, possibly during battle. We pulled a small tooth tip from that hole when we found the fossils. That tip matched this tooth."

"What about scavengers? Couldn't a scavenger have lost the tooth as it ate the body?" I frowned. I didn't want to rock their boat, but dino battles were really hard to assume. Especially when many carnivores wouldn't turn down an easy, free meal of a fresh dead animal if it was available.

"Possibly. If we find more of the *T-rex*, we'll have a better picture. The broken tooth we found in the hole suggests a struggle. Why would a healthy tooth break if the animal was just chomping away at a lifeless body? But if it *was* a battle, the *T-rex* likely died from that wound. It's a hole in a spinal column after all," she said.

Even though it was a dark subject, I grinned back. If Sarah was right, well that was amazing. Actual evidence of fights between dinosaurs was extremely rare.

She took back the cast of the tooth and held it up. I looked at the tooth and then to her intricately tattooed arms. It was like an angry mural of bones, but in the madness, I could begin to pick out species. Maybe there was a disarticulated *Pachy* somewhere in there. Somehow Sarah seemed as interesting to me as the tooth's owner.

"It's not just the matter of our dead *T-rex*. Molly, take a good look at this tooth. It's from a creature that no one has described before. It's out there."

"Yep," Farnsworth said from the tent entrance. He took off his hat and wiped the sweat from his forehead. Like his temples, the rest of his dark hair was flecked with gray, and it stuck up at various angles like ears or horns. He looked like a *Dracorex*. He rubbed his head violently, then put his hat back on. He pointed to the tooth in my hand. "It wasn't another *T-rex*, that's for sure. Whoever owned that tooth broke a *T-rex* in half."

Letter from Gideon Mantell to Rev. William Buckland, 1824

Dear Buckland,

I am off to assist in a birth, but wanted to write to respond to your last letter. The teeth I've found connected to that fractured skull have five serrations. Your Stonesfield specimen has only one or two if I remember correctly? Please confirm as soon as possible.

I have been visited by several gentlemen who wish to purchase my fossils for their personal collection, but I am unwilling to sell. They heard of my finds from the quarrymen. I swear they cannot keep a secret from anyone!

Your humble servant,
Gideon Mantell

GIVE IT YOUR AWL

Molly

TWO HOURS LATER, I felt like an ant dying in a hot beam of sun focused by a magnifying glass. Farnsworth's hat might have kept the sun off my head and face, but it didn't stop me from sweating buckets. As if reading my thoughts, a large drop of sweat dripped down my forehead, mixing with the SPF 30. Before I could stop it with my gloved hand, it flowed down the bridge of my nose and into the crease of my left eye, causing it to water.

The last thing I wanted was for anyone to think I was some kind of emotional teen, so I wiped my eyes on my sleeve and continued to whack at the sandstone pedestal I'd been working on all morning.

After we'd finished talking about the *T-rex*, Sarah asked me to do some dirty work. Literally. A few days before, she'd discovered a hadrosaur femur, probably *Edmontosaurus*. *Edmontosaurus* was a herbivorous duck-billed dinosaur that grew about forty feet in length. It was a relatively common dinosaur, and paleontologists had found their fossils in late Cretaceous–aged quarries across the western United States and Canada.

Because she had a *Triceratops* skull to take care of, Sarah placed the lovely bone in my care. No pressure or anything. She asked me to get it ready to transport out of the quarry and into Glasgow. Apparently we were storing all the fossils we collected at Farnsworth's office until she headed back to Wyoming at the end of the summer.

Finding fossils was the best part of our job. But a close second was actually digging a fossil out of the ground. Lots of fossils were small and could be gathered quickly just by picking them up. But larger fossils, like bones, required a little more time and effort.

I spent the next few hours lying on my side, parallel to the fossil femur. I couldn't get what Sarah had said out of my head. *Molly, take a good look at this tooth. It's from a creature that no one has described before.*

First I had dug a moat around the fossil; then I dug underneath it, essentially creating an isolated, stone mushroom—what we call a *pedestal*—in the middle of the quarry.

It's out there.

I tried to push the thought away so I could focus on the task at hand. Even though I'd put several kneepads under my shoulder and hip, my left side tingled and ached, telltale signs I'd improperly placed my pads. My circulation must have been cut off a bit. *Fantastic.* I hated when my leg fell asleep.

I wiggled my body to wake it up and decided to clean my workstation. I grabbed my paintbrush and swept at the mess of loose dirt and pebbles that flecked off my pedestal. I pushed the debris—what's called *matrix* by those in the know—into a nearby pile. After all, a clean quarry was a happy quarry. Eventually I'd brush all that loose matrix into a bucket and take it to the edge of the quarry. While I'm pretty sure there weren't any tiny fossils in the loose matrix, Sarah wanted us to double-check everything using the giant sieve she'd built. And so, I'd pour the matrix material through the sieve: if it caught something, I'd bag and catalogue it. So far, the team had found a few small teeth fragments, a mammal jaw, and several fish scales using this technique.

I gave the sandstone mushroom a small smack for luck and then stood up. This pedestal was finished. Time to plaster. Plastering a fossil was messy business, but it was unavoidable. Sometimes a fossil would have thousands of miles to go before landing in a lab. It might seem strange, but fossils were just rocks, so they could break—and of course we didn't want that. So, years ago, some genius scientist invented the art of covering fossils in the field with plaster-of-Paris. Once dried, the plaster created a durable jacket around the fossil, protecting it during transportation. And once the fossil made it to a lab, a quick slash with a saw removed the jacket so that scientists could get to the good stuff—the fossil itself.

I wiped the sweat from my nose again and walked to the edge of the quarry to gather the necessary tools I'd need for plastering. A bucket of water, some newspaper, paper towels, a bag of dry plaster, an empty bucket for the mixture, and burlap strips. It took several trips to get everything, and I tried to look more confident than I felt. I had to get this right. I only learned how to plaster by myself last summer, and I really didn't want to look like a noob on my first day.

Before I mixed the plaster, I covered the top of the fossil with wet paper towels and the surrounding stone with wet newspaper. If I didn't do that, plaster would stick to the fossil, which might cause it to break when someone tried to open it with a saw. Once I finished that, I was ready to get plastered. With plaster-of-Paris, of course.

It was a simple enough process. You mixed one-part water with two-parts plaster. But it was done by eye, mixing it by hand and sometimes a painter's stick. It was critical to get the right consistency. Too watery, and the plaster jacket wouldn't protect the fossil. Too thick, and it would be a pain to remove. Not to mention it would also be very heavy and awkward to move from the field to the lab.

I poured the water into the bucket and then slowly added the plaster powder, using my hand to feel the texture as it thickened. As I mixed, white flecks of plaster splashed onto my upper arms and my sand-covered jeans.

Licking my cracked lips, I squished the plaster between my fingers until it was a perfect consistency of thick pudding. I pulled my arm out of the bucket and squeezed my hand into a fist, enjoying the sensation of the plaster dripping through my fingers.

I turned to the stack of burlap strips next to my plaster bucket, picked up a long strip, and swirled it around in the plaster mixture. I pulled it out, using my other hand to squeeze any extra plaster back into the bucket. I carefully placed the strip over the paper towel–covered part of my fossil pedestal. I then repeated the process with the other burlap strips, over and over, sometimes pushing the burlap strips against the pedestal, molding them to its shape.

About ten minutes later, I stood back, shaking my hands of excess plaster. The pedestal with the fossil had disappeared, and in its place was a giant and wet white rock. Awesome. I stretched my back and felt a slight cramp. I'd been at this all morning. I needed to move my body. Paleontologists were famous for having horrible backs, a fate I wanted to avoid. Besides, my awl was dull from hours of use. Digging into sandstone was way easier with a sharp, pointy tool. I wandered over to the supply pile and poked around until I found a bucket with freshly sharpened awls. Knowing my luck, my first job back at base camp would be to sharpen all the awls for tomorrow.

I grabbed a new awl and turned back to the quarry. Above us, the sun shone harshly; there wasn't a cloud in the sky to stop its assault. Like fresh snow, the quarry's light-colored rocks were an intense natural reflector of sunlight. It was almost blinding. I squinted in the bright light and pulled Farnsworth's hat farther down on my head. Just then a gentle breeze flowed mercifully through the quarry, rustling tarps and cooling my face. I took in the fresh air but then scrunched my nose as the chemical smell of Butvar-76 hit me. Glancing around, I saw Karolin squeezing a small plastic bottle, pouring its gooey contents onto a fossil. Butvar-76 was the glue of choice for fossil excavation. If a fossil broke a little, it was used as an adhesive to secure the bone until it could be properly fixed in a lab.

The crew was busy around the quarry. Karolin and Sarah were working on a *Triceratops* skull, plastering it for removal. Dean was sitting cross-legged on the floor of the quarry, his head bowed down as he scribbled in a yellow journal. Across the quarry, Farnsworth's back was bent as he worked on his own bone. I craned my neck, but I couldn't see what he was working on. As if he sensed my stare, his head snapped up. I quickly ducked my head and walked back to my fossil.

As I sat down on my kneepad, I heard footsteps stop behind me, and a shadow crossed over my fossil. "Bored? Missing your Facebook yet?"

"Nah, I'm good," I said. I looked up at Farnsworth. "Ready for Denny's Early Bird Special?"

He grumbled in response but squatted down next to me. He rubbed at the wet cast, moving plaster around, making sure there was an even thickness.

A few seconds later, Sarah sat down next to him. She moved her own hands around in tandem with his, poking my handiwork. My stomach churned. I really hoped I'd done my job right.

Finally, she grunted approvingly and slapped me on the back. "Looks great."

"Thanks," I said.

Don't smile, Molly.

I smiled.

Ugh.

"So what kind of dino do you think it is?" Sarah asked. I knew she wasn't talking about the femur I was working on, but the strange dinosaur that maybe killed the *T-rex*.

"I don't know," I said. I bit my lip. "What are the next steps with the *T-rex* spine?"

"Finish the cast and haul it over to Farnsworth's warehouse in Glasgow," Sarah said. "I just wanted to get it out of the ground to study it as soon as possible. Moving it into a truck will be a pain."

"Should have moved it to the warehouse three weeks ago," Farnsworth growled.

"My call," Sarah said.

Farnsworth glanced at her and held up a hand. "You're the boss."

At that, she smiled. "Damn straight."

"You think the rest of the *T-rex* is somewhere nearby?" I asked.

"Hopefully," Farnsworth said. "It'd be nice if the entire body is a part of this flood zone. If so, I bet we'll find other pieces nearby." He slowly moved a finger across the lip of the plaster cast, removing a glob that was slowly dripping onto the ground. With a practiced flick of his wrist, he sent it shooting toward the ravine.

"Flood?" I asked.

"This bone quarry is an example of a mass mortality event caused during a catastrophic deluge," Sarah said.

"Say that three times fast," Farnsworth said.

Sarah slapped his arm but grinned. Seeing my confused look, she waved the abusing hand around the quarry. "Basically, Molly, a huge rainstorm caused havoc here about sixty-six million years ago. Plants and animals were caught in an enormous flood. I want to understand everything that happened here. That's why this is my PhD project."

I'd been wondering why there were so many different species of dinosaurs strewn together. *Triceratops*, *Edmontosaurus*, *T-rex*. You could find them in the Hell Creek, but so close together? I thought of that pachy fossil in Farnsworth's truck. It was kinda rare. This site was a nice snapshot of what thrived and died during the late Cretaceous period.

Sarah stood up, tipping a bit to the side. Laughing, she steadied herself. "Head rush. Make sure to drink lots of water, Molly. It's hot." She wiped her hands on her pants, leaving a long white mark as she rubbed up and down. "Wouldn't want you to die on your first day."

CRETACEOUS SALAD

Molly

IT WAS EARLY evening by the time we arrived back in Glasgow. I was so tired that I fought to keep my eyes open during the drive back. Not surprising, since I woke up at 3:00 a.m. Pacific time to catch my flights. Even though Sarah had an extra sandwich for me to eat for lunch, my stomach gurgled so loudly that I had to cough to try and cover it up. Didn't fool anyone though. Dean ended up giving me half his Snickers bar on the ride home just to make the gurgling stop.

Sarah pulled off the main road down a gravel driveway and parked behind a large warehouse. Leaping down from her truck, I shouldered my backpack and walked over to Farnsworth's truck to grab my larger bag.

"That's Derek's business and our lab. I'll show you around later," Sarah said, waving at the building. It was a large gray concrete building with a huge metallic roll-up door and a small staircase that led to a red door. On the door was a faded sign with the words "Glasgow Geologic Institute."

"Come on," Sarah said, pulling at my arm a bit. I moved to follow her but stopped for another good look around. In front of me were two large, gleaming Airstream trailers. They were arranged in an L-shape, almost intersecting a large, square house to create a mini-courtyard. The house was gray and covered in patches of off-white and beige as if its painters weren't sure what exactly to do with it and eventually gave up. There was a rickety porch with a few rusting metal chairs, a small table, and a large green cooler.

Farnsworth tipped his hat at Sarah, then disappeared into the home. A line of light flickered through stained curtains.

Sarah and the others tried to make the mini-courtyard as homey as possible. There were a few picnic tables, some camp chairs, a large red cooler, and a barbecue made out of a barrel that had been cut in half. Off to the side was a large fire pit that appeared to be well used from the charred logs and ash in it. Dean and Karolin plopped down at one of the tables, and Dean leaned over into the red cooler, pulling out several cans of soda.

"Come on, Molly," Sarah called from the entrance of one of the Airstreams. I ran up the short stairs and stood in the doorway. I've seen Airstream trailers before in magazines and in movies, but never in person. This particular model seemed rather nice, especially for a university dig. On my last dig, I stayed in a tent all summer.

"Not much to see. Here is the bathroom," Sarah said, waving her arm toward one of the closets. "It's . . . utilitarian, for sure, but at least we have a shower if you really need one at the end of the day. Just use it sparingly, as we'll have to replace the water. You'll have Sundays off, and we use that for a town day. You know, to do laundry, go grocery shopping for the week, that sort of thing. The nearby Gas & Go has a shower that you can rent. They never run out of hot water."

"Why doesn't Mr. Farnsworth let us use his shower?'

Sarah let out a shuddering laugh. "It's disgusting because he doesn't clean it, like, ever."

I grinned. "Not into housekeeping, is he?"

"Nah, too busy traveling the world for fossils to care much." Sarah shrugged her shoulders. "Always been that way. He's a busy man, always hunting." She pointed to the unused bed. "You're sharing with me. Get settled, and come out when you're ready." At the door, Sarah turned back and smiled. "Glad you're finally here, Molly."

Ten minutes later, I opened the Airstream trailer and looked out into the courtyard. This early in the summer, the sun was still out but low on the horizon, painting the sky in bright hues of pink and orange. Above, to the southwest, there was a grouping of dark gray clouds. While we were dry here in Glasgow, I bet our quarry was getting a bit of summer rain.

Sarah was at the barbeque, and Dean and Karolin were sitting at one of the picnic tables, eating chips and salsa and talking. Karolin held a beer in one hand, and playing cards in the other. Opposite her, Dean drank from a Coke can, carefully scrutinizing his own cards. Next to them was a large flat slab of light colored rock. On its surface was a jumble of dark, flat fossils, but I couldn't make out what they were from where I was standing.

Over on his porch, Farnsworth lounged in one of his chairs. His feet were crossed and raised up on a small stool, and his hat sat low on his head, so low I could barely make out his eyes. He sipped on a can of beer.

"Soup's almost on, Molly," Sarah called to me as I approached. She flipped a burger a little too hard, and it tumbled off her metal spatula onto the dirt. "Shoot," she grumbled. On cue, Dean reached into the cooler for another beef patty. Karolin laughed and patted the bench, "Sit down, Molly," she said. "Don't step on the others."

"Others?"

Karolin pointed toward Sarah's feet, where there were several deserted burger patties on the ground. One was covered in ants.

"Oh, shut up." Sarah laughed. "I have two degrees and a black belt in Taekwondo. I can do this."

As I climbed over the picnic bench next to Karolin, I leaned over to look at the large rock on the table. It was round in shape, about two feet in diameter. The rock itself was similar in color to the rock in our quarry. I bet it came from there. But unlike other rocks in our quarry, this slab was only a few inches thick, like it was peeled from the ground, not hammered out. And on its surface, instead of a fossil bone, was a layer of fossilized leaves.

"Pretty cool, right? There are a bunch of interesting plants in there." Dean stacked his cards and used them to point at one of the leaves. "Look familiar?"

While most of the leaves seem to be jumbled on top of each other, the leaf he was pointing at was off to the side by itself. It was large, about the size of a hockey puck, and triangular in shape with rounded edges. It had a long stem that extended down an inch or so.

"Don't know," I said.

"Ancient ginkgo leaf. Not very common in the Hell Creek, but you can find some," Dean said. "Ginkgo species are really old, and they haven't changed their shape very much over time. If you put a modern ginkgo next to this one, it would look pretty similar. Sarah, I forget, when did it first show up in the fossil record?"

"About 270 million years ago," she replied without looking at us, her tongue poking out of her mouth as she flipped a burger.

"So over forty million years before dinosaurs," Dean said.

"And it survived the K-Pg boundary extinction," a voice said behind me. A beer can slammed next to me. I jumped a little at the noise. Farnsworth swung his long legs over the bench and sat down next to me. "Hardy little things. You know about the K-Pg boundary, Molly?"

"Sure." If you want to study dinosaurs, you have to know about the famous Cretaceous-Paleogene boundary. K-Pg boundary was its nickname. It was confusing, but the "K" and the "Pg" came from how geologists label sediments on geologic maps. The K-Pg boundary formed when a giant asteroid hit the planet about sixty-six million years ago, creating a ninety-mile hole in the Earth's crust—roughly the length of Delaware. While we don't know exactly how many years it took, what is clear is that around three-quarters of all life on Earth disappeared. Poof. Gone. Just like that.

"Little?" Sarah laughed. "Modern ginkgos can grow several stories in height, Derek. And ginkgos survived not only the K-Pg boundary but also several other major extinction level events, like the Permian-Triassic extinction." She saw the confusion on my face, and she started laughing.

"Too focused on the Mesozoic, Molly," she jabbed. She put a fist on her hip and twirled the spatula, drawing my eye down to the writing on her apron: *If Something is Gneiss, Don't Take It For Granite.* "Another extinction event. About 250 million years ago, almost seventy percent of all land animals and plants died, and over eighty percent of the Earth's ocean animals also died." She turned back to the barbeque. "We still have no idea exactly what caused it. It's just so old, evidence is hard to come by. But we will figure it out. It's only a matter of time. Ready for a burger? Derek? How about you?"

"Sure." He turned to Dean. "What's the game tonight?"

Dean took a long sip of soda. "Too rich for your blood, Derek."

"What, five-card stud?"

"Go fish." Dean grinned.

"Dear Lord, I'm surrounded by children," Farnsworth groaned, rubbing his face with his hand.

"Yes, you are," Sarah said, and I could hear a warning in her tone as she flipped a finished burger onto a plate. "Remember that."

Farnsworth took a swig of beer and looked at Dean. "How about we play something else."

"Like what?" Dean asked.

"Poker?" Karolin said.

"Nah, I got my Thursday game with the boys at Murphy's for that, and frankly I'd clean you all to the bone." Farnsworth grinned. "Why don't we break Molly into the fold the right way."

I cocked my head to the side. "What do you mean?"

"I think she needs to eat some salad."

I saw Sarah and Karolin frown, and I immediately felt defensive. "What, like a Caesar salad?"

"Derek, that's gross," Sarah said.

"No, it isn't, Sarah. You've done it. I know you've done it too, Dean. Karolin?"

"Just, yuck." Karolin stuck out her tongue and shook her head. "Yes. So gross."

I shook my head. "What am I missing here?"

Farnsworth motioned toward the slab in front of me. "I found that the other day. The southwestern side of the quarry has a ton of sandstone slabs, and each layer has a bunch of leaves on it. We have been excavating slabs like this since we started, and there are way more in my lab." He jabbed his thumb behind him toward the warehouse. "With the exception of that ginkgo leaf, that particular pile of leaves is pretty common. We've got triplicates of every leaf, actually." He looked right in my eyes. "You fancy yourself a paleontologist. Everyone at this table has eaten a bit of fossil leaves. Your turn. Not Caesar salad, Molly. Cretaceous salad."

I stared at him with an open mouth. He wanted me to eat a fossil? He wanted me to eat rocks?

He returned my look, a small smile playing on his lips. I looked at the others. Sarah's mouth was downturned in a frown, and Karolin looked disgusted.

I looked across the table at Dean. He grinned crazily at me. No help there.

I turned back to Farnsworth. I could feel his contempt. I knew he didn't expect me to take the challenge. I mean, who in their right mind would eat a fossil? Especially a teenager, and one who shouldn't be here.

Well, screw that. I raised my chin and reached over, touching the fossil leaf at the very top of the pile. My fingers gently scraped across its surface, and I felt the leaf's texture. This one was long and a bit rounded, several inches in length. It looked familiar. Using my fingernail, I cut into the rock, pushing the leaf's edge up off the rock. I carefully pulled the leaf away from the sandstone slab. I managed to remove it from the pile without damaging it. Instead of a solid leaf, it was more like an intricate web of paper-thin veins that were all connected into a leaf shape.

It's just minerals, Molly, I reminded myself. I could eat a little bit of silica if that was what it took to prove myself.

Turning back to Farnsworth, I put the entire leaf in my mouth, pushing it onto my tongue. It dissolved quickly, a dusty treat for this late June evening. I chewed once, feeling the grit on my teeth. I reached over and grabbed his beer, taking a huge swallow. The beer was sharp as it poured down my throat and washed away the sandy taste of the fossilized leaf. My eyes watered a bit, but I never looked away from him. I placed the beer can down on the table and reached for the next leaf.

"Not bad for a Cretaceous Salad," I said as I pulled up another leaf.

"Okay, stop!" Farnsworth said, shaking his head. "You don't have to eat any more, Molly."

Around me, the others whooped and laughed, and Karolin shook my shoulder with glee. Sarah placed a burger in front of me, and I hungrily took a huge bite, mostly to erase any remaining dirt on my tongue.

After a long moment, Farnsworth chuckled. "Cretaceous salad. For the record, that was an ancient magnolia leaf." He stood up and walked back toward his porch. He opened his cooler and grabbed another beer. As he sat down in his chair, he locked eyes with me, and in a movement almost too quick to see, he brought his beer up to his forehead in a salute.

THUNDER BUMPER

Molly

YESTERDAY WAS A sweltering day. I was sticky and covered in sweat stains. I probably should have cleaned up better in our small Airstream sink last night. Based on how I was feeling—and probably smelling—I regretted that decision.

However, today was very different. While still warm, the sun was hidden behind puffy dark clouds, the air heavy with humidity. While I appreciated the lack of direct sun, the humidity felt oppressive, like swimming in a fish bowl.

"Thunder bumper," I heard Farnsworth say loudly to nobody in particular as he squatted down in the quarry, poking at something with his awl.

I looked at Sarah next to me, my eyebrow raised. "Rainstorm," she translated. *Ah.*

It was mid-morning, and my plastered femur was finally dry. Even if it rained, the plaster cast would do its job and protect it, but I still needed to plaster the other side. If that was going to happen today, I needed to hurry. I couldn't do it in the rain. It would never dry properly, and the fossil inside could be damaged during transport.

Sarah poked at my plastered femur with her awl. After a few jabs, she smiled with approval. "Let's do it. Grab your awl and hammer."

I nodded as Sarah removed her rock hammer from her tool belt. I walked over to the bucket filled with tools and grabbed another rock hammer. After I was settled back next to my femur, we placed our awls at the base of the pedestal, right under the lip of the plaster jacket. If I had done my job right, we'd be able to break the whole plaster cast away from the base of the quarry without damaging the fossil. After a few purposeful hits on our awls with our hammers, our combined force broke the plaster cast away from the base of the quarry with a satisfying crack. We put down our tools and pushed until we capsized the fossil, exposing the fresh rock beneath it. A perfect detachment, if I did say so myself.

"I'll get started on finishing this cast," I said.

Sarah paused for a second, finger on her lip. "No, I can do it. You've done a great job with the other side." She gave me a large smile. "I have a better idea. Derek, can you and Molly grab the box and bring it here? I think she should have a go at it."

Box?

"What? Why?" Farnsworth said.

"Because it'll be fun for her. Something new to try. She's the intern. It's her job to learn."

I heard Farnsworth grunt in annoyance as he stood up, knees cracking in the process. "You don't have to keep her entertained."

"It's just sitting there. She's here to learn. She may as well have a go at it."

"Fine. Get moving," he said, not looking at me as he strode over to the tent.

Rolling my eyes, I followed him to the other side of the quarry and into the tent.

As my eyes adjusted to the darkness, I saw Farnsworth leaning over to pick up something in one of the corners of the tent. Then he whirled around and dropped the object onto the floor as if it were diseased. It was a black suitcase, large and thick, with square gray latches. It reminded me of the boxes I'd seen in movies that contain important weapons or vials of poison. "Nakasogi Industries" was stenciled in gray lettering on the front of the box.

"Like my prize," I said.

"The Nakasogi *Prize?*" he said, his words dripping with sarcasm.

What was this guy's problem? "Yes, *prize*. And you know we're inside a tent that blocks out the sun, right? You can take those off." I pointed at his sunglasses.

"You mean *internship*, kid. You're the intern. To be a *prize* would mean you'd be some big benefit to us," he replied. But he did take off his sunglasses. Small victories.

"I earned the right to be here. I applied for the Nakasogi Prize, and that's what I won. Sarah did the same thing."

The Nakasogi Prize was the brainchild of this billionaire tech guy in Japan. From what I'd read, Nakasogi was a generous supporter of paleontology and education around the world. There were two ways to win the Nakasogi Prize: the graduate-student way, and the high-school-student way. The graduate student who wins the prize receives a full grant to support their field research. The winning high school student gets an internship to learn and support the graduate student's research. The graduate student adds something to the field, and the high school student gets valuable experience.

Farnsworth snorted at my response. But I held his gaze. After a long moment, his eyes flicked down. I heard the click of the briefcase latches. I took a deep breath and looked inside.

Sitting in a bed of dark gray foam was a large, white machine. It looked like a mini-helicopter, but instead of two rotary propellers, it had four. Next to the device was a remote control with several knobs and a small, dark screen.

"A drone?" I said, surprised. I was kinda hoping for poison.

"Amazing observation," said Farnsworth. "As the winner of the Nakasogi *Prize*, you're no doubt aware that your boss, Sarah, gets lots of *tech* to use this summer, courtesy of Nakasogi Industries." He rolled his eyes. "Supposedly, this drone takes video and correlates the surface data with up-to-date geologic maps. She thinks this drone will find fossils for us."

"You don't agree?"

Farnsworth wiggled the drone from its case and carefully handed it to me. It was heavier than it looked. "Using a computer to tell us where to dig for fossils? Pirates know where to dig without some high-tech gadget."

"Pirates?"

"Never mind," he said. He frowned at the drone. "I'm getting too old for this crap." He grabbed the remote from the case and pushed it into my other hand. "Have fun and try not to screw it up." He stood up, his knees creaking and cracking again. He tipped his hat at me and walked out of the tent.

"Have you ever used this?" I yelled after him.

He snorted in response.

I walked out of the tent with my new toy. Now that I was in better light, I took a good, long look at the drone. It was about a foot long and a foot wide, with a small camera lens on its main body. I mean, it didn't look remarkable. Not that I would know. I'd seen people flying these around, but I'd never owned one myself.

"Okay, good. You found it. Quick lesson," Sarah said, walking over to stand next to me. She leaned over and took the remote. "This button turns it on." Using her finger, she pointed to a small button on the side. "These dials move the propellers. One for vertical lift, the other for forward motion." She jiggled two knobs with her thumbs. "This large screen here in the middle is the camera screen, and it will show you what you're looking at. You'll have to play with it a bit to get the hang of it."

She grabbed the drone and walked to the edge of the quarry. She placed it on the ground, turning it on with a flick of her finger. The propellers whirred to life, and the drone rose into the air. The sound of the propellers was louder than I expected, and some dust was kicked up as she sent the drone flying into the gully.

She handed me the remote. "Have fun."

I was so nervous, I almost dropped the remote. "Um, okay."

"Six-thousand-dollar piece of tech there, Molly. You break it, you buy it," Farnsworth called from his fossil.

"He's joking, Molly. You'll do great. Just take it easy."

I bit my lip and turned back to the drone. It was still hovering over the trucks. I moved a dial, and the drone moved forward a foot.

Cool. Progress.

I moved the other dial and the drone dropped several feet, nearly hitting Sarah's truck. *Whoops*. I quickly adjusted the lever a bit and the drone hovered over the bed of Farnsworth's filthy pickup truck.

"Whew," Dean said behind me. "That was close."

Yes, it was. Too close. My heart was beating so fast it felt like it was trying to erupt from my chest and race away. I sucked air into my nose and blew it out of my mouth, trying to remember all the breathing techniques my English teacher had insisted on us learning in class. Something about *mindfulness* and being present in the *moment*. Frankly, she was a wacko who wore yoga pants to school and smelled suspiciously like gin, so I hadn't really paid that much attention. I kinda wished I had now.

Okay, worrying wouldn't help me overcome this challenge. I pressed the dial again, causing the drone to rise.

After a few minutes, and a few close shaves, I finally was feeling okay about managing the drone. In fact, I was pretty proud of myself. I'd managed to keep the machine aloft and relatively stable. I was able to fly it around the ravine, between the trucks, and back up toward the terrace. Pushing the dial, I buzzed the drone up past our quarry, high into the air. Stealing a quick glance down at the remote, I used my thumb to push the big red button next to the screen. The screen flicked to life, and I got slightly dizzy watching the rocks shoot by as the drone's camera captured its ascent. When the drone was finally as high as a white bird in the sky, the small screen showed our group as little moving specks, like ants on an anthill.

Smiling, I flew the drone down to the other side of the ravine, skirting the butte. Just as I got it level with our quarry, my body instinctively trembled as I heard a crash of thunder. At the same time, a strong burst of wind thrashed the gully, almost knocking me over. Tarps, papers, and other loose items flew around the quarry. I heard Farnsworth swearing at the storm.

I turned away from the wind, holding on to my hat while simultaneously trying not to drop the remote. My eyes were just closing to stop the assault of dirt hitting my face when I saw the wind push the drone around the side of the mesa and out of sight.

I squinted down at my remote, and the screen was completely dark. That couldn't be a good sign.

The wind stopped almost as fast as it had started. Whirling around, my eyes confirmed what I hoped wasn't true: the drone was nowhere in sight.

Uh-oh.

The drone must have hit the mesa wall, or crashed in the ravine. It was probably just a pile of plastic and high-tech circuitry now.

Only out of the box for twenty minutes and the drone was gone. Sarah was going to kill me. Worse, I could imagine Farnsworth's told-you-so expression.

I felt my stomach turn cold, and my hands began to shake. Behind me, I could tell that the rest of the crew was trying to manage the chaos caused by the wind.

I had to fix this.

I had to find that drone.

I needed to get away from the others and look around. I turned around and yelled the first thing that came to mind. "Um, I'm going to the bathroom!"

Sarah waved at me but didn't look up.

I bolted down the talus pile, not even concerned about falling on my face. When I reached the bottom, I looked northeast toward the mouth of the ravine, where the drone was forced. My eyes scoured the ground for any sign of the thing, but I didn't see anything. It must be farther. I broke into a run, trying to stay as close to the mesa and talus pile as possible, my feet echoing my internal groans of *please be okay, please be okay, please be okay.*

It didn't take me long to reach the mouth of the ravine. The service road that Farnsworth and I took to get here stretched out before me, all the way to the highway in the distance. But there was no sign of anything white. The drone wasn't on the ground floor, and there weren't many places for it to go, so that meant it was probably on the mesa itself, maybe on one of those ledges I saw earlier. I doubled back but stopped at a point before Sarah and the others could see me. I didn't want them asking questions. I scrambled back up the talus slope. This time I wasn't careful, and the rocks cut into my hands. But I kept going.

Once I reached the top of the talus slope, I saw that I was level with the Hell Creek Formation, which was parallel to the quarry floor. Carefully, I walked northeast along the top talus slope, following the Hell Creek layer. I looked up and saw a red layer of sandstone above the Hell Creek Formation. Automatically, my brain flashed its name: the Fort Union Formation. Unlike the Hell Creek Formation, the Fort Union was very strong. It hadn't broken apart or eroded easily. It was much clearer now that those lips and ledges I saw when I arrived were part of the Fort Union Formation. The Fort Union isn't Cretaceous-aged sediments. It was Paleogene, so no dinosaurs. But that wasn't important right now. The drone was the goal.

Above me, raindrops started to fall, large and fat. The sky was dark and the wind had picked up enormously. After walking along the northeastern part of the mesa for several minutes, I finally saw the drone. It was sitting pretty on a Fort Union ledge, about five feet above me and to the left. It was just sitting there, happy as a clam, like an aboveground fossil waiting to be discovered. I literally hugged myself with relief while taking stock of its position. It was impressive that it was pushed this far from the quarry, around the mesa no less. Maybe it was blown upward, then it fell. It had been a strong wind, after all.

Using the Hell Creek's softer layers as footholds, I scrambled up onto the ledge and carefully walked toward the drone. It didn't look damaged. Hopefully it was okay internally and I could get back to the bone bed before anyone wondered where I'd gone.

Suddenly I heard a loud crack, and I flinched in surprise. *That wasn't thunder.* Frowning, I looked around. I didn't see anything unusual, but just in case I slowed my pace. Once I was within arm's reach of the drone, I leaned forward, finger outstretched. Lightning flashed above me, followed by crashing thunder. I counted the time between the light and the noise. Three seconds. That meant the storm was three miles away, right?

My fingertips had nearly brushed the drone when I heard another loud crack, and I felt the rocks below me give way. My whole body felt like it was floating. But only for a second.

I fell. Around me, rocks broke and crumbled. Together we tumbled several feet and rolled down the talus pile. Sharp rocks scraped my arms and face. Sand entered my mouth and nose as I tried to scream. It tasted like a mouthful of Cretaceous salad.

I landed on my back, a large yucca plant poking my arm. Rain pelted my face, and all the air in my chest was knocked out of me. I blinked a few times, then sat up. I was wet and dirty. But alive. Thank goodness. It could have been a lot worse.

I slowly stood up and immediately sucked at my teeth as I felt a sharp pain. I gently touched my leg. Apparently I hadn't survived unscathed. I'd cut my knees and blood was soaking through my jeans. I shook the dirt and sand from my hair, and I limped around while taking stock of my surroundings. From what I could figure, I was on the other side of the mesa, almost opposite the quarry. I couldn't see or hear the others. The mesa itself looked different from where our quarry was. This side was much more irregular, with several incredibly deep sawtooth divides. In fact, one of them was cut so deeply into the mesa that it looked like there was a . . . cave?

Yup, right at the top of the talus pile, carved into Hell Creek Formation was what looked like a small cave. A long lip of Fort Union layer was right above, capping it.

I remembered what Dean had told me when I'd arrived, about a cave on the other side of the mesa. This must be it. And lying right at its entrance was the stupid drone. That thing was going to be the death of me.

For the third time that day, I climbed the dumb talus pile. As I did, a large flash of lightning brightened the sky, loud thunder immediately on its heels. Then the rain turned into a downpour. I knew Montana summer storms normally didn't last for very long, but I had no idea if this drone was water-proof. The last thing I needed was for the drone to survive two disasters only to die from the rain. I grabbed the drone and moved into the entrance of the cave, slightly shaking from the cooler wind, not to mention the adrenaline that was slowly leaving my body.

After a few moments of standing at the entrance, staring out at flat, rain-soaked plains, it was clear the rain wasn't going to stop anytime soon. I gazed up at the ceiling, feeling glad that the cave was providing some protection. To take my mind off everything, including my throbbing leg, I looked around. The cave was about ten feet deep, maybe ten feet tall. It was sur-prisingly bigger on the inside than it looked from the outside.

Another flash of lightning illuminated the cave. And that's when I saw it. Nestled in the soft, yellow-white rock wall of the back of the cave was the largest dinosaur skull I'd ever seen in my life. Its large eye sockets seemed to follow me as I slowly approached. I reached into my back pocket and grabbed my cell phone. Incredibly, the fall hadn't shattered my screen.

Thank. You. Apple.

I turned on the flashlight app and shined it toward the fossil in front of me. Glossy black bones danced in the light. So different from the brown fossils we had been digging out of this formation so far. I moved my light down from the dinosaur's eye socket. Its massive jaw was filled with razor-sharp black teeth. The skull was perfectly orientated with my face, like the animal was just as curious about me as I was about it. As I reached a hand to touch it, I realized my hands had stopped shaking. It was hard and cool, and I felt the gentle curves and holes that probably connected the ancient bone with living muscle and skin.

And its teeth! The teeth were perfect and terrifying. This animal was designed to tear apart flesh and bone.

I heard Sarah's words again, like she was in the cave, like her words could echo off the walls.

Molly, take a good look at this tooth. It's from a creature that no one has described before.

The teeth appeared to be identical to Sarah's plaster tooth. Using my fingernail, I found a tooth that seemed like it was going to fall out anyway. I carefully dug away some of the sandstone around it. After a moment of digging, I gently pulled the tooth and held it up to the light. Yup. It had five serrations: one in the front, four in the back.

It's out there.

The tooth Sarah found belonged to this dinosaur.

I let loose a squeal and hopped in excitement. Then I winced in pain as the cuts on my legs stung sharply. I looked up at the cave ceiling, trying to focus on something new to distract myself from the pain.

Its giant eye sockets stared at my wound, like it was still alive, a killing machine built to hunt prey and detect weakness. For a moment, though I knew it was impossible, I thought it might emerge from its stone prison and come for me, the girl who had been silly enough to steal its tooth.

Then I noticed a long bone over the skull. It was about five feet in length exposed, and maybe a foot in diameter. The shape was familiar. An arm bone maybe?

The alarms in my head started to clang. The good kind, when you know something is strange, but good. Because in the middle of the bone was a large hole. This hole let me see the internal structure of the bone. A cross section. While the bone looked large and thick, the internal structure of the bone itself was really thin. Probably a quarter of an inch thick, if that. The rest of the bone was hollow.

Now, hollow bones were not really that unusual. Meat-eating dinosaurs and modern birds have hollow bones, for example. But I've personally never seen such a thin wall on a large bone before.

Pterosaurs had long, hollow bones. Their bones were thin, too, designed to lighten their body weight. Because they flew. But they're not dinosaurs. They were flying reptiles, their own species. Dinosaurs did not fly.

No carnivorous dinosaur, even a *T-rex*, ever had teeth like this. At least no carnivore I'd ever heard of. And I think this is even bigger than a *T-rex*.

And the bones were as black as night.

Suddenly, I heard Sarah yelling my name. I tore my eyes away from the fossil and limped toward the opening of the cave. The rain had let up enormously, and Sarah and Farnsworth were at the base of the mesa, looking up at me.

"Are you okay?" Sarah yelled. "We heard a crash."

"Sarah, you know that tooth?"

"Yeah."

"I think I found its owner."

THERE'S A MONSTER UNDER MY BEDROCK

Farnsworth

OUR LITTLE POSSE ran up the talus slope to the cave's entrance. Once we summited, I stopped to catch my breath, my chest rising and falling quickly as I glared at my stomach. I have to cut back on the longnecks at Murphy's. Go for a run. Maybe eat a salad.

Sarah, with all her annoying youthfulness, in a streak of purple hair, raced past me and into the cave. She stopped next to Molly, and I heard her gently swear under her breath. She never swore.

"Okay, hold your horses. I'm coming." I walked into the cave, and frankly I was surprised—the cave was bigger than it looked from below. I'd walked by it several times but never stopped to look inside. Too busy with Sarah's bone bed.

I saw Sarah with Molly at the back. "What is . . ." I started, but then trailed off. They were looking at the largest carnivorous dinosaur skull I'd ever seen. Remarkably, the skull was perfectly oriented so that its side was flush with the back of the cavern. Giving it a once-over, the skull looked complete. I saw a postorbital, premaxilla, maxilla, dentary, teeth, and . . .

"What is that?" While the skull was mostly exposed, its lower mandible had some rock matrix covering it. I pulled my brush off my tool belt. Leaning down, I brushed at the lower jaw, pushing at the rock to remove it. Yep, there was more to the fossil.

"Is that a horn?" Molly said, leaning past me to get a closer look.

Kid was right. Jutting downward from the bottom tip of the dentary were several black horns, at least four or five inches in length. They were conical in shape, looking like stalactites dripping from a cave ceiling. I'd never seen features like that on a carnivorous dinosaur skull before.

"Let me see that." A small hand reached over mine and pulled the brush from my grip. I opened my mouth to protest, but Molly just gave me a smirk. Turning back to the wall, she reached as high as she could, pushing sandstone away from the top of the skull.

"There's another horn here, too," she said, brushing upward and off to the side, sand and dirt falling onto the cave floor below.

Girl was right again. After a moment, another long, dark horn, not unlike an antelope's horn, took shape in front of us. Squinting in the darkness, I leaned forward and used my finger to brush the matrix away right above the eye socket. Yep, the horn attached to the skull right there, growing upward, then extended out parallel to the skull. Molly had already exposed a foot of it, but it looked like it was even bigger.

Bigger.

This whole thing was just . . .*big*. But how big?

I patted my leg, looking for my measuring tape. Drat, I'd left it in the car. Okay, Sarah was about five feet, six inches tall. This skull's length was probably just shy of one Sarah. So at least half a foot larger than the largest known *T-rex* skull. I took off my hat and rubbed the sweat off my brow as I absorbed that. A giant meat-eating dinosaur larger than a *T-rex*, with horns.

As of five minutes ago, *Tyrannosaurus rex*, Latin and Greek for "tyrant lizard king," was the dominant carnivorous dinosaur in this area of the world during the Cretaceous. This horned creature just stole that crown.

But what was it, exactly? Okay, let's break it down. Most likely it was a theropod. *T-rex* belongs to the subgroup of Theropoda, an extensive family of meat-eating dinosaurs. In addition to the *T-rex* and other large meat-eaters, like *Velociraptor*, theropods included animals that were not as terrifying, such as the ostrich-like *Gallimimus*, or the tiny *Compsognathus*. Oh, and don't forget the only dinosaur species to survive the disastrous attack of the nine-mile-long asteroid—the chicken. Well, not literally the chicken, of course. But modern birds are descendants of theropod dinosaurs, evolving and branching away from dinosaurs during the Mesozoic area.

But, the real question was whether it was another tyrannosaurid species? While *T-rex* was the most famous *Tyrannosaur*, it did have several close cousins in the tyrannosaurid family kicking around for the last twenty million years or so of the Cretaceous. Such as the smaller but just as scary North American *Albertosaurus*, *Gorgosaurus*, and *Daspletosaurus*, as well as the Asian *Tarbosaurus* and *Zhuchengtyrannus*.

And *T-rexes* certainly never had horns.

I leaned my face closer to the fossil. While there was a slight degradation on the skull, probably from exposure, it was in remarkable shape. The cave had preserved the fossil. *Thank you, cave.*

"Here." Molly handed Sarah a long dark tooth. "I pulled it out of the skull."

Sarah paused and rocked the tooth in her hand. "It's the same as the one we found, Derek," she said quietly, her eyes not moving from the tooth. After a moment, she handed it to me. Five serration lines on a conically shaped tooth. Yep. Our tooth came from this new dinosaur.

"The skull, the way it's encased in the rock. It's just like in a movie," Molly said.

The kid was right. It was like someone mounted it for us. This type of thing happened, but not very often. The wall was plainly Hell Creek Formation: around the skull was white-yellow conglomerate, a mixture of sand and rocks, just like in our bone quarry around the other side of the mesa. It's possible that this dinosaur was swept up in the same flood that created the mass mortality around the corner. I grinned at Sarah. "Looks like your PhD dissertation just got a heck of a lot more interesting."

Sarah was staring at the creature, intently. Their gazes were locked.

"Sarah?"

Finally, she turned.

"Yeah. Taphonomy is always interesting," Sarah said, turning to Molly. "Taphonomy is the study of what happens to an organism, such as a dinosaur, after its death until it fossilizes." She pointed at the ceiling of the cavern. "Look up there. That looks like a thick lens of mudstone, capping the fossil . . . and what's that?" she said as she moved her finger toward another long, black bone several feet above the skull.

The cave dimmed, the light from the outside broken.

"Wow," said a voice behind me. Karolin entered the cave with Dean. "Dr. Oliphant will love this."

"Dr. Oliphant?" Molly asked.

"My advisor," Sarah said, shooting a look at me. I shook my head slightly back at her, and Molly saw the gesture.

"Like, Dr. Sean Oliphant?" Molly said, raising an eyebrow at me. "The *National Geographic* Explorer guy? Nest Valley?"

I turned to see Dean and Karolin standing at the mouth of the cave. "When you guys didn't come back, we thought we'd investigate," Dean said, leaning forward to catch his breath. Even the youngsters were struggling. That made me feel a bit better, though it was offset by the fact that Oliphant's name was now echoing through the cave.

Focus on the positives. I turned back to the fossil. While the skull was fantastic, I did wonder about the rest of the body. Maybe it washed away with the flood. Or it could all be here, entombed in the rock behind the skull. I again looked up above the skull, and my eyes caught on that other long fossil Sarah had pointed out. I reached up and carefully touched it. It had been broken at some point, exposing a large hole in the bone.

"Hollow," Molly supplied as my finger gently tapped the hole. "Like a theropod or bird's. But the bone was really thin. And both bones were black. So from the same animal? Could a dinosaur have had super hollow bones?"

"No dinosaur this large had a hollow bone like this," Sarah said. "It's too thin. Pterosaurs have long, hollow bones like this," she said. She seemed almost angry. She leaned back and crossed her arms. "Okay, here's my thinking. This is probably just two animals. The skull here belongs to the remains of some new dinosaur relative of a *T-rex*. The hollow bone will likely be from a pterosaur." She reached up and traced the broken, exposed part of the bone. "It's probably a *Quetzalcoatlus* wing that somehow got caught up in the same flood as this dinosaur, so their bones were jumbled together."

"*Quetzalcoatlus*?" Karolin asked.

"Largest known pterosaur. Long. Wingspan was about thirty-five feet, so about the length of a school bus."

I shook my head. "I've seen *Quetzal* bones before. This bone is too big to be *Quetzalcoatlus*. And I've never seen one in Montana."

"Derek, *Quetz* was a huge pterosaur that probably flew everywhere in North America. It was bound to end up in the Hell Creek at some point," Sarah replied, tilting her head a bit as she looked at me. I knew she was probably right, but something about that bone didn't feel like it was from a pterosaur.

"Let's excavate whatever these are and see what we turn up," Sarah said.

Suddenly Dean cleared his throat. "These new fossils could be a good project for the GPR, Sarah."

I groaned. "What is it with you people and technology? Wasn't the drone enough?"

"Nakasogi gave us the GPR and a 3D printer, Derek. He expects us to use them," Sarah chided. She looked at her wristwatch. "In fact, the 3D printer arrives tonight, so we'll have to leave earlier than we normally would so we can meet the truck."

"Does it have to be stored in my warehouse?" I said, scratching the back of my neck with my hand.

"Wow," Sarah said, her mouth twitching. "The man flies around, going into some of the most dangerous places on earth to find fossils. Hurricanes, dust storms, bandits—doesn't bat an eye." She turned from the others back to me and winked. "Confronted with a giant printing machine, gets almost whiny."

"What's a GPR?" Molly asked.

"Ground Penetrating Radar," Sarah replied. "Similar to what they used in *Jurassic Park*, but a lot more sophisticated."

Weeks ago, I had made the mistake of asking Sarah how it worked. While most of it was Greek to me, what I had figured out was that the GPR emitted high-frequency radio waves into the ground. When those waves hit a buried object, the waves were sent back to the GPR's receiving antenna. Apparently, Nakasogi Industries had tested it extensively before sending it our way. They claimed that there would be no damage to any fossils. But I wasn't sure I believed that. And since all we had so far of this specimen was a skull and a long, hollow bone that looked delicate, I didn't like the idea of playing with fire. We should have been taking our time, but I knew I was in the minority.

"What happens after we collect the GPR data?" Molly asked.

I glanced at Sarah, who motioned toward Dean. When Sarah received notice she won the Nakasogi Prize, she arranged for one of her undergrad students to receive training from Nakasogi Industries. Dean volunteered and spent a week in Japan, learning all about GPRs, 3D printing, and how to drink sake properly.

"We will turn it into a CAD computer file back at the warehouse," Dean said. "Once we've set up the machine, I'll upload it and the 3D printer will do its magic."

"How long will it take to set up the printer?" Karolin asked.

"A few hours. They are sending people to set it up," said Sarah.

"I've seen the printer in action," Dean said, a gleam in his eye. "As long as the data is there, we should be able to print out an exact copy of the fossil in about an hour. It's going to revolutionize paleontology."

"How so?" Molly asked.

"Think about it. If every major museum had a printer like this, then we could email fossils files all over the world. They could print out their exhibits versus spending money and time on real fossils or casts of fossils. People are already doing it. I've seen printed fossils before."

"So you want to destroy the fossil casting trade, too?" I said. Most fossils in museums were casts or copies of fossils. Some fossils were too precious to display, so people made copies using plaster or plastic, painted them, then passed them to museums around the world to study and display.

"Not destroy, Derek. Fossil purveyors of all types will still be in demand. But this will just give us a new way of sharing information," Dean said.

Jesus Christ. They were taking the digging out of paleontology.

Karolin clapped her hands together and rubbed them vigorously. "That is really good timing. We can show Dr. Oliphant the printout when he arrives tomorrow."

Surely I misheard her.

"What? He's coming here?" I turned to Sarah.

"Forgot to tell you. Sorry."

The cave felt too small. I looked at the giant skull and sighed. *Soon I'll be as extinct as you,* I thought.

As we approached my warehouse, a large ten-wheeler semi-truck had just turned into the long gravel driveway that ran parallel to my building. Its black cab read "Nakasogi Industries," in white lettering. Below the English, a Japanese symbol gleamed in bright red. I knew from having seen it before that it was the Kanji symbol for *family*. Behind the cab was a sizable white trailer, its interior hidden from the world. Sarah parked behind me and jumped out without closing her door. She ran up to the truck, waving her arms in greeting. She climbed up the cab, and after a few words and hand signals with the driver, she got down, motioning with her head that my job was next.

After giving her an annoyed glare, which she returned in kind, I walked up the small staircase that led into my warehouse and pulled my keys from my pocket. I opened the door, and without bothering to turn on the inside lights, walked along the wall toward the button that opened the bay doors. I pressed it, and a motor hummed to life. The door rattled and creaked as it slowly rose, and the large truck's trailer backed up toward the door. After a few seconds of diesel exhaust and reverse beeping, the truck had lined up the trailer's door with the edge of the bay doors. A shout later and the truck stopped moving, ready to unload.

"Please excuse me, sir," a pleasant voice said behind me. I jumped at the unexpected greeting. The man was Japanese, wearing white coveralls with the Nakasogi emblem on the breast. Behind him was another man and a woman, dressed similarly.

I nodded and moved away. Walking back to the door of my warehouse, I peeked out and saw that behind the trailer was a smaller SUV. I guessed the SUV followed the truck. Another man walked up the stairs and stopped at the top. After giving me a small bow and a smile, he walked past to join the others.

"This is worth several million, so they want to do it themselves. We don't have to help after all," Sarah said as she approached.

"How long?"

"Apparently, once it's out of the truck, only an hour to set up. The printer is a self-contained building."

A ramp with rollers was extended from the truck to my warehouse floor. One of the workers turned to Sarah and pointed to the floor right in front of the ramp.

"That's an okay spot, Derek?"

I gave her a long, level look. "Does it matter?"

The bay door of the trailer rattled open. One of the staff climbed up the ramp and reached a hand inside the trailer. With a groan, the wheels on the ramp rotated, creating a loud buzzing noise. An extremely large, long metal box exited the trailer. It frankly was shockingly large, almost the exact size of the truck's trailer, just small enough to nest inside. As it rolled out of the trailer, the woman ran around the machine, lowering wheels on each of its sides. Attached to the back of the box was a long metal cable; it was extended and probably attached to something deep inside the trailer. The rotating wheels had enough force to cause the machine to push away from the trailer and move on its own. But the cable inside the trailer did its job, pulling taut and stopping the machine's forward motion once it moved off the ramp. The machine was mostly white with red stripes, and it had several windows along its sides.

One of the men walked around, pulling down what looked like large legs from each corner of the box, locking them in place. "Those will keep the printer stable till we want to move it again," Dean said, coming up next to us.

"All right, Professor. Enlighten us on this lovely new addition to Derek's life," Sarah said.

"The entire metal box is called the *housing*. All printing will happen there. See that dark platform in the middle of the room? That is the building field. And that long, gray, wand-like thing to the far left? That is the recoater. That will build the printout: the fossil. We load the printer with a sand-like plastic, called *particle material*."

He motioned to the side of my warehouse where two of the staffers were stacking large bags next to the machine that reminded me of sandbags. "Once the CAD file is uploaded, the recoater moves back and forth across the building field, laying a thin layer of particle material on the platform. That other wand next to it is the printhead, and it will selectively release a binder chemical that will bond to the particle material. The recoater goes back and forth, over and over, slowly building layer after layer of particle material with a binder in the places the computer tells it to. Eventually, whatever we want takes shape in the material."

"It's kind of like geology, or paleontology," Molly said. We turned to look at her. "Slowly, layer after layer of sand is deposited on top of treasures that we'll have to dig out."

Wrong! It was nothing like paleontology.

Paleontology was about sand and sweat, toil and struggle, chasing that perfect moment.

"Exactly, Molly," Dean said.

Jesus.

Dean continued: "This goes on and on until the entire file has been printed. To keep unused particle material from flowing out into the building field, the machine automatically prints sidewalls. Once the entire file is printed, the platform leaves the room over there." He pointed to the far side of the printer. That entire side consisted of a metal door with what looked like a folded ramp blocking it. "That opens up, and the ramp folds out. It's got automatic rotary wheels that push what we've printed onto the warehouse floor. Once the print-out has stopped, I pull at one of the sides. The rest fall down, unused particle material will fall away, and *voilà*! We'll have whatever we asked the machine to print. In our case, we'll have our fossil."

An hour later we arrived back at my warehouse carrying left-overs and Dean's dinner of steak and fries. While the rest of us were starving, Dean didn't want to leave the machine. So I took the crew to Harry's where the great University of Wyoming paid for our dinner of burgers and beers (with a soda for Molly), and we grabbed Dean's meal to go. Nakasogi's team had already left, and Dean was grinning like a fool next to the 3D printer. Based on the loud noise echoing around the cavernous room, that darn printer was working just fine, probably printing off whatever it was that the GPR captured. If I had to put money on it, I would bet that it would be a giant white blob.

"How long will the preparation take once we get the fossil out of the mesa?" Molly asked. "I've never worked on such a large specimen before. Just small fossils that needed cleaning."

"It just depends on how big the fossil is, how complete, how many other creatures are with it. That sort of thing. Months, probably. Maybe years. But we can describe it in a paper as soon as we're sure what we've got," Sarah said. "We need to check all our boxes before we publish anything."

"We? You mean you and Mr. Farnsworth?" Molly said.

"I mean Dr. Oliphant."

"Why is he involved? Isn't this your project?"

I grunted a laugh. Of course he was. I knew better.

"Because he can't support anything that doesn't have either money or fame for him attached to it. He steals the spotlight from the people who actually did the work," I told her.

Sarah gave me that look. "He's coming here tonight. A day early."

In unison, Karolin and Dean turned to look at her.

"Really?" Karolin said, hopefully.

"Sarah, what the—" I said.

Sarah raised her hand, cutting me off. While her face was weary, her eyes were hard.

"He's my advisor, and this site is my thesis. Dr. Oliphant oversees this project. He needs to see it. Come on, Derek. You know that."

"And you know he's an opportunistic, egotistical thief who has no reason to come here except to lord himself over you. All of you," I said, waving my hand at Karolin and Dean. Karolin looked a little alarmed about being included in my rant.

"Derek, please." Sarah rubbed her eyes with the heels of her hands. "Not now."

I scratched the back of my neck and breathed through my teeth, trying to control the anger building in my stomach. I didn't want to lash out at Sarah.

Behind her, Dean waved at me. "Yo," he said, pointing toward the 3D printer, but I didn't care. I turned my attention back to Sarah, crossing my arms across my chest.

"Let it go, Derek. Dr. Oliphant has to be a part of this. Especially now that we have this new fossil to consider," Sarah said.

"Are you going to tell him about the new dinosaur? Seriously? Before we know what's going on with it? You know what he's done in the past."

Now Dean was waving both arms at us, trying to get our attention.

"I'm fully aware of what he did, Derek. You've told me a hundred times. But he's the best person to work on this new dinosaur with us. His expertise—"

"Expertise? You mean what he's stolen from others."

"No! Derek this—"

"Sarah!" Molly yelled. "Dean is trying to tell us that something is happening with the printer." She gestured behind me, and I turned to look. The loud noise from earlier had stopped. The large door along the printer's side was opening, and the ramp was slowly unfolding out over my warehouse floor.

"Oh!" Sarah said, moving quickly toward the printer. She stopped next to Dean, who was typing furiously on a computer attached to the printer.

Once the ramp stopped moving, I heard another loud noise, and a large object flowed down the printer's ramp and onto the warehouse floor. A beat later, the ramp retracted back into the printer, and the door closed.

Together, we walked to the side of what looked like a large white rectangle. Its sides were about four feet in height, but it was long, maybe longer than Sarah's huge truck. This had to be the weirdest thing I've ever had in my warehouse. And that was saying something.

Molly stepped up next to me, peering at the top of the white rectangle. Unlike the sides that seemed like a solid wall of plastic, the top seemed to be made up of a layer of sand.

The particulate material, I guessed. I leaned over and poked my fingers into it, pulling some into the palm of my hand. Each grain was a tiny sphere of plastic. That's what the world needed—more plastic. Like we didn't have an island of the stuff the size of Texas smack in the middle of the Pacific.

"Here we go," Dean said, pulling at his side of the box. "Our cave dinosaur." There was a loud crack and all the sides broke away. A loud boom echoed around the warehouse as the plastic walls hit my concrete floor, and an avalanche of white particle material flowed over my feet.

Lying in front of me, formed in white plastic, was the skeleton of something that I knew did not exist.

A giant winged dinosaur.

The creature was in miraculous condition. Its long neck was arched away from its front, over its back. Dead birds and complete dinosaurs were sometimes found like this. It was known as the *death pose*. Scientists believe it had to do with the neck ligaments contracting during decay. Its articulated tail was wrapped around and under the body, as if creating a circle around itself. Its skull was enormous. During death or fossilization it twisted around and it was perfectly upright, just like how we saw it in the cavern. But most surprising of all were the wings. The bones looked perfectly preserved. One was even arched over the body, as if its last goal before death was to protect this dinosaur.

Dinosaurs didn't have wings, I reminded myself, which meant that the wings had come from another creature, probably a pterosaur. But where was the rest of the pterosaur? It had to be here.

My mind tried to make sense of what I knew was true: Dinosaurs did not fly. Pterosaurs did. But no pterosaur was anything close to this big.

I strolled around the printout. Because Dean had the good sense to make sure to not print the rock that it was situated in, we were staring at a skeleton that hadn't moved in sixty-six million years. It was so lifelike that I could almost visualize what the animal looked like with skin and muscle.

I was so engrossed with the printout that I didn't hear the man's footsteps until he was standing right next to me. Then came the voice that had tormented me for so many years.

"What the hell is that?" said Dr. Sean Oliphant.

CREATURE FEATURES

Farnsworth

I'D HAVE RATHER spent my time one-on-one with the real-life version of whatever that machine printed out than the man who just walked in.

Above us, overhead fluorescent lights flickered intermittently, causing my already aching head to throb. I reached behind me, grabbed my water bottle, and took a long drink. Hopefully it would help, but I knew that dehydration wasn't the real problem. Clearing my throat, I walked back to the printout and squatted next to Molly.

"Holy shit, that's Dr. Sean Oliphant," she said. "I've seen his TED Talk a thousand times." Her teenage voice deepened into a far-too-real impression of the man who had just entered the room: "'Imagine a world millions of years ago that looks almost exactly like this one. Can you do it? Just try.'" She had his arrogant pauses down and everything.

"Oh God, it's like there are two of you," I groaned.

On the other side of the printout, Oliphant, Sarah, and Karolin knelt down near the arched neck of the dinosaur.

"There seem to be some issues with its neck," Oliphant said, pointing at one of the vertebrae with his finger.

Huh. He's right. Several of the vertebrae were smaller than the others. No, wait, they were flatter. Their shape reminded me of that *T-rex* spine back at the bone bed. Oliphant squatted down and gently pushed at a vertebra, his fingers tracing around its mounds and valleys. Suddenly his fingertip disappeared. Holding his finger in place, he exchanged a significant look with Sarah, then slowly moved his finger up out of the hole and along the side of the vertebra.

"There is also a trench here," he said, tapping the vertebrae with his finger. "Something huge punctured and scraped the spinal column of this animal."

"We found a partially articulated *T-rex* spine nearby, Dr. Oliphant. It also had holes in it, and one of the holes was filled with a tooth fragment. That tooth frag matched the larger tooth I found a while back, remember that?" Sarah said.

"Was that the tooth cast you waved under my nose right before I headed out to my department meeting?"

"Well, yes. That tooth frag and that unknown tooth match the teeth found from this species, Dr. Oliphant. Maybe they even came from this dinosaur."

He looked at Sarah, then his eyes tracked behind her, his head moving slightly from side to side. I glanced at where he was looking, figuring he was eyeing another fossil on one of my tables or something. No, it was the glass-windowed cabinet where I kept my chemicals. Things like diluted hydrochloric acid to dissolve limestone, Butvar-76 for fossil repair. That sort of thing. Not that you could tell at this time of night—the lights above shone on the pane of the glass, causing the glass to reflect the room. Oliphant moved his head a little, his fingers reaching up to move the hair away from his forehead. He gave a small satisfied smile.

Dear Lord, he was using it as a mirror.

"Now let's examine your fundamental hypothesis," he said to Sarah, still looking at his reflection. "The chances of two animals attacking each other, both dying and both preserved at the same time, is very . . ."

His students must be used to his vanity; Sarah was purposely not looking at me, even though I was trying to catch her eye. Molly, on the other hand, let out a little giggle. At that noise, Oliphant glared at her and stood back up.

"Very slim," Sarah said. "Not unheard of, though. They are both from the same layer of the Hell Creek, and my initial cursory analysis suggests that they were both caught in the same flood event. There may be no relation, but I thought I should mention it."

That's my Sarah. She was brilliant and a hard worker. Dedicated to the craft. She'd come a long way from the twelve-year-old girl who used to race around the badlands, taunting me that she was going to find more fossils than I could.

Oliphant pointed toward the fossil's leg bones. "Those femurs are very long, while its tibia and fibula are relatively short. And . . . look at the feet. Instead of the usual three claws in the front, one in the back, this creature has two claws pointing forward, and two claws pointing backward. I've never seen that before."

Me neither. Not on a dinosaur, nor on a pterosaur. These feet look like they belong to a modern osprey. And at the end of each toe was a huge, sharp claw. Perfect for grabbing and tearing off the flesh of its prey. I poked at a tip; any further pressure and I was afraid the point would actually make me bleed.

I took off my hat and vigorously rubbed my hair to organize my thoughts. Okay, so this dinosaur had unusual feet. Maybe they were features we'd never seen before. Or perhaps as it fossilized, the fossils became distorted. That can happen. That process was called *plastic deformation*. Rocks get bent or broken due to pressure and the fossils inside the rocks become distorted or bent. Perhaps its feet were a normal three-in-front, one in the back, but over time, one toe moved to the front, and all four toes elongated.

Or perhaps this was another type of dinosaur foot that we'd never seen in the fossil record before.

Then Molly hit us all right in the gut. "Could fossilization cause the hips to look like that?" she asked, pointing at the middle of the dinosaur. It was hard to see from my vantage, mostly because it was a tight jumble of monochromatic white plastic. But my eyes traced familiar shapes, like ribs, vertebrae . . . and the hips.

I heard Dean's intake of breath and a low whistle from Sarah.

"Those are not Dinosauria hips," Oliphant said after a long moment.

"Huh?" Molly asked.

"No, more like a pterosaur," Dean said, turning to Molly. "You know that there are two dinosaur hip structures, right?"

Molly nodded. "Sure. Ornithischians and saurischian."

"These two clades define the dinosaur family tree," Oliphant said, interrupting Dean. "There is some argument that there might be three, but that still needs further investigation. Anyway, Ornithischian dinosaurs are called 'bird-hipped' because their hip structure resembles modern birds. *Stegosaurus* and *Triceratops* are part of that family."

"I know all this, Dr. Oliphant," Molly said, her voice low with a hint of exasperation.

"Welcome to the world according to Oliphant, Molly," I said. *If she only knew.*

Seemingly not hearing her, Oliphant drove on. "Saurischian actually means 'lizard-hipped,' but the term is misleading. Family members include *Tyrannosaurus rex* and *Velociraptor*. You know, I have a chapter in each of my books on this; you should read them. In any event, this creature's hip structure resembles neither ornithischian or saurischian. It looks like what you'd find on a pterosaur. That's not possible, though. Not on a creature this size and shape," he finished. Mercifully.

"So . . . ?" Molly asked breathlessly.

"Not a dinosaur. At least from my preliminary analysis," Oliphant replied.

Not a dinosaur. It should be one. Dinosaurs were the dominant land animal at this point in earth's history. But then, maybe creatures like this had always existed with the dinosaurs. We just hadn't found an example of one yet in the fossil record. We just didn't know the full extent of fauna that existed—230 million years is a very long time to live and evolve. And disappear.

That was the amazing thing about paleontology. While we did know a lot, there was still so much to learn. It was just the nature of the gig. I mean, to be fossilized, you had to have a perfect set of conditions. A dead body. Isolation from scavengers. Water pushing sand and mud over the body, entombing it. Over time, minerals seeep into the bones and occasional soft tissue. So many things could go wrong with that recipe. It was a bloody miracle we had as many fossils as we did. But then, the earth had been around for a very long time. Billions of years. A fossil or two was bound to survive. Treasures locked in a grave of sand and stone.

And it was the hunt for these treasures that made all the pain worth it.

Oliphant cleared his throat, and I started at the noise. "This is something special," he said, more to himself than the rest of the group. A small smile played on his face, and I heard the once-familiar thrill in his voice, a tone that promised adventure. With it brought a tidal wave of horrible memories. I put my head down and closed my eyes, sucking in a breath through my nose to steady myself.

"Then what is it?" Molly asked, pulling out her cell phone, pressing her screen to capture a picture. Karolin did the same.

Excellent question.

SOMETHING NEW

Sarah

OIL AND WATER. Gasoline and fire. Oliphant and Farnsworth.

Sarah, what have you done? I thought to myself.

I put my hands over my ears to quiet the ringing. The ringing must have been in my own head though, because nobody else was reacting. Pulling my hands down, I took a deep breath and the ringing stopped. I shot a glance at Derek. Maybe the stress of the two of them together was getting to me.

Maybe all of it, all of the last few months, was getting to me. I was losing it.

I placed my hands on the printout. The fluorescent lighting above me cast a harsh glow on my bare arms, causing me to glance at my forearm tattoo. A *Triceratops* strangled in vines, dotted with small white magnolia flowers. Angiosperms, or flowering plants, first hit the fossil record during the Cretaceous. Magnolia was one such species.

I put more pressure on the printout as I leaned forward to view the hips. It creaked a bit but held.

"These hips look like they are from the pterosaur *Rhamphorhynchus*," Oliphant said. I nodded slowly. I was no expert on pterosaurs, but I knew enough of the basics to see the resemblance.

"So, you think this is a *Rhamphorhynchus*?" Dean asked, raising his eyebrow. "The tiny Jurassic-aged pterosaur? I thought you—"

"Of course not," Oliphant said. "There are about one hundred million years or so between *Rhamphys* and this animal. But it does give us some thoughts on how it evolved. Maybe this is distantly related to *Rhamphorhynchus*."

"That is stretching it," I said. "Why couldn't those hips just be from the same large pterosaur that supplied those wings?"

"Let's find the arms, if there are any," Oliphant said, plowing on.

"No, seriously. Why can't they be from a pterosaur, and the rest a dinosaur?" I said.

"I've been looking for the arms," Molly said. "There are no arms."

"Or they are there, and you just don't know what you're looking at," I said.

"Keep looking. If we find the arms, then we know for sure that these wings belong to another animal. No land animal besides insects, bugs, and spiders had more than four limbs. Maybe they are under the body, under those wings," Oliphant said, moving toward the belly for a better look.

Molly had the same idea. She dropped to her stomach and wiggled herself right into the rib cage. "Yup, no arms at all, and I can see that the wings were probably attached. The end of the wing bones are right next to that weird-looking bone on each side of the body."

"Weird-looking bone? Oh, for Pete's sake, let me," Oliphant snorted and tapped her leg. She pushed herself out of the rib cage, and he got on his stomach and pulled himself forward.

"Those strange-looking bones are called *scapulae*. Shoulder bones," he called out.

Shoulder bones. Shoulder bones with wings. No. That wasn't right. I craned my head around to see the entirety of each wing. One wing was arched over the body; the printout actually captured the bones seemingly hanging in the air, like they were on display in a museum. The other was driven under the body. The size of the wings were impressive, too. Fully spread, I wouldn't be surprised if the wingspan was sixty feet. More, even. Huge animal. Larger than a *Quetzalcoatlus*. Or maybe we just didn't have an example of how big they got before?

What were you? What were you? What were you? Are you even one animal?

Oliphant climbed out from under the printout and stood up, brushing the dirt from the floor off his shirt and pants. "No arm bones, and those wings look articulated to the body to me."

"The printout might be wrong, Sean," I said. "Or if water was moving fast enough at the time of burial, it could have pushed the dinosaur's body onto a *Quetzalcoatlus*. See? That is a classic pterosaur wing." I pointed up and down the wing over the body for the group's benefit. "They had an upper arm that included a forearm, three small fingers, and an enormously elongated 'pinkie' digit with four long jointed sections. These were designed to support a wing membrane."

Molly shook her head at me and pointed to the creature. "But this has five fingers per hand."

"She's right," Farnsworth called out, leaning into the rib cage to see the wing under the body. "Five fingers on each hand. Four digits and one elongated pinkie."

"I don't know of another flying reptile during the Mesozoic with that hand configuration, do you?" Dean asked.

Karolin just shrugged. "Don't look at me. I'm a mammal girl."

There was a general chuckle at that, and then Oliphant cleared his throat and cracked his knuckles. "Okay, here is my thinking. As far as I'm aware, there are no pterosaurs with five fingers per hand in total. But that could just be because the fossil record is very incomplete. If these are pterosaur hips, and there are wings here, well, this could be an unknown pterosaur."

He shot a glance at me, and gave me the smile I knew all too well. "Or, this is an entirely different animal that is distantly related to both pterosaurs and dinosaurs, and we're just finding it."

"Oh, come on. A brand-new, absolutely huge species that lived at the time of the dinosaurs? The largest land-dwelling animals in history? I get this thing has weird features," I said, and I couldn't stop my voice from rising. This was getting too ridiculous. "The feet are weird. The horns are weird. The hips are weird." I planted my feet apart, my hand punctuating every sentence with a wave. "And yes, even these wings are weird. But again, there could just be a really simple explanation for all of this. Maybe the CAD file from the GPR is corrupted and threw together two animals. Maybe even three."

"No," said Dean. "I was in Japan, Sarah. I watched this thing print out fossils from multiple types of sedimentary strata, and it's very accurate. Arguably the GPR may not have picked up everything, but this animal looks really complete. You can even see that the wing bone near the skull is broken, just like it is in the cave."

Oliphant moved to where Dean was pointing, and gently prodded the hole. The printout had captured it with remarkable clarity. It was a radius by the look of it. And it was obvious that the bone's wall was incredibly thin.

"Hollow bones," Oliphant said, his eyes flashing. "When were you going to tell me that?"

"Pterosaur! Those are pterosaur wings. That's why they are hollow." I rubbed my eyes with the heels of my hands. I felt a headache growing behind my eyes.

"We haven't even mentioned the fact that all the bones are black," said Karolin.

"Black?" Oliphant asked.

"Sarah, why are you fighting this?" Farnsworth said, moving to my side. "This could be something really remarkable."

I pressed my fingers to my temples. "This isn't science! It's speculation. Given the size and location of this creature, it most likely is a tyrannosaurid. Considering its size, if it was something new, we'd have found a lot more evidence of this type of animal over the last one hundred and fifty years. Right? We find dinosaur remains everywhere."

"Well, sure, but—" Farnsworth began.

I pointed toward the skull, interrupting him. "Those horns could be a function of sexual dimorphism of *Tyrannosaur*. Maybe we've only found females previously, and this is a male. I think that this dinosaur is a new member of the *Tyrannosaur* family, and a pterosaur, maybe two, of some kind died on or near it. The hips could be . . . well, they could be from those pterosaurs."

The others just stared at me. I didn't blame them. I was dropping a load of reality on their dreams. But I had to. "We have to do this correctly, or the scientific process is dead," I said, quietly. "Dinosaurs were the land apex in the Mesozoic. If something else existed, we have to prove it correctly. No fantastical assumptions when there could be a logical explanation. And, if this is something new, we have to have a *very* clear logical explanation, or else it will be refuted. In fact, I don't see a lot of evidence that it's anything but two species right now."

Oliphant gazed at me for a long moment, then he looked at Molly. He patted her on the head, and a wave of fine dust rose up into the air. He looked at his hand, twisting his face in disgust, then wiped it on his pants leg. "It's a wonderful find—one for the history books. You found it, I believe? Sarah texted me that you fell down a cliff or something? Unusual technique. Whatever it takes, I suppose."

Molly's eyes widened, and her cheeks turned bright red. As she opened her mouth, Farnsworth came up behind the girl and put an arm over her shoulder, leading her away. Oliphant shot him a smirk, then turned to me. "Tomorrow, let's call Snyder at the lab. She can send a team up to begin excavation."

"Wait, no!" I said, shocked. "I have a team right here. We can dig this out—"

"No, you should focus on your bone quarry." He put a placating hand on my shoulder. "Don't worry, Sarah. All of this is obviously connected. You'll get credit, but I need you to finish your project, and Snyder's team will connect the dots to this new creature. I'll be right there to help her."

The thought came again. *Sarah, what have you done?*

"This is my dinosaur!" I said.

"It's not a *dinosaur*. But I *know* what it is," Molly said, her loud voice from across the room cutting through the warehouse like a knife.

"You know what it is?" Farnsworth said.

"Yes. Of course," she replied.

"All right, then. Care to enlighten us?" Oliphant snorted.

The girl walked toward us, looking around, staring at us in disbelief.

"Seriously? You don't know? Come on. It's the size of a *T-rex*. It has horns on its skull. It's got massive wings." She ran her hands through her hair, a sigh on the border of a scream. "Guys. It's a dragon."

GAME OF THRONES ISN'T REAL HISTORY

Molly

OLIPHANT LAUGHED SO hard that he had to bend over to catch his breath.

"A dragon? A fire-breathing dragon?" He looked at the ceiling and shook his head. His hands reached up through his hair, smoothing it back into place.

I narrowed my eyes at him, but he didn't notice. Too busy being a tool, I guessed. I know it was a crazy idea, but come on. Oliphant could have at least heard me out. I was not a hundred percent crazy here. You'd heard the stories, the myths. They were everywhere, on every continent with humans. These stories have existed for centuries. Okay, so, why would that be?

"Seriously, this *could* be a dragon," I said.

Oliphant's eyes finally met mine. "Young lady, that has to be one of the silliest things I've ever heard." He gave me an appraising look. "Where are you from, anyway?"

"Berkeley."

"Well, there you go."

"What's wrong with Berkeley?"

"The school? Nothing. Great paleo department. The town is full of crystal-loving hippie-dippies though."

"I believe the term is hipsters now, Dr. Oliphant," Karolin interjected helpfully.

"Well, we all can't spend four years partying on daddy's money in New Haven," Farnsworth growled. He stared daggers at Oliphant, and he took a step toward me, almost in front of me.

"Can we hear why Molly thinks this is a dragon?" Dean said. He nodded and winked at me. The knot in my stomach loosened a bit.

I reached inside my backpack and pulled out the old, tattered children's book I always carried with me. My fingers lingered over the raised lettering, *Dragons of the World*. I lifted it for the group to see. "My mom gave me this book when I was a kid."

I opened it to the first page: *European Wyvern*. The dragon had two legs, two wings, a giant skull with several horns over its eyes and jutting from its snout. If it didn't have skin and flesh, it could have been a twin of the fossil printout lying at our feet.

"You all know that people used to think fossils they found in the ground were from mythical creatures, right?"

Sarah nodded her head slowly. "Of course. For a long time."

Thousands of years, actually. Humans have always been curious creatures with active imaginations. There were stories from around the world of people finding fossils and creating elaborate tales about them. I'd read Indigenous tales about Monster Lizards and Thunderbirds, Chinese stories about Longmas and Celestial Stags, and Celtic stories of Kelpies and the Direach.

"Maybe dragons have been here the whole time," I pointed to the printout. "This creature could be the actual inspiration for the myth. Maybe ancient peoples saw these skeletons in the ground for years, but scientists who describe fossils for publications hadn't found one yet."

After a long pause, Oliphant cleared his throat. "Look, from where I stand, this is probably a new species. Maybe divergently evolved from a shared ancestor of dinosaurs and pterosaurs." He raised his eyebrows at me. "Do you know about divergent evolution? Divergent means you have a few species that evolved from a common ancestor. Like a woolly mammoth and an elephant. Convergent is the other side of it, where several species have similar traits, but are not related. Like a bird and a bat. I've written many papers on the subjects. You should read them—"

"Actually I do remember freshman year biology," I replied. I'd also read his papers. Well, tried to. "I just don't understand how that doesn't make this a dragon? I mean . . ."

It had wings like a dragon.

Its skull looked like a dragon.

It probably roared like a dragon.

It was a freakin' fossilized dragon.

"Listen, whoever you are . . ." Oliphant raised his eyebrows and motioned with his hand in a circle toward me.

"Molly," Sarah coached.

"Oh, the Nakasogi intern, right? Okay, Molly-the-Intern. Dragons are something in fantasy books, not science. *Game of Thrones* isn't real history."

Okay, that did it. I took a step forward, and I raised a finger in his direction. "No," I snapped between clenched teeth.

Sarah whipped her head at me, and I saw a warning in her eyes. Next to her, Oliphant pulled out his cell phone, not even bothering to acknowledge me anymore.

"Sean, the kid could be right," Farnsworth said. I turned to him in surprise, and he gave me a small nod.

I looked back just in time to see Oliphant snarl slightly.

"Thinking this is a dragon isn't crazy. Sarah?" I said, driving ahead, weirdly more confident with Farnsworth at my back.

"No, it's a dinosaur." Sarah shook her head in frustration.

"Sarah, it's hip structure doesn't let it fall under Dinosauria," said Farnsworth. "We've gone over it. How do you explain the fact that each wing has five fingers instead of four?"

"Easy, those belong to another pterosaur," Sarah snapped.

"Can we also talk about the usual bone color?" said Dean. "I've seen dark-colored bones. I've even heard of black bones before. There's that Black Beauty *T-rex* at the Royal Tyrrell Museum, or the Tristan Otto *T-rex* in Germany. But this is like a really deep black."

"Coloring of fossils is due to impurities in the surrounding sediment during the fossilization process," Oliphant sighed. "If you'd been paying closer attention in my sedimentology class, Dean, you'd know that."

Dean frowned and looked down.

Clearing his throat, Farnsworth answered. "It's a good piece of data to understand, Sean. These bones are very different from the other fossils we've been pulling out of the Hell Creek just around the corner from this fossil."

I held up the book. "This is a wyvern. This is a Cretaceous-aged wyvern dragon."

"Wyvern!" Oliphant slapped his hand to his forehead. "My apologies, intern. I had no idea you had so much to teach us." He put his hands on his hips and gave me a cold smile. "Tell me again, which of my colleagues wrote that fantasy book in your hands?"

"Sean, please," Sarah chided.

I narrowed my eyes again, but bit back the retort before it could leave my mouth. This man was a piece of work. But he was Sarah's boss, so I'd take the high road. "This could be a new species. I agree with that. All I'm saying is that dragons and dinosaurs might have lived at the same time. And as you say, they even shared a common ancestor, but diverged at some point so that one stayed on the ground, and the other one flew."

"Calling this a dragon is a silly fantasy until we have a lot more evidence," Karolin said. "Dr. Oliphant is right. It's not science."

"Ancient fossils were always called dragons by the first academic paleontologists," I said. "Heck, in the 1800s, English fossil hunter Mary Anning and Oxford professor William Buckland used to call pterosaurs 'flying dragons' and swimming reptiles like ichthyosaurs 'swimming dragons.'"

"Until they didn't because they are not dragons," Oliphant came back fast. "Dragons are a fantasy. This whole conversation is a fantasy. I mean, my God!" Oliphant stared for a moment at the ceiling as if hoping for guidance from above. Looking back down, he waved his hand toward the printout. "Where are the charred logs? Don't dragons breathe fire? Don't they have lairs full of treasure?" Then he looked right at me. "Where are the human bones, Molly-the-Intern?" he said, his eyes flashing in the fluorescent lighting.

"Human bones?" I replied, frowning.

"The token damsel in distress and her would-be saviors. Where are the rusted helmets and heraldic shields? Doesn't your fantasy book talk about all that?" He waved in my direction.

Fine, he asked for it.

"First, it's not a fantasy book. It's just a book of dragon myths from across the world. There are many other books about mythology, and some of them do focus on this kind of stuff. People who study folklore call this *geomythology*. It's the study of myths or stories that contain geological events like volcanos, earthquakes, even fossils. Early humans didn't have scientific explanations for their discoveries, so they invented myths to explain what they were seeing. There is even a professor at

Stanford University who specializes in it. And second, that's not what I'm saying. All I'm saying is that this is a fossilized dragon. This is what the myth is *based on*."

Rage was building up in me. Even in its death pose, wrapped around itself, the creature was fierce. I could see its terrifying eye sockets, and scary though they were, it was like those sockets were telling us it was real, and the great Dr. Sean Oliphant was telling it to shut up after tens of millions of years of doing just that. The words were out of my mouth before I heard the impression I'd quietly practiced so many times.

"Imagine a world millions of years ago that looks almost exactly like this one, except along with dinosaurs and pterosaurs, there's a third creature that every culture that ever existed had a word for. Dragons. Can you do it? Just try."

RAID

Molly

THE NEXT MORNING, I woke to chaos.

I groaned as I moved about, trying to remember where I was.

I was not at home. I was somewhere far. My brain spun as I tried to make sense of my surroundings. I was in Montana, not California. I was here for the summer, living in an Airstream.

We found a dragon.

Then I remembered my dream. It had flying dragons, burning rocks. I walked into a deep hole filled with books and monsters. But it wasn't a pleasant dream. I took a deep breath, and as I released it, the memory of the dream started to die. I focused on the ceiling of the Airstream before turning toward Sarah's bed. It was empty.

I heard a loud crash. And another. There were lots of noises around me. Noises that shouldn't be here. I heard the slam of truck doors, and the crunch of gravel as heavy boots walked around the Airstream, around Farnsworth's lot. Voices shouted at one another, but I couldn't hear exactly what was said.

I leapt out of bed, nearly hitting my head on the low roof of the trailer. I brushed aside the curtain on the small window. A dark shape passed, startling me. I rubbed the sleep from my eyes and took another look. Outside, I could see at least a dozen men and women walking around in dark clothing and sunglasses, looking very official. They were moving in and out the back door of Farnsworth's warehouse, carrying what looked like computers, file boxes, and fossils.

I quickly dressed and grabbed my backpack. But as I rushed out the Airstream door, a strong arm caught me, causing me to lose my balance. Instead of steadying me, the arm pushed me forward.

"What the hell?" I shouted, trying to not fall flat on my face. "Let me go!" I swung around to see who was holding me.

There were two large men, both dressed in black. Each was wearing a vest with lettering on their left pocket, but I couldn't make out the words.

"If you resist, Ms. Wilder, we will arrest you," the taller one said calmly. His voice made me shiver, and my stomach clenched. While he was wearing sunglasses that hid a lot of his face, I could see that he had dark brown hair, a large hook nose, and a mouth downturned in a snarl. He raised a huge arm and pointed toward the entryway of the warehouse. "Walk."

Mostly because I was terrified, I did as he said. But I did scowl and shrug off his hand. As I entered the warehouse, a woman, also dressed in black, walked out with a fossil still encased in plaster. Written in large lettering on her back were the letters "BLM."

BLM.

The Bureau of Land Management.

"Why is the Bureau of Land Management here?" I asked, but neither man answered me. The BLM managed land across the United States, but Sarah said we were digging on private land and that we'd gotten permission from the rancher. What was going on?

Entering the darkened warehouse, my eyes adjusted enough to see that Karolin, Dean, and Oliphant were seated at one of Farnsworth's worktables. Karolin was biting her fingernails and looked like she was about to cry. Dean whispered something to Karolin, patting her back. Sarah stood nearby, typing furiously on her cell phone. Oliphant was leaning against the table, hands in his pockets, watching the BLM move about. I didn't see Farnsworth anywhere.

But as we approached, Oliphant's expression turned from relative indifference to clear rage. "Leave the girl alone," he spat as the BLM guy pushed me forward. He stepped ahead, carefully guiding me closer to Sarah and the others.

"She was in a restricted area," BLM man replied.

I rubbed my shoulder. "Dude, I was just coming out of my trailer. Where I live."

The BLM guy chuckled as he walked away toward another BLM agent.

I turned to Sarah. "What is going on?"

"The BLM says we're digging illegally on government land, not on private land." She looked confused, and her voice was shaking, the tone of every other word was high or low.

I heard rapid footsteps. Farnsworth stalked toward us, his face bright red.

"The Feds are taking everything, Sarah. They're taking fossils that have nothing to do with the bone quarry," he shouted. "What the hell is going on?"

"We are doing it because you, Mr. Farnsworth, have been on our radar for a while now," the BLM agent interjected. Now that he had removed his sunglasses and wasn't pushing me around, I got a better look at him. He was tall, almost as tall as Farnsworth. He had broad shoulders with thick, muscular arms. His face was angular, with high cheekbones that were covered in stubble. But his eyes were what caught me. Dark, almost black eyes. His pupils seemed to have streaks of yellow, like a predator.

"Agent Raley," he introduced himself. He reached into his pocket and pulled out a badge of some sort. "We've recently been informed that you are digging on public land without the proper permits, Mr. Farnsworth. Given our ongoing investigation into your other activities, we're shutting you down. If you have a problem with that, I suggest you take it up with Uncle Sam."

"That's bull. I've always followed the law!" As if to prove his point, Farnsworth waved behind him toward a desk with a computer. In response, a BLM staff member walked over and grabbed the computer. "You can't take that!" Farnsworth shouted.

"Yes, we *can* take that computer," Raley said. He reached into his vest pocket and waved a paper in the air, handing it to Farnsworth. Even from where I sat, I could see the words "Warrant" on it.

Farnsworth reached over and grabbed the paper. "Screw this." He tore up the paper, its pieces floating to the warehouse floor. Calmly, Raley reached into his pocket and pulled out a small white card and handed it to him. "That was your copy. Call this number if you want another one."

Farnsworth glared at the card and slapped it out of Raley's hand. "Go to hell." He turned around, walking toward one of his worktables. He leaned over it, his back rigid and his hands in fists. I jumped as he pounded a fist into his table, the noise loud even over the footsteps and voices of the BLM.

Oliphant turned to Raley. "You said we were 'digging on public land.' How do you know where we've even been digging?"

"We have photographs, Mr. Oliphant," Raley replied.

"What photos? And as long as the landowner grants us permission, we have every right to dig on private land. We have the right to not be harassed if we're following the law." Glancing at Farnsworth's back, Oliphant added, "Even *he* has that right!"

I heard Farnsworth huff, but he didn't say anything.

Raley stared at him for a long moment, a small smile on his lips. "Well, Mr. Oliphant, let me assure you that you were indeed digging on public land, as evidenced in the photos.

Now you and your people are not to revisit the site until all of this is cleared up. Do you understand?" He moved closer, right in front of Oliphant. "If you try, I'll arrest you on sight."

"What photos?" Oliphant repeated, matching Raley's glare.

"Oh no," Karolin said quietly, slapping a hand over her mouth. "I posted some pictures of the site on Twitter last night." I saw her bite her lip, her eyes filling with tears.

Raley's eyes never left Oliphant's. To Oliphant's credit, he also didn't move. Finally, Raley spoke, his voice icy and deadly. "Stay out of our way." Raley shouldered Oliphant aside and walked toward the front of the warehouse. As he did, he moved his left hand to his pocket, and I saw a dark mark on his wrist, but I couldn't tell what it was. He pulled out a phone from his pocket and pressed it to his ear.

I let out a long, shaky breath I didn't know I was holding. But then the bay doors of the warehouse screeched and shuttered, and I jumped again.

I thought of the dream again. I thought of the hole, the books, the monsters. Not monsters.

Dragons.

The fossil.

Farnsworth turned at the noise and pointed to the doors. "What are you doing?" he shouted at nobody in particular. Slowly, the large bay doors creaked open, and a huge eighteen-wheeler pulled back into the warehouse. A group of BLM agents flooded into the warehouse around it. They stood around the printout skeleton, glaring at it like it was something dirty or rotten.

"Wait," Oliphant said, his own voice becoming frantic as we all realized what was happening. His eyes grew wide, and he started toward the printout's direction. "You can't take that!"

A nearby woman laughed at Oliphant and shook her head. She took a position between the printout and us.

"It's not a fossil; it's not even technically Derek's. It's Nakasogi's!" He pointed to the printout. "That is on loan from Nakasogi Industries. You're stealing their property."

"It's evidence," Raley called out. "It's ours."

I watched as the rear door of the truck opened. Men climbed up and extended a metal plank. From inside the truck, one of them retrieved some type of winch, like he was going to tow away our dragon for having parked next to a hydrant. He sauntered down the gangplank like he was picking up regular old boxes and clicked the hook of the winch to the base the dragon was on.

I heard the whir of the motor before tears flooded my eyes. I was watching our dragon being dragged away from us. Last night, all I could see was a skeleton of an animal that terrorized the skies, something that could tear apart a *Tyrannosaurus rex*. But now this creature, our Montana Monster, looked sad and lonely as it was dragged up the truck's ramp. Before I lost sight of its skull, its eye socket reflected the warehouse lighting, and it seemed almost scared. As if it was going to its death. Again.

"They're taking literally everything I own."

Farnsworth's voice made me turn around. His face was buried in his big, rough hands. Sarah put a hand on his shoulder. At her touch, he looked up sharply at a corner of the warehouse, behind the printer. I followed his gaze. I hadn't noticed it the night before, but there were several big boxes stacked against the back wall, as well as some large pictures or posters.

Farnsworth hissed at us. "I need help. Those boxes contain fossils that don't belong to me."

Oliphant scoffed. Farnsworth glared at him but continued on. "The BLM is taking everything. They can't have those. They're from other museums, on loan for my museum. Let's move them into my home."

"Won't they look in your house?" Karolin asked.

"Hopefully they'll need another warrant for that. Go out the emergency back door. Watch for BLM staff, and try to avoid them." He pointed to another door I hadn't noticed before. Above it was a dirty "Emergency" sign. Together, we walked to the back of the warehouse. Now that Raley had moved outside, the other BLM staff didn't seem to care what we were doing.

I immediately grabbed a box labeled *Natural History Museum—London*. "What is all this?" I asked. The box was way heavier than it looked. I stumbled and looked straight into a large photograph leaning against the wall of the warehouse. It was a portrait of a grizzled, older man.

"Why do you have a giant print of Sir Richard Owen, Derek?" Dean asked, pointing to the portrait. I pulled it closer for a better look. It was an enlarged print of a famous picture of Owen. I'd seen it before, in history books. He was standing in black academic robes, holding a crocodile skull. Sir Richard Owen, the renowned anatomist, and one of the most important paleontologists in recent history. He coined the term *Dinosauria. Dinosaurs.*

"Should have said this last night, but welcome to the Glasgow Geologic Institute, future site of the Glasgow Museum of Paleontology."

Confused, I looked around. "This is a museum?"

"Someday, when I have the money," Farnsworth replied, lifting a box labeled *Museum fur Naturkunde*.

I frowned. "I thought you liked being a commercial paleontologist?"

Just as Farnsworth opened his mouth, someone dropped something large and metal, and the noise shook us back to reality. We moved quickly and quietly. Dean grabbed the photograph of Owen as well as several other photographs stacked behind it. We headed toward the emergency door and outside.

I followed Farnsworth up his back porch stairs. He stopped to open his door with his keys, and he held the door open for the rest of us.

The inside was dark and dingy. I stepped into what was probably the main living room. The floor was covered with a dark brown shag carpet, and I could see several dark spots in one corner. Yuck. There was an old TV and a paisley couch along the wall under a line of windows covered with green curtains. The walls were covered with fossils or pictures of fossils. Occasionally, hung in between the fossil decorations, were pictures of people. I saw Sarah in a few of them.

"Something about this whole situation doesn't make sense," Oliphant said, lowering his box to the ground. He turned to Sarah. "Sarah, walk us through what's going on."

"I'm not sure. Our map shows the site is on private land; their maps say its public. Our map is older, and their map is newer. If it does belong to the Feds now, we never saw a clear change in property ownership. It's all a mess," she said, shaking her head. "Derek, you double-checked the map with the owner, right?"

Farnsworth leaned against his front door and banged it with his fist. "That doesn't matter, not anymore. Those jerks are stealing my life."

"Doesn't matter? Derek, what are you saying? We didn't have permission?"

"Look, maps change, you just said so," his voice rose, and he gestured south out his window. Toward the site of our creature. "At the time, that bone bed was more important. Now the most important thing is the skeleton."

Oliphant began to clap. "This is why, ladies and gentlemen, we don't like commercial paleontologists," he said, sneering. "Cutting corners could mean jail time for you, Sarah, and your team, you pathetic hick."

Farnsworth stared at him for a long moment, then pushed off the door, moving slowly toward Oliphant. "Our maps say we were on private land. That is what matters," he growled, baring his teeth. "Call me a pathetic hick again, you piece of—"

"Stop it!" Sarah yelled, and that seemed to snap the two men out of their fight. Farnsworth looked down at his feet, his chest rising and falling quickly. He turned away from the rest of us and placed his hands and head against his front door. Oliphant looked at Farnsworth. His shoulders fell, and he walked over to Farnsworth's couch. As he sat down, a cloud of dust rose, causing him to cough.

"Okay," Farnsworth said quietly. The tension in the room dissipated. "We need to make sure that the BLM doesn't damage the skeleton."

"What? Derek, they already have the 3D printout. There's nothing we can do," Sarah said, her brow furrowed.

"You mean the actual fossil of the Monster," I said.

Farnsworth looked at me, his eyebrows raised. "The Monster?"

"Yeah. Our dragon is a monster. Our Montana Monster. Since we're fighting about what to call it, dragon or dinosaur or pterosaur, why don't we just call it the Monster, so we all know what we're talking about," I said.

Farnsworth's lips curled into a small smile, and his hand reached up to scratch the back of his neck. "Montana Monster. Yeah, anyway the actual fossil. They could be at the site right now. We have to make sure they don't ruin everything."

"But they said they would arrest us if we showed up," Sarah said.

"That's a risk I'm willing to take," Farnsworth said.

"He's right, Sarah," Oliphant said.

We all turned to stare at him.

"While I do question your judgment at times, Derek, I have never disputed the fact that you might be right . . . once in a decade," Oliphant said, shrugging. "Certainly that fossil is too precious to let those dunderheads ruin it." Oliphant turned and walked out the door. "Let's go."

"Wait, I'll grab my keys. We can take my truck," said Sarah, following his footsteps. Dean and Karolin moved toward the door.

Farnsworth took his hat off and ran his hand through his hair. He put it back on his head, then looked at me. "If you're coming, kid, you can ride with me. There won't be any room in Sarah's truck for all of us."

Letter between Rev. William Buckland and Mary Anning, 1829

My dear Miss Anning,

Your discovery of a "flying-dragon" is most extraordinary. I will report your find during our Geological Society meeting in a few weeks. I have never heard of another flying reptile found in England. I will send you a copy of my paper as you'll find a reference to you and your work. I look forward to comparing it to my lithographs of *Pterodactylus* and seeing if it's a match.

You did mention previously that you found another arm of a flying dragon nearby—could you send me a drawing soon?

May God grant and keep you,

Yours etc.

Rev. William Buckland

1829

LOST IN MONTANA

Oliphant

FARNSWORTH, YOU OLD fool, I thought to myself as Sarah broke several laws driving at ridiculous speeds down Highway 24 to her quarry site. *What did you do to get the government so angry with you that they'd bother raiding your sad little warehouse?*

I scanned the surrounding terrain and focused my thoughts. This was the find of the century. No doubt about it. That plastic dinosaur may have been the most beautiful thing I'd ever seen. And that says something, considering I have an original Cole Morgan at home above my fireplace. Every single cell in my body was screaming that this find was a game-changer. I wanted—no, *needed*—this dinosaur. Or dinosaur-like creature.

The fact that I was entangled again with Farnsworth, well, wasn't that just ironic. Forget Derek. Focus on the find.

Sarah said it was a dinosaur. And a pterosaur. I didn't think what we'd found was either of those animals. This was something brand new. This was a giant, flying carnivorous animal who lived at the time of the dinosaurs. This thing may have hunted one of the greatest dinosaurs to ever live.

In fact, this find would change everything we know about paleontology. This was on the same level as Sir Richard Owen naming the family Dinosauria way back in the 1840s. And if I played my cards right, I'd be playing at that same level.

I just hoped they hadn't messed up the actual fossil. The BLM was surprisingly competent for a government agency, but there were dolts in every bunch and certainly no shortage of those with no real idea how to handle fossil excavation. I hope they'd left it in the rock. I really didn't want to have to fix up their mess.

And that warehouse raid was a complete disaster. I needed all of Sarah's data and fossils, including that amazing 3D printout that was carted away by our lovely government overlords. But no matter. It paid to have friends in high places. As we were leaving Glasgow, I'd sent an email to my BLM contact, an old friend from Yale, asking what the heck Farnsworth did to cause this. He'd replied quickly, and said he'd figure out what was going on and get back to me as soon as possible. I'd get the printout for the University to study by next month at the latest. We'd lose a few weeks, but it would be worth it. After all, it would probably mean no Farnsworth!

We hadn't been driving that long on a dusty service road when I saw something that made my stomach flip-flop. "Stop the car," I ordered. "There." Sarah slowed down her truck, and I rolled down the passenger side window, pulling off my sunglasses and coughing as a cloud of dust flew into my face.

"Down in and around those tire tracks," I said, pointing. She looked at me and frowned. Below, scattered about the ground were large pieces of a smooth white material. They contrasted sharply with the surrounding sands that were brown and white-yellow. It was plaster-of-Paris, and I could see more even farther up the trail. I had a sinking feeling.

Damn. We were too late.

In the backseat, I heard Dean spout a string of profanities, his voice shaking with anger. "I bet it's from our bone quarry. It's gotta be—ours is the only site in the area."

"And those tracks are fresh, too," Sarah said quietly. "There was that storm yesterday. Softened the ground. Derek and I always drive along the same tracks to avoid creating new ones. Someone else definitely made those tracks."

Sarah shifted the truck into gear, and it lurched forward. She moved farther off to the side of the service road. We jumped violently over yucca bushes and uneven topography. She was on the chase. How Farnsworth of her.

"Preservation of evidence?" I said wryly, holding on to my armrests.

"If those jerks . . ." She didn't finish her thought though.

After a few more minutes, Sarah slowed down again. I looked up and saw a large hole in the mesa, right above the talus pile line. "Is that our bone quarry?" I asked. "It certainly doesn't look like what you described to me."

"No, that's where Molly found the other fossil," she said. In the backseat, Dean swore again. He really needed to expand his vocabulary.

"They destroyed it," Karolin said.

"No, we don't know that," Sarah replied, but her tone was unsure. "We need to go up and see." We all got out, and Molly raced past me and charged up the talus pile. Sarah and the others followed in quick pursuit.

Sighing, I closed my door and sauntered forward. At the top, I stopped and stared at what was a massive hole. It hardly resembled the site Sarah described to me last night. Somebody came through here moving fast and hard, apparently with little concern for what they destroyed. The cavern roof was gone, as were its sides. It looked like a large team excavated back into the mesa several meters. There were long scrapes in the soft Hell Creek sediments—marks of pickaxes, jackhammers, and other excavation tools. In the Fort Union sediment above, there were large depressions, as if the rock was blasted from the mesa itself. Looking down the talus pile, I saw huge chunks of fresh red rock without any signs of weathering.

"It's completely gone. They took it," Molly said.

Dean touched the rocks. "How can they have done this so quickly? In one night?"

"Dynamite," Farnsworth said. He pointed above the Fort Union. "See those blast marks?" As usual, I was right.

"But that means the fossil is destroyed," Karolin said.

"Not necessarily," Farnsworth said. "It's risky, though. TNT and jackhammer vibrations can damage a fossil. But if they were just interested in getting it out quickly, and repairing it in a lab . . ."

"That's irresponsible. It may well ruin the integrity of the fossil. Who wants to study a fossil that has been glued together from a million tiny pieces?" I said. "Even a fossil hunter wouldn't do that. It would risk their bottom line." Near me, Farnsworth opened his mouth to argue, but then shook his head. In agreement, no doubt.

At that moment, we heard a small propeller plane overhead, flying low. It circled us twice, then flew south. "Do you recognize that plane?" I asked loudly.

"No," Sarah said.

"Derek?"

"No, I don't know it," he replied. "I know a lot of local pilots and their planes, but I don't recognize that one."

"Guys, maybe coming here was a bad idea? That BLM guy told us not to," Karolin said.

"Then we should hurry," Farnsworth said. "Before we leave, we should take a quick look at the bone quarry."

The quarry was probably the source of the plaster-of-Paris I saw in the fresh truck tracks. I looked back up at the sky. The plane was gone, but I couldn't shake a feeling that we were being watched.

Our group cascaded back down the talus pile. I headed for Sarah's truck, figuring we'd drive there and I'd get the opportunity to turn on the air-conditioning. But Molly kept running along the border of the mesa, the others following like ducklings in a row. Sighing, I followed.

As we skirted the mesa, I saw more tire tracks, but not as deep as those on the service road. The bits of plaster were getting bigger. One large piece of plaster the size of a softball made me stop, and I squatted down. I picked it up and turned it around in my hand. On the side was writing from a black Sharpie. As I read the text, my stomach clenched. In my hand was a broken, plaster-covered *Triceratops* horn.

"That was a complete horn yesterday," Karolin said, her eyes forlorn.

Up above, Farnsworth, Sarah, Molly, and Dean were already surveying what I now recognized as Sarah's bone quarry terrace. At the base of the talus pile were the remains of a large white canvas tent, its poles bent and broken. Next to it were three large, red coolers, their contents of crushed soda cans and bottles of water strewn around the ravine. A solitary wheelbarrow lay upside down on the talus pile, its wheel spinning gently in the light breeze.

Reaching the bone quarry, I felt my stomach drop. I dabbed at the sweat dripping from my brow with my pocket bandana and took it all in. The bone quarry was completely destroyed. There were fragments of fossils, shattered bones, and broken rock everywhere littering the ground.

I looked at Sarah, who stared at her ruined work. There were tears in her eyes.

"How could they? I didn't know . . ." She trailed off.

Her pain was well-earned. And it made me think. No responsible scientist would be a party to this atrocity. What the hell was going on?

For a few minutes, the others wandered the bone quarry, moving torn tarps around or shifting fossils here and there.

"This doesn't make sense. The BLM doesn't go around messing up fossils," Farnsworth said.

"In my experience, they are the law," I said. "They can do pretty much what they want in the short run. But I've only had good experiences with the BLM. They protect fossils. This is utterly contrary to their protocol."

"The Monster, the bone quarry. The *T-rex*?" Molly said. I saw Farnsworth nod, and she hugged herself for a moment. She then moved her hands and grabbed at a metal ring hanging from a leather cord around her neck. I saw bite marks on the leather. "This is all messed up. They stole from us!"

At that moment, that small plane flew overhead again, this time much lower.

Molly stared up at it, but her voice was for us.

"We can't let this be the end."

A LAST-DITCH EFFORT

Molly

FARNSWORTH'S TRUCK LURCHED to a jerky stop in front of a two-story red brick building in downtown Glasgow. I bit my lip as I watched Farnsworth throw open his door and run, stopping at the building's bottom stair but not going inside. Not yet.

As I opened my own door to follow, screeching tires next to me made me turn. Throwing open her own truck door, Sarah ran toward Farnsworth. The others didn't follow. Karolin sat in her seat, her hand covering her mouth while Dean stood up on the edge of his doorframe, leaning his arms on the roof of the truck. Oliphant's eyes were on his cell phone as he got out of Sarah's truck, and there was a deep frown on his face. As Oliphant closed his door, he put the cell to his ear, but I couldn't hear what he was saying.

As I approached, Sarah touched Farnsworth's shoulder. He shrugged her off, and he pointed up to the top of the building. My eyes followed his finger. Immediately I made out a familiar gold star that contrasted brightly with the red of the building. In large block lettering were the words "Valley County Sheriff."

"Why are we here?" Sarah said, her voice breathless.

Farnsworth looked at her incredulously. "What the . . . ? Where else would I go? I've been robbed!"

Rising slightly on the balls of her feet, she placed both hands on his shoulders. "The sheriff can't do anything. The BLM took your fossils."

He glared at her. "I had nothing in there that was illegal," he finally replied, his tone low.

Sarah removed her hands and looked down at her feet.

"Well, considering it *wasn't* the BLM, we have a serious problem," Oliphant said from behind us. "Just got off the phone with my buddy at the BLM. Great paleontologist, actually. He and I—" Sarah cleared her throat loudly. "Anyway, I emailed him before we left for the bone beds. He just confirmed that there was no scheduled raid planned today. Nada."

As his words sunk in, a dark cloud blocked the sun, casting us in shadow. I closed my eyes and lifted my face to the sky. The air was cooling, heavy with the promise of rain. Another storm was heading our way.

Farnsworth pulled off his sunglasses and stared at Oliphant. After a long moment, without another word, he ran up the stairs, taking two steps at a time.

Four hours later, we were still at the station, sitting on hard plastic chairs at a desk that was empty except for a speakerphone. Next to me, Sarah leaned back in her chair and ran her fingers through her long hair. Oliphant was on her other side, tapping away on his cell phone. He'd been on his phone almost the entire time we'd been there. At one point he did leave to get some food but didn't offer to get anything for the rest of us. Jerk.

Karolin and Dean weren't there though. By then, they were probably on the road to Colorado. Once they gave their statements to the sheriff, they asked to speak privately with Oliphant. From what I could gather from their quiet conversation in the hallway, they didn't want to get involved with whatever was going on. Sarah told me that another University of Wyoming grad student had a dig just outside of Denver, so that's where they were headed.

She then asked if I wanted to go home. I had to cough to hide my laugh. *Home?* I just started my summer. Why would I want to go home? If there was any chance of saving this dig, I wanted to be around for it. Better this than working for that yogurt shop down the street from my house. She then asked if I wanted to join Karolin and Dean in Colorado, but I just shook my head and told her the truth. "I'm your intern." She smiled, maybe a bit sadly. She seemed to like that.

The speakerphone was silent now, but for the last thirty minutes, we'd been on a conference call with an Agent Porter from the Federal Bureau of Investigation in Billings.

"All you have is a business card?" A man's voice broke the silence.

"Yes, sir. An Agent John Raley, so it says," Farnsworth said, leaning toward the speakerphone, his hands clasped together on his knees.

"Yeah . . . computer searches still show no record of that man. Probably an alias." Well duh. I rolled my eyes. Sarah shot me a small smile. "Did you get any license plate numbers? I mean, you say this man and his team stole thousands of pounds of rocks, correct?"

"Fossils, but yes," Farnsworth replied.

"That would require a large vehicle, such as a semi-truck . . . did you get a color? Make?"

"No, I was busy dealing with Raley inside my warehouse. I think they were white."

"Um, okay. So I'll need an inventory of what was taken, as well . . ."

"My computer and inventory were also stolen."

"Don't you save to the cloud?"

"In the sky?" Farnsworth snapped, raising his hands in the air.

"That would be a firm no, Agent Porter," Oliphant translated, leaning over Sarah to speak into the speakerphone.

"Okay. I'll put out an APB on the two semi-trucks. Both nondescript and white. One contains stolen fossils and various equipment, including computers and files. The other contains a 3D plastic printout of . . . a fossilized dinosaur, you say?"

Not a dinosaur, I almost said, but I clamped my tongue between my teeth.

"Yes," replied Farnsworth. "Also, our bone bed was destroyed, our fossils stolen. We said that earlier."

"Oh, yeah, That's right . . ." A long pause, and I could hear the clicking sound of computer keys. "Any chance on a model or make on the trucks that took them?"

"Oh my God!" Farnsworth yelled into the phone. "Of course not! We didn't see it happen!"

"Please don't yell, Mr. Farnsworth. I'm just trying to get a timeline. But those fossils, they did or didn't belong to you?"

"We have permission from the landowner to take them. Legally, they belong to the University of Wyoming," Sarah said. She glanced at Farnsworth, who shrugged.

"Why don't we plan on meeting tomorrow morning at your warehouse, Mr. Farnsworth? You can walk me through everything in person?"

"Okay," Farnsworth said.

"But I'll be frank here, Mr. Farnsworth. The chances of us finding these trucks is very slim, not without more information. Montana, as you are well aware, is a huge state with thousands of miles of highways and back roads. It's a large ship-ping and distribution state. They have hours on us at seventy miles an hour. They could be in Montana, or in North Dakota, Wyoming. Even Canada."

Farnsworth leaned back in his chair and violently scratched his jaw stubble. For a second, I thought he was going to cry.

Less than an hour later, we were back in Farnsworth's ware-house, sitting in camp chairs next to the 3D printer. At least they left that. Without fossils and computers and papers, the warehouse seemed vast, cold, and lonely. I leaned back in my chair, sipping on a can of root beer. The others had real beers. While Sarah and Farnsworth looked depressed and dirty, Oliphant looked thoughtful as he sipped his beer.

"Hardly a Caymus Cabernet, but this beer is rather tasty," Oliphant said, peering at the label.

Suddenly, Farnsworth stood up and walked to the nearest desk along the wall. He pulled out a piece of paper from one of the drawers and groaned as he got on his knees, bending over to look under the desk. Leaning over in my rickety camp chair, I nearly fell out as I saw him pat around underneath the desk. After a second, he stopped and blurted a grateful grunt. As he pulled his arm out from under the desk, I heard a ripping sound, like the kind you hear when you're tearing tape off a box. He lurched to standing, holding a small item in his right hand. He leaned over the desk and began to furiously write something.

"What are you doing?" Sarah said, moving to look. Whatever she saw made her stand back slightly, her shoul-ders rigid.

"Making a list. I need to make some calls. Need to figure this out."

She glanced at me. "Maybe we should talk about this alone."

Oliphant let out a snort. "Don't bother, Sarah. Derek is nothing but predictable."

I was intrigued. "What is it?" I asked, craning around Sarah who was trying to block my view by waving her arms around. Squinting, I saw that the paper had what looked like a bunch of wavy lines all over it. And numbers.

"God, is that your handwriting? My doctor has neater handwriting than that," I said.

"Always a comedian," Farnsworth snapped.

"Go sit down, Molly." She gently pushed me back toward my seat. "Derek!"

He ignored her and took a few steps away, paper in hand. He opened his other hand to reveal what he pulled out from under the desk: a flip cell phone. Dialing a number, Farnsworth put it to his ear and walked away. I couldn't make out what he was saying, but it definitely was not English. Mandarin maybe?

"What is going on?" I said.

"Oh, just routine black market stuff." Oliphant laughed, sipping his beer.

"Wait, what?" I asked, my eyes growing rounder by the second.

Sarah rubbed her forehead and looked at the floor. "It's nothing, Molly."

Oliphant looked at Sarah. "Sarah, Derek has been involved in black markets since before you were born. We all know about it. So do you."

Well that was news to me. Black market fossils can sell for a lot of money. I heard of a *Tarbosaurus* skeleton from Mongolia selling for over a million bucks a few years back. *Tarbosaurus* was a distant cousin of the *T-rex*, so I guess I could see the reasoning for wanting one. A giant meat-eater in your living room would be quite the conversation piece. But it was illegal to smuggle fossils out of Mongolia. The smuggler was arrested, the fossil returned to Mongolia.

"Besides, someone from the black market world probably stole all these fossils." Oliphant's voice became louder, aimed at Farnsworth who was walking toward us. "Smugglers talk. And he's making sure that if his fossils do end up around more unsavory types, he'll be notified. Am I right, Derek?"

Farnsworth glared at Oliphant, his hands gripping the back of a camp chair. "Fossil hunter. Not a smuggler."

Oliphant leaned back in his chair and took a long swig of beer. He gave Farnsworth a long look. "Semantics. Brass tacks, Derek. What did you have here?"

"What are you talking about, Sean?" He cocked his head to the side.

Oliphant grinned. "Come one, now. Humor me. *What* could you have possibly had in this warehouse that would have caused thieves to descend and steal everything, including your precious mousetraps?"

"Nothing," Farnsworth said to the floor. "Nothing. Honestly. Well, maybe a juvenile *Stegosaurus* skeleton. Other hunters could sell it for some change. But nothing *really* valuable." He glanced toward the back wall of the warehouse, toward his home. "Small pieces really, for my future museum."

His museum. He'd said that before. But before I could ask more about it, Oliphant barked a laugh. "Not true."

Oliphant leaned forward in his chair, a slight sneer on his face. He pointed the beer bottle's neck toward Farnsworth. "Yes, you *did*. You had something so valuable here that once they got wind of it, it took less than twenty-four hours for a group of people, pretending to be government officials with coordinating vests, to steal all your fossils. Not to mention, they took our fossils in the field. And destroyed what they didn't want."

"The printout," I said.

"Ding ding ding." Oliphant saluted me with his free hand. "And the second they knew about it, probably moments after we did, they were ready to strike. I know the government. They are not that fast."

Deadly silence gripped our little group, and my throat was suddenly dry. They did move quickly. I mean, Karolin had just posted those pictures online last night. Not too long after the printout was spat out onto the warehouse floor. Whoever Raley was, he had been waiting. Watching, somehow. I'm no expert, but it probably takes time to organize semi-trucks and the necessary equipment to move massively heavy fossils in casts. Or a printout of a flying creature larger than a *T-rex*. But how? I looked around the warehouse half expecting to see cameras in corners. I suppressed a shiver and squeezed my root beer a little too hard. Brown liquid spouted out and spilled on my already-dirty jeans. I rubbed at the stain with my sleeve.

"So, what now?" Sarah said. "That FBI guy, Porter, didn't seem that hopeful. Did your contact say anything, Derek?"

"He'll keep an ear out. He's on a dig in Australia, so not much he can do till he gets back to the States."

Above us, the pitter-patter of rain on the metal roof was interrupted by a deep crash of thunder. The air around me had noticeably cooled. I looked around the warehouse again as a heavy wind slapped against the walls to the east.

"What next?" I asked.

"We can salvage the bone bed. Those guys weren't BLM. We have the right," Sarah said.

"And that's it?" Farnsworth said. "We just give up?"

"We wait to hear from—" Sarah responded.

"We have to do something," Farnsworth interrupted. "I can't just sit here."

At that moment, I heard a loud buzzing noise. I looked around the warehouse in confusion.

"I'll get it," Farnsworth said, moving toward the front of the warehouse.

"Doorbell," Sarah said to me.

Farnsworth opened the door, signed for a package from a man I couldn't see, and returned with a long, brown paper tube. Written in red lettering on its side was: *Overnight. Open Immediately.*

"What is that, Derek?" Sarah said.

"No idea. Wasn't expecting a package." He looked at the address label. "It's from an 'S.V.'" He looked back at us. "It's from London."

"Overnight from London?" Oliphant asked. "Expensive. Very expensive."

"Probably another package from the Natural History Museum in London. For my museum." Farnsworth carefully placed it on the nearest workbench. "Maybe they'll come back and steal this, too."

Oliphant let out a snort and stood up, snatching the package from the table. "Come on, Derek. The Natural History Museum in London isn't known for overnighting fossils. What in the world did they send you?" And with that, he ripped it open.

"What the hell, Sean!" Farnsworth reached for the tube. While Farnsworth was bigger, Oliphant dodged his hands, pulling out the contents of the tube.

Oliphant grinned at its contents.

"Well, this is unexpected," he said.

OWEN'S TRUTH

Oliphant

"IT'S JUST A couple of pictures," I said, turning toward Farnsworth. "Why would the museum spend money to overnight these to you?"

I glanced again at the pictures in my hand. I recognized the first one. It was a daguerreotype of Sir Richard Owen holding a fossilized skull, the same picture we moved into Farnsworth's home earlier that day. The other was a strange painting of a man on a horse fighting two reptiles.

I felt pressure on my arm. Molly was standing at my side, hand open. "May I?" She scrunched her eyes as she looked at the picture and the painting, holding them up to see them better in the dim light of the warehouse.

I patted my front pocket for my reading glasses. But something was nagging me. Something about the picture Molly was holding. I'd seen it before. And yet . . .

I leaned over Molly's small shoulders and took in the picture again. Oh my God. I put my hand on her shoulder, and she turned to look at me. Her eyes were wide and her mouth was slightly open.

"This is wrong," Molly said quietly, stealing a glance at Sarah and Farnsworth before grabbing her backpack off the floor of the warehouse. Then, she bolted for the back door, her boots squeaking as she ran.

"Molly! Wait," Sarah cried, but Molly had already left, the heavy door banging in her wake.

Sarah turned to me. "What did she mean, 'wrong?'"

"She means that picture of Owen is the same as yours, Derek, but with one huge difference." I motioned toward the door Molly had just left through. "After you two."

Farnsworth shot me a level look.

"Trust me," I said. He scoffed in response, but he pulled at Sarah's arm and together we walked out of the warehouse.

When we opened his front door, my instincts were confirmed. As I knew they would be. Molly was holding up the larger Owen poster and comparing it to the smaller copy. The two pictures matched. The pose, the clothing, Owen's apparent age. Everything looked the same.

Except for the skull.

"Look at the skull in that larger picture of Richard Owen," Molly said. "It's white, and some sort of reptile. A crocodile, I think. It's the photo common in history books. I think it's even on Wikipedia. But in the picture Farnsworth was just sent . . . the skull has horns. And it's black. Like our creature."

Wanting to get a better look at the new picture, I pulled it from Molly's grasp and walked over to the nearest lamp. Holding the image up to the light, I could see horns over the creature's eye sockets, and even small horns on its dentary, almost hidden in Owen's robes. Judging its size relative to Owen, this fossil was much smaller than our *Monster*, as Molly called it. Based on the printout, our Monster was massive, maybe fifty feet in length. The animal in this photo, when alive, was maybe five or six feet in length. Perhaps it was a subspecies of what Sarah's team found? Or a juvenile, maybe?

A smile graced my lips. I gently touched the picture, tracing Owen's robes till I got to the bottom. I squinted in the light. There was something written in elegant cursive just below his body.

Owen's Truth —S.V.

"Whoever sent you these pictures, Derek, annotated this picture," I said. "This S.V. wrote *Owen's Truth*."

What does that mean? Owen's truth. I closed my eyes. Sir Richard Owen. I taught his life story in my historical geology class. In the second half of the nineteenth century, Owen was *the* authority on comparative anatomy. He was in high demand as a consultant for those trying to make sense of the fossil evidence that was then being regularly uncovered. Using three dinosaurs—*Megalosaurus, Iguanodon,* and *Hylaeosaurus*—in 1842, he published the first critical account of these animals and coined the term Dinosauria. Each of these dinosaurs enthralled the world with their strange, fantastical sizes and shapes. *Megalosaurus* was a thirty-foot-long meat-eater that lived about 160 million years ago during the Jurassic period. *Iguanodon* was another amazing dinosaur. It lived during the early Cretaceous, about 130 million years ago. It walked on two legs and had a bony thumb on its front feet to defend itself. A thumb! The third, *Hylaeosaurus*, was an armored dinosaur that lived around the same time as *Iguanodon*. It was huge, with several spikes protruding from its back.

Owen was also a famously intractable curmudgeon. He and Farnsworth probably would have been drinking buddies. Even though Owen enjoyed the patronage of Queen Victoria, he was thrown out of several prominent societies after accusations of plagiarism surfaced. His expulsion was no doubt fueled by his difficult personality. He was best remembered as a superintendent of the British Museum, where he curated the museum's extensive natural history collection and advocated that the collection deserved its own space. The creation of a new Natural History Museum in London was his crowning achievement. A somewhat less known fact is that Owen was the rival of several famous scientists of the day. The most famous feud was with Charles Darwin. Owen and his colleagues were highly vocal challengers of Darwin's natural selection theory. Of evolution. Well, Dickie, you lost that one.

And now in my hand was a picture of Sir Richard, posing with the skull of what Molly would like us all to call a dragon. Quite unexpected, indeed.

"That's Mary Anning, isn't it?" Molly said as she squatted down, gently touching a poster of Mary Anning, the nineteenth-century amateur fossil hunter from Dorset. She pushed the Anning poster aside. "You also have . . . Gideon Mantell?" She read the label on the bottom of the picture. Gideon Mantell was a nineteenth-century English doctor who loved geology and paleontology so much, he used to dig fossils between helping women give birth. He and his wife first discovered *Iguanodon*.

Oh, and he was another Owen rival. Paleontology was a much smaller world back then.

Farnsworth nodded. "Yeah. Artwork for my museum. The Glasgow Museum of Paleontology. I want to open a museum about paleontology and its history. Not just focusing on dinosaurs. I want kids to see the whole field, and understand the journey we've taken as humans to learn about paleontology, our earth-science history. To get to know the players as well as the fossils, geologic timescale, that sort of thing. Most of the fossils and artifacts were donations from France, England, and Germany. But I'm also researching the history of paleontology in China, Russia, Greece, Canada, Argentina. Got lots of interesting stuff already donated. It was going to be great—fun, real, not stuffy."

What was he insinuating?

Even with the potential barb, I could see Farnsworth's passion . . . and his pain.

Molly cocked her head to the side. "That's pretty boss. I mean cool, actually." She sounded surprised. "So these are all from museums?"

"I've got friends in a lot of museums, and they send me stuff, mostly loans. It's all stuff their museum isn't going to be using any time soon."

I shook my head and turned my attention to the other item from the tube. It was a painting on canvas. "And we also have this." I handed it to Farnsworth. "What is your expert opinion of this painting, Mr. Wikipedia?"

He glared at me and grabbed the painting from my hand. But as he gazed at the painting, his jaw went slack, and any sort of retort he was planning to shoot my way flew out the window.

"That's not just any painting," Farnsworth said, his voice low and reverent. "It's *St. George and the Pterodactyl.*"

"Is that supposed to mean something?" I said. The painting seemed unremarkable, to be honest. Just a man on a horse and some monsters.

I leaned over to take another look at the painting. It depicted a man on horseback in a deep, dark cave. He was on a stone stair path that led down to a pool of water, and his head was covered by a helmet. He was dressed in an unadorned robe. A monk's habit, maybe? He was holding what looked like a crucifix in his left hand and was brandishing a large mace in his right hand, over his head, as if he was defending himself. The monk's horse was rearing, in either anger or fear. Below the man, two monsters were rising out of the watery pool, poised to attack. The monster on the lower right was a giant octopus, slithering up onto the rocks from the waters below. The other creature was about the same size as the octopus, but stockier. The creature's head was huge relative to its body, with two small horns jutting from its skull, its mouth open wide and filled with razor-sharp teeth. Two legs with long feet topped with huge talons grasped and clawed at the stone steps beneath it. And its large wings were outstretched, as if the animal was about to take flight to fight the intruder of its damp cave.

I realized Farnsworth was still talking. "It's a famous painting of Saint George, the Patron Saint of England. Saint George was famous in English lore for slaying a dragon? But this painting is by Benjamin Waterhouse Hawkins. Instead of a dragon, he famously painted Saint George fighting a *Pterodactylus*."

"Wait, I know that name." Molly turned to look at Farnsworth. "Why do I know that name?"

Farnsworth grinned at her. "Because he's also the guy Richard Owen collaborated with to design the Crystal Palace Dinosaurs in London."

Oh, yes, those metal monstrosities. It was all coming back to me now. Benjamin Waterhouse Hawkins worked with Owen to create giant statues of dinosaurs and other prehistoric animals for the public in the early 1850s. They were still on display in London's Crystal Palace Park. They were commissioned as part of a plan to landscape Crystal Palace Park. Academic dinosaur paleontology was relatively new when Owen guided Hawkins in the design of the statues. Consequently, the results of the various dinosaurs and other Mesozoic animals are of lumbering reptiles, more closely resembling Gila monsters or weird lizards than what we see in today's natural history museums.

"But . . . he's not though," Molly said, pointing toward the bottom of the painting. "Look at it. The painting is called *St. George and the Pterodactyl* but that's not a *Pterodactylus*. It has . . . horns."

The damn girl was right. The creature's head was crested by horns. Horns just like those on the skull Owen was holding in the daguerreotype.

And the horns on our printout.

"You're right, Molly," said Farnsworth. "This isn't the regular version . . ." He touched the painting. "This feels like real paint. I don't think this is a copy. Maybe an earlier version, like the *Isleworth Mona Lisa*. And there. It says 'BWH.' For Benjamin Waterhouse Hawkins."

"Hold on . . . give me a minute . . ." Molly said unhelpfully, taking out her cell phone and typing in a blur of speed. After a few seconds, I could see that she was looking at the original painting online. "That dragon isn't the only change in this painting from the original. There is lettering on these stone steps that aren't in the original." She pointed to the painting and held out her phone with her other hand. Sure enough, each stone step in our painting has a small line of text, utterly absent in the original.

"What does it say?" I asked. "Read it aloud." Damn Molly and her youthful eyes.

Molly cleared her throat, and read slowly, carefully.

A thousand ages underground
His skeleton had lain
But now his body's big and round
And there's life in him again
The jolly old beast
Is not deceased
There's life in him again

Its mind contains the key
Made of red and crystal bone
Oh woe is the legacy of the Dracosauria

The world has never known
An ancient enemy impedes
Those that will save the truth
But fate will lead the willing
To hallowed halls that whisper of the Origin in sooth
To the dragon you will fall.

"Well. That's a bit overdramatic," I said after a long silence.

Sarah looked bewildered and a bit anxious. "Yeah. Yeah, it is." She turned away from us, repeating the verses quietly.

Dracosauria.

Draco was Latin for *dragon*, and *sauria* was derived from the Greek word *sauros*, for *lizard* or *reptile*. Dragon Lizard. Kind of superfluous, but the name repetition did evoke a visual of primordial terror.

I looked back at the painting in Molly's hands. Saint George looked proud and murderous, intent on slaying a dragon.

I glanced at Molly. Last night she seemed so sure that dragons could have walked the earth at the same time as dinosaurs.

Dracosauria.

Someone else appeared to agree with her.

"The raid. These pictures," Molly said finally. "Sent by someone who signed both the picture and the package as 'S.V.' What is going on?"

I scraped at the beginnings of a five-o'clock shadow on my chin. The timing of everything was crazy. Someone seemed to know a lot. Or multiple someones. They had time to prepare.

"Remind me about something, Sarah. That fossil you found wasn't the first evidence you had of the creature, was it?" I said, glancing at her. "You had a tooth, right?"

Sarah nodded. "Yeah. We found it in the stream bed near the mesa months ago. It's what led us to the quarry."

"Didn't you say you had trouble identifying it? Did you post it on the online forums for ID?"

"Yeah," Sarah replied. "Got skunked, though."

Interesting. Maybe that was what alerted Raley. If he got wind ahead of time that we might find the tooth's original owner, however slim those odds may have been, he could have gotten ready to take it. But why? It was obviously a rare specimen. I mean, I couldn't ID it, and I've been at this for decades! And now this S.V.? Sending us stalker-level pictures with weird poems on them? Were Raley and S.V. the same? If so, why steal Farnsworth's stuff, yet send us the pictures? I grimaced and rubbed my temples. I felt like we were heading down a dark path, and I didn't like not being in control. I needed answers.

"Owen's picture," Molly said, and I looked up at her. Her eyes were sparkling with excitement. "Owen's truth, the poem . . ."

"That's it. I recognize that poem." Farnsworth snapped his fingers. "At least the first part. It's a song that was sung by guests during that famous New Year's Eve dinner in 1853." He looked at us expectantly.

"Derek, this is the part where you'd hear crickets," I said.

"God, read some history, will you? 1853. Richard Owen hosted a special New Year's Eve meal in London with other prominent scientists and citizens in the actual mold that was used to create one of the Crystal Palace *Iguanodons*. That mold still exists. It's on display at the Natural History Museum in London. I believe it's the only mold left in existence."

"Mold?" Molly asked.

"Yeah. Have you ever made a mold before?"

She shook her head and looked at me. I shrugged. "Sorry, too busy with my lecture series."

Farnsworth glared at me and took a deep breath. "Hawkins wanted to make his sculptures out of concrete, so they would last a very long time. But it's hard to carve concrete, right? It's much better to pour wet concrete against something, like a mold, with the shape you want, then remove it and—voilá—you have your sculpture with all the trimmings. So, he made life-sized plaster molds of each animal first. Dinosaurs, flying reptiles, swimming reptiles. Even other more recent animals, like a giant sloth. From the outside, the molds looked like the animal. But inside, they were hollow. He etched details along the interior walls of the mold, such as scales, fur, eyeballs, and talons. Eventually, he had his team press concrete into the mold walls to make concrete casts of what he carved into the plaster. Once that was done, the concrete panels were assembled at Crystal Palace Park. Hawkins destroyed all of his molds. Except for one. That one—one, of his *Iguanodon*—still stands at the Natural History Museum in London."

"What about the second half of the poem?" Sarah said.

"No idea. It's not part of the original song," Farnsworth replied. "We can double-check, but I'm sure it's not."

"I bet Owen wrote it—the second half, I mean," Molly said.

"Now wait a minute." I barked out a laugh. "Owen? Why on earth would you assume that? It could just as easily have been Hawkins. Or a recent jokester. I get that you all see Owen as the man of the hour, but let's have some discipline. We can't just make outlandish assumptions."

"No, you're right. We can't make assumptions about anything, especially after our giant flying Monster was stolen by robbers pretending to be government agents!" Molly snapped.

Wow, she can go from zero to sixty real fast. "Okay, okay. You're right. Strange circumstances and all that, but let's hypothesize. After all, some of us here are careful *scientists*." I smirked. "Please explain your thinking, Ms. Wilder."

She glowered at me and started to pace a little.

"What if, and hear me out, Owen's leaving us clues? That picture of Owen—he's holding what looks a heck of a lot like the Monster we just found. What if that skull is still in the London Natural History Museum? What if Owen commissioned the painting with this poem? The painting, the picture, the poem: What if Owen is leading us to London, to get the skull?"

"Owen's dead, Molly. He can't be sending Derek overnight packages," Sarah said gently.

"No, but someone else could be carrying out Owen's wishes. This 'S.V.' person, maybe. Someone who wants us to find evidence of dragons. The Natural History Museum's collection is enormous. The skull could be there even if no one knows it's there. Like in a box in their basement or something."

Not a dragon, I thought. *But something.*

I looked back at the picture of Owen, his hand resting on the black skull. The Natural History Museum in London is one of the best museums in the world. The intern was right. Their fossil collection was incredible. Maybe we could find this exact skull in their basement, collecting dust. And their paper archive was also just as mouthwatering. Maybe I could find out more about this creature there. Perhaps Owen documented more information about it. I needed as much information as I could get to describe this species. Or else I'd be laughed out the door.

I pulled out my phone.

"Molly, are you a fan of The Clash?" I asked.

"No. Why?"

"Because, my dear, I believe London is calling."

LONDON CALLING

Molly

"WHAT ARE YOU saying?" Sarah asked.

"What does it sound like? I'm saying we turn stage left, and we head out into the unknown," Oliphant replied with a devilish grin. He turned away from us and walked toward Farnsworth's tiny kitchen, typing furiously on his phone. When he reached the refrigerator, he paused for a second, tapping his foot on the stained linoleum.

I had no idea what was going on with Oliphant. But I knew what I wanted. That tube had come from London. The *St. George and the Pterodactyl* wannabe painting by Benjamin Waterhouse Hawkins was made in England, probably London. Owen, the great English naturalist, was photographed holding a dragon's skull. The Crystal Palace *Iguanodon* mold was in London.

All arrows pointed to London.

But how in the world would I get there? It was not like I could just use my dad's credit card . . . or could I? I mean, I didn't think he checked our statement that often. He hated computers with a passion and still used paper checks. Even in the supermarket. People gave him the meanest looks sometimes.

The scuffle of Oliphant's boots on the floor caused me to look back up. "So I have a better idea than wallowing in self-pity and waiting for the FBI to do nothing," Oliphant said, his voice positively cheerful.

He pointed a finger in my direction as he continued to type on his phone. "You spell your last name with an 'i' and not a 'y,' correct?"

"Yes?" I replied.

"What are you doing, Sean?" Sarah asked quietly.

"What *have I done*, you mean. I bought us all tickets to London," he said, putting his phone down and looking at us. "Benefit of being an executive member of United. We leave in the morning on the Glasgow express to Denver, and from there to Heathrow." He started laughing as he looked over at us.

"We can't just go!" Sarah yelled, looking at me.

"Why not?" Oliphant said calmly. "That skull," he held up the picture of Owen still in his hand, "could be in London. Even if it's not, Owen may have kept records about that specimen. A creature I seriously believe is not a dinosaur. It's something else. What we need is evidence. I need to see the damn thing. And frankly, I want to get away from Glasgow as soon as possible . . ." His voice trailed off, looking at Farnsworth.

I knew what he meant. Someone was watching Farnsworth closely. Watching us all, I bet. I realized I didn't want to be there anymore, either. But if there was a way to find more of the Monster, either in print or an actual fossil, I was game for the hunt.

"You have a passport, correct, Molly?"

I nodded. Thankfully, as part of the Nakasogi intern prep package, I was told to pack mine.

"Good. Get packed, lightly. It'll be a short trip. We leave for Denver at seven a.m." He motioned to Sarah and me. He then turned to Farnsworth. "On that note, thank you for your . . .

hospitality, Derek. I know Sarah appreciates it. We'll be out of your hair in the morning."

"What are you talking about?" Farnsworth snapped.

"This is a University matter—" Oliphant started but was interrupted by Farnsworth's bark of laughter.

"I'm coming with you," he said, moving toward his phone on a small table by his couch.

Sarah walked over and placed a hand on his arm. "Derek, he's right. This is really just a University thing. We—"

"I'm coming," Farnsworth said, giving her a look under narrowed eyelids. "Those a—" He turned and looked at me, swallowing his words. "They took everything."

"Exactly, Derek," Oliphant said. "You should stay here and deal with the Feds. That FBI guy is coming over in the morning. You can try to track your stuff. Legally."

"No. We need to track that." Farnsworth pointed to the Owen picture in Oliphant's hand. "You said it yourself. They were organized. They struck when they knew what we had. Whatever *that* is, it's important. We find that fossil, a fossil like our . . . Monster . . . we can salvage . . . something. And besides, I'm not going to just sit here on my rear while—" He narrowed his eyes at Oliphant. "I'm coming."

Farnsworth then opened a small drawer in the table and rummaged around. He pulled out a business card and dialed a number on his landline. I walked closer and squinted at the card, making out the words "Travel Agency." Wow. I had no idea they still existed. I raised an eyebrow at Farnsworth, but he just turned his back to me and waited for someone to answer.

The next afternoon, we were boarding a Boeing 787 Dreamliner to cross the Atlantic. Three of us managed to get seats together in the four-person middle section of the plane. Oliphant waved at us from first class, a champagne flute in his right hand and a croissant in his left.

"Well, this isn't how I thought we'd be spending our summer." Sarah chuckled.

No, it wasn't. Our flight this morning was more of an escape. I hadn't slept well at all. Even though Sarah was in the next bunk in the Airstream, I had kept waking up, half expecting Raley to be standing over me. Before heading to bed, I had suggested we sleep at the airport, but Sarah said, *Derek will keep watch. It's what he does.*

Sure enough, he was sleeping on his porch when I left our trailer at 5:00 a.m.

Now, as the captain began her speech about flight times and how we needed to listen to the air stewards who were there to help, Sarah poked my arm and pointed to my open dragon book. I'd taken it out as soon as we sat down.

"You really do love dragons, huh?"

I leaned back in my own chair and rubbed the armrests. "My mom used to read to me all sorts of myths, but dragons are my passion." I held up the book for emphasis. "We know dragon myths are from all over the world, right? Well, it's really fun to read about what people believed a dragon looked like, or how they acted." I smiled at the roof of our plane. "Except for the poles, there really isn't a continent that doesn't have a dragon story. Including the United States."

Sarah shrugged her shoulders. "I figured there were some, but I don't know any."

Indigenous groups all over the world have dragon myths, North America included. One of my favorites was the Piasa, a dragon from Illinois. Apparently, a strange dragon terrorized an ancient Native American tribe that lived along the Mississippi River. It was a peculiar dragon—a giant flying monster with antlers and the face of a man. But a group of brave young warriors coaxed the beast to the ground and slaughtered it. That particular story was recorded in their petroglyphs.

As the plane rose, my stomach jumped in excitement. England. The land of Camelot and Avalon and dragons and wyverns. Dragons were so important to Britain's history and culture. Dragon stories existed across the island, from Wales to England to Scotland; there were even stories that claimed dragons were still around, like Scotland's Loch Ness Monster. And there was another special connection between the English and dragons, through their love and devotion to their patron saint, Saint George. The man who fought and defeated a dragon. The very man in the painting sent to us.

And I was on a plane flying to England, hoping to find and save a dragon.

NIGHT AT THE MUSEUM

Oliphant

LONDON, ENGLAND. ORIGINALLY called Londinium by the Romans when they settled it two thousand years ago. The greatest city on earth, in my humble opinion.

The early evening air was crisp, windy, and damp as I walked up the stone stairs to the Natural History Museum. I actually hate rain, which was weird because it's such a critical part of fossil discovery: rain erodes rock and exposes the fossils. We find them and dig them up. But I let my students do all that. Why get dirty when I don't have to? I mean, just two days ago, I was happily sitting in my office, drinking a flat white, commenting on a paper about the nesting behaviors of the bird-like dinosaur *Oviraptors* in Mongolia. And now I'm stuck with my grad student, her adolescent intern, and my old frenemy, about to get rained on. All because someone stole Farnsworth's stupid fossils and a plastic printout of what could be the next big thing in paleontology.

"Are you okay, Derek?" Sarah said, not for the first time. He waved her off, but I heard him mumble about aching elbows or something.

"Well, since you're so ancient, you'll fit right in," I said.

Farnsworth turned to look at me, confusion etched on his face.

"Do I have to spell it out? Because you're a fossil. You know, because you're practically . . . never mind." I shook my head and grinned as his lip went up in a snarl.

"Dr. Oliphant, that was just so . . . bad. Like, the worst joke ever," Molly groaned through her fingers.

"Ah, but what is life without bad puns?" I replied.

"Molly, where is your cell phone?" Farnsworth said. "You're a teen. Shouldn't it be attached to your hand? I figured you'd Immediate-Gram or whatever once we arrived."

I shot him a disbelieving look. "Immediate-Gram? Seriously, you say that, and I get crap for a fossil pun."

Molly bit her lip. "No phone, at least not regularly. Roaming. International charges. My dad would immediately find out and kill me."

"He's a good dad," Farnsworth said.

As we neared the top of the stairs, I stopped to gaze at our destination: the Natural History Museum of London.

The exhibits inside have changed through the years, but the building itself displayed the same remarkable Victorian glamour it did the day it opened to the public in 1881. Visitors entered through a giant archway with two large, ornate wooden doors capped with beautiful stained-glass windows. On each side of the arches were columns, each unique with different relief stylizations. Some had geometric designs, others had patterns found in nature, such as scales. All along the side of the building were small arches that framed hundreds of exquisite windows that illuminated the exhibits inside with natural light. Put together, the entire spectacle was incredibly grand.

As we walked up, I saw a visitor standing on the steps. She was on her phone, typing away instead of looking at the building. My heart sank. Humans created something truly remarkable here, yet our society would rather stand right next to it, staring at a computer screen only a few inches wide. Probably bragging on social media about how they were there, but not actually living the moment for themselves. When I saw things like that, I realized that while I loved my life, I was glad I studied the dead rather than the living.

"Owen helped design this museum, didn't he," Sarah said. It was more of a statement than a question.

"Yeah, he did," I replied. "Quite the testament to human ingenuity. It's stunning, isn't it, Molly? And a much better view than your empty warehouse, right, Derek?"

"No," he returned, and walked up the stairs at a quicker pace, pushing Molly slightly ahead of him. "This whole situation is crap, Sean."

"Oh, come on. We're halfway around the world on an adventure. Live a little."

Farnsworth stopped and swung his body toward me, leaning in close to my face, his sunburned nose inches from mine. On the stairs above us, Sarah stood still, her face strained with anxiety.

"Did you forget the last thirty-six hours, Sean?"

"Of course not," I said. "I'm just trying to remind everyone to see the bright side of things."

"Well, you suck at it," he said.

I narrowed my eyes. Farnsworth had a few inches on me, so I rose slightly on the balls of my feet. "Seriously, why are you here, Derek? Yes, your fossils were stolen. But shady individuals stealing stuff is just another day in the life of a fossil hunter. Something you know all about."

Farnsworth raised his hand, and I heard Sarah's intake of breath. At the noise, he stopped, and lowered it. "Pot calling the kettle, Sean. I'm here to make sure you don't mess this up.

Or get someone hurt," he growled. He pulled away and darted up the stairs to where Molly and Sarah were standing.

I felt my insides turn a little as I watched them go. I knew bringing Molly was a mistake. A knee-jerk reaction to anger Farnsworth. But this whole situation was his fault. I wouldn't have put it past any of his old friends to stalk him, figure out he had a priceless fossil in his grasp, and steal it. He should have been more careful. His lifestyle choices may have cost me the discovery of a lifetime. And that made me angry. Spiteful. So I brought the intern. The innocent one. To hurt him.

But if we were able to find another specimen, well, it would be worth dealing with Farnsworth and the intern for a few days.

Since it was near closing time, the museum wasn't too full of visitors or staff. We easily entered the building, quickly passing the main hall, or Hintze Hall. The hall was a giant and stunningly constructed atrium made out of beautiful light-colored stone. Opposite the main entrance, seated on the first level of the museum's grand staircase, was a statue of Charles Darwin. He sat regally on his stone chair, his white beard a testament to his longevity and academic prowess. While he seemed to not be looking at anything in particular, I felt like he missed nothing, a gatekeeper to stop the riffraff from entering these hallowed halls.

I once read somewhere that Owen had insisted that the east side of the museum house the extinct specimens, while the west side house the living specimens. Kind of a "get stuffed" to Charles Darwin because Owen thought Darwin's approach to evolution was stupid.

"It's weird to think that Owen and Darwin were colleagues," Sarah said, looking at the statue of Darwin as we walked.

"Not just colleagues, but friends, too. Owen helped describe some of the fossils Darwin brought back from his trip on the HMS *Beagle* in the 1830s."

But sometime in the mid-1800s, their relationship broke down. Their falling-out occurred over transmutation, which was the word commonly used then to describe evolution. Basically, up until the 1800s, most believed that God created the differences between modern animals and the animals they saw in the fossil record. Darwin saw something else. He saw that over generations, animals passed down beneficial traits, like a beak shape, or a long neck. By passing these traits down their genetic lines, they could outperform their future rivals for food, shelter, and mates.

Many people at the time hated this idea. Not just the Church. Much of the scientific community did too, because it really challenged their own opinions and thinking. To them, God was the first and final word.

"Owen and Darwin eventually hated each other, right? Over evolution?" Molly asked.

"Well, kinda, but actually it was more of a heated disagreement. Owen wasn't totally opposed to the idea of evolution, of species changing over time. He just thought God had more of a hand in it than Darwin's camp did. For Darwin and his group, it was all or nothing.

"Owen still wrote a scathing review of Darwin's book, *On the Origin of Species*," Farnsworth said. "He was the poster boy for the religious side of the argument."

That was enough from he-who-surfs-Wikipedia.

"Darwin's supporters included several famous figures," I said, turning back to Molly. "Take Thomas Huxley, for example. The newspapers at the time branded Huxley as 'Darwin's bulldog.' He was a smart man, and he fought anyone who opposed evolution. Team Darwin, if you will, was composed of men like Huxley who rejected the Church. Owen and others, like Reverend William Buckland, the guy who discovered *Megalosaurus*, well, they were religious and thought differently."

Molly frowned. "So we have the religious camp and the non-religious camp."

"Well, it's more than that," I said.

"Later," Sarah interrupted. "We're here." She halted in front of a doorway of a large yellow room, and motioned for us to follow her inside.

The museum had undergone several major remodels and exhibit changes since its construction. However, our destination hadn't really changed much since the museum was opened in the 1880s. That's because Owen's will stipulated that the mold used for the Crystal Palace *Iguanodon* was to be maintained at this location in the museum. Forever.

The room we were now standing in was known as the Lasting Impressions Hall. It was perfect for displaying the massive *Iguanodon* mold: high ceilings and wide, yellow-painted walls. Along the back wall was a dark glass door etched with the words: "British Geological Survey."

"So that's it," Molly said.

I chuckled. "Yes. Yes. Very impressive."

"It's . . . *something*," Molly replied.

Owen's mold was an incredible relic. It was a huge, imposing reptile-like creature. It had a giant head situated on a stunted neck, and its mouth was open slightly to show several cylindrical teeth. The body was large and lumbering, with a long tail that extended away from the rest of the body.

Nearby, I overheard Sarah quietly speaking to Farnsworth. Snippets of his reply hit my ears: "BLM," "fossils," and "make a call. I'm done after this." Good. Hopefully he'd leave soon. He shouldn't be here anyway. I stole a glance at the door to the room. A docent stood near the door. I gave him a nod. No reason to annoy the local fuzz.

"It seems so fragile. Why was this one preserved? How?" Sarah asked.

Interesting question. There were no other molds still around, as far as I knew. And it was in remarkable shape, considering its age and composition.

"Heh, its thumb is stuck to its nose." Molly laughed, pointing at the head.

I chuckled, too. A silly detail to put on the mold. It showed what Hawkins and Owen believed at the time. They were very wrong. When paleontologist Dr. Gideon Mantell described the first *Iguanodon* fossils in the early 1820s, he didn't know that *Iguanodon* had large conical spikes for thumbs. Instead, he thought that they were defensive horns and added one to its nose. Eventually, Mantell found more skeletal material. However, he failed to convey any new information to Owen and Hawkins. Mostly because he was dead. So, the Crystal Palace *Iguanodon* had a spike that was really a thumb on its nose.

"Did they cut the legs off at its shoulders?" Sarah asked. "I thought this mold was of the standing one?" There were two *Iguanodon* sculptures at the Crystal Palace Park: one standing, and one lying on its belly with one of its front legs raised, resting on a large fallen tree trunk.

"Yeah, Owen cut the legs before positioning the mold here. Due to its size," Farnsworth said.

"How do you know that?" Molly asked, leaning forward to touch the mold.

Farnsworth grabbed her shirt and pulled her backward. "Easy there, kid." He pointed to a sign on the nearest wall that said "DO NOT TOUCH" at the same time the docent echoed the sentiment loudly.

I motioned to another plaque on the floor next to the legs of the *Iguanodon*. "Says Owen wanted the legs cut off so it would fit here." Even with these alterations, the mold was still huge: probably seven feet tall and fifteen feet long, tail to snout. *Imagine the New Year's Eve party inside this baby.* The local press even covered Owen's 1853 New Year's Eve dinner in the *Iguanodon* mold, so there were several drawings made of the night's events. He had invited some of the brightest and most powerful men of the day to dine right inside this mold. In the belly of the beast! What a bash it would have been. For a moment, I mused at time travel. I imagined traveling back in some H. G. Wells machine and walking into the museum almost 170 years ago, knowing everything we did now. What I could have taught them!

Sarah cleared her throat. "Okay. We're here. What's next?"

Excellent question. Why the mold? How was this going to help me? I should be in the basement. The museum's library was unmatched in terms of original documentation. I'm sure a lot of it is digitized, but just in case, I need to peruse through the original paper journals to see if Owen had other documentation about this strange new animal. Or maybe more photographs or drawings of the skull that he had on his lap in that picture sent to Farnsworth. Perhaps even notes on where to find the skull.

I'll give this five more minutes, then head down to the basement.

I glanced at Molly. Since she had come along, I'd put her to work. Interns were notoriously hard workers. Not to mention free. Young eyes coupled with a hungry personality would really help going through all that documentation. Sarah could manage Farnsworth. And I'd have them review the documentation, too. Then, together we'd take a look at the bone room. Who knows, maybe between Farnsworth's weird knowledge of paleontology history and Sarah's eye for detail, they would find what we need. Drawings. Descriptions. Fossils.

"The second part of the poem," Molly said. "Let's read it aloud. It's gotten us this far."

Farnsworth pulled out a folded piece of paper from his pocket. "I copied it from the painting." He cleared his throat:

Its mind contains the key
Made of red and crystal bone
Oh woe is the legacy of the Dracosauria
The world has never known
An ancient enemy impedes
Those that will save the truth
But fate will lead the willing
To hallowed halls that whisper of the Origin in sooth
To the dragon you will fall.

Its mind contains the key.

Yeah. I had absolutely no idea what that meant. I shot a glance at Sarah and saw she'd closed her eyes. Her mouth was moving silently, repeating the poem. Molly was staring at the mold as if the answer would be revealed to her in some strange form on its body, like ghostly letters or glittery runes.

I cleared my throat. "Let's take this in steps. We know this mold held that New Year's Eve party, and distinguished guests literally ate at a table set up inside the mold, but what could 'its mind contains the key' mean?"

"Maybe it's referring to the minds of those who attended. They were all scientists or important politicians of the day, right?" Sarah said. I nodded. "We know Owen was there, what about other scientists?"

"No, that doesn't feel right. Its mind . . ." Molly snapped her fingers. "Its head, maybe?" She walked over to the giant head of the *Iguanodon* mold and stood on her tiptoes, looking intently at its chin. "Owen was seated in the head section of the mold during that New Year's Eve dinner. Maybe there is something inside?"

"How do you know that?" I asked.

"The plane had Wi-Fi," Molly replied. "Sarah and I read about the party on the flight over." She quickly looked around and up near the ceiling. Reflexively I did the same, wondering what she was looking for. Since we arrived near closing time, this room was now entirely empty, except for our docent friend in the doorway. But he looked tired and bored.

That's when I saw it. Cameras. They had a good view of most of the room. Except for the far side of the *Iguanodon*, closest to the door to the British Geological Survey.

"We need to get inside the mold," she said, her voice no higher than a whisper.

"Wait, what?" Sarah said.

But Molly didn't answer her. Instead, she walked up to the docent and spoke to him. She pointed to me, and his eyes went wide, his hand moving toward his mouth. He then walked away, speaking into his walkie-talkie. I couldn't make out what he was saying, but he sounded excited.

"Okay, we have only a minute," she said as she walked quickly past us to the far side of the *Iguanodon*.

"No, Molly!" Sarah hissed. Too late. Molly lunged at the mold, scrambling up its side, using the shoulder as leverage to reach the top. She grabbed the upper lip, and was over its side before I could even blink.

"Molly, what are you doing? Be careful!" Sarah warned.

"I'm okay," her reply was muted by the walls of the mold.

"Not you! She was talking about the mold," Farnsworth said, but he couldn't hide his huge grin. "It's very old and important, and you could have set off an alarm."

"Glad you're concerned. Anyway, in case you all want to know, it looks like the bottom of the *Iguanodon* has been removed. I'm looking at floor tiles that are different from the rest of the room," Molly said.

Oh, what the heck. I was on the same side of the mold, so I grabbed its top edge and pulled myself up. I dropped down next to her with a soft thump. It was very dark inside the mold, but a weak beam of light from Molly's cell phone illuminated her face.

"What did you say to that guard?" I asked.

"That Dr. Sean Oliphant, a *National Geographic* Explorer in Residence, was upset that the director of the museum had missed their appointment."

She shrugged. "You're famous. That docent had been trying to place you for the last five minutes."

This intern was growing on me.

Behind me, I heard the grunts and thumps of Farnsworth and Sarah as they climbed into the mold. Farnsworth helped Sarah stand up. "Ouch," she moaned, rubbing her left leg. "I need to work out more."

"More time with the pickaxe, less time with the dental pick," Farnsworth said.

She snorted and gave him a gentle push. "Yeah, I heard that the first fifty million times you said that to me."

I reached down and brushed my hand against the floor. These tiles weren't smooth like the rest of the room. Each tile was large, maybe a square foot each, and they seemed to have their own texture. One felt like scales, another like carved feathers.

"Well, if they couldn't move the exhibit, it would make sense that it would be the original 1880s flooring," Sarah suggested.

"Maybe . . ." I said.

"This one has fur," Molly said. "Stone fur."

"This one has triangles carved down into the tile as if pieces are missing," Farnsworth said.

"If this mold weren't here, protecting them, these tiles would be worn down, destroyed by visitors walking all over them. They look just like the designs on the facade of the museum, or around the entrance. Owen wanted them this way," I said.

Molly carefully moved toward the head of the *Iguanodon* and squatted down. The head was big enough for all of us to sit in if we were friendly, so I moved in closer to Molly. The head was all waves and bumps—an inverse three-dimensional replica of the creature's face, covered in scales.

"Look—there." Molly pointed to the top of the head. Etched into where the mold would form the forehead of the *Iguanodon* was an inscription in large block lettering: *To the Dragon We Will Fall*. "That's from the poem."

"Looks like we're on the right track," I said.

"And look there. Look at the tile," Farnsworth motioned between us.

This tile was dark with a glassy surface, not light yellow like the other tiles. It was a large mosaic of deep red and black triangles. I leaned forward and used my nail to try lifting one of the red triangles. Surprisingly, with slight pressure, it wiggled. After a few pulls, I lifted it right out from the floor. It was dark red, translucent, and shimmered in Molly's cell phone light.

"I bet that's garnet," Sarah said.

"Not glass?" Molly asked.

Sarah took it from me. "Too heavy. I'm almost positive this is garnet."

Molly removed a black piece and handed it to Sarah. "And this?"

"Onyx, maybe?" Sarah asked.

"Maybe these shapes are the 'blood red and crystal bones' from the poem," Farnsworth said quietly. "Maybe they are the key?"

"Like we have to use them to open something?" Molly said.

"Exactly," he said. "We just need to find the lock."

Suddenly, a loud squeal from a walkie-talkie radio echoed around the room. "Our friendly security guard has returned," I whispered. We traded a series of glances, and I couldn't help but feel like a high schooler in some over-the-top prank, waiting like a statue until the walkie-talkie sound receded and disappeared. Molly nodded and continued to pull up pieces of red and black triangles from the tile.

"But what are they supposed to do?" Sarah whispered. She moved away from the head and held a tile up into the dim light. "How can these tiles be a key?"

I shook my head. I had no clue. But if they were a key, what kind of lock would they work with?

"Wait! What about that tile that had strange grooves carved down into it? Other tiles had raised, nature-themed symbols on it. That one didn't," Molly said. She pushed past us and scrambled the few feet to the tile on her knees. "Here it is." I saw her carefully place a garnet tile into a space on the stone tile. "Dude! It fits! See? All of these pieces are triangles. This tile carving was designed to accept these triangles. If you look carefully down at the tile, they have lines that show where each of the triangles fit."

Suddenly, she slapped her forehead. "I know what this is! Give me the others, will you?" I moved over and handed her the tiles one at a time.

"First, shhh! Secondly, what the heck, Molly?" Sarah asked.

"It's a tangram puzzle," Molly said, biting her lip while she moved a triangle down into the floor.

"A what?"

"I have one at home. It's a type of puzzle from China. You take various shapes—like triangles, parallelograms, and squares—and make bigger shapes with them. Often animals . . ." She pointed down at the figure she was creating. "See, the black onyx triangles are forming a shape, where the red ones form the background. This looks like a lion . . . I think?" She turned her head to the side. "Maybe a horse?"

Farnsworth started to grin. "What about a dragon?"

"Yeah . . ." Molly said, sitting up. "A dragon."

After a few minutes, Molly had almost completed the design. It was crude, but unmistakable—a black winged dragon on a bloodred background. Just as she placed the final onyx into its spot, we heard a loud click, then the movement of gears.

What the hell?

Sarah grabbed Molly's shoulder and pulled her small body back just before the large tile, now covered in a black dragon, dropped down several inches. It threw up a small dust cloud.

After a few moments of silence, Sarah cleared her throat. "Does this tile just drop down and that's it? Is something else going to happen?"

"Well, maybe if we . . ." I leaned forward and poked at it gently. After nothing happened, I tried sliding the tile around a bit. Maybe whatever it was supposed to do was stunted by one hundred years of non-movement. Maybe it needed some WD-40 or something.

Suddenly, the tile moved again with a loud grinding noise, rotating clockwise, sliding beneath the other tiles. It stopped with a decisive click halfway through the circle, but the grinding noise continued for some reason. Then, the grinding noise stopped, and we heard a loud *whoosh* sound. In unison, we turned toward the source of the noise—the head of the *Iguanodon*.

Molly aimed her light at the head. The tile that held the tangram pieces had disappeared, as well as some neighboring tiles, creating a large hole in the floor.

"So, that was the lock . . ." Farnsworth said.

"We knew you'd prove useful eventually, Derek," I said, but I was too shocked to even make a proper joke. I half expected a boulder to fall down from the ceiling on us.

We walked over to the hole and looked down. Molly's flashlight revealed a giant, spiral metal staircase. It was so dark below that I couldn't see farther than its first curve.

"Big hole beneath a mold of a giant *Iguanodon* head." I looked at our strange little group. "Now which of you wants to be the proverbial sacrificial lamb?"

Letter between Mary Anning and Sir Richard Owen, 1830

Mr. Richard Owen
Royal College of Surgeons

My dear Sir,

As you requested, I am sending you a rough sketch of the fossil arm I found. You can see the long bones as well as the smaller hand bones. As we previously discussed, I do believe it is the wing of the *Pterodactylus*, perhaps with bones from another specimen mixed in. Our geologist friend, William Buckland, is in agreement. I will say, this wing is larger than the other that I found nearby. Interestingly, its stones are of the deepest black, which made it very easy to see amongst the light grey cliffs.

The Duke of Buckingham has offered £50 for it, but as your letter arrived the day before his offer, I will consider your claim first. Should you wish to buy, I humbly request £60. Buckland has also offered to purchase, but I told him of your prior claim, which I will honor. He is in agreement. Please send your decision as soon as possible.

I thank you for thinking of my little dog, Tray. He was not lost, as I feared. He came home at midnight, with a slight injury to his leg. We managed to bandage the wound, and he is now very happy. My brother believes he got into someone's chickens as it looks like a pellet shot.

Your most humble servant,
Mary Anning
Lyme Regis, February 1830

OFFICE HOURS

Molly

FARNSWORTH GRABBED MY arm as I moved to lower myself onto the staircase. "I've got a light," I said, shaking his hand off.

"No," Farnsworth said. "Let me."

"Why?"

"Because we don't know what's down there. And you're a—" he started.

"Girl?" I rolled my eyes. "Okay, first off, I'll be fine. Not scared of the dark, not scared of spiders, and this has probably been sealed for a long time. So I doubt anyone is alive down there to bother me." I pointed toward his gut. "Second, I am much, much younger than you, and definitely more . . . fit?"

"Hey!" Farnsworth replied. "All I was going to say was 'intern.'"

"Yes, she's an intern. She's expendable," Oliphant chimed in.

"Hey!"

"No, I think I should go," Sarah interceded. Even in the dark, I could see the strain on her face.

"Too late." I stepped quickly onto the staircase. My feet hit the first step, and I wiggled around, testing it. "Feels safe. See ya."

"Molly!" Sarah whispered gruffly. "Stop!"

No. I wanted to see what was down in that hole. I quickly climbed down the staircase, which groaned as I moved, but held. The staircase seemed to be leading me into a pitch-black chamber of sorts. A large one, based on the echoes of my steps as I clanged downward. I shone the light on my feet so I didn't step on something gnarly. I talked tough, but I *hated* rats.

After a few more careful steps, I could see the stone floor of the room. I stepped off the staircase and aimed my light in front of me.

I was in the middle of a large, stone room. Bookcases covered three of its walls. An imposing wooden desk was pushed up against the back wall. Tacked above the desk were drawings and what looked like maps. The desk was cluttered with papers, books, and other odds and ends. And dust. Lots and lots of dust.

There was also a large silver candelabra with yellow-white candles still sitting in its four tapered branches. I unshouldered my backpack and reached inside for the small book of matches I always carry in my first aid kit. I struck a match and lit the candles. They lit quickly and gently illuminated the room.

What I saw took my breath away.

"Um, guys? You might want to come down now and see this," I called up. I could hear the shakiness in my voice.

"What is it?" Sarah whispered.

"Pictures of our Monster," I replied. "Lots and lots of them."

I carefully moved the papers on the desk. Some were drawings of fossils still in the ground. Others were of individual fossil specimens that were cleaned and free of stone: a femur, a wing, a claw.

Above the desk were more drawings, maps, and notes overlaid on each other. One drawing immediately caught my eye and I pulled it from the wall. It was the skull we saw in the portrait of Owen. I reached down into my backpack and pulled out *Dragons of the World*. I turned to the wyvern page, held the book up, and compared the two.

They were the same. Suddenly I was five years old again, lying in my bed, my mother sitting next to me. She touched the cover of the book as she looked at me. *Ancient mysteries, that is what dragons are to the world. This book reminds me that fantasy is possible, Molly.*

Behind me, I heard the others descending the staircase. I quickly stowed the book back into my backpack. Oliphant loomed over me.

"It's the one from Owen's picture," Oliphant said.

I turned to face him. "Looks like. The fossil in the picture is also black, just like our Montana Monster."

"Remarkable," he murmured. He pulled several drawings down, holding them close to his face.

Sarah stepped up next to us. "Wow . . . maps, drawings . . ." She poked a book on the desk. "This is a personal office."

I took a deep breath and felt my throat itch in response. The air had a musty smell to it. How in the world did this place even exist? Did the museum know about it?

Reading my mind, Sarah said, "It's not that unusual to have lower level rooms like this in a museum, especially older ones. Helps staff move large items around the museum without disturbing other exhibits."

"But a secret entrance that uses an art nouveau mosaic as a lock and key?" Farnsworth said. "No, Owen did this on purpose. He intended to keep this room a secret."

"Art nouveau, *tres bon*, Derek," laughed Oliphant.

Farnsworth's glare was obvious even in the dark.

I put down the drawing and looked at the other papers on the desk. They were so old, they seemed to be crumbling right before my eyes. I carefully lifted the piece of paper. It was a drawing of a femur and a spinal column. In elegant handwriting below the drawings were the words, *Collected from the Isle of Wight, 1838*.

Behind me, Oliphant made a disgusted noise. Turning, I saw him pointing to a large jar on the top shelf of one of the bookcases. I moved closer and took in the whole scene. Old, leather-bound books lined many of the shelves. There were also a few rocks and lots of animal skeletons interspersed between the books. They were white and familiar, probably from Owen's time. One looked like an ordinary house cat. Morbid, but not surprising considering Owen was a naturalist.

So what grossed Oliphant out?

I got a closer look at the jar he was pointing at. I could barely make out some type of vertebrae. Then I read the label.

'Human spinal column. Subject: G. Mantell. Death: 1852.'

My stomach dropped.

Yuck.

I turned away to steady myself.

Farnsworth stood next to me, and I felt his hand on my back. I turned, and I saw his concern, how his mouth was slightly downturned. I shook my head and waved him off, turning back around. "I'm okay," I said.

Farnsworth leaned forward for a closer look. "G. Mantell," he said. "This is Gideon Mantell's spine. That doctor paleontologist who discovered *Iguanodon* with his wife in the 1800s."

"Wait, seriously? What poker game did he lose?" Oliphant said.

"Are you sure it's Mantell?" Sarah said.

Farnsworth nodded. "Pretty sure. He had horrible scoliosis, and this backbone is badly curved."

"And where did you pick up that tidy fact?" Oliphant said, not hiding his amazement.

Farnsworth snorted. "You know, I *can* read."

"Your savant tendencies are a shining light in this gloomy world, Derek."

"Enough!" Sarah's voice was low but cut through the room like a raptor talon.

"Why would he have this?" I asked quietly.

"Well . . . they were rivals," said Farnsworth. "He and Owen had a huge falling-out. It's unclear why. Some say over jealousy. The Royal Family supported Owen generously, and Mantell had trouble making ends meet. I even read that Mantell was forced to sell his fossil collection to pay the bills. Several years before he died, he was hurt in a carriage accident. With his deformed spine, the pain was probably awful. He supposedly died from an opium overdose."

I looked back at the jar with the pickled spine. *Pitiable, really.*

"I read a rumor that at the time, Owen wanted his dead rival's spine to prove that Mantell was, well, spineless," Farnsworth continued.

Sarah gently reached up and touched the jar, her fingers tracing the writing on the label. "Owen is always described as a visionary, but also as a difficult person. This makes him more of a monster."

"We don't know the whole story. Maybe this was sent to Owen, and out of respect, he kept it. We don't know. It's best not to judge matters belonging in the past," Oliphant said as he moved on to another bookshelf, adjusted his reading glasses, and leaned forward to see the titles in the beam of his smartphone.

Inspired, I looked at the shelf below the pickled spine. "'*Comparative Biology of the Nautilus, Mythology of Greeks and Romans,*'" I read aloud.

"This is a copy of *On the Origin of Species*," Oliphant said, pulling a book from the shelf. "First edition, too." He gingerly opened the book to its first page. "It's got an inscription . . ."

Whistling, he looked up at us over his reading glasses. "Charles Darwin, to Richard . . . Jesus, this is worth a fortune!"

Sarah turned back to the desk. "Richard Owen's private office. Well done, Molly," she said.

"Well, we all did it," I stuttered, blushing at the praise.

She gave me a warm smile. She turned and started roughly pushing papers around the desk. As she did, a large, dark book caught my eye, so I reached over to pick it up. It was a leather-bound volume with black-and-gold lettering on the cover. I then made the colossal mistake of blowing on it, sending dust directly into my eyes.

Farnsworth snorted, and someone took the book away from me. "You okay?" Farnsworth said.

"Yeah, I actually like blowing one-hundred-and-fifty-year-old dirt into my eyes." I laughed, looking at him with watery eyes.

"When you can, look at the cover," Farnsworth said, handing me the book.

In the center of the cover, inked in black, was a stylized dragon skeleton. It was arching backward, its neck curved, and its mouth was open wide. The beautifully articulated wings! Like our Montana Monster, the wings were connected to the arms—another black wyvern.

Farnsworth pointed to the gold lettering over the dragon. "I can't read that title in this light, can you?"

I pulled the book close to my eyes and read the title aloud: "'*Evidence of the Fantastical: Dracosauria, 1820 to 1890.*'"

The book was held shut with a leather loop over a mother-of-pearl button. I carefully opened the book, its spine cracking as I did. On the first page were several lines written in elegant cursive. "It's a note from Owen. Written in 1890."

"What does it say, Molly?" Sarah's voice was low, encouraging.

"'In Anno Domini, 1838, I first saw the Isle of Wight Monster. It was a creature even more astounding and strange than its cousin, the dinosaur.'"

I looked up. "Those pictures on the desk, they are labeled *Isle of Wight*."

Sarah moved closer. "Let me, Molly." She gently took the book away before I could protest. She continued to read aloud.

"'Mantel sold the British Museum his collection, even with this treasure. He said his lady wife had made drawings, and he needed the money. I immediately wrote to the regents and asked for permission to review his fossils. It was a dark beast, with glistening black bones and large arms with wings, like a bat. It's skull was angular, with small horns on its mandible as well as over its eye holes. As I was the first to describe it academically, I would name it Dracosauria.'"

Sarah shuffled through the book.

"Owen wrote pages and pages about the fossil, as well as other finds that seem related," Sarah said, squinting at the text. "He's made notes, illustrations, lists, maps . . ."

"It's like a field journal, focused on . . . Dracosauria," I said.

For a few moments, there was complete silence as that sunk in. I knew our Monster wasn't the only dragon ever discovered.

"Why didn't Owen publish?" I said. "What stopped him?" Neither Farnsworth nor Oliphant said anything. They looked just as confused as I felt.

I looked over Sarah's shoulder as she continued to turn the pages. I saw other drawings of dragons, from crests that looked like British and Welsh aristocratic heraldry to Asian-stylized dragons without wings.

"There is correspondence in this book from all over the world," Sarah murmured. Suddenly she stopped and let out a frustrated hiss. "This book is incomplete."

"What do you mean?"

"Look at the binding. Like someone ripped out half the pages. Here is the last entry." The page was filled with blocks of handwriting, going in various directions. I remembered seeing a note written by the nineteenth century author Jane Austen once online. People used to do that to save paper space. And on that last page was a drawing of what looked like a serpentine animal curved in a circle. The central passage was dated 1890 and read:

Dracosauria, unlike Dinosauria, remains hidden even today because of the Order's power. My only regret is that I waited too long and failed to tell the world. While I could find no more bones, there is evidence of its presence across the globe. I am an old man now, but with the support of Huxley's S.V., what they now call "Owen's Truth" will be revealed, and Dracosauria will rise from the ashes.

"Who is the Order?" Farnsworth said.

"And what does he mean by Huxley's S.V.?" I said. "Who is 'S.V.'? And how can a note from one hundred and fifty years ago mention a person that sent Farnsworth a package just yesterday?"

Farnsworth shook his head. "I don't know any S.V., as far as I can recall."

Stealing a glance at Sarah, I could see that she seemed rattled. None of it made any sense.

"Someone else has been here before us," Oliphant said ominously.

"Maybe, but everything is under, like, six inches of dust. Nobody's been here for a while," I countered, looking around.

Oliphant gestured to the book. "But they used those exact words. 'Owen's Truth.' Just like in that picture Derek was sent of Owen. And now we're here. How do you explain that?"

I shrugged my shoulders. "Magic?"

He chuckled.

"And did you all notice that while there are tons of pictures, there isn't a single Dracosauria fossil here?" Oliphant said. "Pictures are great, but we need a fossil to analyze."

Oliphant was right. There were a lot of dead animals in this place, but only the reconstructed skeletons of modern animals. If this was a secret, protected place, why wouldn't Owen have kept some Dracosauria fossils here?

Sarah was gently touching the book, her finger tracing a circle on the page. No, she was outlining a stylized circle. That serpentine animal. It had scales and a head that was arched to bite its own tail.

"Is that an ouroboros?" I said.

"A what and a who now?" Oliphant asked.

"The famous snake coiled in a circle, eating its own tail."

Oliphant and Sarah stared at me with blank faces. "Come on, am I the only one who reads mythology?"

"Do you really want to know my answer for that?" Oliphant smirked.

I rolled my eyes. "The ouroboros first appeared in ancient Egyptian texts, and myths of a circular serpent eating its own tail are found in Norway, Greece, and India. Basically, it's a symbol for the unity of life and death."

"Now that *is* impressive. Jeopardy-level knowledge there. Good job, intern. See, I told you it was a good idea to have her here, Derek." Oliphant slapped Farnsworth's back. Farnsworth grimaced.

"But this is a dragon, not a snake," Sarah said.

"I've read ouroboros can be represented as either," Farnsworth said. I raised an eyebrow, and he gave me a small smile.

I leaned closer in the dim light. The dragon was dark in color, and it had front and back legs, but no wings. However, it had a dragon's head similar in shape to the skull in the drawings around us. More importantly, it closely resembled the dragon's head we found in Montana. There was one big difference, though.

"Why is it not eating its tail? This dragon has its tail wrapped around its neck," I said.

"Good question. And why is its back drawn like that, with a blanket?" Farnsworth pointed to the dragon's back. Sure enough, it looked like the dragon had a strange open blanket on its back, with white sticks pointing outward.

"That's not a blanket," Oliphant said. "It's cut open. This dragon has been strangled and dissected."

I wrinkled my nose. Gross. Underneath the drawing in elegant but fading script were six words.

Beware the Order of Saint George.

"The Order of Saint George?" Sarah said.

The Order. This must be what Owen wrote about. The Order of Saint George.

"Isn't that some fraternal order in Hungary or Austria or something?" Oliphant asked. We turned to look at him. "What? I think I met one of the members at a conference once. Nice guy."

"Maybe it is now, but back years ago, it could have been something else," Farnsworth said.

"Hmmm. We should do some research. Maybe there's something about them online," Oliphant said. "Maybe keyword it with 'S.V.' Maybe there's a connection."

"Huxley's S.V.," I said again, biting my lip. "What do you think that means?"

"No idea, but Huxley is Darwin's guy, as I said earlier. Considering their history, it's strange that Owen even mentioned him."

"History?"

"But why risk damaging the journal by tearing part of it out?" Sarah blurted out. "Owen put a lot of time into this."

"Sarah, can I see the book?" Oliphant grabbed it before she could answer. "What do you make of this?"

To find the rest, amongst the blue cliffs, Mary's flying-dragons are Common Place.

"Mary . . . who is Mary?" Sarah asked.

"Mary Anning!" I shouted. "I bet it's Mary Anning. The blue cliffs." Farnsworth nodded in agreement, holding his chin with his hand. "She—hey, what was that?"

We fell silent, listening. Sure enough, we heard a loud voice above, and the screech of a two-way radio. "Find the kid first! Molly Wilder. She'll be easier to spot." My name echoed across the room above.

"They said my name," I hissed. "How does a museum guard know my name?"

Farnsworth shook his head. "We need to get out of here."

"Can we call anyone?" Oliphant asked. "I get cell reception here. Maybe we can get the police?"

"And tell them what? We've broken into a secret room of a long-dead scientist filled with priceless items because we're looking for dragon fossils?" Sarah said.

"Didn't you say that these museums would sometimes have rooms built below exhibits to help move larger exhibits around?" Farnsworth asked. Sarah nodded. "Maybe there is a hidden door?"

Our group broke apart and began pressing on the walls, the bookshelves, anything that might move. I even tried moving a few books, but no secret door swung open.

"Hey, this desk is on wheels," Farnsworth said. I quickly turned. He was right—there were small wheels on each of the desk's legs.

Together, we slowly moved the desk. It groaned and creaked with the effort. I waved for them to stop, to listen. Thankfully, we didn't hear any voices or noises from above. After we moved the desk, I got on my hands and knees and looked at the intersection between the wall and floor. Sure enough, I saw a crack of light from the next room.

"I think if we push together, it'll move." I was actually guessing, but who knows. Maybe it did follow the rules of mysterious houses.

"Worth a shot," Oliphant replied.

After a single push, the wall swung open and outward into another room. The fluorescent light blinded me for a moment.

"The fossil room! Owen's office is next to the fossil collections room of the museum," Oliphant said, his voice loud and sure. "I know this place. Follow me."

As we left, I grabbed Owen's journal and opened my backpack. Oliphant handed me several Dracosauria drawings that he had taken from Owen's office. "Evidence." I nodded, stuffed them into my backpack, and walked into the bright light. Thankfully, the room was deserted.

"We need to hide this," Farnsworth said, motioning toward the open office. Oliphant and Farnsworth pushed the wall shut, and I grabbed a broom to sweep up any dust we had left behind. Sarah grabbed some boxes and stacked them against the wall. Satisfied with our efforts, we quickly headed out through a side door. After climbing a flight of stairs, we found ourselves right outside the Lasting Impressions Hall where the

Iguanodon mold was kept. I quickly peeked inside as we walked by, but I didn't see anyone, not even the docent.

Overhead, we heard a polite voice saying the museum was now closing and we needed to exit. We walked out of the museum as inconspicuously as possible, blending in with a group of loud tourists. We headed down the stone steps, but as I walked, I felt the hairs on my arms rise and saw goose-flesh appear.

I turned around and then stopped so suddenly that my boots squeaked on the stone steps. A few feet behind Sarah, a man leaned against the wall of the museum, smoking a cigar. His eyes were dark and hard, and his posture was stiff under his black overcoat. Clouds of cigar smoke encircled him, swirling in the early evening gloom.

My whole body froze, and my heart threatened to thump out of my chest.

It was Raley. In London.

His eyes didn't leave mine as he lifted his cigar to his lips. That's when I spotted it. A dark mark, on his wrist.

I saw it before, in Montana, but I didn't get a good look at it then. But now, only a little ways away, I recognized it.

It was a tattoo of an ouroboros.

ESCAPE FROM THE MUSEUM

Farnsworth

AS WE RUSHED down the museum stairs, the cold wind whipped around us, rustling nearby trees. I walked in step with Sarah, Oliphant in front of us. But where was Molly? I turned and saw her running down the steps. And that's when I saw him twenty or so feet behind her, staring at me over her head.

Raley.

The "BLM agent" from Montana.

A loud sound roared in my ears. This man stole my fossils, my work. Our Monster. I had to do *something*.

But as I moved forward, Molly grabbed my arm, causing me to jolt backward. I turned to wrench her off me, but as I did, I looked at her face. She was terrified.

"Look," she whispered. Raley lifted his jacket slightly, and I saw a gun in a holster attached to his belt. He moved his eyes from me to Molly.

And suddenly my rage was drowned by fear. For her.

I grabbed Molly's hand and pulled her down the stairs. Oliphant and Sarah were already at the sidewalk.

"Let's move," I said as we ran by.

"What is going on?" Sarah called as we rounded the corner where Oliphant parked our rented SUV. I didn't answer. Instead I ran faster. When we arrived at our car, Molly doubled over, breathing hard, hand on her side. I looked behind for Raley. The tree-lined street was quiet, almost empty.

I motioned to the car. "Open it. We're leaving right now."

"What happened?" Oliphant asked.

"Raley. We saw Raley," Molly said, her breath coming back.

Oliphant scoffed, his eyes narrowing.

"No, seriously, we saw him. He was on the museum steps. He had a gun."

Oliphant unlocked the doors, and we got into the car. As I climbed into the backseat with Molly, I saw Raley at the corner, not moving. I pulled out my cell from my back pocket and took a photograph. Evidence for Agent Porter. "Flip a U-turn here. He's on the corner."

"Okay, Mr. Paranoia." Oliphant pulled out of our parking space at an angle, quickly completing a three-point turn. As we rounded the corner, Raley disappeared. I released a shaky breath and leaned my head back against my seat. Rain started to splatter on our windows and roof. Oliphant sped up, the outside world a blurry mess of colors.

"We were followed," Molly said quietly, looking at her lap.

"Are you sure you saw Raley?" Sarah asked, turning in her seat to look at us.

"Um, a large, scary man who assaulted me just yesterday? Yeah, I remember him," Molly snapped.

Sarah reached behind her seat and squeezed Molly's leg. "I'm sorry, I didn't mean to make it seem like I didn't believe you." Molly looked up at her and gave her a small smile. "I'm just trying to figure this out. Why would he follow us here?"

"Why would he take the Monster? Why would he steal my entire life's work, Sarah?" I said.

The SUV made another sharp turn. We were now in the heart of London, surrounded by large gray and glass buildings glittering with rain. I stretched my body, trying to get comfortable in a seat not made for men with legs this long.

Raley. In England. The man who'd pretended to be a government agent had followed us over four thousand miles to England. Across an ocean. What the hell was going on?

"Should we call the police?" Molly asked.

"Probably not the local constabulary. You could send Agent Porter a note," Oliphant said. "But don't expect him to do anything."

"Why not?" Molly asked.

"Because what can he do? We're out of the country, *very suddenly* I might add. Right after Derek's fossils were stolen. We don't have any evidence it was Raley—"

"I took his picture," I said.

"Okay, you took his picture. Just now. When it's nearly dark and still rainy. It's useless."

"It's almost like you don't want me to get my fossils back, Sean."

He glanced at me in the rearview mirror. "Well, Derek, I do think contacting the cops is a waste of time. A random grainy photo of a man who you say stole your fossils yesterday in the United States, but who is now here in London, will not only get you laughed out of Scotland Yard, but probably the J. Edgar Hoover Building back home, too."

I leaned back and pulled out my cell. I composed an email to Agent Porter and attached the photograph of Raley. It was not the clearest image, for sure, but it did capture his dark hair, angular face, and muscular build. Hopefully, they could match it to a picture of him in their own files. If he was a fossil thief, I'm sure he had a file.

After all, I had one.

I hit "send" and rubbed my eyes. I was tired, and drained. I had a lot on the line. Raley. My fossils. Oliphant. Sarah could lose her fossil site and new specimen, but her career was on the right path. Oliphant was Oliphant, doing what he does, no matter the cost. Molly was young and would be fine. But me? I'm the one who was getting screwed. In the last forty-eight hours, I'd gone from finding a new species to financial ruin. Potentially millions of dollars just gone. Some of the fossils in my warehouse were worth a lot of money, at least to the right buyer. I'd spent hundreds of thousands of hours digging fossils out of the ground. Years of backbreaking work that now accounted for nothing. I needed something spectacular to turn it all around. I held up my hands and frowned, my pale skin covered with veins, freckles, early liver spots, and smudges of dirt.

I was too old to begin again.

And it made me angry. Maybe we should go back. Confront him. Next to me, Molly put her hand on my arm, and shook her head. "He *followed* us," she said, her voice low. I held her gaze for a second, and slowly nodded. He *did* follow us. Whatever he was after wasn't in my warehouse or our bone bed.

What does he want with us? My eyes traveled to Molly's backpack. The journal, maybe? How would he know about that? No, it must be something else. But what?

Oliphant looked up into his rearview mirror. "So what is the next move? Raley stalking us aside for a moment, we didn't get any fossil material. We didn't even check out the Natural History Museum's archive."

"Molly has the journal," I said.

"And those drawings you stuffed in here, Dr. Oliphant," Molly said, opening her backpack and pulling out the journal. She handed me the Dracosauria sketches that Oliphant had pulled off Owen's office wall, and then opened the journal. "So we have some things."

"I'd prefer actual bone material to describe," Oliphant said. "While we can absolutely use the drawings and journal as evidence, many will argue that we raided a Renaissance faire prop store, not that we found Owen's secret catalogue of Dracosauria. So we need more."

"I think we need to find more of the journal. Have a complete book, and then go from there," said Molly.

"Interesting idea. But where do we find the rest? That journal is over one hundred and fifty years old. The rest of it could be anywhere," Oliphant said. "If it exists, at all."

Molly read aloud: "'To find the rest, amongst the blue cliffs, Mary's flying-dragons are Common Place.'" She then looked up at me. "Sounds like Mary Anning may have the rest of Owen's journal."

"I'm not following," Sarah said. "Mary Anning? What does she have to do with that line?"

"The 'blue cliffs' and 'Mary' together is a reference to the Blue Lias Formation," I said.

Sarah nodded slowly in understanding. "Blue Lias. Mary's old stomping ground. Got it."

Mary Anning was one of the greatest fossil paleontologists that you've never heard of, at least until recently. She was born, raised, and died in Lyme Regis, a sleepy vacation town where, two hundred years ago, people used to travel to "take in the waters" for their health. It sits in the shadow of the Blue Lias, a layer-cake looking stack of limestones and shales that look blue when wet. These deposits occurred during the late Triassic, early Jurassic periods (about 195 to 200 million years ago) when the area was underwater. As such, the rocks contain the fossils of aquatic creatures such as fish, crustaceans, and larger swimming reptiles, like long-necked plesiosaurs. Even the occasional land-dwelling animal washed out to sea. These cliffs were now a World Heritage Site, dubbed the Jurassic Coast.

In the early 1800s, Mary Anning explored these cliffs and made some of the period's most significant finds. Just like me, she was a fossil hunter who sold her discoveries to make a living and support her family. She was good at it, too. Sadly, at that point in history, most women were not accepted within scientific or academic circles. Her contributions to science were largely ignored, and credit was taken by men. Idiots. She could have run circles around most of them. Mary was a blue-collar worker who loved what she did, and she did it well. She worked hard to provide for her family, fossil hunting until the day she died at the age of forty-seven in 1847. A true pirate.

"Mary Anning's dead. Has been for about almost two centuries," Sarah said, tapping her finger on her window.

"We should go to Lyme Regis," Molly said, riffling through the journal.

"Lyme Regis. That's not nearby. That's southwest of here by several hours," Oliphant said. "If we go there, it will be quite late when we arrive. Are we sure that is what the line means?"

"Maybe," I said. "Pretty sure."

Next to me, Molly leaned forward, her seat belt straining with the effort. "Dr. Oliphant? Can I borrow your cell phone?"

Holding one hand on the steering wheel, Oliphant reached into his back pocket and pulled out his cell. He used his finger to unlock the screen and handed it back to her. "Why mine?"

"You can afford international charges," she said. "And I can't." She typed furiously and started nodding. "Definitely, Lyme."

"Why?" I asked.

"That 'Common Place' line was screaming at me," Molly replied. "Why was it uppercase while the rest of the sentence wasn't? Put the words together, and you have 'commonplace,' and a commonplace book is an autograph book. Mary Anning's happens to be on display at the Lyme Regis Museum."

"It's a book?" Sarah asked. "Like, a journal?"

"Yes and yes," Molly said. "Pre–social media people would write their thoughts or wishes to others in these books. Like a yearbook." She looked at me and shrugged. "What? I love Jane Austen."

"Lyme Regis it is," Oliphant said from the driver's seat. He jerked the steering wheel hard to the left, causing a nearby vehicle to swerve and honk in alarm. He made a few more turns at reckless speeds, and I saw more than a few fingers flipped our way as we streaked by.

After a few minutes, we were on the M25. I stole a glance at Oliphant. He was grinning, and his tongue was sticking out one side of his lips. He was always happy when he drove like a maniac. I wonder if he still had that classic Porsche 914. That was a fun car.

Memory lane was an ugly street, though.

"We'll stop for the night in Southampton. Sarah, go online and save us some rooms. Preferably with views of the piers and a balcony." He handed her his wallet.

Next to him, Sarah pulled out her own phone and began to type. Oliphant looked in his mirror at Molly and me. "Lyme is a three-hour drive from here. Southampton is halfway, so it's a good place to stop and rest. Sea air is both invigorating and restful after a long flight." He started to grin. "And I know that Derek gets grouchy without sleep."

THE WORST IDEA EVER

Oliphant

IT WAS VERY late when we reached the outskirts of Southampton. The road we were traveling on was dark and murky, wet with rain and mud. An owl swooped gracefully through the high beams of our SUV without bothering to give us a passing glance.

I pulled up to our destination: the Pilgrim Inn. It was a large Tudor-style pub adorned with a brown thatched roof as rumpled as a hedgehog. Soft firelight flickered through the cut-glass windows. As I turned off the ignition, I caught a glimpse of a large group of late-night revelers enjoying a pint at tables in the back.

"Here?" I remarked. "Surely, Sarah, you could have chosen a venue that doesn't have sixteenth-century plumbing."

"I tried," Sarah replied. "Apparently three cruise ships are leaving from Southampton harbor tomorrow, so everything is booked up. This was the only place available."

"This is so cool," Molly chirped from the backseat. She unbuckled her seat belt and practically tore down her door as she got out. "I've always wanted to see a real English pub. Maybe order a pint."

"Well, now you've seen a real one," Farnsworth said as he tossed her backpack toward her. "But you're still too young. The drinking age here is eighteen."

Molly rolled her eyes. "Okay, Mr. Farnsworth, I won't. I'll also be sure to not run with scissors, either. Where do we check in? Are we staying above the bar?"

"I'll find out," Sarah said, charging ahead. They entered the building and walked up to a small counter. Behind it, a grizzled but friendly-looking man greeted her. Farther down the hallway, the Pilgrim Inn opened up into a large room sectioned with tables and large pillars decorated with pictures, wall sconces, and dartboards. In the far back was the main bar, a lot of noise, and happy patrons. Over the fireplace hung a flea-bitten but fearsome-looking wild boar's head with enormous yellow tusks.

"Okay, that will have to do," Sarah said, her voice high and wavering.

"What's wrong, Sarah?" Farnsworth reached for her elbow, but she shook him off.

"The rooms are in another building," she said, reaching for the keys the innkeeper held out. Then, without a backward glance, she turned around and walked toward the front door.

We walked a short distance across a grassy courtyard toward another building. It was built in a similar style to the main pub, except this one was made of red brick. We entered the reception area, a small but clean room. Opposite the entrance was a large brown desk covered in papers. Behind the desk sat an older woman with gray hair. Sarah greeted her, and showed her our keys.

She smiled and pointed toward the stairs next to her desk. "Head up, down the hallway."

Farnsworth tipped his hat as we walked up the stairs, Molly's backpack bounced as she took two steps at a time. *Oh youth. I've missed you.*

When we got to the second level, Sarah slowly walked down the hallway, reading numbers on the doors aloud, finally stopping at the last two rooms.

"Okay, here we are," she said calmly.

"Sarah, I think you are mistaken," I said. I looked at the two doors, then back at her. "There are four of us. We need four rooms."

She finally looked me in the eye. "I told you these were hard to get. Everything else was booked; these were the last two rooms in town."

"So you are saying I have to share a room with . . . him?" I said, pointing at Farnsworth. He stared back at me, his hands at his sides.

"No way," Farnsworth snarled.

Oh my, was that a snarl?

Sarah put her hands on her hips. "Look, it's just for one night. Molly and I will take this room, you have that one." She tossed Farnsworth our key, and quickly opened her own room. Molly stood between us, looking back and forth with her mouth open. Sarah grabbed her arm and dragged her inside their room. "Good night. Please don't kill each other," Sarah called as she shut her door.

Farnsworth was just standing there, staring at Sarah's door, his face a brighter red than a tomato. After a long moment of seriously wondering if Farnsworth was going to burst into flames, I reached over and grabbed the key from his hand and opened our door. I walked inside and left the door open, mostly for him, but also just in case I needed to get out quickly.

Well, looks could be deceiving. The Pilgrim Inn had rather nice rooms, and they had obviously been updated since Shakespeare was spinning yarns at the Globe Theatre. There were two twin beds with wrought iron bed frames, covered with fluffy white comforters. Off to the side, a slightly open door suggested a possible bathroom. Next to it, a small desk. I dropped my bag on the bed closest to the window. Turning around, I saw that Farnsworth had followed me inside and was standing next to the other bed.

My bed groaned and squeaked as I sat down, but the mattress was firm and comfortable.

I looked back up at Farnsworth. His mouth was stretched into a deep frown, and his eyes were thunderous under creased brows.

"Look, it's just for one night . . ." I said slowly.

He didn't answer but instead threw his backpack onto his bed. He put his hands on his hips and breathed heavily out of his nose.

"Seriously, Derek," I said, but the only response I got was another push of nostril air. I really didn't want to fight, not after a day like today, so I tried another tactic. "TV and room service? Couple of hamburgers and you can pick the movie . . ." I trailed off as his breathing became even faster, and his face became even redder. What is redder than a tomato? That was Farnsworth. "Fine, do you want to sleep downstairs? That carpet in the front lobby looked rather comfortable."

"Better than sleeping here," he said between his clenched teeth.

"Dear Lord, you big lug. I'm not going to kill you."

"No, you just take and take."

I shook my head. "Come on. I'm tired, and this is getting really old. That was over twenty years ago."

"What? Let bygones be bygones?"

"'We learn from our past to strengthen our future, to be better people.'"

"You're actually quoting your own TED Talk?"

I pointed at him and let out a loud, barking laugh. "I knew it! You did watch it."

He glowered at me, his leg twitching like he wanted to stamp his foot and charge like a bull. "You hurt people to get what you want. Adults can take it, but kids?" he said.

I looked down at my lap. Now I know he's not talking about our past.

"Sarah's an adult. And Molly's—" I began.

"Too young to know better. What were you thinking? The minute my fossils were stolen, you should have sent her away. To Colorado with Dean and Karolin, or back home to California. You know that."

I knew that. I'd made many decisions in my life I was proud of, but several of them I wasn't. No sixteen-year-old kid should be here. Especially if Raley was following us. I knew I should put Molly on the next flight home.

"Derek . . ." I started, but the words were stuck in my throat. I wanted to agree with him, but I couldn't. Finally, I stood up. "Okay. I'm going to the bar for a nightcap. Get some sleep." But before I could even move around our beds, Farnsworth turned around and stormed out the door, slamming it behind him. The effort caused a small portrait of a man fishing near a stone bridge to fall down onto the floor.

I shook my head as I yelled at the door. "You better not still snore!"

SOME FAMOUS INFLUENTIAL MOVIE

Sarah

MY ARM FELT wonderfully cool as I pressed it onto my tired eyes. The mattress under me was soft, like I was lying on a springy cloud. A definite step up from dozing sitting up in coach on a transatlantic flight. Hopefully I wouldn't have to do that again. That was horrible. My spine was still screaming at me.

The voice in my head was relentless.

What are you doing here?

How did all this get so messed up?

What are you doing here?

How did all this get so messed up?

I just wanted it all to stop.

On the other side of the room, I heard Molly's fingers dance over my laptop keys, the telltale clicky-clacky noise the only sound. A funny juxtaposition of modernity in a room that was probably built around the time the United States was founded.

Something about Molly pushed the voices in my head back.

"Good email?" I said, my voice raspy. I cleared my throat and reached for my water bottle next to me.

"No," Molly said, letting out a long sigh. "I have no idea what to say."

"The truth?"

"Yeah, right. 'Hi, Dad, how are you? Got that Harley finished yet for that client? Oh, by the way, I'm not in Montana anymore, but instead in England on a wild goose chase to find a dragon—'"

"Dinosaur."

"*Dinosaur*. Whatever. 'I'm good. There is a strange man following us who is pretending to be from the Bureau of Land Management, but don't worry, I'm good. Will call soon.'"

That made me laugh. "Yeah, you're screwed."

She was such a good kid. She reminded me of me, or of the me that Derek saw. Back then.

She turned around and hit the "delete" button, erasing the email. "Probably."

I sat up and gave her a long look. She looked back, chin raised. Fire in her eyes. The girl had so much potential, and I was probably getting her into a world of hurt here. *Do the right thing*. "Do you want to go home? We can get you home—"

"No!" Molly replied quickly. "No."

She beamed at me, and my stomach churned. This could end really poorly. Time to change topics and dive into calmer waters that have nothing to do with traveling around the world hunting errant fossils. "Your dad fixes Harleys for a living?"

"He's a mechanic. Specializes in old motorcycles."

"That's pretty cool. You know how to ride?"

"Yeah. I grew up sitting pillion on his old Triumph. When I was big enough, he got me started on an old dirt bike."

"Triumph?"

"Triumph Bonneville. Type of motorcycle. Made in England, actually. Dad got it in a trade."

"You guys close?"

She nodded vigorously. "Dad's really supportive of me being here. Digging dinosaurs that is. He loves that I love dinosaurs."

I doubted he'd be supportive of her flying across the world without his permission.

"I could never tell him about Raley. He'd probably burst a vein in his brain due to worry and bankrupt himself flying out here to get to me," she continued.

I sighed in agreement. "What about your mom?"

She shook her head, her voice low and sad. "Not in the picture. She left when I was a kid."

I knew how that felt. I had my parents, but they were busy all the time. I had been lucky to have Derek. He took an interest in me, making sure I was busy after school and on weekends. Forced me to do my homework. Gave me skills that I could use in the future. Unlike so many other kids I knew growing up. Some left, but most stayed. I saw them when I visited Glasgow, trapped in time.

Not a chance would that ever be me.

"So, why do you think Raley is here?" Molly asked quietly.

"I have no idea. I would think he had everything he wanted from his raid on Derek's warehouse, but obviously, that is wrong," I replied, picking at a string on my comforter. It was all so strange, honestly.

She nodded and pulled her legs up against her body on the chair, resting her chin on her knees. "Dr. Oliphant said back in Montana that Derek dealt with black market stuff. Could that be what's happening here?"

"Maybe," I replied.

"You knew about that stuff?"

I knew Derek would kill me if I told her the truth. Derek really tried to keep me out of it. But even I couldn't ignore the calls or the last-minute trips to countries the United States warned against visiting.

"His main commercial fossil business is legit," I finally answered. "But, I honestly think that over the years he just pulled a few strings in some undesirable countries to gain access to lands that he shouldn't have. I know that that part of his life was years ago, and he's moved on."

"The job on Farnsworth's warehouse was very fast and calculated. Someone with a lot of experience stealing fossils was behind it. I'm no expert, but I'd bet my dragon book a person used to dealing with black market stuff could manage it," Molly said, her whole body rigid with energy.

"Where do you get that idea?" I said. "You sound like someone from *CSI* or something."

"And Raley was in London, looking right at us as we ran away," Molly continued, seemingly not hearing me. "What else does he want? The journal? There is no way he could have anticipated us finding that, right?"

Good point. "Can I see the journal?" I asked.

Molly handed it to me and I carefully opened it. It was really quite stunning, a fantastic example of nineteenth-century artistic penmanship fluidly mixed with scientific observations and evidence. I turned several pages that contained illustrations and maps, stopping on a note glued into the journal. It was really hard to read because it was so faded, so I read aloud what I could. "'The Order has woven itself into the very fabric of our scientific society, smashing the advances of men in their efforts to eliminate what they deem to be false idols . . .'"

What are you doing here?

How did all this get so messed up?

The voices again.

"I bet whoever wrote this means the *Order of Saint George,*" Molly said. "They were trying to stop scientific progress." She sat back and gave out a huff. "Well, they didn't succeed. We know all about evolution and dinosaurs and stuff."

"Charles Darwin wrote this," I said, squinting at the text. Well this was a new angle. Charles Darwin.

"Wait, what?" Molly said, sounding just as surprised as I felt.

"Yep," I replied, smoothing my hand over the letter. No mistaking his famous neat signature. "This is a lot to process. I mean, Darwin and Owen hated each other, yet Owen kept a letter from Darwin?"

"And it's about how the Order was trying to hide the truth."

I rubbed my temples. My head was spinning and my knees ached.

It was just fatigue, I told myself. Just fatigue.

Yeah, Sarah, keep telling yourself that.

I closed the journal with a thump. "Okay, let's do something fun. There is a menu next to the computer, Molly. Why don't you bring it over and we can order some junk food and watch some TV?"

Molly bit her lip and gave the journal one last pensive glance before looking at me. I nodded toward the table and she grabbed the menu, handing it to me before throwing her body on the other bed, its springs screaming in protest.

"Find something on TV, and I'll place our order."

After a few flicks with the TV remote, Molly stopped on a familiar scene. On the screen were two dirty, windswept young children enjoying dessert. Suddenly, the girl's smile froze and turned to horror. On her spoon, the green Jell-O shook rapidly. The girl and her brother were not alone in the room. Behind them, a dark, bipedal shape stalked slowly behind a screen, snorting and screeching, calling to its mate.

"*Jurassic Park*," I said approvingly. I grabbed the phone and pressed a button that connected me to the front desk. While the kitchen was technically closed, they told me they could bring up some fish-and-chips. I ordered two sets and settled down to watch the movie.

"How old were you when you first saw this?" I asked, trying to ignore the rumbling in my stomach that was ignited with the promise of fish-and-chips.

"Six," Molly said, her eyes not leaving the screen. Right then, the *Velociraptor* breathed on the kitchen door window, causing us to jump slightly. I knew it was coming, but it was still terrifying, no matter how many times I'd seen it.

"That's young," I replied. There was a knock on the door. Wow, that was quicker than I thought it would be. At the door was a man with a large tray. I took it from him. He tipped his hat at me, and I closed the hotel door.

Molly practically vaulted off the bed to the tray. I guess she was as hungry as I was. Smiling, I lifted off the tray's top. "Violá!" Wrapped in newspaper was a mouthwatering array of fried fish covered with French fries and some sort of vinegar.

"So how in the world did a six-year-old get away with watching *Jurassic Park*?" I asked after we had gathered up our food and sat on our beds. Greasy fingers and face be damned tonight. I had an actual working shower I could use, and I planned to use it well.

"I did it on the sly, in the middle of the night."

I put a chip in my mouth and pointed another one at her. "You sneaky girl. Have you read the book?"

She nodded. "What about you?"

"High school. You know, it's really crazy," I said, swallowing then frowning.

"What's crazy? The book?"

"No. Just the appeal," I said. "I know *so* many people that got into this business because of those movies. And that book."

She narrowed her eyes at my words. "You sound like that's a bad thing." I guess she could hear the edge to my tone. Oops.

"No, it's a good thing," I replied, smiling. But in truth, it was and it wasn't. There were so many people at this now. And that was good. There was a lot to do and find and argue about in this business. But at the same time, it had become a difficult world, especially academically. Paleo could be a difficult place. Undergrad, grad school. Post-grad, finding a steady job. There weren't a lot of jobs in this field. Money could be very tight, and competition for funds cutthroat. And *Jurassic Park* and its sequels created a lot of interest in this field. There were a lot of new, hungry players. Many of these new paleontologists were willing to do whatever it took to make their name in the field. To get the best positions and the grant money. They needed the major finds to do this, of course. Derek called it "making their bones." And sometimes, good people got trampled and broken.

Molly was still looking at me thoughtfully, waiting for me to say more, but I just turned back to watch the movie. Just in time to watch the *Tyrannosaurus rex* scream her dominance from the *Jurassic Park* lobby.

What are you doing here?

How did all this get so messed up?

YOUTH IN ALL ITS GLORY

Oliphant

MOST OF THE patrons had left the inside of the pub when I finally made it downstairs. There were still plenty of people outside, laughing and drinking in earnest.

"And how are you, sir?" the barman said as I sat down on a stool. He was young, barely old enough to drink himself. He had a pasty complexion marred with red spots and a wisp of what could be a beard if it had fertilizer. His hair was greasy and pulled back into one of those fashionable man-buns.

I shot him a wide smile. "Very well, my good man. Ready to imbibe some ridiculously expensive wine."

"Oh? Are you celebrating tonight?"

"Maybe," I replied, my eyes skimming the wine list he laid in front of me. "I see you have Chateau Margaux, 2003." Quite a find.

"Only by the bottle."

"That'll be fine."

The man raised his eyebrows. "It must have been an excellent evening."

"More . . . *intriguing*."

"Oh? Care to share?" the man said, pulling a dark bottle from a locked cabinet behind him. He grabbed a glass from under the bar, and after holding it in the light to make sure it wasn't dirty, filled it with the bottle's red liquid.

"You wouldn't understand," I said. I held the glass up to the light to see its color. After swirling the wine in my glass and smelling its bouquet, I took a long sip. Perfection.

"Maybe not, but still curious," the barman said, pouring a beer for a waiting customer. "And anything that requires Chateau Margaux is sure to be fascinating." He handed the pint to another customer and then leaned on the bar. "Try me."

I gave him a smirk. "Well, in the last twenty-four hours, I've lost probably the most important paleontological specimen since 1842. I've traveled almost five thousand miles at the behest of an anonymous package. I've found one half of a journal of one of the greatest paleontologists of all time. A journal that would seem to upend the fossil record and also contained a number of strange poems, by the way."

I took another slow sip, savoring the wine's chocolate tones. After swallowing it, I turned back to the barman.

"And now, I'm traveling with my favorite grad student, a kid intern, and my worst enemy—who, by the way, I'm forced to share a room with because apparently there are no room vacancies in all of the south of England. Oh, and we have a stalker who pretended to be from the United States government to gain access to our sites and steal our new specimen before we could publish anything. And he followed us to England. Apparently."

The man gazed at me, his mouth slightly open.

"Yes, I know. It'd be almost too fantastical if I weren't present for all of it." I sighed and put my elbows on the bar. "Hence, the need for Chateau Margaux. Lyme Regis is, what, two hours or so from here? I need to get there in the morning. Any traffic?"

"Usually no traffic in that direction, sir," he replied.

I took another sip of wine. "Do you have a pen?"

The man pulled a pen from his front pocket and handed it to me. "Thanks." I looked back down and started to draw on my napkin. In this day and age, scientific illustration had been basically replaced by real-time photographs and video recordings. A natural progression. But there was something so elegant about scientific illustrations. During college and grad school, I took art lessons as much as my schedule allowed so I could supplement my own publications.

After a few moments, I frowned at my drawing. I wasn't sure what I was doodling, but its head was angular, and its teeth were sharp. I drew scales on its neck, and my pen made a large arch on its side. I took another sip of wine, enjoying the warmth that flooded my body. The slam of a book on the bar startled me, and I spilled a little of my wine. A dreadful waste.

"Excuse me," I snapped. "This is expensive."

I rotated to see Molly on a barstool next to me.

"Sarah just went to sleep, and Farnsworth has disappeared."

"Maybe you should be doing the same," I said, using my small cocktail napkin to clean the spill. Yes, she was much too young to be here. I'll book her on the next flight out of Heathrow to Denver tomorrow evening, after we check out the Lyme Regis Museum. I'll email Dean, have him pick her up and take her to the University's other fossil dig in eastern Colorado. Sean Oliphant, responsible adult.

"There's more," she said, ignoring my pointed statement. Her gaze went to my napkin. "Is that a dragon?"

"What?" I said, narrowing my eyes.

"On your napkin. Did you draw one?"

I shook my head and crumpled the napkin in my hand. "No, it's a dinosaur. It's just a doodle. Now, what do you mean 'there's more'?"

She slid Owen's journal in front of me and opened to a familiar-looking page. "Look what I found in tiny handwriting on the same page as that 'Common Place' notation. 'Philpot's Fafnir.'" She looked up at me expectantly.

"Philpot," I said. "Never heard of any Philpot, let alone a Fafnir."

"Elizabeth Philpot!" Molly said, her voice raised. She reached for my cell phone, which I had placed next to me. Ignoring my protest, she tapped the keyboard screen and brought up the search engine.

"How the heck do you know my password?" I asked, baffled.

Ignoring me, she continued typing, then turned the phone around to show me the screen. I squinted in the dim light but only saw squiggles and what I think was a woman's face.

"I looked it up on the computer in my room. Elizabeth Philpot was Mary Anning's close friend. She was also a fossil hunter who corresponded with some of the experts of the day. Her collection of ancient fish is on display at the Oxford Museum of Natural History."

"We're not driving to Oxford," I said, a warning in my tone.

"I did an internet search using the key terms Philpot, Mary, and Fafnir. Now, nothing came up with those exact terms together, but some exciting things did pop up. Some of the results were about Mary's commonplace book. We have to get to the Lyme Regis Museum. I think we'll find some answers there."

"Well, it's a good thing we're going to Lyme Regis in the morning," I said, watching as she bounced in her seat. I chuckled and brought my wineglass to my lips. "You love to research, don't you?"

She nodded vigorously. "I mean, it's kind of an important part of this job, right? You have to think about the whole puzzle, about how a dragon could exist with the dinosaurs."

"Not a dragon. A new species, sure. But not a dragon."

She let out a *harrumph* and leaned an elbow on the bar. "Dr. Oliphant, you even admit that this is something new. A new species. Why are you fighting against the actual possibility of it being a dragon from mythology?"

"Dragons are just that, Molly. Myths."

"Why can't this be a dragon? I just don't understand why you can't say that this new species isn't a dragon. Owen literally called it Dracosauria." She waved her hands around, her fingers spread wide. "If you can believe that there was an apex predator the size of a school bus that walked the earth seventy million years ago, and you can believe that there were herbivores over half the length of a football field that lived 150 million years ago, then why can't you believe this? Just because *you* haven't studied it, doesn't mean it's not real."

Answer: Because I'd have seen it by now. I'd been doing this kind of work for a long time. Not as long as the old man, but long enough to have been around the block, as they say. But this girl won't hear that. Time to inspire from another angle. Be the professor I love to be. That I was meant to be.

I turned my body toward her and looked her in the eyes. "To be a dragon of myths, you have to have certain attributes, right?" I held up my hand, counting off fingers. "Breathing fire, killing humans, right? Or if you were a water dragon, breathing boiling water. That sort of thing, correct? You're the expert, after all."

"I guess," she said.

"Well, by that definition, we do not have a dragon." She opened her mouth to argue again, but I waved her to stop. "You have to think of this critically, Molly. What you stumbled

upon was definitely a strange creature. We've never seen anything that size or shape in the Hell Creek before. There are
enough attributes, such as the strange hips and the five fingers,
to suggest that this animal, our Monster, is remarkable. Do you
follow me?" She nodded. "Okay. But—and this is being really
honest with ourselves—Sarah could be right. We can't defini-
tively prove that it flew—those wings and hips still could have
belonged to a pterosaur. Correct?"

"I guess."

"And flight is a hallmark trait for dragons."

"Not all dragons flew—"

"But you are arguing it is a dragon because it had wings
found with the body, right?"

"Well, yeah," she replied, lowering her eyes.

"Molly, we don't know for sure what is going on because
the specimen is gone. Both the printout and fossil. And all
we've seen of other potential 'monsters' are a picture of a skull
on Owen's lap and some drawings. Nothing concrete. Honestly,
if we published what we have, a critical scientist would argue
we just hired someone off that DeviantArt website and tried to
pass it off as science."

I took another sip of wine, collecting my thoughts. "But,
assume that those hips were really attached to the specimen,
like I'm hoping, then yes, it's something truly remarkable. It's
not a dinosaur. It's a giant meat-eating creature that competed
with the dinosaurs. That is special, Molly. And if it flew, then
that would be remarkable. History-book-altering remarkable."

"Still, how can you not call it a dragon?" she asked. "It's a
flying carnivore with a long neck."

I shook my head and smiled, turning back toward the bar.
"Because if we can find more specimens like the Monster, we'll
have a real creature to describe and study. It didn't breathe fire.
It didn't hunt humans. It didn't hoard gold. It lived sixty-six

million years ago and died out like all the other large animals at the K-Pg boundary when the asteroid hit."

"So you're stuck on the fact that it's a real thing, and so can't be the myth."

"Myths were inspired by our natural surroundings, as you've said, Molly. But it's just another animal. Nothing fantastical."

"Oh yeah? Then how do you explain the color of the bones?"

My glass was halfway to my lips as I turned to look at her. "Color?"

"Yes. The Monster's fossil had a glossy black color."

"I already told you, surrounding minerals influence the color of bones during fossilization."

"Yes, but Owen's skull was the same black color as our Montana Monster. And I don't think that skull came from the Hell Creek."

I put my wineglass back on the bar and interlaced my fingers. The girl was right. How did I miss that? Black fossil bones were not common. Extremely rare, honestly. I know of two complete specimens. Out of hundreds. Thousands. Tens of thousands. And to have two different specimens of the same new animal the same color, found in different parts of the world. Well, that was a very strange coincidence indeed.

I took another sip of wine and gazed thoughtfully at the liquor display in front of me. The last few hours had been enough to warrant me to make a call to New York. And, based on that conversation, my publisher was drooling for the story, and *National Geographic* was circling for the property. The black bones. It definitely would be useful to continue on.

I turned to Molly and handed her my glass. "Want to see what the good life tastes like?"

She took it and looked at it skeptically. I nodded encouragingly. "Just don't overdo it. That's expensive."

Molly carefully moved the rim of the glass to her lips and took a sip. Scrunching her face, she handed it back to me. "Yuck. That is horrible."

"Two hundred and fifty pounds a glass is not horrible. It's sophistication. It's the culmination of geology, biology, and time coming together to create a perfect beverage. But you are young, so I'll impress you about its importance in a more academic fashion, considering your interests." As she rolled her eyes, I simply pointed at the glass. "That wine is grown from grapes whose deep-rooted vines have thrived for hundreds of years in carefully cultivated soils. Thousands of years before, those soils were once the stomping ground of ancient humans, and before that, ancient mammals like mammoths. Millions of years before that? The classic spread of Mesozoic Animalia—dinosaurs mixed with swimming and flying reptiles. You know the drill. And even before that, over 300 million years ago, a plethora of strange creatures all lived and died so that their bones and shells and skins could decompose and fossilize into rocks. That mineralogy would eventually provide the right combination of stratigraphy to grow grapes that would cause people like me to shell out beaucoup bucks just to take a sip. You're drinking complex history right there, Molly. A billion-year-old story of life and death that had to happen in just the right order to create this moment. Savor it."

Molly gazed thoughtfully at the glass and brought it to her lips. "Savor it," I repeated. But my smile turned to an indignant frown when she tipped her head back and downed the entire glass in one gulp.

It was almost one in the morning when I finally made it back to the room. I stood in front of the door, the key in my hand, but I didn't move. I leaned my ear against the door, but I didn't hear anything on the other side. So either Farnsworth was asleep, or he was not there.

I put my key in the lock and quietly opened the door, slowly entering the dark room. The light from the hallway spilled around me, and my body casted a shadow across Farnsworth's prone form. He was lying on top of his blankets, his back to me. I closed the door and headed into the room, turning into the bathroom.

The face in the mirror seemed tired and old. Not surprising considering we'd been traveling for a day straight. I needed a good night's sleep.

I splashed some water on my face, then turned off the bathroom light. As my eyes adjusted to the dark, I saw that Farnsworth was still lying there, now on his back, his arm covering his face.

I sat on my bed, scrunching my face as the mattress creaked. Farnsworth didn't move, but I saw that he was breathing. I watched his chest rise and fall, and I knew that he was awake. You didn't spend years working with a person without knowing their ticks, their ways of passive-aggressiveness. Our collaboration happened years ago, but some things never changed.

I let out a long sigh and lay down on my own bed without changing my clothes. To be honest, I didn't have much to change into.

The still of the room was deafening, and I clasped my hands over my face. After a moment, I sat up on my elbows. I turned to look at Farnsworth, and my stomach sank. Years ago, this man was my best friend. Now he was fake-sleeping just to avoid talking to me.

I stared at the dark television screen looming in front of my bed. My voice was barely louder than a whisper.

"I'm sorry, Derek."

THE BASEMENT IN LYME REGIS

Farnsworth

IT WAS EARLY in the morning when we arrived in Lyme Regis, a quaint brick-and-stone beach town on the edge of Lyme Bay. The weather was murky and cold, the air heavy with salt and moisture from the nearby sea. Knee-aching, teeth-chattering weather. Montana winters can be cold and ruthless, but after a blizzard, the sun comes out and it lights up the land and brings warmth to your face. This was the type of cold that soaked into your bones and never left.

Walking with a coffee cup in my left hand, I stretched my right arm over my head, rubbing my neck, and I let out a long yawn. Thank goodness the Inn provided free coffee to go. I needed it this morning.

"Sleep well, Derek?" Oliphant called from behind. "You're looking a little scruffy this morning."

Ignoring him, I walked quickly along the cobblestone streets toward our destination: the Lyme Regis Museum. Next to me, Molly was practically skipping. As she walked, her backpack slapped against her back, its insides rattling and shifting with every movement. I glanced at her, and she looked back up at me, her face shining with anticipation. Exhaustion aside, I had to remember that while I was here to find my bones, there was more at stake than my financial future. Molly was just a kid along for the ride. I had to watch out for her.

As if reading my mind, she grinned at me. "This is so much better than working at the frozen yogurt stand this summer."

I snorted in response and kept walking. She might have been having the time of her life, but I wasn't. No word yet from my various contacts about seeing my fossils on the markets. I'd always etched them with my small brand: a *T-rex* skull with rock hammers crossing behind it like an X. It's the same symbol on the hat Molly was wearing, the emblem of the Glasgow Geologic Institute. Everyone who sold fossils knew that I found them, and if there were ever any problems or questions, they talked to me. Wherever they ended up around the world, I'd know immediately.

And this morning I had received an email from Agent Porter with the FBI. He said that the picture I sent of Raley hadn't matched anything in their database, but that he'd keep looking. He also advised me to come home for another interview, that he'd talked to a few other people and had more questions for me. I had a sinking suspicion that he might know more about my past than he let on.

I replied, in the nicest possible way: find out who stole my fossils. I was staying here for now. I had my own job. I had to make sure Molly and Sarah were okay, and I had to keep Oliphant in line. And if I helped discover a new giant species of carnivorous animal from the Mesozoic, that would help make up for all this madness.

The Lyme Regis Museum was just opening as we arrived. The building itself was an L-shaped, towering, twisted sort of structure. It was obviously ancient but well kept. At its front were several brick arches that contained glass doors etched with the words "Lyme Regis Museum" and "Museum Shop." Peering near the entrance floor, I saw that the pavement was decorated with an artful display of the mollusca ammonite. Ammonites were related to our modern squids and octopuses, although they looked like a modern shelled *Nautilus*.

As I reached the front door, a larger man walked toward us. He was bald, bulky, and had big brown eyebrows that protruded over his eye sockets, making him look more like a Neanderthal than a man. He glanced at me and stopped, pulling one of his hands out of his jacket pocket. He kept the other one hidden.

Sarah was not paying attention because she walked straight into my back, making a *humph* sound as she skittered backward a bit. She stepped around to apologize but stopped when she saw the man.

Molly was oblivious to the man, however. She pushed past me to open the front door of the museum, mumbling something about us being slower than a herd of sloths. The man's eyes followed her as she disappeared into the building, a small smile playing on his lips.

The whole scene caused the hair on the back of my neck to stand up. Why would he look at Molly like that?

Next to me, Oliphant stood rigid. After a long moment, the man motioned for us to enter the building. "After you."

"Do you recognize him?" I whispered to Oliphant inside the museum.

Oliphant shook his head. "No, but he feels familiar."

"Yeah. Maybe," Sarah said. "Let's not drive ourselves crazy. He's probably just some creep. Every place has them, even Lyme."

Inside, the museum was quiet and empty. Our rubber-soled shoes and boots squeaked on the cold marble floor. It was not a large building. A slim, older woman with graying hair and periwinkle blue eyes stood near the front desk. As we walked forward, she immediately approached us.

"Dr. Sean Oliphant?" she exclaimed in surprise, reaching her hand out toward Oliphant.

"You presume correctly," he replied. "And you are?"

"Dr. Leah Smith. I'm the director. I saw you present a few years ago."

"A great pleasure," he said, bowing slightly. Oh, dear Lord. Next to me, I heard Molly stifle a laugh. Behind us, the Neanderthal man had entered the building. He walked past us and picked up a brochure at the front desk.

"What brings the famous Dr. Oliphant to us? Forgive me, we didn't have an appointment, did we?" She looked frazzled. She didn't even spare the Neanderthal a second glance at her station behind her.

"No, Doctor. I'm here with my colleagues. And intern." He motioned toward Molly, who looked a bit put out. "We're here . . . because my next book is about famous paleontologists. A history of paleontology, if you will," he said. "Our research indicates that you have something of Mary Anning's here. Not a fossil, but an actual book of hers. Something called a commonplace book?"

"Oh, of course! Her commonplace book!" Dr. Smith tittered loudly.

"Shh!" Oliphant said, quickly looking around. "Please, this is very sensitive. Because we are working under the gun, Dr. Smith. We've been told that another colleague might also write about this particular angle. We have . . . some unique interest in this work."

He lied so easily.

Dr. Smith nodded and tapped her finger against her nose. "Say no more. I'll take you right to it." She motioned for us to follow. "It's on display in our Mary Anning Wing. It's not far, just upstairs."

"As we walk, Dr. Smith, could you please tell us a little about this museum? To help with our research?" Oliphant asked.

"Of course! You're standing on what used to be the location of Mary Anning's home and office, the Anning Fossil Depot. But I wager you already knew that?" Dr. Smith led us through a rotunda and up a spiral staircase. "Today, the museum focuses on the history of Lyme Regis, both ancient and more recent. In addition to being *the* Mary Anning experts, we also have exhibits, paintings, and pictures that detail Lyme's history as a fishing community and tourist destination. Did you know that Jane Austen, for example, was a fan of Lyme?"

"I did," burst Molly. "She set part of her novel *Persuasion* here."

"Well, aren't you rather well read for a young Yankee," came back Dr. Smith.

Molly swallowed the compliment before she tasted the jab.

A few turns later and we were in a tall, narrow room filled with exhibits. Fossil skeletons of plesiosaurs and ichthyosaurs were attached to the walls; ten-foot replicas of these same creatures hung from the ceiling as if swimming above us. On my left stood a huge glass shelf that housed a variety of cleaned fossils, including a particularly beautiful ancient ammonite. It was about a foot long, with a white spiral shell that seemed to glow under the soft overhead light.

"This museum was built in 1902 by Thomas Philpot," Smith continued as she walked farther into the room.

"Excuse me, did you just say Philpot?" Molly blurted.

"It used to be called the Philpot Museum. Our founder was a relative of Elizabeth Philpot, a local woman who lived in Lyme Regis during the 1800s. Thomas was her nephew. Elizabeth was also a fossil collector like Mary Anning. They were great friends and often looked for fossils together." Dr. Smith stopped and motioned toward a large book on display in a protective glass box. "This is Mary Anning's commonplace book. Inside, Elizabeth wrote several messages to Mary. I suppose you know what a commonplace book is?"

"People used to have their friends and family write messages in their commonplace books as keepsakes," Molly said.

"Exactly, young lady," Dr. Smith beamed. "Ms. Austen served you well, I see."

People seemed to always take a shine to this girl.

"Look, we need to see that book," I said, reaching for the glass that surrounded it.

Dr. Smith reached over and slapped my hand. "Excuse me, sir. That book is for display only." Dr. Smith gave me an appraising look and frowned, stopping at a stain on my shirt. "Not to be touched by the public."

I looked down and brushed at the stain, a mixture of plaster and sand. Okay, I probably should have changed into my cleaner shirt this morning. But we were in a hurry. And what the heck? This uptight academic had no reason to judge me.

Just as I opened my mouth to respond, Oliphant leaned forward and caught her eye. "Please excuse my friend, Dr. Smith. He's not house trained." I snorted as he gently put a collegial hand on her shoulder. "For my book, please, would it be possible if we take a quick look at it?"

"I don't know, Dr. Oliphant . . . it's very delicate."

"What I meant earlier is that *National Geographic* has spoken of a documentary based on my book and is *very* interested in Mary Anning's contributions to science. There would be a lot of press about your museum. And surely an on-screen interview with you. Filmed here in Lyme Regis. All for science."

Dr. Smith scrunched her face. Finally, she broke. "Oh, all right, you may," she said. "But let me get some gloves—"

"Thank you, Dr. Smith. Don't bother about the gloves. We'll be careful," Oliphant lifted the glass. He handed it to Dr. Smith and carefully pulled the book toward him. Gently, Oliphant turned the pages of the book.

Squinting at the small print, I could see blocks of notes addressed to Mary Anning. The handwriting was very faint, worn with age, but I could make out several names and dates. Many of the entries were by Elizabeth Philpot herself.

"What are these entries about a rockslide and a dead dog?" Sarah asked.

"Oh, Mary was out fossil hunting with her dog, Tray—he was her constant companion," said Dr. Smith. She pointed to a large portrait near the front of the room. It was of a woman in a long dark dress, her hand on a rock hammer. At her feet was a small black-and-white dog. I had a copy of that same portrait sitting in my house. I wanted to use it for my future museum. I had a whole section planned on Jurassic fossils and Mary Anning's contributions.

"There's Tray with Mary in that picture," Dr. Smith continued. "Anyway, Mary was fossil hunting, and the cliff overhead suddenly collapsed. Mary managed to escape, but the landslide killed poor Tray. Mary was devastated, but she continued prospecting for fossils for many years. Brave woman. I'm not sure I would have gone back," Smith said sadly.

Of course she would. Mary was a pirate. She understood the thrill of the hunt, the need to dig. She was the best commercial fossil hunter of her time, digging and selling fossils to get her family through rough times. It would make sense that she would continue to hunt. Even with the risk to her own life. I admired someone like that.

Several minutes later, Sarah shook her head. "This notebook seems like a bust. That rockslide is the only drama in this entire thing. Plenty of notes about who visited Mary for tea if anyone is interested."

Molly pushed past me and turned a few more pages.

"I'm sorry, young lady, but really!" Dr. Smith said with annoyance.

Oliphant leaned toward her conspiratorially. "Interns. They have a mind of their own." She chuckled in response. Why did people find that bastard funny?

"What's this?" Molly said.

Oliphant and I leaned over her shoulders at the same time.

"'Philpot's Fafnir bones protect the notes,'" I read aloud.

"'Philpot's Fafnir' again . . ." Molly said. "And the script is familiar. That's Owen's handwriting."

"As in Richard Owen?" Dr. Smith asked.

"Yeah," I said. "Owen."

Smith nodded. "I know they were contemporaries, and I know that Mary corresponded with some of the same people Richard Owen did. I also remember reading that they met at least one time, but I don't remember the year. Maybe he did write it. We always thought that was such a strange entry. Are you sure that's Owen's handwriting?"

"Oh, I'm sure," said Molly. Her smile was sly; for a second I thought she would pull Owen's journal out.

"What could it mean that 'Philpot's Fafnir bones protect the notes'?" Molly said.

"I'm not sure, young lady. Nobody has been able to figure it out. Others have seen it, of course. You can't study Mary Anning and not read the commonplace book at some point. Wow. Richard Owen. Well, he was quite the important figure, at least later on that century." Dr. Smith paused and tapped her finger against her chin. "Owen may have written this strange note, but he wasn't a huge influence in her life, as far as we know. But, the mentioning of bones and the fact it was written by Owen . . . I wonder."

She turned to face us. "See, Elizabeth Philpot was Mary's biggest advocate in the academic world, both before and after her death. Elizabeth often argued with the men that Mary deserved public credit for her work. Only William Buckland from Oxford University even mentioned her in his presentations. The others ignored her for the sole reason that she was a woman," Smith said. "She's left a huge legacy for this museum and for others. You may not realize, for example, that Mary found the first pterosaur ever discovered in England." She smiled. "Early on, it was called *Pterodactylus*. You know it now as *Dimorphodon*. Richard Owen renamed it, but actually, Mary always called it the 'flying-dragon.' She found the fossil in 1829. The artist Benjamin Waterhouse Hawkins used that skeleton as an inspiration for the Crystal Palace flying reptile models. They are right next to the dinosaurs in Crystal Palace Park. Have you ever been? You've probably seen the famous *Iguanodon* mold in the Natural History Museum."

"We've seen it," I said. I could practically feel Molly's body bursting with energy next to me. "Do you have the *Dimorphodon* fossil here?"

"Well, not the one that Anning found that was used for the species description, but we have the bones from another specimen. They just might be the 'Philpot's bones' Owen mentioned here. According to our records, Elizabeth owned these fossils, but I believe Mary found them initially, near where she found the other *Dimorphodon* skeleton. According to my predecessor, we received them from the Natural History Museum in London years ago. The museum had found the fossil in storage, and there were instructions to return them to Philpot, at the behest of an *R. Owen*." She shook her head. "I never put two and two together, actually. *Richard Owen*. I just assumed that this Owen was a curator of some kind, cleaning out the basement." She shook her head, as if to clear away the stars. "Anyway, the bones are incomplete. They are just a *Dimorphodon* wing. I saw it years ago when I started here." She rubbed her chin thoughtfully. "It's funny, the bones are deep black. Polished-looking. Bizarre considering fossils from this formation tend to be a dull light or dark brown color. It's in our collections room, in the basement. Would you like to see it?"

"Oh, yes, I think we would," Oliphant said emphatically.

The museum basement was dark and a bit cool. Not surprising, considering the only natural light came from several small windows near the top of the room. Boxes, books, and filing cabinets cluttered the basement. Cords of rope hung on some of the walls and shelves; relics of Lyme Regis's naval connections, I guessed.

"Here it is," Dr. Smith said. She moved a few boxes off a large, old trunk. She then unsnapped the clasps and opened it. "Voilá."

Inside, resting on a bed of yellowed paper shavings, was a large slab of rock. It was bluish-gray, about two feet in length and width. Encased in the stone were several fossils. They were a deep black, with a slight sheen to them. They formed the shape of a wing.

Next to me, Molly knelt down to study the fossil more closely. I heard her counting quietly to herself. But even standing, I knew exactly how many fingers this wing had. I felt it in my gut. This was precisely what we'd been looking for.

Apparently, Dr. Smith had excellent hearing. "Oh, you've seen it." She chuckled and pointed toward the finger bones. "This fossil is made up of several individual pterosaurs. See, instead of the usual four fingers, there are five. We all know pterosaurs had four fingers, but I don't need to tell you, Dr. Oliphant, how it's not unusual to find multiple fossil specimens in one place, do I? That explains the extra finger."

Oliphant, Molly, and I exchanged a look, while Sarah frowned and crossed her arms across her chest. Finally, Oliphant cleared his throat. "Dr. Smith, would you mind if I have a few moments alone with my colleagues to discuss how this fossil relates to our studies?"

Smith nodded and backed up. "Of course, Dr. Oliphant. Please take as long as you'd wish. By the way, I saw your TED Talk the other day. *Can you imagine? Just try.* I did! I can! So inspiring! I'll be upstairs if you need anything."

Only when her footsteps faded away did Molly speak. "I bet my life this is a dragon wing. It's a smaller version of our Monster."

"Pterosaur," Sarah said.

"What are you talking about? This is literally a five-finger wing made of black bones, just like our Monster!"

I squatted down next to Molly and gently touched the bones. "These are much smaller than our Montana Monster's, but identical in shape, at least from what I remember."

Molly pulled out her phone and opened the photo app. She handed me her phone and pointed to the screen. Clever girl, she took photographs of the printout the other night. I'd forgotten that. I increased the magnification on the screen and looked at one of the wings.

"Yep, the scapula is almost identical, except in size," I said, holding the phone out to the others. Oliphant took it from me and looked at Molly. "You have photographs? Raley didn't make you delete them?"

Molly shrugged. "He never asked, right? He just said Karolin had posted her photographs online. I didn't."

Oliphant looked down at the screen, then at the fossil in front of us.

"Or, it could just be a pterosaur wing," Sarah said, a strain in her voice. She pulled out a yellowed piece of paper from the crate. "Here is a list of people who have viewed this fossil. I recognize some of the names. They are all pterosaur paleontologists." She pushed it into my chest.

I frowned at the paper. "Some I haven't, though. Ever hear of 'Ryuunosuke'?"

"I don't get it," Molly said. "Why wouldn't those scientists have argued this was something new? I mean, a five-fingered 'pterosaur' wing?" Molly put air quotes around the word while rolling her eyes.

I smiled. "Well, we come to this party after seeing other evidence, including our Monster. Others don't have that background. This is exactly what we need. We can use this."

Oliphant reached for the list, and I handed it to him. He looked down and raised his eyebrow. "This is quite the list of who's who in the pterosaur world." He looked up at me. "Sarah's not wrong. That could be from a pterosaur."

I turned and looked at him incredulously. I pointed to the fossil. "What the hell are you talking about? A five-fingered wing? Made of black bones? Look at its shape! That's no pterosaur."

He held up a hand at me. "There are a lot of highly respected people on this list. I'll admit I'm no expert at pterosaurs. But people on this list are, and if nobody claimed this wasn't a pterosaur, it's hard to argue that."

"But it's a black wing!" Molly nearly shouted at Oliphant. "We talked about that last night!"

He lowered his chin to look at her. "However, having said that, I gotta admit this wing is . . . *interesting*. People have been wrong before. To describe a new family of animal, an animal different from dinosaurs and pterosaurs, yet one that shares convergent or similar traits of both, we need more evidence than just a wing. People could argue it's just several specimens of pterosaurs jumbled together, like Dr. Smith said. Just as some could argue they are from one animal. We need more of a body. After all, Owen used three species—*Megalosaurus, Iguanodon,* and *Hylaeosaurus*—to describe Dinosauria. We need more than just a wing."

Damn. He was right.

As much as I wanted this to be the smoking gun, we needed more fossils. I turned around and leaned against one of the shelves. I gently banged it with my fist, and a slight clang echoed around the room.

"We probably can't take this with us, can we?" Molly asked.

She sounded sad. I didn't blame her. I'd like nothing more than to pack this rock up and head home, back to Montana. I could see myself sitting in my warehouse, air scribe in hand, cleaning it out of the stone. I'd take some measurements, maybe cut part of the bone to see if it was hollow like our Montana Monster. We could get to the bottom of what this animal was and its place in the ancient world. It might not be enough of a bone to describe a new species, but it would be an excellent first step at getting my life back on track.

Back on track.

I grabbed the shelf, gripping it tightly enough to make my knuckles turn white. When we finished this, hopefully with enough information so we could publish, I still had to figure out my next move. I mean, publishing a paper or two about this new flying carnivore species would help me, assuming Oliphant didn't figure out a way to cut me out, but I was still screwed. What if I couldn't get my fossils back? I mean, the BLM had no hand in this. What was I going to do?

I gave the shelf one more squeeze. I turned around and looked at Molly. She gazed at me, her head tilted slightly. It was her tell when she was trying to figure something out. For her sake, and Sarah's, I had to be strong. I gave her a small smile. She returned it, then her gaze dropped back toward the fossil.

"Something tells me this museum might not like us to take away a Mary Anning fossil without an extensive legal agreement," Oliphant said. "Plus, it's a massive slab of rock. It's rather heavy."

"We should take some photos," Molly said, taking her cell phone back from Oliphant.

"I thought you didn't want to use your phone because your dad would know you were using it abroad or something?" I asked.

"It's on airplane mode normally, Mr. Farnsworth. And you don't need cell reception to take a photo," she replied. "Besides, I hardly turn it on anyway because there is no reception in the badlands."

I reached for my cell phone in my back pocket. Sarah patted down her body, a strange look on her face. "My phone. It's not here?" She moved her hands, frantically up and down her pants legs, pulling at her jacket pockets. "I must have left it in the car."

"Don't worry, Sarah. We can do a group chat or a secret Facebook group." Oliphant smirked. "Call it 'Mary Anning's Flying-Dragons.'"

Molly laughed. As I leaned down to get a close-up of the fossil, a thought hit me, and I blurted, "The other half of the journal."

"What?" Sarah said.

I started to put it together.

The other half of the journal.

The note from the commonplace book.

The bones protect . . .

"Owen's note in the journal, and in the commonplace book. The bones. The missing half of Owen's journal." I dug around and under the fossil, reaching down through the paper shavings as best as I could. A whitish object caught my eye. It was wedged under the slab of rock, and my movements looking for the journal must have shifted it out. A letter. I gently reached over and opened it.

It was hard to read the faded writing in the dim light. "It's dated 1857." I cleared my throat and started to read.

"'Dear Miss Philpot. Thank you for this wing. I remember communicating about it, but it never ended up in my hands, and I am glad to see it finally. While tenuous due to its isolated nature, it does provide an important hint to the truth that you and Miss Anning have glimpsed in the ancient rocks above your home. I look forward to showing you the newest evidence, how Siegfried can prove that Fafnir existed, as we discussed in our last correspondence. I think you will find it very illuminating. Yours etc. R. Owen.'"

What was Siegfried, or for that matter, Fafnir?

"Richard Owen," said Molly. "How come no one has found this note before? You'd think a note from Owen to anybody would be an important find!"

"Wait, there's more," I said. "'Written but not sent. Just heard of Philpot passing. A sad day for those who seek the truth. I pray our foe was not involved, like MA. I will provide instructions for the bones to be returned to Elizabeth's family in due time, for its safety.'"

"Foe?" Molly said.

A *foe*. Owen's journal also mentioned something about an enemy, the Order of Saint George. Could that be it?

"MA? What is MA?" Oliphant asked.

"MA . . . as in Mary Anning?" Molly said.

"She died of cancer, she wasn't murdered," I said. "She died of breast cancer."

"Maybe she didn't die of cancer," Molly said.

Interesting idea. Mary died way back in 1847. Back then, medical science was pretty primitive, and it probably wasn't standard practice to do an autopsy. Jumping from cancer to murder seemed extreme, but then it would be hard to prove otherwise at this point. Did someone commit a perfect crime, and Owen was calling out the injustice from the grave?

God, focus, Derek.

I needed to wrap my head around the task at hand. Speculating about a death that occurred in the mid-nineteenth century was useless at this point. Besides, we were here for hard evidence—fossils, documents, or other artifacts. That was what was going to save my career. Not fantasy. "Let's get out of here and into the fresh air." The others nodded, and we replaced the trunk. Together, we headed back up the stairs to find the exit.

SENECA'S WISE WORDS

Molly

THE OCEAN WIND whirled around my face as we slowly walked along the shoreline of Lyme Regis. I loved the sea, how it was the same but different all over the world. The sound of the waves was the same as in California, but everything else was different. I looked at the blue-gray cliffs and thought about the history and records contained in them.

"If only we had more time," Oliphant said with longing.

I looked down at my feet, nodding. I got it, I really did. I mean, the Jurassic Coast was really famous for its fossils. But after seeing that Dracosauria wing, and reading that note from Owen, I just couldn't focus. Finally, I turned to the others. "Could Mary Anning have been murdered?"

Oliphant looked at me. "Doubtful. Besides, there is no way to prove either way. One note written over a hundred years ago does not equate to an Inspector Poirot moment," he said.

I stared at him blankly. "Who is Poirot?"

Sarah coughed to hide her laughter. Next to her, Farnsworth walked with his hands in his pockets. His body was slightly tilted against the cold wind.

"Molly, it's unlikely she was murdered. Someone would have figured that out. Even back then. And why would anyone murder a woman over a few fossils? They could have just bought them from her. She used to sell them," Sarah said.

"Well, fossils can be really valuable to the right people, and if there was like a bidding war or something—"

"It's unlikely," Sarah said, interrupting me with a wave of her hand.

"But Owen seemed to think the Order had something to do with Mary's death," I replied, my voice rising.

"We don't know the whole story. Nor do we even know for sure that 'MA' means Mary Anning," Sarah said with finality. I frowned and kicked some sand.

"Let's work on something new. The term *Fafnir*," Oliphant said, bringing out his phone. "We've seen that term in Owen's journal, and now in the commonplace book and Owen's note to Philpot. We should look that up."

"It's the name of a dragon," I said, not looking up.

In unison, the others stopped moving and stared at me. I gave them a small smirk. "When I was researching online last night, I didn't find any hits of 'Fafnir' with 'Mary Anning,' but there is plenty about Fafnir alone. He's pretty famous."

"Oh, please enlighten us," Oliphant said, an edge to his voice.

"Fafnir. Okay. See, my dad's an opera nut, and I'm an only child. I get dragged to a lot of shows. Have you ever heard of *The Ring* by Wagner?"

"Sure, never seen it though," Farnsworth said. "That's the one with the tune used in the helicopter attack in *Apocalypse Now*, right?"

"'Ride of the Valkyries.'" I nodded. I pulled my backpack around and reached inside. "Four operas make up *The Ring*. The operas are loosely based on Germanic mythology and tell the story of Siegfried."

I opened my dragon mythology book and flipped to a page with a giant dragon breathing fire at a man. A knight dressed in armor, with a sword in one hand and a shield in his other. Above the picture, written in Gothic-style lettering, was the word *Germany*.

"It's in here, too. In the story, Siegfried follows the dragon's tracks to its cave, where it guards a large treasure. Siegfried kills the dragon and takes the treasure. The dragon's name is Fafnir."

"Let me see Owen's journal again," Farnsworth said. I put my dragon book back in my backpack and pulled out the journal. I handed it to him, and he riffled through the pages. "Are there any other mentions of Fafnir we should look at?"

"Yep, there is one." I leaned over Farnsworth's arm and stopped him. "Here." I had spent a good chunk of time looking at the journal last night and in the car this morning. While there were a ton of letters, notes, and drawings that mention dragon lore, one thing stood out to me because of Owen's earlier note about Fafnir. That, and it actually indicated a physical location. "Right here. He has an entry about Germany. A whole section about a castle in Germany called Drachenfels. It's near a town called Königswinter on the Rhine River."

Farnsworth leaned forward, his finger skimming the pages. "The opposite page has some drawings of footprints. Molly, didn't you say something about tracks?"

"That's how Siegfried found him. He tracked Fafnir's footprints to his cave."

"These footprints," said Farnsworth. "They look like bird footprints. An osprey, actually." He looked up at me. I knew exactly what he was thinking.

Just like the Montana Monster.

"Yep."

He continued, "There's a note here: 'Fafnir's footprints are at Drachenfels.' But the handwriting is very different.

More blocky. This is someone else's writing. Someone sent this to Owen."

Oliphant looked down and typed furiously into his cell phone. "Drachenfels translates to *Dragon Rock*."

I started to pace. "I think Owen is sending us on a quest from the grave. We need to go to Germany."

"What?" Sarah said, her mouth dropping open. "Molly, let's not get too far ahead of ourselves and start looking for the Holy Grail or something."

"Look, this journal is a road map or guide of some sort," I replied, my voice raised a little. "Owen spent his life collecting evidence about dragons—"

"Dinosaurs, Molly!" Sarah said, closing her eyes in frustration. She huffed and turned around to look at the ocean. The gray waves churned, and the wind peppered our faces with sand.

Oliphant looked back and forth between us and sniffed. "Listen up. By no means do I think that what we're looking at is a dragon—and don't look at me like that, Molly. Just *no*. But it *is* a new family of animal, whatever it is. Agreed?" He looked at each of us.

Farnsworth closed the journal and held it at his side. He glanced at Sarah and grunted, "Agreed."

"All right," said Oliphant. "Let's go to Germany and look at those tracks. If this picture is accurate and the prints are clear, then we'll start work on an abstract. We'll have enough to start the process. We'll have the wing in the Lyme Regis Museum, as well as what we found in Owen's office. Not to mention those pictures you and Karolin took of our Montana Monster, Molly." He rubbed his unshaven chin and looked at the slate-gray sky. "Assuming Karolin's are still up online, of course."

"I checked before we left Montana. They aren't," I said. I was curious about what she had posted, and wondered how much attention they were generating. But either Karolin took them down, or someone else did. My thoughts drifted to Raley, smoking a cigar on the stone steps in London. His dark eyes staring at me, and his mouth twisted in a cruel grin. I shivered.

"Bummer. I'll email her to send me copies. Sarah, do you think the CAD file you made using the GPR might be saved somewhere else?"

Sarah stamped her foot and started to pace. "No. This is all insane. For whatever reason, we've lost our perspective, our objectivity. This is a stupid, crazy chase for what is probably just a new species of dinosaur."

"Sarah, this could be something really new. I mean, I've never seen a dinosaur with feet like what we saw in Montana. And if these prints exist in Germany . . ." Oliphant frowned at her and crossed his arms against his chest. "Look, I completely understand why you'd think our intern might be jumping the gun with this mythological crap—"

"Hey!" I said. "That's—" I started to respond, but Farnsworth put his hand on my shoulder and shook his head slightly, motioning toward Sarah. Oliphant's speech fell into the background as I took her in. Her eyes were wide and distressed, and she was biting her lip.

Oliphant was ranting. "—this could be something monumentally important to paleontology, to all of our careers."

"I understand, Sean, and coming from you, well, that's not insignificant," Sarah replied. "But all this traveling, this . . . *lying.*"

"What lying?" Oliphant asked.

She pointed at me. "We're lying to Molly's family, Sean. She's just a kid! She shouldn't be here. And my God, the warehouse! They took Derek's fossils. Derek saw Raley in England. This is just too much—"

Sarah suddenly stumbled and fell face-first into the sand. Farnsworth tried to help her up, but she flung his hand away, rubbing her bruised knee. "Stupid rocks!" she hissed. "I'm so tired, I can't even see straight. We should go back to Montana. We should get out of this place!"

I stared at her.

"Sarah, you don't really want to go back, do you?" Farnsworth asked.

"Don't you?" She turned to look at him sharply.

"No."

"Why not? Even for you, Derek . . ." She looked down at her feet, trying a different tack. "Derek, there are no fossils here. Not for you, that is. That wing we just saw could be from a pterosaur. And it belongs to the Lyme Regis Museum. Owen's office was cool, but come on, you're a *fossil hunter*. What do you need books and drawings for? And they belong to the Natural History Museum or Owen's family. You literally make your money in the field. The almighty dollar, right? There is nothing here you can sell. Don't you want to go home?"

Farnsworth looked at her, startled, then he narrowed his eyes. "They took everything, Sarah. I don't have any home to go back to."

Oliphant rolled his eyes. "Okay, so putting Derek's dramatics aside for one second. We need to make some decisions here. About our next move. My vote is Germany. Hopefully we can find those footprints and have a variety of information to publish. Bingo: we're the toast of the next Society of Vertebrate Paleontology meeting. Sarah, I know you have doubts, but trust me on this. Let's see this through one more path, then we can reassess. Besides, when was the last time you were in Germany?"

"Well, never," Sarah murmured. She lowered her head, breathing hard. A few seconds later, she snapped her head up and gazed out over the ocean. "Fine."

Oliphant slapped his hand on her shoulder. "Boom, we're going to Germany. And number two." He looked right at me. "I agree with Sarah. I don't think Molly should be here anymore."

I stared at Oliphant. "What?"

"You're too young, Molly. And you shouldn't be in England. Not without a parental permission slip or whatever kids need these days."

"Dr. Oliphant, that's not fair." I cringed at the whine in my voice. "I can't go home now!" I turned to Sarah. "Please don't send me home."

"Molly—" Sarah started, her tone low and sad.

"I don't think she should go," Farnsworth said firmly. "Molly's been nothing but helpful. Maybe a bit in the way." He smiled at me. "But she's got an impressive skill set about mythology that none of us have. It's been useful. I mean, she figured out that Fafnir bit. I highly doubt any of us would have, or at least as fast as she did. She should see this through." He nodded his head toward me. "I'll pay her way."

My mouth dropped. Wow, that was unexpected. And flights and hotels were expensive. "I have some savings, Mr. Farnsworth," I said quietly. Actually, I had very little. But it would be worth it to go to Germany and see the Dracosauria tracks in person. But I couldn't let Farnsworth pay for me, not when his fossils were just stolen.

Farnsworth shook his head. "Molly, I can manage."

Oliphant snorted and looked up at the sky. "Oh, stop the martyrdom, Derek. I see what you're doing. Fine. If you want to herd the intern, I'm completely okay with it. And I'll pay. I've got more money than you do."

He turned to me. "Nothing personal, Molly, but you're just young, and it had to be discussed. And once in a blue moon, I am forced to agree with Farnsworth. You've been very helpful," he said, tapping me on the shoulder with his finger.

I smiled back. I glanced at Sarah, who was looking down at her shoes.

We walked in silence along the beach. Oliphant was typing on his phone again, probably purchasing plane tickets for us to go to Germany.

Farnsworth had the journal open as he walked, but after a few paces, he stopped. He moved his fingers and tapped at a page like a woodpecker. "What's this line?" he said. I looked over his arm to find what his finger was pointed at. It was a small line right below the footprints. "It's in Latin, I think. '*Ducunt volentem fata, nolentem trahunt.*' I wonder what that means."

"'The fates lead the willing and drag the unwilling,'" I replied automatically. I started to walk on but realized the group wasn't moving; they were staring at me. "What?"

"You know Latin?" Oliphant asked.

I shrugged. "I've got two years in high school, so far." Seneca is required reading. Easy, poetic sentence structures, or so Mr. Collins said. I didn't think so.

Farnsworth laughed. "Reason number six hundred and sixteen to keep you around, Molly! I mean, who knows Latin these days?"

Smiling, I looked at the sky. I took it as my foreign language elective because I wanted to understand scientific names, most of which used Latin as the root.

Honestly, Seneca's words kinda fit our situation. And they were familiar. Why were they familiar? Oh my God. I turned to Farnsworth. "Do you still have that poem in your pocket? The copy you made of the poem from the Hawkins painting?"

Farnsworth reached into his pocket and took out the heavily crumpled piece of paper. I unfolded it, and started to read:

> An ancient enemy impedes
> Those that will save the truth
> But fate will lead the willing
> To hallowed halls that whisper of the Origin in sooth

"I think there is a connection. That Seneca saying, 'the fates lead the willing and drag the unwilling,' part of that saying is in the poem, right here." I pointed at the line in the poem for the others. As they leaned over to look, we heard a voice yelling at us from behind.

Turning, I saw a guy running toward us, his right hand raised and holding something metallic.

Farnsworth immediately stepped between our group and the approaching man. "Whoa there, buddy! Just stop right there." Farnsworth raised his hand like a traffic cop.

Sarah pulled my arm forcing me behind her. What was going on?

"Easy there, guv. It's all right," the man said with an English accent. "I was just walking on the beach with my mate, when I found this." He held out a cell phone with a metallic purple cover.

"Oh my God, that's mine," said Sarah. "You guys are lifesavers."

Farnsworth grabbed it from his hand, never taking his eyes off the man. He handed it to Sarah. As I looked at the man, my stomach began to roil, and I instinctively took a step back.

"No trouble, man, just helping the lady," the stranger said, stepping backward away from us. We watched him walk to the seawall, where he entered a staircase that would take him to street level.

Once he was far enough away, Farnsworth turned to Sarah. "You know that man?"

"No, the first time I've ever seen him was just before we entered the museum."

"I've seen him before," I said, clutching my stomach with my arms. "In London. He was near Raley, at the Natural History Museum."

"He came *into* the Lyme Regis Museum after us," Sarah said breathlessly.

We watched the large man emerge from the stairwell onto the street. Immediately, another man walked into view and stood next to him. I couldn't see the man's face, but I didn't think it was Raley. They stared at us intently. After a moment, the stranger pulled out his phone, and his lips moved silently as he watched us. Then, he and his buddy turned around and walked out of sight.

"We're definitely being followed," said Oliphant, his face grim. "The stakes have officially been raised."

Farnsworth glanced at Oliphant, then at me. "Hold your cards close, kid."

I gave him a smile. After all, he went to bat for me. I wanted to show him that I wasn't scared. But I was just pretending.

"I suggest we get out of here," said Farnsworth, turning to Oliphant. "What's the plan?"

"I've already arranged our exit from England," said Oliphant. "Lucky for you all, my American Express card has a very high limit."

Letter between Elizabeth Philpot and Richard Owen

Mr. Owen,

I have just received your note. Providence was truly on our side. We are just fine. Whatever you may have heard, we are safe. There is no need to visit us at this time, although your company is always welcome. You are correct that Mary was caught in a landslide. They are common around here, as you know, but we do not let that deter us from fossil hunting. Especially for Mary, who must sell fossils to provide for her family. In any event, Mary survived the landslide by digging herself free. But her poor, lovely dog, Tray, did not survive the catastrophe. Mary is very upset, as you might imagine. Besides myself, that dog was her closest friend.

I must admit that your letter frightened me. How else would a rockslide occur?

Sincerely,

E. Philpot
Lyme Regis, 1833

THE FOOTSTEPS OF FAFNIR

Farnsworth

THE RUINS OF Castle Drachenfels clung to the craggy summit of Drachenfels Hill. While time had decimated the central structure of Castle Dragon Rock, we could still see its grandeur among the fallen walls and vine-covered staircase to nowhere. Built over eight hundred years ago, in its heyday it must have been an impressive sight. We could have hiked up, but we chose to take Drachenfels Railway to the summit. I'm glad we did, because my body felt like it had been hit by a bus. I was creaking and cracking and my joints ached. Lack of sleep and plenty of stress didn't help.

I leaned against a metal railing and took a deep breath, letting it out slowly through my nose. Trying to calm my nerves. My nostrils sniffed involuntarily, and I smelled that damn smell again. Schnitzel! Yeah, that was it. I'd been trying to figure it out for the last ten minutes. The aroma was fantastic and held the promise of something greasy and delicious. I checked my watch. It was almost lunchtime.

Yesterday we flew from Exeter Airport to Cologne. We spent the night in a hotel, then drove here in a rented Mercedes, outside the city of Königswinter. While I did sleep, I had a disturbing dream that someone—or something—was chasing me. I didn't remember a lot, but I do recall feeling trapped and anxious. Something black and huge, just out of my peripheral vision. This so-called dragon hunt was really churning up my subconscious.

I heard Oliphant on his phone about twenty feet away. I caught the word "property," whatever that meant. He'd been on his phone a lot since we left England. He was staring at me, with an inscrutable look on his face as he talked to whoever it was. I stared right back at him until he looked away.

Farther away, in another clearing, I caught a glimpse of a large modern building that looked like it housed a restaurant. Must have been the source of the smell of cooked meat. As an unrepentant carnivore, I headed that way.

"This isn't right," Sarah said. She stood at the base of one of the castle walls, inspecting the ground.

"What do you mean?" I said, altering my path toward her.

"Look at the rocks."

I walked over and squatted down next to her, pulling out tufts of grass to expose the rock formation below. Sarah was right. How did I miss this? The rock below the grass was trachyte. Trachyte was an igneous rock, from volcanic activity.

"No sedimentary rock, no fossils," Oliphant said above me. I hadn't heard him walk over. "And no footprints."

"Obviously," I grumbled.

This didn't make any sense. You needed specific conditions for fossilization, for both bones and trace fossils, like footprints—water, sediment, time. You found fossils in sedimentary rock. Igneous rock comes from lava or magma. You couldn't find fossils in igneous rock.

So why did Owen think those tracks came from here? There is no way they could have been made here millions of years ago. The geology didn't fit. I'd looked at Owen's journal again last night, and while the scribbled entry about Drachenfels was vague, it was one of the better leads we had. There was the drawing of footprints, with the accompanying note written in a stranger's handwriting explaining that they were Fafnir's and were located at Drachenfels. And there was a small entry by Owen farther in the journal mentioning Drachenfels. Molly had done a little internet research and found an interesting article describing the local mythology. Apparently, the cave where Siegfried killed Fafnir was supposed to be somewhere on this hill.

Yet, it looked like we'd hit a brick wall. Or igneous wall, you could say. I kicked the ground, scattering the pebbles. Maybe Sarah was right. Maybe coming to Germany was a mistake, our tunnel vision for treasure blinding us from what this really was: a fool's errand.

Sarah turned to Oliphant, using her hand to shield her eyes from the bright sunlight. "Who were you on the phone with?"

"Listening to my messages, talking with Michelle," he replied smoothly. I recalled that Michelle was the University's Geology department administrative assistant.

"Anything important?"

"Nah, just informing her I am out of the country unex-pectedly for a bit—"

"Excuse me, sir," came a voice behind us. "I couldn't help but overhear what you were saying about footprints." I turned to find a young Asian man, probably in his mid-twenties, with a slight build and dark hair. He had a fancy camera hanging around his neck, and what looked like a brochure in one of his hands. I detected a Japanese accent in his voice.

"Howdy," I said.

"And how do you do, sir? I believe there is a cave nearby, at the base of Drachenfels Hill. Our tour guide told us about it." He pointed to a large group on the other side of the castle. Standing on a rock in front of the group was a young woman in a blue uniform with a large yellow flag. "Supposedly, it's a dragon's lair because there are footprints on the floor, or leading to it, or something. Just take the train to the bottom of the hill, then look for the markers. It's a bit of a hike, she said."

"Thank you," I said. "We appreciate it."

He nodded in reply, walking away from us. "Happy to help out another fan of GOT."

I stared at his retreating back. "GOT? What's that?"

Molly came up next to me and whispered, "Dude, *Game of Thrones*. Don't tell anybody that you didn't know that."

I ignored her, watching the man as he strolled away. My instincts were screaming. Maybe he was just a helpful tourist. Why would one of Raley's people tell us *where* to go? I thought they were following us, not leading us? The man stopped at the railing overlooking the valley for a moment, brought his camera to his eye, and pressed a button. Looking at the screen on the camera, he smiled, then turned to rejoin his tour group.

Oliphant grabbed Molly's arm and gently tugged her toward the train track. "It's okay, Derek. Don't be so paranoid." He smirked at me and shook his head. "He just heard us talking about the footprints. If people like dragon mythology, then this is probably a stop on the grand world tour of dragon relics. Let's take the next train down to the base."

About an hour later, we were standing in front of an enormous cave. It was cut directly into the light-colored trachyte rock of Drachenfels Hill, a mystery unto itself because caves usually formed when water percolated and carved out the rock over time. I was no hydrologist or geologist, so call it my gut, but the cave just didn't feel natural. Its opening was too round, too ideally situated. It was fifteen feet in diameter, and deep. After only a few feet, the cave features dissolved into complete darkness.

It wasn't easy to find this place. The overgrown trail led us through an old forest, so dense that the leaves and branches seemed to swallow the light, casting a foreboding gloom over the area. It wasn't hard to imagine Hansel and Gretel dancing along the path to a gingerbread house, complete with a witch who dined on children.

We were the only ones here, which was good because we were about to do something that was probably very illegal. There was a rusty old gate blocking the cave entrance, covered with signs proclaiming in various languages the words "Verboten! Kein Eingang! Danger! Stay Out!"

"This looks more like a death trap than a stop on the magical mythical dragon tour," I mused aloud.

Oliphant wrinkled his nose. "Apparently the tour guides haven't correctly sold its attributes to the masses."

"Time to change that," Molly yelled as she ran ahead. I was starting to think that it was her default mode: charge! She pulled at the gate, and it swung open with a groan.

That kid. Here I was, creakin' up a storm, and she was blazing ahead, no holds barred. Youth was not wasted on Molly.

I was a stupid man. Oliphant was going to send her home, and then my big mouth had to open up and argue with him. I mean, she'd been useful. Incredibly so. Weird knowledge of myths, dinosaurs, and apparently Latin. Not something you usually see in a sixteen-year-old. But she was still a teenaged kid. Probably collected Pokemon or Magic cards, like Sarah used to do. Too young to be running around the world, breaking into places she shouldn't, being followed by a man who lied and stole my fossils.

But one question was seriously scaring me: that man on the beach. He had been with Raley. It was obvious we were being followed. If we did send Molly home, would they follow her there? Raley and his people hadn't physically attacked us, but he'd flashed a gun at Molly and me in London. Better to stick together.

In a single file, we squeezed through the gate and walked into the dark cave. Nearly in unison, Molly and I turned on our flashlight apps and walked deeper into the darkness. Oliphant and Sarah walked a few steps behind us. The cave was massive, and our shadows danced on its light-colored walls as we moved.

"Just the right size for a gigantic dragon," Molly said, her words echoing slightly.

"This still doesn't make any sense. There won't be footprints here," Sarah said. "Trace fossils form in sedimentary rock. Footprints, shell casts, impressions on mud. How can that happen in volcanic rock?"

"It can't," Molly said. "But that doesn't mean rocks can't be moved." She had stopped and was staring at the ground.

At our feet was a huge, thick slab of brown rock. Following the slab with my phone's light, I could see that it extended toward the rear of the cave. I could barely make out its end. I knelt before it, noting that it was several feet wide, and about half a foot thick. And, inscribed on its front side were two large, block letters. "S.V." I fingered it gently.

"S.V. strikes again," I said.

Next to me, Molly let out a squeak of excitement. "S.V.! Same person that sent you the package, the one that contained Hawkins's drawing! And in Owen's journal!"

"Yep." I grinned at her.

"This is mudstone," Oliphant said. "Sedimentary rock."

"Look," Molly whispered as she illuminated the surface of the slab. "Footprints!"

Along the surface of the slab were footprints. Four huge footprints. "Look at them," I said, touching one with my finger. "Two toes on the front, two in the back, just like an osprey. And our Montana Monster. Huge, too. Probably over forty inches in length."

Fossilized footprints have always fascinated me. Unlike bones, which showed the moment an animal died, tracks record a moment when the animal lived. They were a Polaroid in time, capturing a monster as it strode across the earth. Was it hunting? Was it just going for a stroll? We'd never really know the answer, but it was fun to speculate and imagine the scene.

"There's more," Oliphant said. I heard his voice at the rear of the cave. From where I was squatting, I could see that he was on his knees, with his cell phone light out. "My God," his voice carried around the cave. "This animal is *landing*. From flight. These footprints started when the animal made contact with the ground."

I joined Molly and Sarah who were squatting next to him. "How can you be sure?" Sarah said.

"There was that discovery in Australia a few years ago, remember? Small Cretaceous-aged bird prints were found near other dinosaur footprints. Some avian paleobiologists asked me to review their paper. The biologists identified a small groove behind one of the footprints. That groove showed the animal had landed, sort of skidded a bit, and then walked away, creating footprints captured in the mud that turned into rock."

He pointed at two long grooves in the mudstone. "There seem to be similar grooves behind this footprint. The next one is closer, like the foot was put down to steady itself. Then, normal stride. And note the distance between each print. Whatever made this was huge." He stood up, hands on his hips. "And it had been flying."

"Dracosauria," said Molly, also standing.

"A giant flying creature," Oliphant said.

I looked down again at the footprints. From this angle, I was watching the creature walk away from me. I could imagine that if locals from centuries ago saw these footprints, they would probably conclude they were made by the dragon described in local legends. Legends that became the tale of Siegfried killing Fafnir.

How in the world did this get here? It was massive. The slab alone was probably sixty feet in length. I walked along it slowly, shining my phone's light along its edge. Wait, it wasn't completely in one piece. There was a crack, right across a footprint. So the same print track, but in two pieces. Much more manageable to move. Okay, but who moved it? And when? Did "S.V." do this? How? This was here when that note in Owen's journal was sent, over a hundred years ago. How could the same person be alive to do this, and also send the Hawkins painting to me in Montana?

"But how does this help us?" Sarah said, throwing her hands up in the air. "We don't really know where these footprints came from. We don't even know that the footprints are real. No responsible scientist would rely upon this as any form of proof that dragons existed." She looked at Oliphant. "You know what, Sean. You'll be laughed out of the Society of Vertebrate Paleontology before you can snap your fingers."

"Well, I doubt that," Oliphant said briskly, but his face seemed troubled.

"Sarah, I know it's frustrating," I said, putting my hand on her shoulder. "But this is another step—another clue. Between the wing in Lyme and this—"

"Honestly, I see a whole lotta nothing." She shrugged her shoulder away from me. Her eyes were hard, and her breath seemed shaky.

"Maybe the journal has more info about this, and we just missed it," Molly said. She took off her backpack and pulled the journal out. As she did, Sarah reached for it.

"No, I'm done," Sarah growled. "Give me the damn thing." She reached for the book.

"Wait!" Molly shouted, clutching the book. The two of them pulled at the book for a moment. Molly's face was etched with complete confusion, a stark contrast to Sarah's red and frustrated appearance. Finally, Sarah pulled hard enough that the book flew from their hands, landing on the cave floor with a loud thud. Pages flew from the journal, like birds escaping a predator.

"What the hell, Sarah?" I snapped, completely shocked. "What's gotten into you?" I walked over to help Molly gather the scattered papers.

"I'm . . . tired, Derek. I'm sorry, Molly." She placed her head in her hands. "Am I really the only one who's wondering if this is a huge waste of time?"

"How are these footprints a waste of time?" I returned.

Sarah gave me an icy stare, then turned and walked toward the entrance without saying another word.

"Look!" Molly shouted. "Look at this!" She held up a drawing of the footprints. "This was glued into the journal, but the adhesive gave away when the book hit the floor. There is more writing on the other side and other drawings, folded under. I didn't see it before."

Molly was practically dancing as she handed the papers to me. "This is the same handwriting as the one on the side with the footprints! It's a letter from a man named Lorenzo Meyer, from Atessa, Italy. Dated 1857. It's in English," Molly continued. "He wrote to Owen—can I see it again?"

I removed the drawings from the letter and handed it back to her. She began to read.

"'Over the years I've heard that you are a learned man with a keen interest in natural objects. Particularly those oddities that cannot be explained by current scientific understanding, but that you wish to rectify. Because of this, I have a great desire to write to you about my family history. Please see the enclosed sketches by my ancestor, Cornelius Meyer.'" Molly paused and pointed to the drawings in my hand.

I separated the drawings, holding one in each hand. The one in my left hand showed a sketch of a mounted dragon skeleton. It was large, with two legs and two wings. A wyvern, as Molly would say. It had a long neck and a very long tail, curved upward in a curlycue. The skull had two horns over its eye sockets, and what looked like a downturned horn on its upper snout. While most of the skeleton was exposed bone, its long neck and wings were covered with scales; its skin looked as if it were in the process of rotting off the skeleton. The drawing in my right hand was the same dragon but visualized as if it were alive in modern times. This dragon, imposing and lifelike, was covered in dark scales and sat on a hillside. Far in the background was a stone bridge crossing a river. Even farther back was a town in the shadow of a mountain.

"'Cornelius published these pictures in 1696 to help secure a contract from the government of Rome. A dragon had been harassing the local villagers, and Cornelius provided these drawings to the government as evidence that he took care of the problem. According to my family's reliable history, he displayed these bones in his home and boasted of his exploit, until . . .'" Molly's voice trailed off as she read the next passage.

"What?" I said.

"'Until he was forced to hide the bones and keep silent because the Order of Saint George had threatened him.' There is a symbol here, at the end of the sentence. It looks like a small ouroboros."

She bit her lip and looked up at me. "The Order. It keeps getting mentioned. Connected with bad things. Not sure if you all have seen it yet, but there is a letter in the journal between Owen and Elizabeth Philpot discussing the landslide Dr. Smith mentioned back in Lyme Regis, the one that nearly killed Mary Anning? Philpot asked why Owen said the landslide wasn't an accident. And there is that letter between Charles Darwin and Richard Owen. About scientific progress. And the Order."

Oh, yes, the Darwin letter in Owen's journal. Molly showed it to me on the flight over. That was quite a surprising and unexpected thing to find. "Molly, can I see the journal for a second?" She handed it to me. I skipped around till I found the letter. I read it aloud:

My dear friend Owen,

I had to write to say that your anonymous review in the Edinburgh Review of my <u>On the Origin of Species</u> *was as cruel in print as we might have hoped. While I dislike asking you to write such horrible things about me and my book, it had to be done. Our enemy will do everything they can to stop us. The Order has woven itself into the very fabric of our scientific society, smashing the advances of men in their efforts to eliminate what they deem to be false idols. We can only trust a select few.*

This is a war we must win. Together, we will destroy the great lie, and preserve what we are now calling Owen's Truth. Ducunt volentem fata, nolentem trahunt.

Yours faithfully,
C. D., 1859

I looked up at the others.

"Darwin believed this Order was trying to destroy scientific progress," said Oliphant. If that other letter from Philpot is true, Owen also believed they would do that by any means necessary. Including murder."

Deep in the cave, a heavy silence settled over us. I read aloud the Latin text above Darwin's signature in his letter again. "'*Ducunt volentem fata, nolentem trahunt.*'"

"'The fates lead the willing and drag the unwilling,'" Oliphant intoned, then he chuckled loudly. "If I didn't know better, I'd say that Darwin and Owen were in cahoots with each other. Not the enemies that history has made them out to be."

Cahoots? Who said that?

"What are you, Dick Tracy?" I said.

"No, I'm Perry Mason. The fact you even know who that is speaks volumes about your advanced age, old man." He smirked.

"You're only a few years younger than I am," I snapped.

"Is there more to Lorenzo's note, Molly?" Oliphant opened his hand toward me, shaking it a little, silently asking for a drawing. Sneering slightly, I gave him the skeleton drawing.

Sarah slowly walked up next to me. Her features were much calmer, but her face was still slightly red, and her hands were shaking a bit. I saw her clench her hands into fists to stop the tremors.

"According to Lorenzo," Molly continued, skimming the letter, "the family believed that Cornelius Meyer hid the bones somewhere in their country home in Atessa, Italy. He died not long after drawing these pictures. At the time, it was rumored that he died protecting the bones. The stories prompted Lorenzo's fascination with dragons. He met others who shared his passion. With their encouragement, he moved to the town of Atessa to be near his family's land. He was delighted to discover dragon mythology was still alive and well in Atessa, specifically at the local church. His interest in dragons eventually led him to visit Germany. 'S.V. told me about the site with

Fafnir's tracks.'" Molly looked up at us. "'S.V.' again? Why be anonymous? Why not just say who 'S.V.' was?"

"Or is," I murmured. After all, they sent me that picture of Owen and the Hawkins painting. I tapped the drawing with my finger. "Take a look at this. Owen wrote on the drawing of the mounted skeleton, see? He wrote *Dracosauria*."

Sarah looked at the drawing I was holding out to the others. "The skull shapes are similar, that is for sure. Different crests, though."

"These are from the *Nuovi Ritrovamenti Divisi in Due Parti* by Cornelius Meyer," said Oliphant. "I knew that name was familiar. Lorenzo's letter said that Cornelius used these pictures to get a contract, correct?" Molly nodded. "Yeah," he continued. "I now recall that Cornelius was a seventeenth-century civil engineer who worked on hydrology projects, like draining the swamps around Rome. The Rome you know today was made possible by Meyer."

"Seriously? You know about these pictures?" Sarah said.

"Yep," replied Oliphant. "A few years ago, I was asked to peer-review an article that argued that the mounted dragon skeleton in the picture was a collection of bones from various animals: mammals, reptiles, and fish. A 'chimera,' if you will. It introduced me to the work of Cornelius Meyer."

Interesting. I wondered whether these were actually the real deal. While there were a few differences, such as the horn on its nose versus the horns on the bottom of its mandible, this skull looked similar to our Montana Monster. And Cornelius had drawn a four-limbed dragon. Most dragon drawings I'd noticed online were dragons with six limbs. Four legs and two wings. Unless you were an insect, six-limbs were impossible. To be fair, there were spiders with eight legs, and some crustaceans like the lobster with ten legs, but insects had six. Our Montana

Monster had two wings and two legs, like this one. They were tetrapods, like mammals and reptiles.

"These bones could be the real deal! Maybe Cornelius was a terrible artist and got the rest of the fossils wrong, or he put bones together wrong," Molly said.

"Perhaps, but it also may be that he simply mixed up modern bones with ancient fossils to bolster his story that he vanquished some creature," Oliphant said.

At that moment, Oliphant's cell phone rang. He held up a finger for silence and answered. "Oliphant. Yeah, just a second." He turned away from us, passed through the gate, and walked toward the surrounding forest.

"What is he doing? He's always on the phone," I snapped.

"Derek," Sarah warned.

"No, open your eyes, Sarah. Here we are, trying to work, and he's probably arranging a book tour! Don't you roll your eyes at me, young lady."

"Oh, leave her alone, Derek. Take your insecurities out on me," Oliphant said, walking back up to us.

"Who was on the phone, Sean? The press? It's business as usual, right?"

"Derek!" Sarah said.

"Okay, old man, keep at it." Oliphant narrowed his eyes at me. I stepped forward.

"What is he talking about?" Molly said, confusion evident on her face.

"This man is a liar and a thief," I said, pointing at Oliphant.

"Derek," Oliphant began. "You shouldn't talk."

"Will you two give it a rest? We're all here for the same thing, right?" Sarah said.

"Are we, Sarah?" I said, exhaustion finally smacking me in the face. "Why are you here?"

My statement hit her right between the eyes. Her shoulders sagged, and her mouth downturned slightly. Her strong hands shook again, and she stretched her long fingers in response.

Sarah-the-minion. Sarah-the-dinosaur-hunter. Sarah-the-scientist. Sarah-the-friend. Heck, Sarah-the-daughter, whom I'd stupidly put right in the middle of my own personal war with Oliphant. My stomach churned. Suddenly, it was as clear as day. I was pushing her away. To Oliphant. I was losing *again* to Oliphant.

"I'm here for the truth, Derek."

Oliphant aside, why is she suddenly positive about this trip? Only a few moments ago she was against it. Why the change? Was it for me?

Molly cleared her throat loudly. "Dracosauria, if we can prove it exists, is enough for all of us."

"I agree," said Oliphant. "Not about the Dracosauria. Well, maybe we'll call it that if we can get a skeleton and describe it, but we need *something* concrete. A skull, or the hip bones. Preferably several specimens. To make this work, we have to do this right." He looked right at me. "Together."

"Can you two stop fighting then?" Molly asked.

I desperately wanted to punch something, but instead I focused my attention on my feet.

"Look, I wasn't on the phone with the press, the BLM, or even the fake BLM. I have some news," Oliphant said gravely. "I was just sent an email by a colleague, and they called to follow up. It had a link to an article from this morning's *London Times*. It's about the Lyme Regis Museum. Here, Molly. Read it to us, please."

"'Lyme Regis Museum looted,'" Molly read aloud. "'Museum officials reported the burglary last night, claiming that while the main part of the museum was untouched, the Mary Anning Wing was ransacked. Museum Director Dr. Leah

Smith said the storage area was also raided. "Whoever broke in destroyed several casts of fossils, and took valuable fossils from our main exhibit as well as our basement."

Anxiety wound itself like a coiled rope in my stomach. My own warehouse was ransacked by Raley's people. Raley was at the Museum in London. Those sinister men at the beach in Lyme Regis. And now this.

"There is an ouroboros symbol on Lorenzo's note, so it is connected to the Order," said Molly, staring out at the forest. "Owen has the symbol in his journal. And I'm almost positive Raley has an ouroboros tattoo on his wrist. I saw it as we were leaving the London Museum."

I nodded. Kinda hoped it was a coincidence, but the evidence was mounting.

"So you think this Order still exists," Sarah said quietly.

"Yeah," I said, kicking the dirt. And I'd bet my fossils, if I still had them, that S.V. still exists, too. Who or whatever that is."

"We need to go to Italy and find the dragon bones described in Lorenzo's note," said Molly, her voice clear and steady. "We know Cornelius had at least a partial skeleton. If we can find these bones, we'll have the best evidence ever. We'll have a skull. We can then put the information out there so that it can't be stolen by Raley. Like a press conference, maybe, Dr. Oliphant? Get pictures all over the internet as quickly as we can?"

"Sure," said Oliphant. "Show the world what we've found."

"That's a long shot. We could also just go back to Montana and dig for one," Sarah said quietly.

"Okay," Molly said. "But you know the chances of finding a dragon—" Sarah cleared her throat and Molly rolled her eyes. "Or a creature like our Montana Monster in the ground is much slimmer. Not impossible, but unlikely. Like a needle-in-a-haystack unlikely."

"Yeah, I know," Sarah muttered.

Italy. I had to agree with the kid. It was the best lead we had. And carnivores, while not rare, were hard to find in the fossil record. You were more likely to find herbivores. If we had a skeleton of a monster like our Montana Monster, like Cornelius Meyer's, that could save years of work.

"One more thing," Oliphant said. "The truth. I wasn't *exactly* lying to Dr. Smith in Lyme Regis. I've been on the phone with my publisher. I've told him that we're trying to find evidence of a new type of species that can rival dinosaurs. And there's already been interest in this, apparently. Film rights for the story. Don't worry. I've been very vague, but I wanted to get the ball rolling. I'm sorry I've been so secretive. He says they will pay our expenses from here. Consider it my contribution to our team's welfare." He clapped his hands together and rubbed them vigorously. "So, how about I purchase some ridiculously expensive plane tickets to Italy?"

Owen's Journal, 1855

Near Konigswinter, Germany—the supposed location of Fafnir. But this connection to Drachenfels Castle must be attended to. The drawings I've been sent are remarkable. And hereto protected.

S.V. is exceptional.

BURIED HISTORY

Molly

ONCE WE HAD left Drachenfels, we went straight to Cologne Airport. After Oliphant purchased our tickets, I had scoured the area for the nearest outlet to our departure gate to charge my phone. There was this young backpacker dude who had his eye on it, but I was quicker. After creating a makeshift camp of airport snacks and water on the floor, I settled in to wait for our flight.

"Can you move over a bit? I need to charge my phone, too," said Sarah. I snapped my head up to look at her. The late afternoon sunlight shone brightly through the large windows across from me, and it backlit her body.

I squirmed to move over and immediately regretted that decision. Ouch. My butt had totally fallen asleep. Wiggling a little more than necessary to wake it up, I settled down, and Sarah sat down next to me. I pulled my phone charger out of the outlet but left the European adapter Oliphant gave me to use. Sarah plugged her own into the wall.

"Thanks."

"No worries. Mine was done anyway."

Sitting crossedlegged on the floor, I picked at the dark, well-worn carpet. My hand grabbed at the gold ring on my necklace, and it glinted as I swung it back and forth, catching the light. My mom's ring. Sometimes I'd find my dad glancing at my necklace, a look of sadness etched on his face. He didn't like to remember her. I wondered what he was doing right now. He was probably puttering around the apartment or in our shared yard, weeding or cursing the voles who kept eating our vegetables.

As Sarah typed on her phone, I gazed around the airport. Even though it was in Europe, it wasn't that different from the United States. It felt familiar: the same typical setup of airports across the world. That was kind of comforting, in a way. It had the same food kiosks, the same magazine and newspaper stands. There was a considerable display of *National Geographic* on the stand closest to me. On each glossy cover was the same picture of a man holding a dinosaur skull on the palm of his hand out in front of him as if holding it out to the world. The man was well-built, with stylish hair, a clean blue shirt, and pressed khakis.

Holy crap, it was Oliphant.

Of course it was.

And just a few yards away stood the man himself, chatting on the phone, while gazing at his own reflection in the tinted airport window.

Out of the corner of my eye, I saw Farnsworth stalking in our direction. I waved to grab his attention, but the magazine stand was brighter and shinier. He stopped and stared at the magazine stand, and his body tensed as he spotted the photographs of Oliphant. He picked up a copy of *National Geographic*, then jerked it away, muttering as he clenched his fist. Finally, he grabbed the only non-Oliphant magazine on display—a magazine about farm tractors. In German. He turned and saw us looking at him. Scowling, he walked to the nearest metal bench and sat down so hard that it shook. He slapped open the magazine on his knees and stared at it, not even turning the pages.

Farnsworth was so angry and distracted at seeing his rival on the cover of the world's most famous magazine that he didn't even realize he just stole a magazine about German farm equipment.

Ever since we left Drachenfels, I'd been dying to ask Sarah about Farnsworth and Oliphant. While they seemed to be allies in this crazy adventure, there was obviously bad blood. It was none of my business, but at the same time, I couldn't help but wonder what happened.

"Sarah, what is the deal with them?" I asked, nodding toward the men.

"Why do you want to know?"

I looked at my feet. "They just seem to really hate one another."

Sarah chuckled.

I turned my head to look at her. "But why?"

"Long story, Molly. It happened years ago."

"Please?"

"It's not a nice story."

"I want to know."

She let out a long sigh and clasped her hands in front of her. "Years ago, Derek and Oliphant were friends. Derek had a good reputation as a successful commercial fossil hunter. But Derek didn't want to be just a commercial hunter. He wanted to publish papers about the fossils he found. To teach people about paleontology."

"His museum?"

"Exactly." Sarah smiled. "Anyway, when Oliphant was just starting out, he knew that Derek was an excellent fossil hunter. He also knew that Derek could access private lands other scientists couldn't. I think they both wanted a mutually beneficial partnership. Oliphant could get to great fossil localities, Derek could gain respectability.

"That changed when an old client of Derek's in Montana showed him some fossils she had found on her ranchland during the winter," Sarah said, looking away from me. "They were eggshells."

"Wait," I said, feeling bile rising from my stomach. "Eggshells in Montana. You don't mean Nest Valley?"

"Yeah. Nest Valley." She wiped her nose with her wrist. "Derek invited Oliphant to see the site with him in early spring. Realizing that they had just discovered the first dinosaur eggs in North America, they agreed to dig together. They'd decided to start in early summer because Derek had other commitments in South America. However, according to Derek, Oliphant struck an inside deal with the landowner to dig in the spring and brought out his own crew. Digging in the melting snow was difficult, but before Derek knew anything was wrong, Oliphant already identified several nests and arranged for the PR campaign. It effectively cut Derek out of the find."

I rubbed my eyes as I absorbed this information. Nest Valley. Oliphant's famous dig. He discovered not just egg nests, but fossils demonstrating the entire life cycle of *Triceratops*. He found fossils from birth until adulthood. It was a game-changer. Until Nest Valley, there was hardly any evidence that dinosaurs cared for their young. The find made Oliphant's academic career and also catapulted him to broader stardom in the media. Farnsworth definitely wasn't in the story I read about.

"I had no idea," I said quietly.

"Why would you? It's now a rumor more than anything. Oliphant denies it, but Derek says he somehow got the landowner to shut up. She probably didn't want to get involved. Anyway, this was over twenty years ago. She's not around to contradict the story."

"So why are you working with Oliphant?"

Sarah gave me a long, appraising look. "He's not all bad, Molly. You're too young to get this, but everybody makes mistakes. Even good people."

Farnsworth could have had a very different life if the cards had fallen another way.

"That was the first dig I was ever on," I said.

"What do you mean?" she asked.

"There is an established field camp at Nest Valley, did you know?"

She nodded. "Yeah, I went once a few years ago for a few days. Oliphant wanted me to see it."

"Well, they have a youth program, and when I was fourteen, my dad arranged for me to attend. We don't have a lot of money, and they agreed to give me a scholarship."

I smiled at the memory. Then the weight of Sarah's story hit me again, settling in my stomach like a block of ice. "It's hard to believe that I worked at the place that triggered their fight."

"Derek thinks of all paleontologists as pirates," Sarah said. "He has a point. Pirates aren't nice, Molly. Oliphant seized an opportunity. Maybe Derek understood that might happen, maybe not. Now is a different story—both of them are extremely skilled paleontologists. Don't hate Oliphant for the past. Derek and Oliphant both have their share of fame. They just approach things a little differently."

I looked up to find that Farnsworth was standing above us, his large arms crossed over his chest. He'd taken off his hat, and his dark hair was sticking up at all angles again.

Sarah sighed. "Derek, it was a very long time ago. He's changed."

"Like a leopard can change his spots?" Farnsworth snorted in response.

"That's right. People change," Oliphant said loudly, walking over. I wonder how much these guys overheard.

Farnsworth's face reddened as he barked, "Seriously, Sean? Just how have you changed? By butting in on our discovery of the Monster?"

"No, by taking on your understudy as a protégé."

"Oh, so you agreed to work with Sarah because you felt guilty?" Farnsworth said.

"Hey!" Sarah said, looking indignant.

"No. What I mean is— Sarah, you are extremely talented. My team is lucky to have you. Having you at my University has been great."

Sarah glanced away.

"Okay, let's do this here and now. Let's get the cards on the table," Oliphant said, more to himself than us. He looked Farnsworth in the eye. "Derek, look, I know you're still angry."

Farnsworth glared at him.

"And you have every reason to be." Oliphant paused. "I was a stupid kid, and I'm not that much smarter now. Look, we can't change the past," Oliphant said in a more professional tone. "I admit that I was focused too much on my career. It's a competitive world, and I didn't want to wait. I thought taking on Sarah would help with what happened."

Farnsworth gave Oliphant a look not unlike the look a lion gives a zebra before he pounces. Oliphant moved back slightly.

"You're apologizing now?" Farnsworth finally said.

"No. Yes. Well, I'm trying to. But it's hard. It's been over twenty years, Derek. Don't you think it's time we buried the rock hammer, as it were?"

"Twenty years too late, Sean," Farnsworth said.

"Why?" I nearly shouted, slapping my hand against the thinly carpeted floor. The two startled men turned to look at me. A few other passengers also glanced my way.

Slightly embarrassed, I lowered my voice. "Look, can't you just let it go? We may have a chance here. We've got to do this together."

"You say that like it's nothing," Farnsworth said in a low voice.

"It's not *nothing*, Derek," Sarah said gently. "But she's right. Fighting with each other is only making this harder." She stood up, rubbing a cramp from her leg. She took a jerky step toward the men, still working the heel of her hand into her leg, wincing slightly. "What matters now is that we work together—as a team. That means you two have to stop fighting."

Farnsworth grunted. "Easier said than done, Sarah."

"Why? Why is it so hard for you? Sean is willing to move on. He apologized!"

"He didn't have his entire life destroyed!"

"No, Derek, but neither did you," Oliphant said, his gaze unwavering.

"What do you mean?" Farnsworth said.

"I mean, look at yourself, Derek. You might not be famous in academic circles, but you're famous in your own right," Oliphant said, taking a step closer to Farnsworth. "Everyone knows museums call you all the time for help, or if they want to train staff for digs. Heck, my department head at the University often asks me to coordinate with you!"

"I must have missed that call," Farnsworth snarled.

"No, you're right. I never called."

Farnsworth looked at him incredulously. "You gotta be kidding me. So you're still cutting me out of work?"

Oliphant's eyes flicked toward Sarah. Just as he opened his mouth, the loudspeaker announced in German and English that our flight was boarding.

"Look, we have to get on that plane," Sarah said. She looked at Oliphant and Farnsworth. "Can you both calm down? I'd rather not get thrown off the flight. You two can duke it out in Italy."

"Let's go," Farnsworth said stiffly, moving toward the gate.

After a deep breath, Sarah reached down for her backpack. As she did, it tilted to one side, and its contents spilled out. As I reached down to help her gather her belongings, I saw a large orange pill bottle roll away. I grabbed it and handed it back to her. As she took it from me, she looked down, embarrassed.

Oliphant looked at Sarah for a long moment. He'd seen the bottle, too. He opened his mouth a bit, like he wanted to ask her about it, but didn't. "Time to board," he said, turning toward the ticket counter. Spotting the magazine stand, he chuckled. "That turned out well, didn't it?" he said, pointing to *National Geographic*.

Without a word, Sarah walked toward the airplane gate.

THE ITALIAN JOB

Molly

NASCAR LOST OUT when Oliphant chose paleontology as his career. As we drove toward Atessa at ninety miles per hour, I was seriously wondering if he had a death wish. He treated the other cars on the highway as if they were obstacles in a video game, zipping and braking around. He'd nearly crashed into one car.

"Ciao, Bella!" Oliphant laughed, looking at me in the rear-view mirror. "When in Rome, Molly, do as the Romans do. In this case, drive like a maniac."

Atessa, as it turned out, was a small village on the eastern side of Italy in the Chieti province of the Abruzzo region. Since this was my first time in Italy, I'd basically glued my nose to the car window and took it all in. Italy was stunning. Yellow-colored hills covered in flowing grasses were punctuated with picturesque buildings. The occasional vineyard poured around these obstacles, brown stalks and vines heavy with green leaves.

Sarah seemed just as nervous about Oliphant's driving as I was. Her hands curled around her armrests, knuckles white. Farnsworth wasn't fazed though; instead his eyes were on his phone. Since we arrived in Italy, he'd been scouring the internet for the dragon connection Lorenzo Meyer mentioned in his note. According to a few websites, in ancient times, a man named Leucio, Bishop of Brindisi, was asked to deal with a dragon that was terrorizing the area. After supposedly subduing it with just his enormous willpower—aka his massive ego—he killed it.

"'According to the legend, the local church is built over the dragon's lair,'" Farnsworth read aloud. He let out a barking laugh. "Dragon bone, my behind. Here is Atessa's dragon bone rib." He turned the phone's screen toward me and used his fingers to enlarge the picture. On a red velvet stand sat a large, brown fossil. It was cylindrical, curving slightly to form a sharp point at one end. The other end looked broken, as if it was detached violently from its owner.

I narrowed my eyes at the picture. "But that's just—"

"A mammoth tusk. Definitely not a dragon bone," said Farnsworth. He passed his phone to Sarah, who held it up for Oliphant. Oliphant shook his head and turned back to look at the road.

"According to the story, Saint Leucio himself pulled it from the dragon," said Farnsworth.

"You mean from Pliocene sediments in the area, about two to five million years in age," Oliphant said. "So the time of early hominids, like Lucy the *Australopithecus*."

"Yeah. Anyway, even though it's quite old, apparently it was 'rediscovered' about three hundred years ago by a parish member. He claimed he found it while hunting deer," Farnsworth paraphrased as he read.

"It's geomythology at its best," I said. Creating myths to describe natural phenomena. But something Farnsworth said made me pause. "That rib was supposedly brought to the church three hundred years ago? Wasn't that the time that Cornelius Meyer disappeared in Atessa with his own dragon fossil?"

Farnsworth slowly nodded. "Yeah, I think it was."

Maybe there was a connection.

The Meyer estate was only a few miles northwest of Atessa. We drove through spikey, wrought iron gates down a gravel driveway. There was a large pile of stone ruins at its end. Next to the ruins was an impressive, modern-looking building with orange roof tiles, white walls, and a brown front door. As we parked, a young woman exited the building and headed for our car. A caretaker, maybe?

Since Oliphant spoke a little Italian, we sent him out as our ambassador. He could charm a scale off a snake; I hoped he could get us some new intel on where we might even start looking for Meyer's long-lost dragon fossils. Who knows, maybe she'd tell him all the deep dark secrets of the Meyer family, and we'd have our dragon skeleton in the next ten minutes.

While Oliphant talked to the woman, Sarah, Farnsworth, and I walked slowly along one of the many gravel trails cutting through the estate. It was enormous, with tall yellow grass punctuated with oak trees as far as I could see. The entire area was mostly flat, except for a weird hill in the distance, maybe less than a mile away. I wondered what could have caused that. It just felt a little off. Not natural.

I looked at the pamphlets the woman handed me before we walked away. What was clear from the pictures was that we could rent the property for weddings. Since the text was written in Italian, the other information was a little more challenging to decipher, and Farnsworth and Sarah gave up immediately. However, one of the benefits of taking Latin as my language credit was that it was the foundation of the romance languages, including Italian. Lots of similarities, and I was sorta proud of myself for being able to read a bit of it.

According to the brochure, the estate had been in the Meyer family for centuries, only recently opened to the public as a museum and event venue. In the early 1700s, there was a terrible fire that destroyed the entire property. For some reason, the family never repaired the ancient Roman villa that existed before the fire. Maybe they weren't around often enough to want to rebuild, or they just didn't care.

I heard a small crack and looked up. Sarah was throwing pebbles from a small pile in her hand toward the ground. From her hunched stance and scrunched-up face, I'm pretty sure she was back to pondering whether coming here was a stupid waste of time.

I was worried about her. I really liked her. I hadn't known her that long, but she seemed to be a kind, honest person. And a good boss. Farnsworth and Oliphant both trusted her, and from our conversations, it was obvious she was passionate about dinosaurs. About paleontology.

But ever since England, she had been hot and cold. I thought that finding the truth about a potential fossil dragon would be amazing. Or even just discovering a huge new carnivorous dinosaur. I figured she'd want to work hard to prove exactly what it was. Be supportive of its discovery, no matter the strange journey we'd have to take to get there.

But instead, one minute she was all about it, another she was yelling at us that we needed to go home. What was going on?

Of course, Oliphant and Farnsworth were not helping. She was clearly stuck in the middle of two strong personalities. I bet it was hard for Sarah not to feel overwhelmed and frustrated between these two men. Plus, worrying about me wasn't helping.

As if she'd heard my thoughts, Sarah raised her head. She walked over to me, put her arm over my shoulders, and gave me a squeeze. "How are you holding up?"

"I'm okay. Tired. Wondering where someone would keep a dragon skeleton in a place like this."

"Maybe it's in the storage room." She giggled, nodding to the pile of rubble near us.

I glanced over my shoulder. Oliphant was walking toward us. I caught his eye, and he shook his head.

"Long shot anyway. Let's keep moving."

Farnsworth walked in step with me, his eyes scanning the estate. He started as his eyes fell on the large odd-looking hill of dirt I noticed when we arrived, and he plowed off the path toward it. I followed, unsure of where else to go. The grass gently rustled as it brushed against my legs.

As we walked, I turned to Farnsworth. I had to say something. The last time I brought this up was in Lyme Regis, and the adults basically dismissed me. *Inspector Poirot*, whatever that meant.

But a lot had happened since Lyme Regis.

I took a deep breath. "Do you believe what Darwin wrote in that letter to Owen? About the Order being everywhere? Do you believe they would . . . kill to stop people from learning about science, like evolution? Or even dragons?"

Farnsworth didn't look at me. "I don't know," he said. "Maybe. People have killed for less. If this Order was threatened by scientific progress, then maybe."

"But evolution is fact," I said.

"Well, now it is. You have to remember, Molly, times were very different back then. For centuries, people were taught since birth to believe that God's power controls everything, down to the smallest decision. Even as late as the nineteenth century, the great scientific minds were devoutly religious men. Take William Buckland, for example. He was one of the greatest paleontologists ever, but he was also an Anglican priest. To Buckland, science was a part of natural theology. Species were static and fixed, and any differences between species were God's plan to deal with local conditions. Humans, well, they were made in God's image, so no reason for change."

"I guess I can see that, but if the Order is still around, why are they threatened now?" That seemed kind of stupid. Evolution was widely discussed and accepted. Heck, I started to learn about evolution and Darwin way back in elementary school.

Farnsworth sighed. "I'm not sure, but my guess is the old standby: that people fear losing power and control. Ignorance is a tried-and-true strategy for controlling people. Maybe the Order still believes it's their duty to stop other scientific revolutions. Maybe there is a money angle, or they just need to control and shape the world."

"Scary," I said.

Farnsworth nodded. "Yup. Zealots are always frightening, religious or not."

"I just don't understand how anyone could still be tied to some old religious idea. You can't ignore evolution just because you don't like it."

"It's hard to deal with people who want to stay ignorant. *But*, I do think that, at a minimum, our job as scientists is to explain phenomena so that people without our background can clearly understand it. If we still have doubters, it means two things. One, we've failed those who are logical because we were not clear enough in arguing our finds. In that case, we need to do a better job. Or two, they are idiots who do not want to change, no matter the evidence right in front of them."

He shrugged as if shaking the weight of the world's stupidity off his shoulders. "It was the same problem, back in Darwin's day. The logical thinkers wanted to see the evidence. It caused a lot of fights. Darwin's book, *On the Origin of Species*, was popular. He participated in debates to discuss his theories and encouraged his supporters to do the same. They were exciting events. One such friend was Sir Thomas Huxley." Farnsworth chuckled. "He was a crazy man who loved to argue with anyone who didn't believe in evolution."

"Thomas Huxley?" I asked. "Oliphant mentioned him before in London. He's also mentioned in Owen's journal too, connected with that acronym 'S.V.' we keep seeing, on things like your package, or on that slab of mudstone in Drachenfels."

"That's right," Farnsworth replied. "Huxley was known as Darwin's 'bulldog.' He famously debated with a man named Wilberforce in the 1860s about evolution. And guess who coached Wilberforce . . . ?"

"Owen?" I said, my mouth twitching. Wilberforce. Why was that name also familiar?

"Yep. Wilberforce was a bishop of the Anglican Church. He believed that all creatures of the world were designed to perfection by a Divine hand. As an opponent of evolution, Owen supported Wilberforce. In fact, when Darwin published his book, Owen immediately wrote an anonymous, scathing review."

"Sorry to interrupt," said Sarah from behind us. "But everyone knew that Owen wrote that review, and the two became highly public rivals for the rest of their lives. Owen famously debated Huxley too, about human ancestry and our evolutionary connection to apes."

"But notes in the journal suggest a different relationship, a hidden friendship perhaps," said Oliphant.

I nodded. "Yeah. I think you were right at Drachenfels, Dr. Oliphant. They seemed to be working together." I pulled out the journal from my backpack and flipped to the page that held Darwin's note to Owen. "This was sent in 1859. When was *On the Origin* written? It talks about an anonymous review."

"Same year," Farnsworth said, looking over my shoulder as we walked. "1859."

My mind was whirling, and I broke away from the others, not looking where I was going. I could hear them behind me, their legs swishing the grass. "Maybe they both realized that the Order was trying to stop them, to stop scientific progress," I said, thinking out loud. "The world was changing, right?" I turned back to the group.

"Sometimes relationships are not what they seem," Sarah said.

"It does make sense," said Oliphant. "By attacking each other in public, they ensured that people discussed evolution, and as a related subject, dinosaurs and other prehistoric animals."

"Power of the press," said Farnsworth. "The average person wouldn't read an article in a scientific journal, but they would read an article in *The Times*. Debates between Huxley and Wilberforce, and later Owen and Huxley, got a lot of press, particularly in London. Those articles would probably have been translated all over the world."

I recalled what I read in the journal, and I was struck by an idea. "Maybe Owen also fought Darwin in public to keep him safe. If Owen and Darwin made sure that the theory of evolution was talked about everywhere, it could protect Darwin."

"Protected Darwin from whom, the Order? Why not just kill him to shut him up?" Sarah said.

Farnsworth slowly nodded. "That strangely makes sense, Molly. It would be harder to kill someone famous than a nobody. Not impossible, as history has shown, but definitely harder. Darwin would be surrounded by people after *Origin* was released, powerful people who would demand that he give presentations on his work."

Oliphant let out a loud laugh. "Owen publicly toed the party line, all the while secretly promoting evidence that challenged the Church. It makes for a great story. The villain is actually a hero."

"And maybe they were working together to make sure nobody else got hurt," I said. "I gotta show you something." I pulled Darwin's 1859 letter from the journal and turned it around.

"I found this drawing last night. After discovering the drawings on the back of Lorenzo's letter, I'd wondered if there was anything else glued on the back of other letters. Well, there was."

Everyone leaned forward to examine the paper I held out. On the back of the letter was a drawing of a spinal column, horribly bent. Underneath was a note in Darwin's handwriting: *Remember your old friend Mantell. The enemy did this. They can kill you, too.* Next to the spinal column was a drawing of an ouroboros.

"Why didn't you show us earlier?" Oliphant barked.

"I was going to . . ." I trailed off. "Honestly, it scared me. When you're looking at a picture of someone's spine with the words 'they can kill you too,' well . . . it freaked me out. Even if this happened over a hundred years ago. Plus, we saw that same spine floating in the jar in Owen's office." Gross.

"This note implies that the Order killed Gideon Mantell," Farnsworth said, his voice hard. "Perhaps Mary Anning . . . maybe even Elizabeth Philpot."

"Assuming our new theory is true . . ." Oliphant trailed off, his hand stroking his chin. "Perhaps Owen was too young when the Order turned on Mantell, Anning, and Philpot. I mean, Owen was not yet that prominent when they died. Maybe he couldn't save them because he didn't yet have the right connections."

"But why kill them?" Sarah asked.

"Maybe Mantell discovered something that threatened the Order," Oliphant said. "He unearthed the Isle of Wight dragon mentioned in Owen's journal. That could have been it. Anning could have been a threat because she came across that Dracosauria wing. Maybe she stumbled upon other fossils too. And Philpot was Anning's best friend. Maybe she knew too much."

The question we'd asked ourselves repeatedly hung over me, so I voiced it aloud. "Why not publish the evidence of Dracosauria? Wouldn't that ensure everyone's safety? Why would a dragon be any different than a dinosaur?"

"Not a dragon, Molly," Oliphant said, putting his hand over his face and looking toward the sky.

"A flying animal with black bones, Dr. Oliphant!" I snapped. "Explain that! Maybe something about the fact they breathed fire—"

"Coincidence and speculation! A weird geologic phenomenon! Animals don't breathe fire!" He threw up his hands in exasperation.

"Dragons, Dracosauria, new species of Cretaceous-aged animal . . . let's just continue for now," Farnsworth said, stepping between us, like a boxing referee. "Sean?"

Looking a bit astonished at Farnsworth's attempt at peacemaking, Oliphant continued, "Maybe Owen needed more evidence. Like us. He had plenty of dinosaur fossils to withstand criticism. Three species, remember? *Iguanodon*, *Megalosaurus*, and *Hylaeosaurus*. But why didn't he even publish what he had, well . . ." He trailed off, his voice unsure. "In any event, maybe the Order made sure he didn't have enough of the specimen or specimens to do his job."

Around us, the wind gently caressed the grass into rolling waves. We were almost at the hill I saw earlier. There was a flat slab of stone with several irregularly shaped, soccer-ball-sized rocks at the base on one side of the hill. The rest of the hill was covered with grass and small shrubs.

That strange hill. Suddenly it hit me. I knew what that hill was—a tumulus. I remembered reading about them in *Scientific American*. They could be found all over the world. They vary in size and shape, but they were usually the grave of a prominent ancient person or a family. Some were just mounds of dirt or stones. Others could have a room for bodies or treasures.

I started walking toward it, and Farnsworth joined me. Oliphant and Sarah were several steps behind us, so I walked a little faster to put some space between us.

"Can I ask you something?"

"Sure, kid."

My palms were sweaty, and I bit the inside of my cheek. The words I wanted to say wouldn't come, so I tried a different route. "Are you worried about how the Order seems to know where we are?"

"Well, we don't know if they knew that we were in Germany or that we're here," he said.

"But Montana, and then England. They also destroyed the Museum in Lyme Regis! They were at two places that had real Dracosauria evidence. I wouldn't be shocked if those dragon footprints—"

"You're wondering if they are tracking us?"

I took a deep breath. "Do you think Oliphant is with the Order?"

"What?" Farnsworth stopped. Sarah and Oliphant had fallen far behind, out of earshot.

"I mean, you're so angry with each other, and he's always on the phone. I trust you and Sarah, but Oliphant . . . He stole from you."

Farnsworth turned to me, and his face was severe. "You don't really believe that."

I immediately looked down at my feet, and I felt a blush creeping onto my cheeks. That wasn't the response I expected.

"Well, sorta. They do keep finding us." I knew it was a leap, but they seem to be just one short step behind us, breathing down our necks.

"You could say the same thing about Sarah or me," Farnsworth pointed out.

"You're not that type. Annoying, sure, but with Oliphant's past . . ."

Farnsworth chuckled. I looked up at his face. His head was tilted gently to the side and he had a small smile on his lips. "Annoying, huh?" He gently grabbed my arm to get me walking again. "No, Oliphant's not Order. He's a jerk, and he's been fast and loose taking credit other people deserve, but no, he's not a traitor to science."

I grimaced at the word. *Traitor.*

His voice was low and gentle. "Molly, no matter what I say when I'm angry, I'm positive he's okay. Sean might sell his mother for the publicity or some award, but he wouldn't ever destroy a fossil. Think of the bone bed in Montana. He'd never do that. Paleo is his life. Just like it's mine."

"But—"

"Sarah trusts him, and that's all I need. You can trust family."

"Family?"

"Sure. I mean Sarah's practically my kid."

"I wondered about you two."

"Her dad was my best friend in high school. When she was about six years old, her parents asked me to take her out with me fossil hunting. She became my minion."

"A daughter," I said, grinning.

Farnsworth turned to look at her, and Sarah waved, still speaking quietly with Oliphant.

"It's been hard to have her away at school, but I don't want her to just be a fossil hunter. I love my job, but academia is the better way to go—less drama, more respectability." He sighed deeply. "In some ways, Oliphant is a good mentor for her. He can give her what I couldn't."

Suddenly it clicked. All that anger. Oliphant wanted forgiveness, but Farnsworth couldn't. It was not just about reputation or careers, or even money.

No. Farnsworth was afraid he lost something even more precious. He was worried he lost Sarah. She left their life in Montana for Oliphant, his worst enemy. While her reasons may have made sense, and he supported her, that must have really hurt.

"You haven't lost her," I said.

He looked away, but not before I saw his eyes glisten. He looked back at me. "What about you? What's your family like?"

"Well, Mom left when I was a kid. All I have left of her is this ring." I held up my necklace, and the gold glistened brightly. "And my *Dragons of the World* book. She used to read it to me and tell me that dinosaurs were distant cousins of dragons. She had no idea how right she would end up being. It's just Dad and me now. He works a lot, but he's very supportive of me. Of all this."

"That's good. What we do isn't easy—being away from home for long periods, hard work in the sun. It's nice to have someone in your corner."

"Yeah."

"I'm sorry about your mom. That's rough."

"Thanks."

"Molly," Farnsworth said, his voice soft. "What you're doing here, with us, well, we're all impressed. You're like Mary

Anning. She also had it rough, but she kept going and really changed the world. You will too, if you keep at it. Hopefully, this Monster, this Dracosauria, is your moment."

"Yours, too." I playfully punched his shoulder. "Finally turned to the dark side, huh?"

"I have no idea what you mean," he said with a grin.

That's when I saw it. Over his shoulder, at the base of the tumulus.

The skull.

I sprinted to the tumulus. "Look at this," I shouted. I stood next to a large flat slab of rock on its side, leaning against the mound. At its base were smaller boulders, one in particular that took on a very familiar shape.

"What?" Farnsworth asked as he trotted up to me, catching his breath.

"See those crumbled statues on the ground? Take a look. Look at this one. It looks like a skull of a—"

"Hey, now. Dragons!"

Letter between Charles Darwin and Sir Richard Owen, 1860

My dearest Owen,

I am very grateful that you supported Bishop Sam Wilberforce during that fantastic debate against Thomas Huxley. It is important that we keep up appearances. You might recall that I informed Huxley and others that I was too sick to attend the discussion, but I managed to disguise myself to see the debate. My favourite part was when Wilberforce asked whether Huxley believed that his great-great-grandfather was once an ape or gorilla. And Huxley's response! To quote, he said

"I would not be ashamed to have a monkey for an ancestor, but I would be ashamed to connect him to someone who uses his talents to hide the truth. *Ducunt volentem fata, nolentem trahunt.* The fates lead the willing and drag the unwilling." After those words were spoken, I gazed around the crowded room and was greatly pleased to see more than one face slack with anger and horror.

Ever yours,
C. Darwin July 2, 1860

Post Scriptum—S.V. will meet next month. I shall forward you details as soon as possible. As the expert, we will follow your lead about when Dracosauria's secret should be divulged. Were you able to acquire that sample we discussed?

INSIDE THE TUMULUS

Oliphant

IT WAS LATE in the afternoon, and the sun had just started its descent into the horizon. This part of the day was what photographers called the golden hour, when the light was just right and it cast a dewy glow on its subjects.

The Meyer estate was huge, and all the walking was making me hungry. Not to mention sweaty. While it was very beautiful, it looked like every other Italian estate I've ever seen: a Mediterranean landscape of grasses, shrubs, oak trees, and vineyards in the distance. If you've seen one, you've seen them all.

But at least we had found something that was a bit promising.

In front of me were broken marble dragon statues. Pieces of their bodies were scattered in front of the dirt mound. Some of the shapes were familiar: a wing, a claw, a skull with horns. Other parts were just mounds of white-gray rock, some weathered so badly that I couldn't make out what they were supposed to be. I touched one of the rocks and a fine layer of marble dust rubbed off on my finger.

Marble was notoriously strong. Many buildings and sculptures around the world were made of marble because it was a metamorphic rock that could take a beating. Something happened here to cause this kind of damage to these statues.

In front of me was a massive mound of dirt, at least a story high. It was covered in the same brown-yellow grasses as the rest of this place, but it was obviously not a natural formation—the surrounding terrain was as flat as a pancake. The closest hills were miles away. There was a large slab of light-colored rock decorated with geometric designs set into the side of the hill. Earlier, the caretaker had told me there was a tumulus on the property that was used as the burial place for an Etruscan family. If this was it, the hill was hollow inside, and this was the door to the burial chamber.

"This looks like a good bet," Farnsworth said.

"Once again, Derek, I thank you for confirming the obvious," I said. Molly shot me an annoyed look, and I returned it with a smirk. Flippancy aside, something was nagging me. We knew Lorenzo never foundCornelius's dragon remains. How come Lorenzo never checked the tumulus for the dragon? Seemed like a rather logical place to look, what with the dragon statues practically screaming, *Come look inside me!*

"Tumulus, right?" Sarah asked the group. "It's a clever idea—hiding bones in an underground crypt. People are generally respectful enough not to disturb a family gravesite, aside from grave robbers. Maybe Cornelius hid his bones here thinking that they would be protected."

I knelt down and looked closer at the statue's remains. Some of the pieces were very weathered, their exposed areas crumbling under even a gentle touch. Yet other parts looked relatively intact. "Maybe something fell down onto the statues, breaking them apart."

"Or someone broke them?" Molly said. "We don't know for sure that the tumulus was never opened. Maybe it was, and now it's empty."

"So you don't want to check?" Farnsworth said skeptically.

"Well, duh, of course I do," she replied.

"Can we please focus here?" Sarah flared. I turned to look at her, surprised by the outburst. She was staring at the tumulus door, rubbing her hands on her legs. Her body rocked gently from one foot to another.

I was worried about Sarah. Her outbursts and emotional swings were becoming more prevalent. That pill bottle. She could be suffering from anxiety or depression. More than most, I knew what a difficult path she'd chosen. Obviously, I'd had my share of good fortune. These days I hardly noticed the accolades or the money people threw at me, or the invitations to join boards, media interviews, or the movie-consulting gigs. And let's not forget the honorary degrees.

But Sarah was still trying to find her breakthrough moment. I was helping her, of course, but that only took a person so far.

"So, I guess we know what's next," Molly said, her eyes alight with excitement.

"What, breaking and entering?" Farnsworth smirked.

Molly shrugged. "We've done it in every other country we've visited. Why change now?"

She turned toward the marble slab and pushed her body against it. After a few seconds of watching her struggle, I stepped in to help her. Farnsworth moved to her other side. "On three: one . . . two . . . three!" As one, we pushed and pulled at the door, but it didn't budge.

"Shocking that a three-hundred-pound marble door doesn't want to move," Sarah said, shaking her head. She looked around and then started walking toward a nearby oak tree. When she reached it, she scoured the ground. She returned with two large branches. "Physics 101. Simple levers."

I laughed and helped dig two little channels beneath the marble door. We wedged the branches under the door. Together, Molly and Sarah pushed down on the branches, and slowly the door rose and shifted a bit. Farnsworth and I then pushed and guided the slab far enough away to expose part of the tunnel underneath. As it moved, I heard a slight whooshing sound as fresh air rushed into the tumulus. Finally, we backed away. In front of us was a hole large enough for us to squeeze through, especially if we all sucked in our guts.

Molly reached into her backpack and grabbed her cell phone. A blink later and she'd tossed her backpack into the tunnel and squeezed past the door into the darkness.

"There she goes again," Farnsworth said with a hint of admiration.

I took a deep breath and sucked my own gut in, swearing to go on a diet when I got home. I wiggled through the small entryway, ducking into a low squat so I didn't hit my head on the roof. Ahead of me was Molly's back, her flashlight illuminating the brownish-red, earthen walls of the tumulus. I shone my own phone's flashlight toward the wall and touched it as I walked by. It seemed to be made of a mixed mortar material, a combination of mud, sand, and small stones. However, there were also streaks of black. They reminded me of that ash you'd find around a well-used campfire.

After about twenty feet, we walked into a much larger, open room. It was circular in shape, with several columns constructed of the same rock-mud mortar material that I saw in the tunnel. They didn't look all that sturdy. I leaned closer to one and saw that the same black material that was in the tunnel also covered these columns. There were long tube-like holes in the columns, with more black ash.

Scorch marks. There was a fire in here at some point. As my eyes adjusted to what dim light our phones provided, I saw dark ash lines along the ceiling and walls too. I guessed that these were wooden support beams that the ancient Etruscans used to buttress the tumulus walls and ceiling, later burned away in some fire. Didn't look very sturdy.

I didn't feel very safe. I really hoped some cow didn't decide to walk on the tumulus for its afternoon snack. This whole thing might come crashing down on us—what a way to die.

All around us, cut into the walls of the tumulus were small alcoves. Except for an empty alcove to the right of the entrance, each alcove was filled with relics. Some contained stone busts of a person, their dignified eyes watching their gravesite intruders. Others included small artifacts on stone tables, or rocks of various shapes.

But what caught my eye was in the middle of the room. Right in the center, stacked into a giant heap, were fossils. Glossy, black fossils.

Molly crouched next to a giant skull. It was nowhere near as large as our Montana Monster's skull, but it was still huge—probably three feet in length. Two large horns rose above the black eye sockets. I reached over and touched its teeth, immediately feeling their sharpness. The serrations on their sides.

Holy shit, I thought. *It's a damn dragon.*

Grow up, Sean. There's no such thing.

"Let's compare," Molly said, her voice carrying throughout the room. I turned to look and saw that she was holding up a large white tooth. "It's from our Montana Monster."

"That's the plaster cast of the tooth Sarah found last spring," Farnsworth said. "You had it with you this whole time, Molly?"

"Yeah. I grabbed it back at the warehouse before Raley's goons nabbed it. I mean, I thought it could come in handy if we found another tooth. I didn't want to leave it in Montana."

"Fantastic," Sarah said. "I need it." Molly handed it to her.

"I can see verts, leg bones, arm bones, wings, the same pterosaur-like hip structure . . . This could be an articulate specimen," Farnsworth said, slowly walking around the pile of bones.

"You've done it," Sarah said. "You've found an actual Dracosauria."

"Dragon! Not a dinosaur." Molly beamed at Sarah. She then turned to me. "And black bones, Dr. Oliphant!"

Yep. Black bones. Just like the others. I leaned down to pick up one of the fossils—a foot bone. It was small and had a familiar shape, one I've seen thousands of times. But the bone was smooth and much lighter than I'd expected. What was going on with these fossils?

"No, not a dinosaur," Sarah agreed in a low voice. "It's too bad we don't know exactly where it came from."

But it was a good start. We could glean a lot of information just from the bones. We could at least start the process of describing this creature.

"Where did it come from?" Sarah repeated to herself, staring at the animal skull. "It's just such a jumble. If it's not complete, I wonder if more of it is still out there."

"Well, it wasn't uncommon during the Renaissance for rich families to display fossils in their homes," Farnsworth said. "Maybe it came from around here. Or maybe from around Rome. Who knows."

I pulled out the brochure the docent foisted on me when we'd first arrived. "Indeed. The Meyer compound belonged to a wealthy Tuscan family before the Meyer family purchased it three hundred years ago."

"Did you say three hundred years ago?" Molly asked.

"Yes," I replied.

"Huh. That was when the Atessa dragon fossil showed up, according to the church website."

"That was a mammoth bone," I said.

"Yeah, but did you notice? In the nooks around us? There are other fossils."

I turned around and walked over to the nearest alcove. Sure enough, I saw a fossilized mammoth foot bone placed next to a beautiful clay urn. Looking around, other alcoves held fossils or artifacts, save one. The largest alcove near the entrance had an empty pedestal.

Okay, I got what Molly meant: perhaps we were not the first visitors to this tomb in the last three hundred years. I wonder why they never came back? There was a ton of treasure in this room.

"Oh no," Farnsworth said, his tone strained.

"What's wrong?" Molly asked. That's when she gasped.

I rushed over and looked down. At our feet was a human body.

THE FATE OF CORNELIUS MEYER

Oliphant

CORNELIUS MEYER. AFTER so long, I would have expected a skeleton. Instead, I was staring at the man's face. His skin was pulled taut across his cheeks. His hair was still dark and wavy and was covered with a velvet cap.

Next to me, Sarah gagged, and Farnsworth reached over to touch her arm.

"He looks mummified," Molly said. She squatted down for a closer look. She'd gotten over her shock pretty quickly. "I guess the dry air of the tumulus helped that along."

"So now we know why Cornelius went missing," Farnsworth said. Yep. Stuck in this big dirt mound for all eternity.

"There was a fire in here. Why didn't he burn?" I said.

After a round of shrugging, Molly pointed to the area next to the body. "There's a dagger." Glints of red and gold sparkled in the dim light; I could see a long silver blade fixed to an ornate handle. "And he scratched something on the ground."

I moved closer and saw words carved into the stone and dirt floor. The writing was angular and erratic.

Even in death I protect the truth. They will try to destroy. We will stop them.

"It's in English? Why not Italian?" Farnsworth asked after a pause.

"He wrote to Owen in English, too. Maybe he didn't know Italian?" Molly said.

"No. Cornelius lived in Italy for years. He wasn't originally from Italy—I remember reading that he was born in Amsterdam. Given his status, he should have been conversant in several languages." No, that was strange. Why wouldn't he write in Italian, the language of his adopted country?

"There's more," Molly murmured. I watched as she pulled a large paintbrush from her backpack and gently swept the floor near the engraving. "It's that Seneca line again: 'Ducunt volentem fata, nolentem trahunt.' And there's a circle with a head eating its tail. It's rough, but . . . it's an ouroboros," she said and looked up at us. "I think that Cornelius hoped we'd find him."

"We?" I said.

"Someone who knew about the Order."

"Because of the Latin?"

"That and the ouroboros." She pointed at the drawing etched in the ground. "I think he left this as a warning for anyone who found him."

"Look at his clothes," Sarah said.

I followed her finger and saw her pointing toward Cornelius's stomach. His thin, dark hands were crossed over it. He was wearing a light-colored tunic with a dark sash around his waist when he died. The clothes were in remarkable condition, considering they had been here for about three hundred years. However, there seemed to be some dark stains on his shirt, so I gently pulled up one of his hands. Blood. It was dried and centuries old, but still unmistakable.

"So, did he do this to himself?" Molly said.

"No, I don't think so," Farnsworth said, holding up the knife. "Stomach wounds are notoriously painful."

"That, and the fact that people had threatened Cornelius because of his 'dragon,'" I said, my fingers wiggling air quotes as I said the word. "I'd say we're looking at a murder."

There was a long pause. "Here's my guess," started Farnsworth. "After he bought this property, Cornelius took advantage of the tumulus. Maybe he realized what it was when grave robbers busted in and stole that mammoth tusk. So, to protect his treasure, he stored it inside. Hiding in plain sight, you know? The Order figured it out. They stabbed him, then sealed him in here. As he died, he scraped out his last words using the knife that killed him."

"Wouldn't pulling the knife out cause him to bleed out faster? How could he have written this so fast?" Molly asked.

"Do I look like *CSI*?" said Farnsworth. "I might be totally off the mark here, but look at the evidence: we're in a tumulus in Italy, looking at the body of a man who has been missing for three hundred years and died right next to a fossilized dragon. I don't mean to overplay my hand here, but I'd say this has the Order's stench all over it."

"If it was the Order, wouldn't they want to destroy the dragon?" Molly asked. "That seems to be their M.O."

"I think they tried to destroy it," I said. "See that rod there? In the middle of the bones? I bet that was part of a torch. I think they set fire to this tumulus with the hopes that the fossil and everything in it would burn or crash down."

"The body didn't burn. Maybe the fire died out for lack of oxygen, so Cornelius either suffocated or bled to death," Farnsworth said. "The endgame is still the same: Cornelius dead and the dragon never found."

"What the hell!" Molly said, standing up and stamping her feet in frustration. "Mary Anning. Gideon Mantell.

Cornelius Meyer! All these people were murdered because they found dragons."

"Surprisingly correct statement, for such an ignorant person," a loud, male voice echoed around the tumulus. I turned toward the entrance in surprise.

THE DEVIL YOU KNOW

Oliphant

EVEN SLIGHTLY BENT over, Raley's large frame filled the entrance to the tumulus. He was cool and calm, and his feet moved purposefully. He was wearing a gray suit with a white shirt and brown leather shoes. After surveying the room, he turned to us, raising a handgun. Behind him, the outline of another man and a woman came into focus as they emerged from the tunnel. As the man came into view, I recognized him immediately. It was the man from Lyme Regis who'd had Sarah's cell phone.

Raley finally stopped walking and gazed at the pile of bones at our feet. His face turned hard with hatred. "Another pile to break. Head out and call in the trucks," he said softly. The woman at his side nodded and headed back outside.

"No!" Molly cried.

"Ah, but I think I will." He laughed.

"Why are you doing this?" Molly said. Her hands were shaking, but her voice was strong. Farnsworth was right. The kid was gutsy.

"Because dragons don't exist, little girl. Except in fantasy. And it's going to stay that way."

"There is literally a dragon right in front of you," I said. "Well, at least an animal that looks like a dragon."

"Um, no. It isn't, Dr. Oliphant. That isn't a dragon. It's an abomination."

"What are you talking about? The evidence is right there," I snapped. Probably not my brightest move, but frankly, I was tired of this. Not to mention scared. And I wanted to understand the "why" of everything that had happened. I took a step forward, and in response, Raley also moved.

"Evidence?" Raley chuckled. "I see no evidence." He kicked the bones with his shoe. "At least there won't be. This creature will soon be gone, like the others. Another dream or story that parents tell their children before bed. Because we don't want the truth getting out, after all."

"What truth?"

"Oh, Dr. Oliphant." Raley shook his head. "Imagine what could happen if the world knew that dragons lived side by side with dinosaurs. That these creatures actually were real." He put his arm around Farnsworth's shoulders and leaned toward his ear, the gun pressed into his side. Farnsworth stiffened his body and the color drained from his face. "How that would excite the imagination of man!" he shouted, spittle arcing into Farnsworth's ear.

"Why would knowing about dragons be a bad thing?" Molly asked. Raley pushed Farnsworth away and walked up to her.

"Dragons are instruments of the Devil, Ms. Wilder. God struck Satan down to dwell under the earth. Not up here. As long as the Order exists, it's going to stay that way." He stepped back and used the muzzle of the gun to scratch the side of his temple.

This guy was a nut job.

Fantastic.

"I want to thank you. Seriously." Raley pointed toward the fossil. "Meyer's dragon? Wow. I was under the impression that it had been taken care of, but hey, my past colleagues weren't as careful as we are now. And now we also have Owen's famous journal." Raley reached over Molly and grabbed her backpack, dragging her down slightly. Before she even had time to cry out, he'd pulled her backpack off her shoulders and pushed her away. With a flourish, he ripped open her bag and pulled out Owen's journal.

"Others will eventually find dragon fossils," Molly said. "You can't stop this."

"Maybe. But we'll take care of them. We always do. We are very good at our job." He aimed his gun at us. "This conversation is becoming tiresome."

"You're insane," I spat out, shaking with anger.

"I disagree. So does God."

"Did you destroy the fossil dragon we found in Montana?" Molly said, her voice quivering.

"What do you think?" Raley narrowed his eyes at her. "Of course we did."

"How do you keep finding us?" Farnsworth asked. "Are you tracking our phones?"

"Phones? No need. Do you want to tell them, Sarah?" Raley turned abruptly to Sarah, gesturing his gun at her.

What?

Sarah moved slowly to stand beside Raley. The whole thing was happening in some slow-mo, out-of-body affair. Nausea wormed its way into my gut. I had to keep myself from gagging. I felt a chill in my joints, and I had to blink repeatedly to resolve the double image of Sarah standing with Raley.

I could hear Sarah speaking, but I couldn't make it out. It sounded like she was talking through water. It sounded like she was telling him to let us go, that we wouldn't tell.

After a moment, Raley and the man raised their guns again at the three of us. "Where were we?" I heard the click of the hammers as they cocked their pistols, ready to fire.

BETRAYAL

Sarah

HOW IN THE world did I get here? Here I was, in an ancient Etruscan tumulus in Italy, looking at the man who raised me, my mentor, and a girl who could have been me once. I could hardly bear to see the three of them, their eyes wide with fear and panic—and the shock of my betrayal. Derek wasn't even looking at Raley. He was looking at me, with that puppy-dog look he got when he's been hurt. He was trying to find the right words, and I didn't have the courage or heart to hear them. It was too late, anyway. I'd made my deal.

Raley told me this could happen. If they learned too much, then he would have to act, whatever that might mean. If it happened, I was counting on my fear to push through it. To deal with everything. But strangely, now that I was here, I didn't feel anything. For the first time in days, my hands were steady. I wasn't holding a gun, but if I had to shoot, I'd shoot straight.

Had I lost my mind? The man who raised me was about to be shot, and I didn't feel anything. It was like I was standing next to the body of someone else who looked just like me, complete with purple streaks in her hair and the tattoos that I'd been getting because I liked the pain. I saw myself: Sarah Connell. Paleontologist. Geologist. Traitor. What happened to me?

Pull yourself together. You have to do this.

They said that the truth would set you free. I was no longer sure I even knew what that meant.

"You're with them?" Derek said, his voice low and shaky.

I couldn't look at him.

"Sarah, these people are killers."

"Only when necessary." I looked up, but kept my eyes on a spot between his eyebrows. I didn't know what I'd do if I looked into his eyes.

"Why?" Molly said, her voice high, disbelieving. She was so very young. "They destroy fossils! They aren't like you."

"We eliminate only those who serve Lucifer, Molly," said Raley as if lecturing a small child. In many ways, he was. "The Order protects God's will."

"God's will?" Oliphant barked a strangled laugh. Brave man. "And what exactly is that, Raley? Murder innocents while breaking rocks that make you feel bad? Sounds more like a massive tantrum with a high body count than an epic and righteous religious quest. But, as history has often demonstrated, those can be the same thing."

"What is the Order?" Farnsworth interrupted, but I knew what he was really asking. *Why are you doing this?*

"God has laid out the path for those who crusade in his name," Raley answered. "We are his earthly servants. We strike those who promote blasphemy." He shuffled toward Farnsworth. He didn't move. "You fossil types are all the same. Excavators of disgusting relics. Promoters of misinformation, lies. The Order of Saint George takes care of all that. We protect his Church."

How did I let this get so far?

"God doesn't want this," Oliphant scoffed. His nostrils flared, and he took a step forward. "Believe in religion or don't, but your wrathful God is as outdated as the Inquisition. *You* want this."

He turned to me, a disgusted look on his face. "Sarah, you can't believe this nonsense! You're not some religious lunatic."

No, I'm not. But the contempt on his face made me furious.

"You don't know me." I pointed to his chest. "I came to you, begging you to be my advisor. To help me. I had the grades, but you were too busy. Too famous to take the time to help me, to guide me! It wasn't until I won the Nakasogi Prize that you took any real interest in me. Do you have any idea how hard I had to work to get that prize?"

"They award it to the best scientist. That's why you won!" Oliphant said.

It wasn't just their egos. They didn't know what I was going through. What I had ahead of me, without the Order's help.

"You don't know what it's like to start to lose control of your body, Sean. I tried to tell you that I wasn't well. What do you think those pills are for? But why should I be surprised? Nothing matters to you but the glory of Dr. Sean Oliphant!" I knew I had to pull back. I was too raw and exposed. But I didn't. Too far down the rabbit hole. I wasn't even sure what I was saying. "Do you two have any idea of how much attention you steal from others? Do you have any idea of how tired everyone is of hearing you and Derek whine about each other? Grow the hell up!" I purposely didn't look at Derek as I yelled, but from the corner of my eye, I saw his shoulders sag.

"Is that what this is really about, Sarah? Fame?" Oliphant asked.

Had he even heard me?

"Shut up, Sean," said Derek, concern spread across his face. "Sarah, the pills. What's the matter? Tell me what's the matter."

He was too late. It was too late to be concerned for me.

They say politics makes for strange bedfellows. Try debilitating disease.

Farnsworth made a little noise, and I finally gazed into his eyes. Decades of love, frustration, and disappointment boiled to the surface, so much that it took the edge off, and my leg stopped trembling. For years, people thought of me as Farnsworth's little sidekick. The cute kid who could rattle off dinosaur names like a pro at trade shows while selling her babysitter's cheap fossils. I was never treated seriously then. Or now. It didn't matter what I did in college or grad school. A few months ago I overheard one of the other students whisper that Oliphant is the real reason I got the Nakasogi Prize. Not because I worked my ass off. But because he needed a new prize on his shelf, and I was the female grad student who could help make that happen.

It was then I came to a realization. Farnsworth and Oliphant were the same. Peel back their layers of blue-collar determination or Ivy-League respectability, and you'd find the same person, the same pirate. Derek took fossils from naïve ranchers who had no idea how valuable the fossils were and then sold them to the highest bidder. Oliphant just craved more book deals, bigger grants, high-profile TV shows, and graduate students to stroke his ego.

I made the decision that I wouldn't end up like either of them. The trembling hands and diagnosis had just made it easier, a faster and more necessary decision that would have been made eventually.

I told myself what I'd been telling myself all along. They weren't loyal to you, Sarah. They didn't help you. Look out for number one.

While you still can.

I saw Oliphant's eyes darting around, searching. He was probably looking for an exit, but there wasn't any way out, except through Raley. "You don't need to do this."

I thought back on how I arrived in this moment. So many things converging. The egos of these two men for whom I had worked and who cared so little for me, I told myself. The one-in-how-many chance that I would find this tooth waiting for me in all that bedrock. An organization that I could never have dreamed of, hiding a secret I could never have believed. And offering me an experimental cure for a disease that would surely ravage me.

I was still in that same dream state that I'd lived in for these many months. Thinking none of it was true. That Derek and Sean did care about me. That this organization and the creature it sought to hide were only in storybooks. That I wasn't bound for a wheelchair.

But I looked at Molly, at her fear and anger, and I knew.

It was no dream.

"Well, this has been fun, but it's time to move on." Raley motioned toward the other Order member he brought with him. It was the same guy from Lyme Regis, the one Raley had sent to make sure I wasn't straying from the mission.

I watched Derek pull Molly toward him. A twinge of jealousy burned through me. I could see his jaw working, and his eye was twitching as he tried to restrain himself. He wanted to curse us and scream at us, but he stopped himself. Instead, he was trying to shield Molly.

"Sarah," Farnsworth said, turning his head slightly toward me. There were tears in his eyes. "Please."

I felt bile burning up my throat, and my heart was crashing against my chest. No, I couldn't do it. What was I thinking?

"Wait," I said, my voice weak. "Maybe—" Raley turned the gun toward me, and his cold stare stopped my words.

"We have to clean this up. It's time to finish it."

"No!" Molly shouted as she threw herself against a pillar that held the roof up above us. Thinking that she was trying to hide, Raley's pal moved to grab her; he stopped the moment a loud crack echoed around the room.

There was another loud crack. As one, we all looked to the ceiling. It was collapsing.

Dirt, rocks, and mortar peppered my face. Instinctually, I turned toward the entrance to run, barreling toward the outside world.

ALL FALL DOWN

Molly

IT WAS CRAZY that the hill hadn't collapsed years ago. If the Order had burned a fire in this tumulus over three hundred years ago, any surviving wooden support beams would have been damaged. The mortar holding it up wasn't very strong either. I could see cracks everywhere. Pieces crumbled away from the wall.

It was probably a mixture of fear, adrenaline, and stupidity that made me throw my body into that column. I'm not even sure why I did it. Maybe to distract them enough so that they wouldn't shoot me. Maybe to get them to focus on me so that Oliphant and Farnsworth could disarm them, or something.

It was a really lame plan.

But, as my shoulder connected with the column, I heard a loud crack. My shoulder screamed with pain, but I didn't care.

I landed on my side. Dirt and small rocks fell from the ceiling as it began to crumble. Raley gave me a bewildered stare until a baseball-sized rock landed on his shoulder.

As the ceiling began to sag, more dirt and larger rocks tumbled to the floor. The other columns started to buckle, unable to hold up the roof. The noise was like ice breaking on a frozen lake. Larger chunks crashed into the ground around us.

"Let's go, you idiot!" Raley screamed, pushing the other Order guy toward the entrance.

"Molly!" Farnsworth cried, reaching for me, pushing me in the same direction, the only way out.

The whole back of the tumulus collapsed, scattering plaster and rocks across the floor. Dust and dirt filled the cavern, and my eyes stung. Raley's back was in front of me as he followed his man into the tunnel. But before he could duck down to enter himself, I felt a huge rush of anger, and I bolted forward. *Screw the pain.* I connected my hurt shoulder with his back, and he wobbled and fell, dropping his gun and Owen's journal. I grabbed the journal, stepping on Raley's hand in the process. I heard Raley scream in pain, but I was already in the tunnel of the tumulus. I didn't look, but I heard something behind me. I really hoped that it was just Farnsworth and Oliphant.

A few more feet and I was out, half blinded by the sunlight, sucking in oxygen. Trying to catch my breath, I struggled forward. We had to move. Oliphant raced past me, pulling at my arm, and we ran around the tumulus, away from the entrance. Farnsworth raced at my side. I looked back in dread for Raley, for his gang.

But I didn't see anyone. Nobody. Not Raley, or that man or woman. Or Sarah. Just the tumulus and trees and a bright pink sky, turning dark with the setting sun. The tumulus looked wrecked, though. The grass-covered dome had caved in, exposing layers of soil as well as some of the tumulus's interior. It looked like a giant, deflated soccer ball. It wouldn't be long before the docent noticed.

"Where are we going?" I yelled as we ran. We seemed to be heading back toward the ruins and the house. I wondered if that was a good idea. I mean, that was the location of the parking lot. Wouldn't Raley have parked there, too?

"To see if we can get to our car," Farnsworth yelled, his voice cracking. "We need to get safe and make some calls." My heart broke for him. I sniffed as I ran, fighting to keep my tears from falling.

"The Order probably has our . . ." Oliphant said, his voice rising in panic. "Oh, God. No!" From behind, a large SUV screeched around the tumulus, careening toward us. In front of us, a row of black vans roared in our direction.

Trapped. We stopped and formed a circle. The vans skidded in the tall grass around us, and their doors opened. Out of the vans poured several heavily armed men and women. One of the vans turned a spotlight on us, and I was temporarily blinded.

Farnsworth reached for my hand, and I held him tightly.

"Get into the van," a loud voice said. It was male, young, and disturbingly calm.

"And if we don't?" Farnsworth yelled.

I heard a loud metallic *kerchunk* in response. I recognized it from movies. I'd never heard it in person. A shotgun shell being pumped into a gun chamber.

A person moved behind me and grabbed my arms, pulling my hands together. Something tightened around my wrists. Owen's journal was gently removed from my hands, and as I turned to complain, a steady hand pushed me forward. Next to me, Farnsworth and Oliphant walked, their hands also tied behind their backs.

The van they led us to had no backseats, only seats for the driver and a front passenger. We were pushed inside, and I moved to sit on the floor close to Oliphant and Farnsworth. A woman started the engine, and a man sat in the passenger's seat. With a roar, the van lurched forward, bouncing across the rough grassland.

We eventually left the estate and pulled onto a smooth road. Then silence. Our captors didn't speak, even to each other. Just horrible silence. Next to me, Farnsworth pushed his thigh against mine. A sign of solidarity and a reminder in the dark van that I wasn't alone. I sniffled back tears and leaned into his shoulder.

We were only in the van a short time before it lurched to a stop.

The van door opened with a loud screech, and through the opening I saw two men standing in front of us. I didn't recognize them from the warehouse raid in Montana. Maybe the Order had an Italian branch?

"Please, come out," one of them said, backing away from the van door. Oliphant stood up and walked out first. I followed, ducking my head down. I jumped out onto the pavement and looked around. We were in some sort of alley in Atessa. All around me were the white- and cream-colored buildings with tan roofs that I saw as we drove past on our way to the Meyer estate. Nearby, I could hear a jumble of cars, buses, and voices, but the alley we were parked in was deserted, save the vans and our kidnappers.

The woman from our van put her hand on my shoulder and guided me forward after Oliphant. Behind me, Farnsworth shrugged off his handler, using a few choice words to emphasize his anger. My stomach clenched, and I couldn't stop myself from shaking a little bit.

We were pushed into an ordinary but empty office building. We passed several dark rooms with closed blinds over the windows. I considered shouting, but I didn't think it would do any good. There was nobody around.

They led us into an empty room that had a large table in the middle. There were three chairs on one side and two on the other. It smelled dusty and stale.

"Are you arresting us?" I asked nobody in particular, trying to sound intimidating. I heard footsteps behind us.

"Why would you think that?" a low voice said. It was the same voice that told us to get into the van. The man came into view, and he stood on the other side of the table. He motioned for us to sit, but I ignored him. This was so messed up. Even though I was terrified, my temper was rising, and I could feel my face getting red. Farnsworth and Oliphant ignored his suggestion. I felt my heart beat faster. We were a team, no matter what.

"Well, it's either that or you've kidnapped us at gunpoint," Oliphant said. "I think I prefer to be arrested."

I looked closely at the man. He was Asian and looked familiar. In fact, we just saw him yesterday. "You!" I shouted, leaning forward.

"Oh?" the man said, almost casually. I heard the Japanese accent clearly.

"You told us where to go at Drachenfels, to find the dragon's cave," I said.

"Yes. Now, please sit down." He sat and motioned again toward the three chairs, but we remained standing. Another man walked by us and took the other empty seat.

"Sit," he said with finality after a long moment. "Let us talk." I quickly looked at the others. Oliphant shrugged, and together we each sat in the empty chairs in front of us.

The man cleared his throat. "Why were you trespassing in Meyer's tumulus? Italian law protects that site. Surely you knew that."

"Look," Oliphant said, leaning forward, "I don't know who you think you are, but you should know that while I may look like I can't defend myself, I do have friends in very high places. United States government places. I'm a very famous scientist. People will be looking for me."

The interrogator seemed bemused by Oliphant. He reached down into the briefcase next to his chair and pulled out a large book. He dropped it on the table.

"Where did you find this journal?" he said calmly.

"Hey!" I sputtered before I could stop myself. In front of us was the very familiar red-and-black journal of Richard Owen. "That's ours!"

"Where did you find this? I assure you the authorities here take theft and destruction of artifacts very seriously."

"What theft?" Farnsworth said, looking confused.

"This book clearly doesn't belong to you or your friends, Mr. Farnsworth. Now tell me, where did you get this journal?"

"How do you know my name?" Farnsworth asked.

The interrogator sighed and stood up, his chair scraping against the bare concrete floor. "We know who you all are." He paced for a moment, then turned, spreading one of his hands on the tabletop, the other on the journal. Looking right at me, he pushed the journal to the man next to him.

"Please remain seated, Ms. Wilder." The accomplice stood and walked next to me.

Farnsworth's body tensed, ready to act. But I was surprised when the man leaned down past me and grabbed my backpack at my feet. He opened it and put the journal inside.

I didn't even notice anyone putting my bag there. They took it from me when we were forced into the vans. Why would they give me back my stuff? Or the journal? They just said we stole it.

"Okay, please tell me about the Dracosauria in the tumulus. Was it larger than the one you discovered in Montana?" the interrogator asked.

Deadly silence. I quickly looked at Oliphant. He was leaning back in his chair, gazing at this man thoughtfully. Farnsworth, on the other hand, was as impassive as a brick wall.

"Please. Was it larger?" the interrogator said again, his voice low.

"Your man Raley destroyed it," Oliphant said, looking the interrogator right in the eye. "Ask him."

Our interrogator gave Oliphant a long look and said something to his friend in what I thought was Japanese. Then, he leaned his forearms on the table. "Please answer the question. Was the one you found in the tumulus—Cornelius Meyer's dragon—as large as the one you found in Montana?"

"No. Ours was bigger," Farnsworth finally said.

"I thought so." The interrogator grinned. "This is good." He turned and spoke rapidly to his friend.

"What are you saying?" I asked suspiciously.

"Just confirming our theory, Ms. Wilder," the interrogator said.

"Your *theory*?" I snapped. Frustration and fear were finally getting the best of me.

"I'm sorry for all this, but we needed to know," the interrogator said, his eyes not leaving mine.

Then it clicked. Not sure why it took so long. I'd blame adrenaline and the lack of food and sleep.

These people were not with the Order of Saint George.

The man nodded at me as if confirming my silent assessment. Then he spoke. "*Ducunt volentem fata, nolentem trahunt. We intend to expose Owen's Truth, whether you help us or not,*" the man said.

Owen's Truth.

"S.V.?" I said, my eyes widening as I fell back into my chair.

He didn't answer. Instead, the man leaned over to grab a briefcase that had been sitting at his side, then stood up. He said something in Japanese to the other man, who grimaced and stood. Together they walked around the table. I bit my lip, unsure of what was happening. While his teammate stood at the entryway of the room, the interrogator moved next to Farnsworth.

"Where is Sarah Connell? We know she made it out of the tumulus," he said to Farnsworth in a quiet tone.

Farnsworth's body jerked in response, but he said nothing.

The man gave Farnsworth a sad look. Then he pulled out a photograph from his briefcase and placed it on the table in front of us. It was a black-and-white photograph of Sarah. It was obviously taken in secret. I could see out-of-focus leaves around the edge of the photograph, as if the photographer had been hiding in a bush or something. Sarah's face was in profile, but it was obviously her. I could see her tattoos peeking out from under her winter jacket at her wrist. On her head was a woolen cap, and snow sparsely covered the ground. She was talking to a man.

And that man was Raley.

The man put a hand on Farnsworth's shoulder, which he violently shrugged off. The man didn't seem offended, though. Instead, he just stood up and clasped his hands in front of him. "Do you know that Ms. Connell is sick, Mr. Farnsworth?"

At that, our heads shot up.

"She said something about that in the tumulus," Farnsworth said. "What do you mean?"

The man pursed his lips. "I would suggest you take a moment to comprehend exactly what is going on here. Your friend Ms. Connell has betrayed you, and her colleagues intended to kill you. You didn't even know your friend was seriously ill, but we did. Please, wait here." He gave us a small bow, then left the room with the other man.

We sat in silence, alone in the room. I tried to absorb what I'd just heard, but it was hard. I'd been right about one thing. One of us was a traitor. I just never thought it would be Sarah. I mean, I'd been naïve to think that because she'd been so nice to me, so welcoming, that she couldn't be the bad one.

"I'm sorry," Farnsworth said.

"For what? You did nothing wrong," I said.

"I should have known something was wrong with Sarah. I just figured she was stressed out." His face seemed more lined, older than I remembered.

"She hid all this from everyone, Derek," Oliphant said.

Farnsworth didn't answer but instead bolted up and began to pace the room. It was an effort because his hands were still hog-tied behind his back. After a few moments of pacing, he stopped. "I've known that girl since she was little. I thought I knew everything going on in her life. She had everything going for her."

"Including a chance to break into prominence by working in my program," Oliphant said. We both turned to stare at him. "Oh, you know what I mean."

"To think she'd join the Order . . . I can't believe it. I mean, the Order destroys what we do," Farnsworth said. I heard his breath quicken, and he sniffed a few times.

"Well, this illness must be the explanation. I agree. The fame and money angle doesn't make any sense. Not with Sarah," Oliphant said.

"I guess she's just following your example. You take whatever you want. Money, power, help, access to medical resources. Who cares who gets hurt?"

Oliphant turned and narrowed his eyes at Farnsworth. "Look, Derek, I know this is hard. But Sarah is an adult. She made her choice even if neither of us understands it."

"They wanted to kill us," Farnsworth growled. "Not to mention she let them take all my fossils. Dear God," he said, his face etched with horror at his realization. "She helped them take my fossils."

"That's not Sarah, Derek. Whatever she's suffering from, it made her desperate, and desperate people do crazy things. Me included, once upon a time."

"She literally let a man who wanted me dead hold a gun to my face, Sean," Farnsworth shouted.

"She tried to stop it at the end, right before Molly became the human pinball machine and broke the tumulus," he replied. "No, she's a better person than that. I know it, you know it." He looked Farnsworth right in the eye. "Don't give up."

"Give up?" Farnsworth said quietly.

"Don't give up on us. On me, or Molly, or Sarah, or yourself. I meant what I said in Germany. For all your faults, you're a great . . ." Oliphant cleared his throat, trying to get the words unstuck. "A great paleontologist. One of the very best. I wish I had told you that many years ago."

Farnsworth swung his face toward the wall.

"Come on, Derek. You've known me—well, *hated* me—for over twenty years. I don't give out praise lightly. We need to keep going rather than dwell on Sarah. We'll deal with that later. We'll figure this out and help her if we can."

In response, Farnsworth lowered his head, and I heard a shaky breath.

"So, a truce? We can duke it out later. Let's just get through this, whatever this is. Come on, I'll even let you choose the weapon— pistols or swords," Oliphant said.

After a long moment, Farnsworth turned back to us, his eyes on the floor. "Fine."

I let out a breath I didn't realize I was holding. The tension in the room let up a bit, but we were still there. I'd been pretending that I was not terrified to my core, but now I was shaking.

"Molly." Farnsworth was the first to notice. "We'll be okay." He was calmer now, but the sadness hadn't left his eyes.

I nodded, probably a little too forcefully. He studied me again. "You're one heck of a kid. I don't know how you're even still standing after all this."

I gave him a small smile. "Working on pure adrenaline." And its effects were fading. My legs were shaking like twigs.

"Okay. If these guys aren't the Order, who are they?" Oliphant asked.

Farnsworth retook his chair. "Not Italian authorities. Perhaps the CIA?"

"Maybe, but I'm not getting that feeling," Oliphant said. "If they were, where are the dentist drills and pliers for our fingernails? S.V., perhaps?"

"That's what I think," I said. "But I'm still confused about how this guy could be S.V. if S.V. is referenced in Owen's journal almost one hundred and fifty years ago."

"Maybe it's not a person, but a thing?" Farnsworth said.

The door opened, and the driver of our van entered the room. She was carrying a big tray of food. A large man walked in bearing another tray with three glasses and a carafe of water. They placed the trays on the table, and then walked around to our backs. I heard a clicking sound like a pocketknife unfolding. I felt a slight tug, and then my arms were free. I rubbed my wrists, looking at our captors.

"Eat, drink. You need energy," the woman said in English, motioning to the trays as she backed out of the room. "Those are delicious pastries from a bakery just down the street."

"Well, I'm no expert, but if they wanted us dead, I don't think they would feed us pastries," Oliphant said.

"Perhaps they're trying to lull us into a false sense of security," I said, eyeing a puff pastry with interest. "Is that a cannoli?"

Oliphant poured water and handed glasses to Farnsworth and me. I took a sip. No, they'd had ample time to kill us. They wanted us alive and talking.

But Oliphant and Farnsworth were quiet, lost in their own thoughts. I took another long gulp of water. It felt lovely on my dry throat. I hadn't realized how thirsty I was. Probably from all the stress. A sudden movement startled me, and I watched as Farnsworth dropped his glass and fell over, hitting his head on the table. Oliphant had his own head in his hands and was whispering, "Dizzy." At least, I thought that was what he was saying. All I could think about was the fact our water glasses weren't shattering when they hit the ground. They bounced. I was on my hands and knees when I realized the answer.

"Oh, they're plastic. Good planning. Very clever."

That was when I passed out.

Richard Owen's Journal, 1865

They destroyed my Dracosauria.

They told me that they wanted to discuss British Museum business. They came into my home and found the Isle of Wight Dracosauria. They smashed it into pieces, and took the resulting dust and rocks with them. Why, I do not know.

When questioned as to why I had the specimen, I had told them I was holding the Monster safe until they had time to collect it. I do not think they believed me. More likely I was spared because of my connections to the Crown.

Thankfully this journal remains hidden.

I don't intend to say anything more publicly. But I will deliver my work at the right time. The new museum is already under construction, and we are designing a new office below one of the main chambers. I shall have a safe place to continue my work, and protect important secrets until I can expose the Order.

THE TALE OF NAKASOGI

Farnsworth

AS I SLOWLY woke, the first sensation was a horrible stabbing pain in my head. My body felt like I had stood in the way of stampeding cattle. My hands slowly crawled to my temples and rubbed at them. While it hurt to move, I risked opening my eyes. Huge mistake. Another wave of pain and the room began to spin and my stomach roiled with nausea. A string of four-letter words left my lips before I could stop them.

"Careful, there is a child present," Oliphant chastised me.

"Dude, I've heard it all before," Molly groaned.

I opened my eyes again and carefully turned my head in the direction of their voices. Molly and Oliphant were sprawled out on floor futons, although Molly was starting to sit up.

"Ow. This must be what a hangover feels like," Molly said. She pushed the brim of her cap off her forehead.

"After a particularly intensive bender, yes, this is pretty close," Oliphant said.

"Then I'm swearing off alcohol," she said miserably, putting her hands over her eyes.

"I doubt that promise will make it through college."

I took a deep breath and sat up. We were lying on several futons in a large, dark room. Soft floor lighting illuminated the walls, which were adorned with large tapestries and paintings. They looked familiar, at least in style, but everything was still a bit blurry.

"So, the food was drugged," I said, stating what seemed obvious.

"Or the water," Oliphant said. He had stood and was slowly walking toward a large window covered in thick drapes. Next to me, I heard the sound of a zipper.

"My pack is here, along with . . . wallet, keys . . . passport . . . Owen's journal. Everything seems to be here . . ." Molly sighed in relief. "That's good."

"But no cell reception," Oliphant said, waving his phone above his head.

"Where the heck are we?"

That was the question of the hour. I stood and began to walk around the room. My dad taught me the best remedy for a hangover: get your butt up and moving. But slowly. Very slowly. Otherwise, you'd have to get moving to a bathroom.

Clearing my throat, I pointed to the nearest wall. "These are Japanese paintings, and those are tatami mats on the floors," I said.

"How do you know?" Molly asked.

I didn't answer. I stopped to look at one of the more striking paintings. It portrayed a battle between warring samurai. Men with swords struck at each other, while others loosened spears and arrows. Above the fighters, flying in a circle, were a dragon and a peacock-like creature: a phoenix.

Molly moved to stand next to me. "A four-legged dragon without wings," she murmured. "Asian."

"Yep," I said as I turned from the painting. Oliphant had opened the window drapes a little and was looking outside. His mouth hung open as he turned to face us. For once, he was speechless.

I quickly crossed the room. I pulled the other drape aside, and found myself staring through a window at the snowcapped peak of . . .

Mount Fuji?

"Didn't expect that."

"So we're in Japan now?" Molly said. "Great. Where next, Antarctica?"

Oliphant turned away from the window and started pacing. "Well, that explains our interrogator."

"Who?" I said.

"Our interrogator, the leader. In Italy. He spoke with a Japanese accent. I bet he and the others are based here."

"Maybe," I said. But why bring us here? I mean, they had us in Italy. Why drug us and move us halfway around the world?

Suddenly there was a noise behind us. Turning around, I saw a door that I hadn't noticed before. It creaked open slowly with great deliberation. From where we were standing, we couldn't see through the open doorway, but light shone through it into our room, beckoning us forward.

I reached out and grabbed Molly's shoulder.

"What?" she said, her eyes wide.

"You tend to charge ahead in these situations, kid. Let me take this one for a change, okay?" I smirked.

She bowed her head and gracefully motioned toward the door. "After you, ancient leader."

Chuckling, I peeked through. The doorway apparently led to a cavernous room. Panels and tapestries covered most of the light-colored walls. They were accented by LED spotlights, similar to what you'd see in a museum. The floor plan was open, but pedestals and tables were situated along the walls, displaying artifacts and other relics. I saw an urn or vase of some kind on one of the pedestals, and a large book lying open in a glass-covered case on another. There were pictures and paintings on the walls. The air smelled clean with a hint of incense.

"May I have the privilege of welcoming you, Mr. Farnsworth, Ms. Wilder, and Dr. Oliphant."

I was startled by a voice that seemed to fill the chamber. Peering around the room, I saw that we were not alone. Someone was standing near the back behind a large desk.

Molly pushed past me, heading toward the man, and Oliphant and I fell into step with her. The stranger was an older Asian man. His hair was iron-gray, and his face was gently lined. He had his hands clasped together in front of him and a small smile on his face.

All my anger from the past few days raged through me at the sight of this smiling man, whoever he was. I just knew he was the reason for everything. The reason why we were there, the reason for all the chaos of the last few days. I pushed Molly behind me. All I saw was red, and I wanted to punch something. But I couldn't. Whoever this guy was had us trapped. He could hurt us, and nobody would know. So for Molly's sake, I swallowed my anger. I put my hands flat on the desk and leaned forward, baring my teeth. "Just who the hell do you think you are?"

"His name, Dr. Oliphant, is Ryuunosuke Nakasogi," a voice said behind us. I turned around and saw our interrogator from Atessa striding toward us. After walking around the desk, he stood next to Nakasogi and bowed.

"Nakasogi? As in the Nakasogi Prize?" Oliphant asked.

"Yes. The very same," the young man replied, his tone quiet and respectful as he looked at the older man.

Nakasogi. That name was enough to shake me from my rage and push me into a zone of confusion and disbelief. Nakasogi. The famous paleontology supporter. The renowned recluse. This man had underwritten more paleontology projects than anyone in the world. And hardly anyone in the world had actually met him personally.

"I deeply regret our deceptions," said Nakasogi. He looked sad, and he leaned forward slightly as if to meet me in the middle. "I understand how difficult our meeting here must be for you all. I would be honored if you would sit." He waved at some chairs in front of the desk. None of us moved. "Maybe some food? Or some tea perhaps?"

"No, thanks. Still working off that Mickey Finn your guy there doped us with in Italy," I growled. Oliphant snorted, but next to me, Molly was slowly repeating "'Mickey Finn.'"

I guess she was too young. "Drugs, Molly," I said as I glared at the man next to Nakasogi. He looked back at me, his eyes guarded.

"I apologize," said Nakasogi. "We needed to be cautious. We had to confirm that you were not members of the Order, like Ms. Connell. Once we realized that the Order intended to harm you, we quickly acted to ensure your safety. I am impressed that you escaped the tumulus. My team was on the verge of storming the room and extracting you. As it stands, my team is currently removing Cornelius Meyer's dragon from the collapsed tumulus."

"Your team?" Molly said.

"Yes, Ms. Wilder. If you can forgive me and my *tomodachi* for your discomforts and our deceit, I will explain everything."

"Bated breath," Oliphant said.

"Everything you've been working toward, the fossil treasures you've been hunting for, are important not only for your understanding but also for the entire world. The Order of Saint George, their mission, and their followers stand in the path of important progress not just in your field but throughout all academia."

Dramatic much? After a pause, I pointed at Nakasogi. "What makes you think dragon fossils will change anything?"

"Because myths are tales of imaginary creatures and times, yes? The world accepts that myths are not real because the creatures that inhabit them never existed. But what if they did exist? What if we can prove dragons existed and we have fossil evidence of that truth? What new secrets will be exposed? And what dangers do those secrets represent to the doctrine of organized religions?"

"Dragons didn't exist. People made myths about them, but what we're seeing is an ancient dead animal, no more," Oliphant said, the exasperation practically dripping from his lips.

"Oh, but they did, Mr. Oliphant," Nakasogi said quietly. "They lived at the same time as dinosaurs, pterosaurs, and other large animals. They died when the asteroid hit sixty-six million years ago."

"Semantics!" Oliphant shouted, clearly frustrated. "Applying a mythical term to a real animal isn't science. Dragons, according to myths—and correct me if I'm wrong, Molly—breathed fire, hoarded gold, ate humans!" He rocked back on his heels. "And many had six limbs, not four. We've now seen evidence of at least two specimens with four limbs. Six limbs in nature on non-insects and non-arachnids are impossible."

"They were also aquatic, Dr. Oliphant," Molly said helpfully.

"Okay, they swam in the ocean."

"And rivers."

"Okay! There is a lot of diversity in mythology! But it's all just fantasy!" he snapped.

Nakasogi remained quiet, studying Oliphant. Finally, he let out a little chuckle. "This is why you are the best scientist, Dr. Oliphant. You see the world as ordered, structured."

Oliphant rubbed his face with his hand and barked, "Sure. Ordered. Structured. I know. I have, like, four degrees that tell me that."

"Dragons. New species. Agree to disagree. But back to the Order," I said, steering the topic away before Oliphant lost it. "The Order destroys the fossils of dragons—that is, ancient animals that they believe are dragons. That's a given. But we also know that the good guys will eventually get one of those fossils, right? Someone is bound to be lucky. When that happens, the good guys will publish the results. Then, the Order folds its tent and disappears. Maybe they get tried for their crimes, maybe not. As far as mankind is concerned, problem solved, right? *National Geographic* will run articles on this new species that lived at the same time as the dinosaur."

"That has been our hope for generations, but we are not there. At least, not yet." Next to him, our original interrogator stood like a soldier at rest, his hands behind his back. Our eyes locked. His eyes held no intimidation. Just curiosity. Which was strange considering he'd kidnapped and drugged us earlier.

"Why are we here?" I asked.

"I wish to ask you all to undertake a task that will not be easy. It will not always be pleasurable. But, I can promise you that your experiences will be astonishing."

"What task?" Oliphant asked.

"To join us in a war against the Order," Nakasogi said. "To become soldiers in the fight for the truth."

The three of us were silent for a long time. Nakasogi didn't seem to mind, though, and continued to stand calmly behind his desk. I felt like he had given this speech to others before, and he knew how we'd answer even before we did.

Still, I pushed. "What do you mean?"

"You must see that the stakes are enormous: the quest for a broader knowledge of human history. Dragons appear in many of our oldest stories. They are often intertwined with tales of primal forces that we barely understand. The Order of Saint George seeks to block that research. It preserves powerful institutions that promote ignorance and greed. I have been on this journey for many years, but we require new blood and strong, open minds to stop the Order. We require warriors trained in today's scientific technology who can decipher the clues of the ancient world. I am asking for your help, Mr. Farnsworth, Ms. Wilder, and Dr. Oliphant." He then leaned over as if to grab something underneath his desk. I heard a click and the lights in the room brightened.

That was when I saw the fossils on display, in addition to the paintings and other art pieces that dotted the room. Some fossils were on long tables along the walls, while others had been placed in individual alcoves built into the walls. I could see skulls, a strangely curved horn, and what looked like a giant claw. I looked back at Nakasogi, and he motioned again with his hand.

"Please feel free to examine my collection."

I moved toward the nearest print to the right of the desk. It depicted men with shovels removing dirt from a large hole. Other men and women moved buckets or cloth tarps around the hole. One woman carried a rock in her arms. Except for the period clothing, this scene could have been from any of the digs I'd been on. These were paleontologists.

And rising from the hole was a dragon.

"You are looking at one of my favorite pieces, Mr. Farnsworth," Nakasogi said, walking up behind me. "This print is over three hundred years old. It's from China. Note that the dragon seeks to fly from the excavation to gain its freedom. While the artist has rendered an imaginary dig, we both know that there is truth to this. This captures an actual moment in time, not someone's dream. Just like your team's discovery in Montana. Remember, my team and I created the technology that your team used. We have retained access. I was quickly informed of the CAD file Ms. Connell uploaded into the 3D printer."

"Dude! You provided all of the expensive technology just so you could spy on us?" Molly said.

"Not just you. I support paleontological and archeological digs all over the world looking for creatures, Ms. Wilder. I have come to know and trust many of those scientists as fellow warriors. Where I'm not sure about allegiances, my money and technology allow me to observe their loyalties. Ms. Connell's dig was one. I had hoped for a different outcome, but alas, here we are."

With the mention of Sarah's name, I turned slightly from Nakasogi and lowered my head. Poor Sarah. To be caught up in all this. I felt his hand on my shoulder.

"Mr. Farnsworth, I know you and Ms. Connell were close. You are aware that Ms. Connell is suffering from multiple sclerosis?"

This had been coming since the tumulus. It felt like the roof was collapsing again.

Suddenly, the world began to spin like I was on a carousel. I thought I saw Oliphant say something to Nakasogi, but I couldn't hear him. I knew Molly's hand was on my back, but I couldn't feel her. My senses were a jumble, and I couldn't breathe. I smelled fire, but I knew I was hallucinating. I leaned over and placed my hands over my eyes.

"It's okay," I heard finally. It was Molly's voice. "Take a deep breath."

Sarah had multiple sclerosis. My baby was sick. How can my girl dig if she couldn't walk? Couldn't hold a hammer? Why wouldn't she tell me the truth? We could have figured this out together, as a family.

"How do you know this?" I choked out.

"As part of our background check on Ms. Connell, we noticed an increase in medical bills. A little digging and, well, we put two and two together," Nakasogi said, his tone sad. "We know that the Order is paying for her medical treatment. In return, she now works for them."

"Don't you see, Derek? She sold us out to get healthy," Molly's voice whispered in my ear. "She's getting *help*."

My pain was morphing into that familiar rage. In my mind's eye, I saw Sarah standing there next to Raley, pointing a gun at us.

"Help? Molly, she let her guy try to kill us! The only thing that stopped him was the collapsing tumulus," I snapped, my voice cracking.

"No. No, Derek. Remember, she began to try to stop him," Oliphant said. "And treating MS is very expensive. The best treatments that aren't covered by insurance can cost thousands of dollars. When one is diagnosed so young . . ." He trailed off, his own voice clogged with emotion.

"We can find her. We can help her," said Molly. "Pirates don't go down without a fight." She bit her lip and tilted her head slightly. "Right?"

I wiped my eyes with the back of my hand and stared at the ceiling into an overhead fluorescent light. It burned my eyes a bit, and I blinked black spots as I looked away. Next to me, Oliphant didn't say anything more. Instead, he slapped his hand on my back a few times.

"Okay. Back to spying on us," Oliphant said. "Mr. Nakasogi, if you wanted to get us here, why not just . . . I don't know . . . send us an Outlook calendar invite so we could set up a time to meet up?"

"Well, I did reach out. But carefully. The Order is everywhere," Nakasogi said.

Then it clicked. "You sent me the package with Owen's picture," I said. Nakasogi nodded gently.

"You are S.V.! But how could S.V. be mentioned in Owen's journal all those years ago? Or even on the footprint slab in Germany?" The rambling questions spilled out of Molly in a vast wave, as if a dam had burst.

"S.V. actually stands for Salva Veritate," Nakasogi said. "If you turn around, you will see the picture of Owen from your text." Sure enough, on the far wall to the left of the desk was a large portrait of Sir Richard Owen, draped in black robes, holding the dark skull. I was shocked that I missed it when we came in, but it had been pretty dark.

"This picture is identical to the other one," I said. "To his other portrait. The famous one. Except for the skull."

"Yes. Owen had them done at the same time, 1856. One for the public, one for Salva Veritate."

"Salva Veritate?" Oliphant said.

Molly said. "Salva Veritate . . . that means *with truth intact*, right?" Molly said.

Nakasogi moved his body erect, his hands clasped in front of him. Next to him, the interrogator straightened his shoulders. "Yes. Or *saving the truth*. The fight against the Order has spanned the world over many centuries. The Order's soldiers have crossed many generations. Over the years, we too have had different individuals fight them, all under the wing of Salva Veritate. We work to stop the Order of Saint George.

"Salva Veritate works to protect these critical fossils. But they are found worldwide, and it's hard for us to be everywhere at once. The Order is crafty and devious. My sources say that they scouted your warehouse, Mr. Farnsworth, after hacking into your computer systems. They probably discussed what you had with Ms. Connell, as well. They hoped to locate other fossils like your Monster. Because they weren't sure what might be hidden, they took all of your fossils," Nakasogi said.

"I don't have other fossils like the dragon."

"That you know about, Mr. Farnsworth. For centuries, humans have been encountering evidence of what we'd consider mythological. Do you blame the scientists for not knowing that they should be separating the large bones of a dragon from their more ubiquitous cousin, the dinosaur? And are not most fossils you find incomplete?"

"Sure."

"Then why is it so hard to believe that maybe even distinguished scientists like Dr. Oliphant and yourself have inaccurately cataloged dragons with dinosaurs?" Nakasogi asked, talking to us as if he were teaching a class. "Mankind has barely scratched the surface of our world, and sadly the Order works hard to prevent many startling revelations."

"Tell us what you know about the Order," Oliphant says. "I mean, its origins."

Nakasogi nodded, and then he told us their story.

Apparently, the original purpose of the Order of Saint George was to destroy all evidence of the mythological so that the world would follow God's word and reject what many viewed as Satan's monstrosities. For almost two thousand years, these self-declared servants of God destroyed all fossils, anything they encountered. Their beliefs held no room for animals that no longer existed. There was no reason to distinguish between the fossil of a dragon and the fossil of a dinosaur. To the Order, all fossils represented forces of hell and damnation.

The founder of the Order was the venerable Saint George. Turns out his story was true, from a certain point of view. He did slay a dragon. It just wasn't a live one. He destroyed a fossil skeleton of a dragon that had been showcased in some wealthy Roman's home. To the Christians of that time, especially

George, these creatures were blasphemies. So George and his followers went on a fossil rampage, and the Order was formed.

Over time, the Order grew and changed. Zealots from all over the world from various organizations of power and governments joined. Like the Masons, they kept their rituals and activities secret, recruiting selectively, retaining whole families in the Order. Today, members of the Order are men and women, young and old. It doesn't matter.

Over the years, the Order had to refine its targets. Owen and Darwin were successful, in most respects. Dinosaurs and most other extinct creatures were tolerated because of the widespread evidence of their existence. But animals that had spawned stories that challenge orthodox views of creation or promote myths of ancient and supernatural powers were the Order's primary focus. The Order believed people must be protected from myths, particularly if there was evidence that the creatures that inhabited the myths might have actually existed.

They were efficient and cruel. Evidence of a single dragon fossil could lead to the destruction of entire quarries. Men and women who uncovered such evidence could be killed if the Order deemed it necessary.

He motioned toward the print. "Please, all of you take another look at the dragon depicted in this print. What do you see?"

"It has five fingers," Molly said. "Just like our Montana Monster and that wing in Lyme Regis." Judging by Nakasogi's look of understanding, I'd guess that he already knew all about our adventure in Lyme Regis.

"This painting is very special to my family. In 1957, my father was on a dig near this very mountain in China. He had special dispensation to be there—unusual because the Chinese were still embittered by our occupation in World War II—but my father was a famous archeologist. A true scientist. Shanghai

University invited him to assist in the dig." I heard the pride in Nakasogi's voice.

"On his way to the dig, my father stopped in the nearby village for supplies. He saw this painting and decided to buy it. It was ancient and had been at the shop for many years. He knew that dragons are lucky and wanted good luck on this dig.

"The very next day, he discovered a strange, black fossil that led to a small skeleton. It was a dragon, a *Tatsu*, as it is known in Japanese," Nakasogi said.

Nakasogi explained that his father was shocked by the similarities of the skeleton to the print he had just purchased. Obviously, other dragons in other times had been discovered here.

While Nakasogi senior was an eminent archeologist, and not a paleontologist, he realized this was a significant find. So, he published his work in a respectable journal. But by the time it was printed, the fossil itself had disappeared into the Chinese government bureaucracy. Without the actual bones to prove that the fossil was real, the scientific community branded him a liar. For years, controversy haunted him professionally and personally for the rest of his life. How could dragons actually exist?

"What is clear from my father's experience is that we have thousands of documents created by humans over the centuries to guide our fossil journeys," Nakasogi said.

"Like your father using that print," I said.

"Yes. The artist captured the mountain in the background exactly as it stands today. If you had the inclination, you could find my father's 1957 excavation site using that painting. Also, you could just download a geologic map onto your phone to find it." Nakasogi chuckled. "We must meld the old and new."

Our walk had taken us to the back of the room, and we were standing in front of another door. Frowning, I stared at it. "How big is this place? Where are we, exactly?"

"You are at my private estate. Nobody knows about it, as it's owned by a shell corporation under a false name. We're just at the edge of the Aokigahara forest, a place known for *Yurei*. Ghosts, Ms. Wilder," he told her, seeing her confusion. "I thought its reputation would keep people away. We've moved this collection many times."

"Collection? You mean all this?" I said, waving my hand around the room.

"I store other fossils here. All as special as my father's *Tatsu*. I've spent a lifetime cataloging and trying to protect them." He opened the door and waved us through. "If you please," he said.

I walked through the threshold and was immediately standing in front of a large fossil display.

"Shut the front door, is that a griffin?" Molly said.

THE HARD TRUTH

Sarah

THE PACIFIC OCEAN twinkled below me. A vast, endless abyss of water, covering thousands of miles of ocean floor. Most geologists would love a chance to dive down into its depths to catch a glimpse of its rocky treasures. The Mariana Trench would be a good place to start. The Trench is a huge convergent plate boundary, where two mighty tectonic plates fight for dominance. The Pacific plate and the Mariana plate. But, like life, there is only one winner. Slowly, ever so slowly, the Pacific plate dives down under the Mariana, and as it does, mysteries of the ancient earth are slowly melted back into the mantle, never to be seen again. A dynamic reminder that our planet had always been in motion. Changing into something new.

For much of its existence, the ocean has contained a plethora of life. Some hot, some cold, some large, and some small. Some only visible with a microscope. Some larger than a school bus. Reminders that life always moved forward. Evolving into something better.

It contained countless dead bodies. Whales, fish, seals. Even humans. Carcasses that either died naturally or violently. Some bodies fed surface animals—a feast for the lucky seal or shark. Those bodies were torn apart, victims of a cruel fortune. But the *lucky* ones floated down, hitting the ocean floor, nearly intact. A final resting place. At that point, other sea life scoured their remains, leaving behind only white bones. Over time, sand and silt covered those bones. Pressure turned the sediment into rock, encasing the shells and bones into their forever home.

Maybe millions of years from now, a paleontologist would dig up a fossil from today, and ponder what life was like when that animal was alive. How it died. Use taphonomy to speculate its history. Maybe wonder if there was someone like me, flying over an ocean, thinking about evolution and dead things.

Someone who was a traitor to her closest friends, leaving them behind to die.

My leg just wouldn't stop *shaking*. I pressed my hand on it, held it, forced it down. But it still shook violently, almost throwing itself against the arm of my seat. Muscles contracting. Spasms. It was as if my leg contained nightmares, threatening to burst out.

Giving up, I rubbed at my eyes, turning toward the window so that Raley wouldn't see the tears. He did, of course. He never missed a thing. He was sitting across from me in a matching beige leather seat. The second the shaking started, he'd looked up from his tablet, mouth downturned. Probably thought I was an inconvenience. That trusting me was a terrible idea. That I'm not really loyal, not one of them.

I just willingly left my friends to die. He should remember that.

Raley opened his mouth, as if wanting to say something. He closed it, then opened it again, but I cut him off.

"What?" I said. I didn't want to deal with him, but I didn't have a choice.

He reached over to poke at my leg, but I pulled away abruptly. He raised a hand in a placating gesture. "Relax. We'll fix that," he said. "No more shakes."

But I knew the truth. The *problem* wasn't my disease.

No. It was the mud on my jeans. The dirt on my face. The small chunks of rock in my tangled hair.

Multiple sclerosis wasn't causing this shaking. Not this time. This time I couldn't blame my body.

No. It was what I had done. *My* decision.

We were on our way back to the States, aboard a private jet. Princes have sat in these seats, sultans too. Perhaps even presidents. Now me.

Surprisingly, we didn't fly west. Or maybe not surprisingly. I didn't know. I just figured we would head straight back to the States to finally take a real look at Farnsworth's fossils from the warehouse. Be made to watch as Raley and his goons destroyed things. I knew that the Order had followed this path since ancient times. But, as a scientist, it would still be hard to watch.

But first we made some stops. I didn't recognize any of these places from my window, but I thought I heard a familiar name or two over the loudspeaker. First somewhere in eastern Europe. Croatia maybe. Then Delhi. A stop in Mongolia, and then Shanghai. People got on and got off. But I never left the plane. I had no reason, and Raley never invited me to leave. Instead, I just sat in my seat, ate my food, and slept or looked out the window. I was a good little soldier. For hours. Days probably. I didn't know. It was all a blur.

With every mile we flew east, I tried to forget. Forget Italy. Forget Germany and England. Not think about Montana. Especially not Montana. When I did think about them, I started sweating, and my heart hurt like it was broken. Because it was. His eyes, her face. Even Oliphant's annoying remarks. Their pain matched my own.

But I had to do it.

Think about anything else, Sarah.

Like that damn doctor's visit. I'd been stumbling around the hills during my teaching sections for weeks. I thought it was just exhaustion from trying to be the best in the department while simultaneously trying to have the social life of a normal twentysomething. But the clincher was a bad fall during a class field trip. That nosedive cut my head open. I needed stitches, so I went to the campus infirmary, fingers crossed that my school insurance would cover it. I'd walked down the clinic's hallway toward the doc's examination room and looked out the window at the cold fall foliage and dreamed of summer heat, of next year's field season. My favorite time of year. The resident's voice startled me out of my daydream, causing me to jump slightly. He'd noticed something about my gait. About my leg. He asked me how long I'd been dropping my foot.

"Dropping my foot?" I was so confused. I thought the guy was taking drugs or something. I mean, it was Laramie, Wyoming. Drugs and alcohol were a problem here, what with the large student body and the long winter nights. Maybe this guy was a stoner.

"How long has your foot been falling down like that when you walk?"

I answered his questions. He asked me to think back and try to remember.

Did I have any problems with other body parts shaking?
Tingling of my extremities?
Blurry vision?

As I answered yes to all, my heart felt like it was turning to ice.

"Do you have any cognitive failures?"

"What?"

"Are you having trouble remembering?"

At that point, I knew. I didn't have Derek's eidetic memory. I didn't think in pictures. I didn't remember crazy weird facts about people or things long forgotten. But I had a good memory. Paleontology—heck, most sciences—required a lot of memorization: geological terms, biological families, plant parts. I had to be perfect and know it all, especially for Oliphant.

But I *was* having memory problems. First, it was little things like losing my sunglasses. Or forgetting to lock my apartment. Stuff one can wave away as absentmindedness due to stress. But it had been getting worse. I'd be teaching and forget a simple definition, like the visual difference between conglomerate and breccia. There wasn't much, but there was a nuance between the two—one layer has rounded rocks, the other more angular. *And I'd forgotten that difference.* My best freshman student had to raise her hand to remind me. It was embarrassing, stumbling up there in front of thirty undergrads, most of whom would rather be drinking than learning about how our earth functioned. I was supposed to inspire, but I couldn't even remember the basics.

I walked out of class that day horrified. I went hiking to forget, and after a few miles I began to stumble. I trucked it up to being tired and distracted. But in that doctor's office, I realized the truth. Something was very wrong.

After he scratched the bottom of my foot and frowned, he ordered an MRI and a battery of other tests. A few days later, the diagnosis. I could hardly walk out of his office. When I did, I could barely breathe. That night, I screamed into my pillow. How could I dig if I couldn't use my hands? How could I hunt if I couldn't use my eyes? How could I be in the badlands if I couldn't walk?

Logic told me I was ridiculous. I could work as a geologist or paleontologist from a wheelchair. I'd seen it happen. And new technologies and resources were being developed to allow formation access for everyone. And I did love working in a lab.

But as a young child, I was trapped at home a lot while my parents worked late shifts. They couldn't afford a babysitter. Finally, Dad asked Derek for help. They were old buddies, and my dad knew Derek was lonely, out there in the field by himself, day after day. He didn't have any other family, save my dad, his good friend from high school. My dad thought Derek could help by getting me outside. That we could help each other. He was right.

At first, Derek would take me out into the field only a few days a month. He'd toss me my backpack and yell at me to keep walking, eyes to the ground. Turns out I had an excellent eye and could spot a fossil almost as fast as he could. *The Lucky Girl,* he called me. I worked hard, didn't complain, and was a fast learner. Plus, I'd yell back at him a lot, and I think he liked that. He enjoyed a challenge.

Not so lucky now.

Eventually I stopped heading home after school, walking a few more blocks downtown to his warehouse instead. Either we'd run into the field or work on specimens. Often late into the night—once my homework was done, of course. During summer breaks, we were in the field from sunrise to sunset. He watched over me but gave me freedom. Taught me what he knew. How to hunt the most precious treasures of the land.

Through his guidance, I became me.

But this sickness would change all of that. It felt like my life was over—at least as I had envisioned it. I was still young. It didn't seem fair. I wasn't ready for it. I wasn't sure I wanted to go on living, eventually stuck in a wheelchair for the rest of my life.

At first I reacted to the diagnosis by drinking. When I went back home to Glasgow for spring break, I couldn't hide my skin's sallow coloring. The bags under my eyes.

Derek, bless him, assumed it was due to being an over-worked Oliphant minion. He ranted about him for hours at Murphy's. About how I was the best, and Oliphant was ruining me just to get ahead. I kept my mouth shut and handed him my glass for refills. I wasn't ready to tell him or anyone yet, and besides, Derek never asked.

But we went hunting—every day. Even though there was still snow on the ground, Derek and I could always find some exposed rocks to look at. And hunting was the medicine I needed, a balm for my spirit that Derek was happy to help provide. As long as we didn't venture too far from his truck, I could hide my disability.

I found that Dracosauria tooth during one of those hunts, the one I had casted and that Molly carried around in that backpack of hers. The tooth had been exposed in a dried-up riverbed, a distinct shape and color nestled in the sand. I knew at once it was something special. I knew even then. I just didn't realize how *special.*

Or how much it would change my life and lead to that fateful phone call.

The day I made a deal with a devil. A deal that traded my loyalty for access to an experimental trial that might take me off this bullet train to a degenerating nervous system. A deal that killed innocent people. *Derek.* Tears burned my eyes, and I caught one with my finger before it trickled down my cheek.

I had no choice.

THE ROOM

Molly

NAKASOGI'S LAUGHTER FILLED the room. "Yes, it's what a geomythologist would call a griffin."

I felt like my eyes were practically falling out of my head with shock. "Besides dragons, there are other creatures from myths that lived on the planet?" I said.

Nakasogi motioned toward the skeleton I was looking at. "Many. Including this griffin."

I couldn't keep my mouth closed, and I felt Farnsworth reach over to push it shut. In front of us was a vertical slab of gray rock. On it was a plethora of light brown fossil bones, and I could see ribs, vertebrae, and what looked like an avian skull. I mean, I saw a beak and everything. It had four legs, ending with sharp claws. The front legs were graceful, thin with three-toed feet—two in the front, one in the back, like a bird. The rear legs had five fingers, built with stocky bones—a lion's paw. And wings were protruding out of its shoulders. A long tail curved over and around the body. "This was discovered in Mongolia. Interestingly, speculation concerning a real *Protoceratops* fossil eventually led us to the discovery of this fossil."

I nodded slowly. That made sense. I'd read a book that argued that the griffin myth's inspiration might have come from travelers on the Silk Road, thousands of years ago. Travelers saw the fossils of *Protoceratops* in Mongolia and thought they were dead griffins from local legend.

Realizing that our group was missing someone, I looked behind us. While the rest of us had walked to the griffin, Oliphant hadn't left the doorway. He stood silently, his face slack with shock.

I walked over to the doorframe and stood in front of Oliphant. "Come on," I said, my voice calm as I pulled Oliphant forward, and he stumbled after me. "Come look at it up close." The interrogator from Italy followed a few steps behind us.

"A griffin?" Oliphant finally said, sounding slightly hysterical.

"Oh, yes," the man said as we walked. "We have several confirmed skeletons, but this one is the most articulate in the world."

"My friends, may I introduce to you my confidante and eventual successor. This is my son, Yoshiaka," Nakasogi said.

"Please, call me Yoshi," the young man said.

His son. We were followed and captured by Nakasogi's family. Now that they were standing close together, there did seem to be a family resemblance between the two men. And by the way Nakasogi was looking at his son, they were close.

But I was still ticked about the kidnapping and the drugging and the threatening, so I just turned away and moved closer to Farnsworth.

"This is so bizarre," Farnsworth said, still looking at the griffin.

"And a giant flying dragon is normal?" I laughed.

"It has wings in addition to four legs—six limbs," Oliphant said, sucking in his breath. I turned around to see he had his back to us. He was leaning over, nearly hyperventilating.

I rushed over and rubbed his back, murmuring, "Breathe."

"Now you are beginning to understand the mysteries," Nakasogi said, his eyes glowing with excitement. "Creatures like dragons and griffins are puzzles that we and others need to solve. They defy many of the rules science has developed over generations to define different species. Essentially they appear to be new members of the animal kingdom."

Oliphant turned around, but then took a step back, looking off behind the griffin.

I followed his gaze, letting out a squeak in surprise. Behind the griffin was a giant mounted black skeleton. This animal was about two stories high and maybe thirty feet in length, with a long neck that arched upward. At its end was a giant skull with two long horns and a large horn on the tip of its nose. The animal's body was stretched up, rearing on its hind legs while its wings were stretched out like it was about to take flight.

But what caught me was that this dragon, so obviously a dragon, had another set of legs. These legs were located in the front of the body, just below where the wings were attached to its back.

Our Montana Monster had only two legs and two arms. One arm set was the wings. It was a wyvern, according to my book *Dragons of the World*. This dragon had six limbs.

"Five fingers," Farnsworth said.

Oliphant gaped at him in disbelief. "Five fingers? Is that what catches you? Not the fact that it's got four legs and a pair of wings?" He turned and reached for the nearest steady object. Unfortunately, it was my head and shoulders.

"Hey," I protested, trying to wiggle away. Oliphant was heavy.

"With time, I could explain the Montana Monster creature . . . dragons," Oliphant said to my shoulder. "Wings versus arms. Argue that dinosaurs and . . . Dracosauria . . . at one time shared a common ancestor and diverted at some point . . ."

He was droning on, barely finishing his thoughts. Oliphant seemed like he was losing touch with reality, overwhelmed with what was standing before us. Finally, Farnsworth sighed, pulled Oliphant away from me with a jerk, and forced him to stand in front of him. The noise of Farnsworth's slap against Oliphant's face echoed around the room like the crack of a bullwhip.

Oliphant immediately brought his hand to his cheek and stared at Farnsworth, his eyes first full of confusion, then anger. "What the hell?"

Farnsworth glared at him and motioned to the rest of us. I'm sure I looked scared. Nakasogi seemed a little worried. Oliphant took a deep breath. "Thank you, Derek, I believe that may have been exactly what the doctor ordered." He walked a few feet from us and stopped.

I exchanged a look with Farnsworth. Poor guy. I think all this broke Oliphant a bit.

But he was full of surprises. After a moment, he swung back around and crossed his arms. "Okay, Mr. Nakasogi. You say that is a . . . dragon, like the one we found in Montana, correct? You've seen enough identifiers to conclude this for a fact?"

"Yes, Dr. Oliphant," Yoshi responded. "So far, two divergent families. Much like the ornithischians and saurischians of dinosaurs, there seem to be two different families of Dracosauria. One with four limbs, one with six."

Oliphant returned to stand next to me and stared at the dragon. "Okay. Molly, I am going to eat crow here. This is a dragon. You were right." He gave me a nod. "But here's my problem with all this. These two animals will literally turn science upside down." He pointed back toward the griffin. "For example, that griffin is literally a flying bird-mammal. Not a bird with wings. Not a mammal with wings. This has huge implications for our world. Not just for paleontology, but biology as well. There is no such thing as a mammal, bird, or reptile with more than four limbs. The only creatures on earth with more than four limbs are bugs, insects, spiders, or crustaceans."

Oliphant walked away from us and put his hands behind his neck, rubbing it almost violently. His voice carried to our ears. "If this information gets out, the controversies will last a lifetime. None of us would be spared the accusations that we are involved in some elaborate hoax." He turned around and peered at Nakasogi. "Because that is why you're showing us all this. To tell the world."

Nakasogi slowly nodded. "S.V. works to collect real, scientific information about these fossils. When the time is right, we want to publish our studies in peer-reviewed journals."

"Why did you contact us specifically? And why now?" Oliphant asked.

"Several reasons. We are at a crossroads. Your Monster, as you call it, was a catalyst. When I knew that the Order was planning on moving in, I sent you Owen's picture and the painting. To nudge you. To start your journey to discover the truth." He motioned farther along the wall, toward another display case holding a thick stack of papers. "I have neglected to show you this. Owen's journal. I know you have the other half, Ms. Wilder. May I see it?"

As I reached around into my backpack to pull out the journal, Nakasogi opened the display case and removed the other half of Owen's journal. We exchanged papers, and Oliphant looked over my shoulder as I slowly turned its pages.

"There are more mythical animals here," I said. I saw drawings for a griffin. More dragons. And other fantastical animals.

"*Evidence of the Fantastical: Dracosauria.* As his journal title suggests, Owen's main interest was dragons," Nakasogi said.

"As he got older and had more access to various collections, he learned of other creatures."

"Tell us more about Salva Veritate," Oliphant said. "You say it is a group fighting against the Order. When was it formed?"

"It originated around the same time as the Order, actually. Since then, we have recruited individuals who take an oath to resist the Order and promote and protect scientific and mythological truths by promoting the study of geomythology, the study of the legends and myths that were created to explain natural history. Our motto is *ducunt volentem fata, nolentem trahunt.*"

"The fates lead the willing, drag the unwilling," Farnsworth said quickly, smirking at my open mouth. "Beat you to it."

Nakasogi paused and spoke very slowly and deliberately. "My friends, we need your help. We must recruit prominent scientists and others of courage who are willing to risk their careers to reveal these profound truths."

"Us?" I said.

"Yes. You three each bring a unique strength. Mr. Farnsworth, you are our adventurer. You are well-grounded in the history of our field, and your skills at locating and uncovering fossils are unparalleled," Nakasogi said. "You also have, shall we say, created unique connections with individuals who travel in less orthodox circles. Those connections will be helpful."

Farnsworth raised his chin but didn't respond.

"And you, Dr. Oliphant, have both the reputation and analytical eye we need. You've built an enviable reputation as a scientist. Although there were some questions concerning your integrity many years ago, the faith Mr. Farnsworth now places in you has alleviated those concerns." He raised an eyebrow at Oliphant and then looked directly at Farnsworth. Farnsworth remained silent but gave his head a slight nod. "You also have academic and social connections that will be helpful, including those in the media industry.

"Finally, Molly, we have decided that you are also an essential element." Nakasogi turned to me, a bright smile on his face.

"I am?" I replied, feeling my heart quicken.

"Yes, you are. You see, you represent the most important part of this. You are the believer. Your faith opened your eyes to what others failed to see. You've never once doubted that what you uncovered was a fossil of a dragon even though the others refused to believe their eyes."

"Now, you three, if you wish . . ." He paused and cleared his throat. "What I mean to say is . . . Salva Veritate needs your help. The next stage of this war, the Bone Wars, as my comrades are calling it, is about to commence. Will you join us?"

"Absolutely!" I said quickly.

Together we turned to look at Oliphant. He pursed his lips but gazed thoughtfully at me, then at Farnsworth. After a long moment, he nodded his head in agreement, a small smile gracing his face. "Fine. Let's take a wrecking ball to my career. In the name of science, of course."

As one, we all turned back toward Nakasogi.

"When do we start?" I said.

Lost section of Owen's journal, 1888

Received a drawing today from an old acquaintance of Charles Darwin. Discussed our lost friend before moving onto business. This gentleman has spent significant time in Asia, and is participating in a fossil dig in China. He is sending remains of a scaled animal, including the skull, upper femur, and a scapula with a significant groove—for the wings. A reptile-like flying horse that looks like a dragon! According to local myths, they are called longma. I cannot wait to see this for myself. According to my research, seeing a longma was an important event in China, as it was an omen that whomever saw it would become a legendary sage-ruler.

I shall inform Salva Veritate to coordinate and store the fossil. The Order is growing bolder each day.

But so are we.

AFTERWORD

THE ESSENCE OF this book is really summed up by a quote from the late, great Michael Crichton: "It's fiction, except for the parts that aren't."

The Bone Wars is fiction, but I'm a lover of science. I've loved it as long as I can remember, and while some people, events, and places in this book are fictional, I've tried to make the science, folklore, and geomythology as accurate as I possibly could. I also tried to bring in real people and real historical locations. For example, you can go to Mary Anning's old stomping grounds along the Jurassic Coast, and visit her workshop and home, which is now the Lyme Regis Museum. Or drop by Atessa in Italy and go see the "dragon bone" on display in their beautiful church. Sadly, Gideon Mantell did die of a drug overdose in 1852. His curved spine was collected by the Hunterian Museum (which was overseen by Richard Owen at the time). According to reports, it was actually destroyed in 1962 due to "lack of space." *Or was it?*

There are lots more to dig into, so I highly encourage you to use whatever trusty internet search site you'd like and spend some time learning about the history, people, and places of paleontology. It's a fascinating subject.

Below is a selected bibliography of books and articles that I used while writing this book, and I hope you enjoy them as much as I did.

Barrowclough, G. F., J. Cracraft, J. Klicka, and R.M. Zink. "How Many Kinds of Birds Are There and Why Does It Matter?" *PLoS ONE* 11, no. 11 (November 2016): e0166307. https://doi.org/10.1371/journal.pone.0166307.

Horner J. R., and M. B. Goodwin. "Extreme Cranial Ontogeny in the Upper Cretaceous Dinosaur *Pachycephalosaurus.*" *PLoS ONE* 4, no. 10 (October 2009): e7626. https://doi.org/10.1371/journal.pone.0007626.

Johnson, Kirk R., Douglas J. Nichols, and Joseph H. Hartman. "Hell Creek Formation: A 2001 Synthesis." In *The Hell Creek Formation and the Cretaceous-Tertiary Boundary in the Northern Great Plains: An Integrated Continental Record of the End of the Cretaceous.* Geological Society of America, 2002.

Martin, A. J., P. Vickers⊠Rich, T. H. Rich, and M. Hall. "Oldest Known Avian Footprints from Australia: Eumeralla Formation (Albian), Dinosaur Cove, Victoria." *Palaeontology* 57 (2014): 7–19. https://doi.org/10.1111/pala.12082.

Mayor, Adrienne. *The First Fossil Hunters: Dinosaurs, Mammoths, and Myth in Greek and Roman Times.* Princeton University Press, 2000.

McGowan, Christopher. *The Dragon Seekers: How an Extraordinary Circle of Fossilists Discovered the Dinosaurs and Paved the Way for Darwin.* Cambridge, Mass.: Perseus Publishing, 2001.

Norell, Mark A., Laurel Kendall, and Richard Ellis. *Mythic Creatures and the Impossibly Real Animals Who Inspired Them.* New York: Sterling Signature, 2016.

Owen, Richard. "Report on British *Fossil Reptiles.* Pt II." In: Report of the Eleventh Meeting of the British Association for the Advancement of Science, held at Plymouth, July 1842, 66–204.

Padian, Kevin. "The Rehabilitation of Sir Richard Owen." *BioScience* 47, no. 7 (July/August 1997): 446–453.

Pim, Keiron. Dinosaurs—*The Grand Tour: Everything Worth Knowing about Dinosaurs from Aardonyx to Zuniceratops.* New York: The Experiment Publishing, 2013, revised 2016.

Senter, Phil, and Pondanesa D. Wilkins. "Investigation of a Claim of a Late-Surviving Pterosaur and Exposure of a Taxidemic Hoax: The Case of Cornelius Meyer's Dragon." *Palaeontologia Electronica* 16, no. 1 (2013).

Schulte, Peter, et al. "The Chicxulub Asteroid Impact and Mass Extinction at the Cretaceous-Paleogene Boundary." *Science* 327, no. 5970 (March 2010): 1214–1218.

Shuker, Karl. *Dragons: A Natural History.* New York: Simon & Schuster, 1995.

Rose, Carol. *Giants, Monsters, and Dragons: An Encyclopedia of Folklore, Legend, and Myth.* New York: W. W. Norton, 2000.

Royer, Dana L., Leo J. Hickey, and Scott L. Wing. "Ecological Conservation in the 'Living Fossil' *Ginkgo.*" *Paleobiology* 29, no. 1 (2003): 84–104.

The idea for this book hit me in the face years ago, when my oldest was just a small newborn, and I was an exhausted parent. To pass the time when I was rocking her to sleep and to not go insane from lack of REM, I'd tell her tales of when I was a kid myself, digging dinosaurs in Montana. As the years passed, the story grew into something more outgoing and adventurous, and, at some point, dragons entered the picture. Dead dragons, but dragons nonetheless. It wasn't a huge leap. My mother had given me Adrienne Mayor's amazing book, *The First Fossil Hunters: Dinosaurs, Mammoths, and Myth in Greek and Roman Times* when I was in college. At the time, I was a full-time geology student who also worked as an intern with the Denver Museum of Nature and Science. Between studying and working, when I had a moment to breathe, I'd devour Mayor's work. Realizing natural phenomena might have influenced our mythology was a brand-new concept to me. Mayor's book caused me to view the world, and my chosen field, in an entirely different way. It was exciting.

Although life drove me away from geology, paleontology, and geomythology, Mayor's work has always been in the back of my mind and it became my nerdy party trick, describing to the innocent how the myth of the griffin may have come from the skeletons of *Protoceratops* in Mongolia. You can imagine I was the life of the party after I pulled that out of my sleeve. Joking aside, twenty years later, the concept of our natural world influencing our mythologies weaved itself into what would become this story.

I have a huge list, as many authors do, of people to thank, so I'll start with the family that really pushed me to do this at all. Thank you, Nassi family, for encouraging me right from the get-go. Mark and Jen, your early support and edits were incredibly useful, and I still have Izzy's drawing of a dragon in my collection. I can't wait for Izzy and Talia to read this book.

To my friends, Karolin, Claire, Alexandra, Kristie, Sara, Allison, Sarah, Cheryl, and many others. Thank you for all your support, especially so early in the process. For some of you, our friendship began in our high school years, and you've stuck with me all this time, something that I'm forever grateful for. Karolin, you especially, sitting there while I bored you with discussions about dinosaurs. You were a saint. At least we ate Safeway cupcakes through it all. Anyway, it's taken me years, my friends, but we're finally here. I can't wait for you and your kids to read it.

Early in the process, Matt Harry was a huge supporter and editor. I must have written thousands of words on this story in various forms, and you really helped with the dramatic beats. I am not a fiction writer by training, so your help was really appreciated.

Sarah Nivel, you really picked through the story and helped me round out my characters in ways I never dreamed. Thank you for your help and your cheerful guidance. I always enjoyed our conversations!

Dr. Kirk Johnson, thanks for taking a chance on an eighteen-year-old kid and letting me tag along for years as a minion in Colorado and beyond. Your mentorship was one of the greatest of my life, and it helped me become the person I am today, which I feel is pretty great. So, good job.

Kristine, you were also an amazing mentor, and I'm so proud to know you. Thank you for your support and friendship all these years!

To the original Pirates of Montana: my pseudo-sis Sarah Montani, Rob Gay, and Jim Lehane. I'm so happy that we met all those years ago at Camp Makela as a bunch of crazy teens. While life has brought us together and at times taken us apart, we have a deep connection and friendship, one that I'll forever be thankful for. OLIM! Out into the badlands with you!

Sean Faul, although you were not a direct member of our small teen cohort, we all benefited from your support, friendship, and grad school guidance. Thank you for your constant support, humor, and just being you, you Pirate. And also for introducing me to Loreena McKennitt. You still have no idea how much that impacted my life. Well, if you're reading this, now you do.

Adam Gomolin, it's been a journey, but you've been the best cheerleader / guidance counselor / editor a writer could ever want. Thank you for taking a chance on me and this story.

Sarina, Yaron, Ely, Noam, David, Lauren, Natalie, Tessa, Jacob, Bryan, Ronin, Steve, Terri, and Jonathan: you all have been such a wonderful support system for me during this long process, and I'm forever grateful and thankful to call you my brothers, sisters, nieces, and nephews. Eileen and Shabtai, thank you so much for your unwavering support, guidance, and humor. I love you both.

I wish you were here, Mom and Bill, to see and read this. I know you'd both be tickled pink. Thank you, Mom, for your gift of *The First Fossil Hunters*, and for purchasing every single dinosaur book possible for me in middle and high school. Thank you for driving me to see all the western National Parks from an early age, and thank you for supporting my love of dinosaurs, writing, and X-Men comics. You are with me every day, and I love and miss you both. The world is not the same without you two in it.

Dad, you are the reason I was able to go to Montana that fateful summer in the first place, and I'm forever grateful for your support and love. This book wouldn't be the same without your thoughtful comments and edits, and I look forward to discussing the team's further adventures with you. Kris, thank you for all your support and love and being the best stepmom and Obachan to me and my family. We love you!

To my husband, Adam, and our wonderful children. Thank you for your patience, love, and understanding when I'd disappear for hours at night or early in the morning to work on this book. You are the reason I'm doing this, and I couldn't be more proud of you all. I love you—so much. Go Team Evan.

GRAND PATRONS

Jim Lehane
Julia, Jeremy, Josephine, & Wilder Gross
Mark Nassi
Sean Faul
Eileen and Shabtai Evan
The Montani Family
The Iwasaki and Steele Family

INKSHARES

INKSHARES is a reader-driven publisher and producer based in Oakland, California. Our books are selected not by a group of editors, but by readers worldwide.

While we've published books by established writers like *Big Fish* author Daniel Wallace and *Star Wars: Rogue One* scribe Gary Whitta, our aim remains surfacing and developing the new author voices of tomorrow.

Previously unknown Inkshares authors have received starred reviews and been featured in *The New York Times*. Their books are on the front tables of Barnes & Noble and hundreds of independents nationwide, and many have been licensed by publishers in other major markets. They are also being adapted by Oscar-winning screenwriters at the biggest studios and networks.

Interested in making your own story a reality? Visit Inkshares.com to start your own project or find other great books.